THE
PRICE
YOU PAY

TITLES BY NICK PETRIE

THE
PRICE
YOU PAY

NICK PETRIE

G. P. PUTNAM'S SONS
NEW YORK

PUTNAM
— EST. 1838 —

G. P. Putnam's Sons
Publishers Since 1838
An imprint of Penguin Random House LLC
penguinrandomhouse.com

Library of Congress Cataloging-in-Publication Data

Names: Petrie, Nicholas, author.
Title: The price you pay / Nick Petrie.
Description: New York : G. P. Putnam's Sons, 2024.
Identifiers: LCCN 2023044798 (print) | LCCN 2023044799 (ebook) |
    ISBN 9780593540558 (hardcover) | ISBN 9780593540565 (ebook)
Subjects: LCGFT: Thrillers (Fiction). | Novels.
Classification: LCC PS3616.E86645 P75 2024 (print) |
LCC PS3616.E86645 (ebook) | DDC 813/.6—dc23/eng/20230929
LC record available at https://lccn.loc.gov/2023044798
LC ebook record available at https://lccn.loc.gov/2023044799

Printed in the United States of America
1st Printing

For all those men and women who love their kids more than life itself. Sometimes love hurts, but it always makes you stronger.

Everyone has a plan

until he gets punched in the mouth.

—MIKE TYSON

THE
PRICE
YOU PAY

1

PETER

Peter Ash opened his eyes in the dark, listening.

Some sound had pulled him from sleep. Not one of the normal noises of the old house. His subconscious mind was used to the wintery clank of the radiators, the wind's rattle of the loose windowpane that he hadn't gotten around to mending before the weather turned. This was something different.

Peter often woke in the night, pillow wet with sweat, mind racing, the war returned in his dreams. He'd come to terms with it, mostly. Had learned not to fight it. It helped to look over and see June Cassidy snoring softly beside him, buried under a mound of quilts, to think of the life he was making with her every day. Sometimes that was enough.

Other times, his chest was so tight he could barely breathe. So he'd get up and pace the unlit house, heart pounding, skin flushed and damp. Fighting to pull air into his lungs, he'd feel the desert sun baking his skin. He'd see the faces from those gone-away days, good friends who had died or men he had killed. He'd smell the stench of unburied bodies. Breath after breath, he let it all come. The cost of war.

But Peter wasn't sweating now. He felt cool and alert, his senses searching the night. He glanced at the clock on the nightstand. It was a quarter to four. Then came a soft clink, like metal on stone. Someone downstairs.

Slowly and carefully, not wanting to wake June, he untwined himself from her naked body and eased himself out of bed. He knelt beside the nightstand and slipped a Browning Hi-Power pistol from the holster he'd mounted to the underside, then took a cylindrical suppressor from a leather sleeve beside it and threaded it onto the pistol's barrel. No reason to wake the neighbors if this got ugly.

Gun in hand, he stepped into the pair of raggedy blue boxers that June had peeled off him the night before, then left the bedroom and walked barefoot across the sloping wood floor toward the stairs, the night air cold against his bare skin. As he crept down the steps, he stayed tight against the wall, where the wide oak treads wouldn't squeak. His scalp tingled and his heart thumped in his chest. The Browning's safety was already off.

He heard the sound of running water from the back of the house. He ghosted down the long hall toward the dim electric glow of the kitchen stove. The faint rumble of a drawer, closing softly. He rounded the corner with the Browning up and his finger on the trigger.

A shadow stood staring into the open upper cabinets, hands on his hips. His starched white shirt glowed against his dark skin. Peter had thought he'd been utterly soundless, but Lewis spoke without looking at him. "Where's your big thermos at?"

On the counter, the coffeemaker gurgled and began to drip. A loaf of brown bread stood on a cutting board beside a jar of peanut butter and a plastic bear filled with honey.

Peter lowered the Browning, felt his heartbeat slow. "I thought you were in Detroit. That investment conference."

"Left early." Lewis's voice was slippery and dark, like motor oil. "Big thermos?"

Peter put the pistol on safe and set it on the counter. "Above the coffeemaker. Top shelf." The cabinets were custom and went all the way up to the nine-foot ceiling. Peter had built them himself. He and Lewis had renovated most of the old house together, adding big new windows that opened up the back to the forested ravine that dropped down to the river below. Outside, the Wisconsin landscape shone white with moonlit snow.

Lewis found the dented green Stanley thermos, set it in the sink, and filled it with hot water, pre-warming the cold metal. His movements were quick and clean, his sleeves rolled exactly twice. His polished black combat boots moved silently across the slate floor. "You busy today?"

Peter was in the middle of a spec project on the expensive side of the river, a gut remodel. The electrician was starting the rewire at seven a.m. The plumbing inspector was due after lunch. Before the drywall delivery, scheduled for midafternoon, Peter had sagging floor joists to reinforce in the dining room and a new beam to install in the basement.

But whenever he'd needed Lewis in the past, calling from California, or Denver, or Memphis, or Nebraska, Lewis had always showed up, no questions asked.

So Peter just smiled. "I'm all yours. What's up?"

Lewis nodded. "Take a ride with me. Should be back tonight."

Peter picked up the Browning again. "Let me get some clothes on."

He was waiting for Lewis to look him up and down, make some crack about Peter in his underwear. But it never came.

"Dress warm," Lewis said. "Leave the phone. Bring the gun."

—————

Peter left a note on the counter for June, sent three quick emails to rearrange his day, then shrugged into his coat and walked out the side door, locking it behind him. The wind made his eyeballs ache. Dirty snow was piled waist-high beside the shoveled driveway where Lewis's black Yukon idled, the powerful engine rumbling low. Peter opened the door and climbed inside, grateful for the heat. The dashboard thermometer read five below zero. Early February in Milwaukee.

Lewis wheeled the big SUV through the darkened city toward the freeway. He hadn't said a word since Peter got in the car. Two cheap phones lay charging on the center console. The thermos and a brown paper sack full of food sat on the floor by Peter's feet.

"Are you going tell me what this is about?"

Lewis turned onto the on-ramp, headed north. "We're going up past Crandon, see a guy I used to know."

Crandon was four hours away in good summer weather. "Used to know?"

"Used to work with," Lewis said. "Back in the bad old days."

The highway was brightly lit, the pavement clear. Southeastern Wisconsin hadn't seen fresh snow in almost a week. But the sky hung low on the overpasses, the clouds brushing the high tops of the tall, curving streetlamps, which meant snow was coming. Peter was surprised, as he always was, how many cars were on the road at this early hour, people living their unknowable lives. Where were they all going?

"This guy got a name?"

"Upstate Wilson." Lewis sighed. "First name, Teddy. Ray started calling him Upstate because Teddy was a country boy, always talking about his place upstate, the hunting and fishing upstate, what he was gonna do when he got back upstate. Plus he was usually wired high on some kind of ups, burning that candle. So Upstate Wilson kinda stuck."

"I always thought it was just you and Nino and Ray. Keeping things simple."

Lewis raised a shoulder in a shrug. "That's how it was, usually. Business model wasn't complicated. Target criminals, keep the civilians out of it. If nobody calls the cops, they don't know to come looking for you."

"What about the criminals you targeted?"

Lewis flashed a mirthless smile. "Dead men don't cause no trouble."

Peter knew some of this, but not much. Lewis almost never talked about his old life, at least not at the level of detail that might be used in a court of law.

"Anyway," Lewis said, "when you're in business long enough, you get to know a few people. Opportunities come your way. We get a good one, we maybe diversify a little. Rules were the same, though. Don't steal from nobody can't afford it, don't hurt nobody don't deserve it."

Peter had always known that Lewis was more than he seemed. The better he knew the man, the more clear this became. The fact that Lewis had held himself and his crew of killers to a code of conduct? Icing on the cake.

"So where does Upstate Wilson come in?"

"Nino knew him from the service. Huge guy. We'd bring him in when we needed extra muscle. An asshole generally, but good with a gun, good under pressure. He was also a safe and lock man, alarms and electronics, so we'd use him for that. Self-taught, but talented— when he wasn't high. When he was using, he was prone to weirdness. Conspiracy theories. Paranoia."

They were out of the city now, the suburbs low and dim behind walls and fences and lines of trees. After they passed Good Hope Road, the high lamps fell away and the night grew darker.

"Anyway, a couple years before you and I met, we were going after these bikers in Cali. This was Pagans territory, but these bikers were too nasty to be official members. So they had their own little group, doing the kind of stuff the Pagans didn't want their name on, the real dirty work. Murder for hire, running guns and meth up and down the Central Valley.

"Their clubhouse was a shithole bar outside of Bakersfield. We went in late one night wearing body armor under these FBI jackets we bought in a costume shop. That usually gave us about three seconds before they all scrambled for their weapons. We took care of things, but in the process, Teddy got shot in the head. He actually stepped in front of me, so he took a bullet that probably had my name on it."

Lewis shook his head. "Blood everywhere. Overpressure from the round popped one eyeball out of its socket, left it hanging by the nerve bundle. Ugly as hell. We were sure he was gonna die, but we weren't going to leave him there. So we got him in the car and drove him to an ER in Fresno.

"Somehow, Teddy didn't die. He had some brain trauma, they put him in a medical coma for a week, and he lost the eye, but he survived. So I kept in touch, made sure he knew he had a friend. I figured I owed him 'cause he took the round instead of me. Plus we didn't want him to start talking to the feds, you know? When he was ready to go home, Nino and I got him there."

"He's still upstate?"

"Middle of nowhere. Because of the brain thing, he's got some challenges, but he's doing okay. I check in on him, send a little money if he needs it. We're on this encrypted messaging app." Lewis picked up one of the cheap phones and thumbed in a passcode. "Eight hours ago I get this."

He showed Peter the screen. *Bad men are here. Need help.*

In the headlights, the first fat snowflakes began to fall.

2

Lewis had been in Detroit when he got the text.

He'd texted Teddy back right away, but had gotten no reply. Then he'd called Nino at his restaurant in Minneapolis, which was five hours from Teddy's, but still a lot closer than Detroit. Nino didn't pick up, and his voicemail was full, and he didn't respond to a text, either.

"I think Nino's a little over his head with that place," Lewis told Peter now.

"Teddy ever send you messages like this before? He's not playing you?"

Lewis shook his head. "Usually it's stuff like 'I'm making chili and corn bread today.' Or 'My dogs have fleas.' Then I know he maybe wants some company. It's just him and the dogs up there."

"Who else might come to the house?"

"Nobody," Lewis said. "Teddy don't like visitors. He's got this heavy chain across his driveway. Nino and I are the only people he unlocks it for. He goes to town maybe once a month for supplies. On the way home, he used to stop off for a few drinks at this roadhouse that had a female bartender he was sweet on, until some locals tried to mess with him. Teddy's gotten a little quirky, you know?" Lewis gave Peter a tilted smile. "Brain injury or no, my man's still Upstate Wilson. So things didn't go well for the locals. The bartender saw the whole thing, so Teddy never got arrested, but it put him on the sheriff's radar. Now he don't even go to the bar." Lewis sighed. "I was hoping he'd get hooked up with that woman, not spend all his time alone, but Teddy doesn't even have indoor plumbing."

Peter raised his eyebrows. "In northern Wisconsin? With these winters?"

"You don't know the half of it," Lewis said. "Like I said, he used to be a real asshole. Big talker, alpha dog. But after he got shot in the head? He turned into a different person. Still a talker, real excitable, but almost sweet. Like he's gone back to being ten years old. Like a little brother, you know?"

"A little brother who used to be an armed robber," Peter said.

Lewis gave Peter that tilted smile. "You say that like it's a character flaw."

The highway branched and Lewis took 57 toward Kiel and New Holstein. White fields rolled past on both sides, barns and farmhouses still asleep in the dark. The roads were well salted and clear enough for Lewis to keep his speed well above the limit. With the snowfall lit up by the headlights, the speed of the car made it look like the fat flakes were coming horizontally. As if Peter and Lewis were in outer space, flying through a star field toward an unknown planet.

Six hours later, slowed by the weather, they were thumping along an unplowed county road, with only a half-dozen recent sets of tire tracks.

They'd traded off driving so each man could catch some sleep, and now Lewis was back behind the wheel. Eight to ten inches of fresh snow on the ground, with two-foot drifts in places. The cloud cover had blown away and the sky was a bright, pure blue. The thermostat on the dashboard read fifteen below.

The four-wheel-drive Yukon barreled along at forty, the heavy vehicle absorbing the punishment. If Lewis minded the conditions, he didn't show it. The rolling fields had been replaced by hills covered with dense evergreen forests that grew right up to the ditches, their branches hanging low under white weight.

Their most recent pit stop had yielded the unexpected bonus of a gas station breakfast. Foil-wrapped breakfast burritos, made Wisconsin-style with chopped bratwurst and hash browns and eggs and too much cheese, in a greasy white paper sack. The peanut butter sandwiches could wait.

Peter finished his burrito and drank some coffee. It was fresh and hot. He'd had a nap. He felt almost civilized. "Still nothing from your friend?"

Lewis shook his head. "Tried him three times while you were asleep. I'm hoping the weather took out a cell tower. The storm was worse up here last night."

"Did you come up with a reason someone would go after him?"

"Not unless he made an enemy at the grocery store. Far as I know, he don't really go nowhere else."

They came to a four-way intersection. Most of the tire tracks turned left or right onto the county highway, which was wide and well plowed. On the far side of the intersection, a big white Jeep appeared, the sun turning its windshield into a mirror. The Jeep slowed for the stop sign and turned left onto the highway. Lewis feathered the accelerator and drove straight through. The Jeep's tracks were the only ones remaining.

A faded brown sign read CHEQUAMEGON-NICOLET NATIONAL FOR-
EST. The road narrowed and wound through rocky hills. The wind
rocked the Yukon on its springs. The trees leaned toward them, as if
hungry for any available light. The temperature dropped one degree,
then another.

Then Lewis stood on the brakes. Peter braced himself with a hand
as the vehicle slid to a halt. Ahead of them, the tracks rolled out of an
unplowed driveway. There was a large homemade sign nailed to a tree.
With uneven red brushstrokes, someone had painted, KEEP OUT! NO
TRESPASSING!

"What is it?"

"That's Teddy's driveway." Lewis looked grim.

"That white Jeep," Peter said. "It's not his?"

"Teddy ain't supposed to drive. He's just got an ATV. I don't s'pose
you caught the license plate?"

"Caked with snow. You want to go after them?" It had been ten
minutes since they'd seen the Jeep.

Lewis rolled his shoulders. "Oh, I do. But first, I need to find
Teddy." He turned the vehicle into the Jeep's tracks and goosed the gas
as he lowered his window. The cold hit like a slap. "Do me a solid and
grab my ten-gauge from the back seat."

The Yukon leaped and lurched through the deep snow. The tracks
curved away into the trees. Peter unbuckled his belt, twisted around,
reached into the folds of a green Mexican blanket for the sawed-off
pump gun, and passed it forward. The weapon was awkward in the
enclosed space. Lewis racked the slide, then laid the gun across his lap
with the shortened barrel nosing out the window like a hound sniffing
for rabbits.

Peter bent to pick his Browning off the floor and chambered a
round, then hit the button to drop his own window. His eyes stung in
the frigid wind, and his lungs filled with frost. The air smelled like

cedar and something else Peter couldn't identify, something chemical. It clung to the insides of his nostrils like a combination of fryer grease and cheap perfume.

"You smell that?"

"Teddy's got a woodstove, but that ain't it."

The driveway curved tightly back the other direction, so that evergreens blocked the view ahead and behind. The lane was narrow and unmaintained. Cedar branches thwacked against the fenders and windshield and into the open windows.

After a half mile, the trees gave way and the land opened up. A simple log house stood at the base of a high rocky outcropping that sheltered it from the north wind. The front faced the driveway, and Peter could tell the door was broken off its hinges. Thin smoke came through smashed windows, backlit by a faint orange glow. Someone had tried to start the place on fire, but it hadn't taken off yet. Log homes were harder to burn than most people thought.

The tar-papered outbuilding was another story. Hastened by the wind, fat flames licked the tops of the broken windows, and greasy black smoke boiled around the silhouette of a fat-tired four-wheeler just inside the ruined roll-up door. The stench of burning petrochemicals filled the air, gas and oil and rubber. One long side of the shed was lined with cord after cord of firewood, cured and dried and neatly stacked under a deep sheltering overhang. Evergreen trees had been planted as a windbreak on the other side, but they were already smoking. Soon it would all go up.

Lewis opened his door and stepped outside, the shotgun raised and ready.

Peter got out, too, pistol up, hands bare and aching in the cold, his unzipped coat blowing open in the wind. He scanned his side of the treeline for human shapes. He saw nothing, so he turned his attention to the clearing. The tire tracks ended in a confusion of footprints that filled the yard. Four dark shapes lay in the snow, with red stains below them. The snow past his knees, his breath a dense plume of fog, Peter walked forward to see.

The shapes were dogs, and they were dead. Each big rangy mutt had been shot multiple times, the bodies contorted with pain, but finally at rest. The wounds were big, probably buckshot.

Lewis saw them, too. "God*damn* it." He was bare-handed and bareheaded, too, but if he felt the cold, it didn't show.

Behind the house lay a heap of green-painted boards, topped by the remains of a plank door with a crescent moon cut into it. The outhouse, tipped on its side and kicked into pieces. At the northernmost edge of the clearing, where it would catch the most possible sun, stood a long prefab greenhouse made of clear plastic stretched over aluminum struts. The plastic had been slashed into ribbons that flapped like cruel pennants in the breeze. Anything growing inside was now frozen.

For a moment, the wind let up. Peter swiveled his head, listening. Over the rumble of the Yukon, he heard something out of place. He looked at Lewis. "Kill the engine."

Lewis leaned into the cab and turned off the ignition. Somehow that made the clearing seem even colder. Peter felt an irrational fear that the truck wouldn't start again, that they would be stranded in this cold, dead place, but he pushed it down and listened harder. The deep thrum of the wind softened and he heard it again. Somewhere below the crackle of the fire, there was a high sound that carried. A keening. Like a wounded animal.

"You hear that?"

"Teddy?" Lewis raised his voice. "Teddy, where you at?"

There was no answer.

3

While Lewis ran to the greenhouse, Peter ran to the cabin.

The front door had been broken down with a sledge-hammer. Despite the smashed windows, the building was filled with smoke. The cast-iron woodstove was shattered, and the metal chimney hung bent from the ceiling. The remains of the fire had somehow been shoved across the rough stone floor and against a log wall, which was charred black. Moving fast and low with the front of his sweatshirt pulled over his nose and mouth, Peter searched for signs of life, but found none.

Outside, Lewis returned from the greenhouse, shaking his head. Together, they circled the structure, trying to read the footprints. They followed several sets that looped into the trees, but the tangled tracks always returned to the house. It wasn't until Lewis stepped around to the back and saw scuffed, windblown prints climbing the steep roof from a loft window that they realized what had happened.

From the roof's peak, the prints jumped eight feet from the house to the tall outcrop behind it. They circled the outcrop and found no tracks leading away. The only other way to the top was a vertical scramble up ice-slick rock to a jumble of boulders and a single tall cedar that had somehow taken root in the crevices of the stone.

They found him sheltered under its snow-weighted branches, curled up into himself like an oversized child. He wore ice-crusted sweat-pants and a greasy green parka with the snorkel hood zipped up tight. The sound from his mouth reminded Peter of a dog he'd seen on the road to Mosul, badly wounded by shrapnel from a rocket attack. When he'd knelt at its side, it had thumped its tail in the dust as its heart pumped its blood from its body. Peter had poured a little water from his canteen into its mouth, rubbed its ears for a moment, then put a mercy bullet in its head.

Lewis bent over the man. "Teddy, it's Lewis. Look at me."

The wind was much worse on the top of the outcrop. Despite the effort of the climb and the modest shelter of the tree, Peter couldn't feel his fingers or his face. His toes were a distant memory. "Is he hurt?"

"We gotta get him someplace warm." With bare hands, Lewis swept the windblown snow off Teddy's parka and sweatpants, looking for blood or bullet holes. "I don't see nothing." He thumped the big shoulder. "C'mon, Teddy, we gotta go. I ain't leaving you for dead, and I sure as hell can't carry you down off this rock."

The keening softened, then went away. From inside the hood, a quiet voice said, "I'm cold."

Lewis snorted. "No shit, Sherlock. You get off your redneck ass, I got a nice warm car down there. Hot coffee, peanut butter sandwiches. They shoot you someplace I can't see?"

Teddy remained in his curl. "They killed my dogs."

Lewis patted his shoulder. "I saw. Hurts, don't it?"

"Yeah. I want to kill *them*."

"You can't do nothin' to nobody if you dead yourself, Teddy. Come on, let's get down from here before the cold gets permanent."

After a moment, the man on the ground began to stir. Lewis backed up to give him room.

It was like watching an elephant get to its feet. A vague swimming motion of the legs, a shift of weight, then the greasy green parka, led by its snorkel hood, rose into the air and pushed through the branches of the tree, shedding snow like a minor avalanche.

A bare hand reached for the zipper and unfastened the hood. A big round face emerged, with a mournful look. His left cheek was marred by a curved, puckering scar that the bristly blond beard didn't cover. His right eye was brown and the left was bright blue. He knuckled tears from the brown side. "I didn't even *do* anything," he said. "Who were those guys?"

"We'll figure all that out," Lewis said. "First we get warm."

Teddy let out his breath in a sigh, then stomped his boots in the snow. "Okay, let's go."

He took a few quick steps and leaped off the rock and onto the sharp ridgeline of his house, sliding to a stop like an ice dancer. He stood looking back at them, his breath rising. "Are you guys coming or what?"

Back on the ground, Teddy took a pick and a shovel from a tangle of tools on the porch and began to clear the snow at the base of an oak tree. Lewis and Peter stood warming themselves by the burning outbuilding, which was now fully engulfed. "It's too cold to dig by hand," Peter said. "The ground's frozen."

Teddy raised the pick and took a swing. The impact sounded like a pile driver. Dirt flew into the air.

Lewis shook his head. "The laws of nature may not apply."

Teddy kept swinging. The hole got bigger.

"I'm gonna lend a hand," Lewis said. "We get that done, maybe he'll tell us what happened. Meantime, you want to see what you can do with the house?"

"On it."

The interior was still full of smoke from the ruined woodstove. Peter ducked into the kitchen area, found a dishrag, and tried to wet it with water from a pitcher, but the water was frozen solid. He dampened the rag with snow as best he could, then tied it around his nose and mouth to act as a filter, wondering how long it would be until his face got frostbite.

With a shovel from the porch, he pitched the hot brittle shards of the cast-iron stove out the back door and into a deep drift, then followed it with the coals and firewood still smoldering against the blackened timbers. He dumped a half-dozen scoops of snow against the charred logs, then climbed to the loft to open the remaining unbroken windows to help clear the smoke from the house.

If Teddy's attackers had thought to add some of the accelerant from the utility shed, the house would be an inferno. With the cabin in the middle of the national forest, Peter supposed they'd figured it was enough to deny Teddy shelter and transportation. Winter would finish the job they started.

Whatever Teddy had done, he'd pissed off some very unpleasant people.

They'd killed his *dogs*.

Peter didn't need to know the why, not yet.

He just needed to find these assholes.

As the air cleared, he walked through the house taking a closer look. The main floor was one big room with well-used furnishings. A sagging old couch and a scratched leather recliner by the woodstove, a single plastic chair at a folding table with an unfinished puzzle on top, and a pair of rough plank shelves that held an eclectic mix of paperback thrillers, true crime, and books on Buddhism and traumatic brain injury recovery. The sleeping loft had only a mattress on the floor, a row of hooks for sweatshirts and jackets, and two smaller plank shelves, one with folded pants and shirts and the other empty. The only luxury was the wide windows on every wall, so the trees could keep him company.

It was surprisingly neat, Peter thought. Whoever these guys were, they hadn't trashed the bookshelves or ransacked the kitchen with its propane fridge and stove, the hand pump mounted over a sink that drained into a five-gallon bucket. If they'd come to steal something, they hadn't needed to upend the house. Maybe they'd just come for Teddy.

Even under the smoke, Peter could smell the dogs. Their hair was tufted in the corners of the couch and matted into the round dog beds lined up behind the woodstove. He imagined Teddy reading in the recliner by the window, his hand reaching out for the creature sitting beside him, leaning into his leg. They would wake him in the morning, lick his face and remind him of his purpose, to feed and care for them. They would keep him company while he split firewood and tended his greenhouse. When the fire burned low, they'd curl up on his bed at night, warming Teddy and each other with their body heat.

A simple life. Even with the dogs, it would be lonely. Without them, it would be desolate.

If Peter hadn't met June, his own life might look like this one. No, he corrected himself, it'd be worse. When he met her in the redwoods, he'd been living in a tent in the mountains, suffering badly from the post-traumatic stress he called the white static. It was a crippling claustrophobia that made him unable to go indoors for more than a few minutes, barely able to walk into a grocery store for supplies.

June was the one who had motivated Peter to get help, to find a way forward into a different life. He'd wanted to sleep beside her, indoors, in a real bed. And now he did. Although, the war still lived inside him, a high-performance engine on low idle. It would always be there, he knew. Most of the time, he barely noticed it. He noticed it now.

Whatever warmth he'd gained from the burning shed had dissipated, and he felt the chill grow deep in his bones. Outside, Lewis leaned on a shovel by a large pile of black dirt. Teddy knelt by the last dark shape in the bloodstained snow, lips moving as he talked to it, or to himself. Then he gathered it into his arms, cold and dead, and carried it to the grave beneath the oak tree. The wind lifted the snow from the ground and swirled it through the clearing. It was already beginning to collect in the house's frozen corners.

When Teddy was done, he and Lewis walked into the house, looking around as Peter had done. Indoors, the facial scar was less noticeable, although the mismatched eye color was still disconcerting. Teddy's work in the snow had left his greasy green parka and sweatpants covered with smears of blood and dirty granules of ice. He reminded Peter of a polar bear: thick and round, slow and fat, right before it leaped twenty feet to pounce on a seal sunning itself on the ice.

Teddy opened the fridge and took out a Coke, but the can was split open, the soda frozen solid. He sighed, opened a kitchen drawer, and pulled out a Snickers bar. It was also frozen, but he gnawed on it anyway, using his molars. That same polar bear with a caribou rib.

Lewis said, "You ready to tell us what happened today?" He had his hands in his pockets, his shoulders hunched against the cold, his breath like smoke in the frigid air.

Teddy swallowed some candy bar. "Four guys in a white Jeep. The dogs heard them first. I let them out. You know I don't like visitors." His face fell. "They shot my boys before they even came close to the car. Then they just walked up to the house like they owned the place."

Lewis said, "What'd they look like?"

Teddy shrugged, chewing. "New coats, new boots, fancy winter hats. They looked pretty comfy with those guns, though."

Not locals, Peter thought. City people. "What kind of guns?"

"Two had shotguns," Teddy said. "With those box magazines that hold ten shells. The other two had machine pistols, maybe Uzis."

"Did you fire at them?" Peter couldn't imagine a guy like Teddy not taking a shot at the men who killed his dogs.

"Teddy gave up guns when he got out of the hospital," Lewis said.

"Somebody might get hurt," Teddy said. The blue eye didn't seem to track, so Peter figured that was the prosthetic. "I gave up meat, too. I used to get real angry. Now I don't even swat mosquitoes. I mean, bugs gotta eat, too."

That explained the books on Buddhism. Peter understood the impulse toward nonviolence, and thought it was a good one, but he'd never been able to stick to it. Sometimes things just get ugly. Like when some asshole shoots your dogs and sets your house on fire. For example.

Lewis said, "You really got no idea why they came? What they wanted?"

Teddy looked around. "I don't think anything's missing. What would they take, anyway? I had to sell everything to pay the medical bills. The only reason I got to keep this place is 'cause it's in my dead brother's name. Although I do have a little cash buried in the yard." He flashed a goofy grin. "My memory's so bad it's like a treasure hunt every time I go look for it."

"So maybe you pissed somebody off," Lewis said.

"I can't think of who," Teddy said. "Since I got shot in the head, everybody likes me." The candy bar was gone. The tips of his nose and ears were pale. He had to be freezing.

Peter's own stomach trembled, and his arms and legs ached from the cold. He looked at Lewis, who nodded and said, "Let's talk in the car. Teddy, maybe you want to grab a change of clothes?"

"Okay," Teddy said, and bounded up the stairs to the loft. At the top, he stopped. "Oh no," he said. "No no no no."

Peter and Lewis ran up the stairs behind him.

"My notebooks," Teddy wailed. He stared at the empty shelf. "They're gone."

4

ewis stepped toward him, his voice low and gentle. "What notebooks, Teddy?"

The big man looked at his feet. "Just, you know, notebooks.
For writing stuff down."

"And what are you writing down?"

Teddy shook his head, eyes still down. "Nothing."

"Teddy." Lewis got right next to him, a hand on his shoulder. "Talk
to me."

Teddy took a breath, then let it out. "Well, you know I have a brain
injury. Because I got shot in the head."

"I remember, I was there. What about the notebooks?"

"Well, I have trouble with my memory. So Leanne, my speech
pathologist—I mean, I don't know why they call her a speech pathologist, she's the one who helps with my memory. Anyway, Leanne told
me to start a journal, to write down everything I could remember." To
Peter, he said, "It helps make new neural pathways. Neurons that fire

together, wire together, that's what Leanne says. I also write down things I'm grateful for."

He turned to Lewis. "Like, I'm grateful for you, Lewis. I'm glad you're my friend." Before Lewis could move, Teddy was on him, arms wrapped around him in a hug.

Lewis was a big man, but he was dwarfed by Teddy's bearlike embrace. He shook his head at Peter and patted Teddy on the back until he could extract himself from the hug. "Thank you, Teddy. I'm glad you're my friend, too. Now, what's in the notebooks?"

Teddy shrugged. "I told you. Everything I remembered."

"Everything?" Lewis stared at him. "Even the jobs you and me did together? You write those down, too?"

Teddy's voice got small. "Uh-huh."

The muscles flexed in Lewis's jaw. "You give details? Names and places? *My* name? Nino and Ray?"

"Well, yeah. Leanne said even the smallest details would help. She said write down everything. So I did. It turned out, after a few years, I remembered a lot."

Lewis closed his eyes. "How did someone know about the notebooks, Teddy? Who would do this?"

"I don't know," Teddy said. "I don't go to the bar anymore. You know I don't like visitors. The only guys I talk to are you and Nino." He gave Peter a belligerent look. "I don't even *know* this guy."

"I'm Peter. A friend of Lewis's."

Teddy's face lit up like a sunrise. "You're the jarhead? Can we be friends, too?"

For Marines, the term *jarhead* was an insult, unless it came from another Marine. Peter made an exception for Lewis. Now, he figured, he'd make one for Teddy. "I'd like that. But I have a question. About your speech pathologist, Leanne. Does she know what's in your notebooks? And how long ago was your last appointment with her?"

Teddy's pink complexion turned pinker. "Um," he said.

Lewis looked at him. "Teddy, that was years ago you got shot. Why're you still seeing your speech pathologist?" Then he sighed. "You're sleeping with her."

Now Teddy was bright red. His gaze rose to the ceiling. "Um, we don't really sleep, Lewis. We just screw. I mean, like bunny rabbits. She's real skinny, so mostly she likes to be on top. Unless we do it doggy style. That's my favorite, woof woof."

Lewis put up a hand like a traffic cop. "Please stop talking."

Peter cleared his throat. "Has Leanne read your notebooks?"

"Oh, gosh, no," Teddy said. "Those are private."

Unlike their sex life, Peter thought. "But you talk to her about what you remember?"

"Well, sure. I tell her stories. I mean, we got to talk about something when we're done screwing."

"What was the last thing you told her?"

The tip of Teddy's tongue crept to the corner of his mouth, like a cartoon of a child in thought. "I've been trying to remember what happened the day I got shot. I'm making some progress. I know who was with us and where we were, and who we were taking down."

Lewis closed his eyes and massaged his forehead with one hand. His gun had somehow appeared in the other. "Teddy, I swear to God—"

Peter took hold of Lewis's shoulder. "It's already done, Lewis. All we can do is clean it up."

Peter sent Teddy back upstairs for a change of clothes, then took a burner phone from the Yukon and put the name of Teddy's speech pathologist into the search bar. He found her on a medical network's website, with five different locations listed. He held out the phone to Lewis.

"Hi, honey," Lewis said. "How you doin' today? My name's Bob and I'm lookin' for Leanne Parnell?" His voice was pure country, warm and white as Wonder Bread. Lewis could sound like a Pakistani cabdriver or a plummy English broadcaster or anyone else he wanted. "I was supposed to pick her up at the clinic after work today, but like a dummy, I forgot to ask which clinic, and I'm kinda embarrassed to call her. Can you help me out?"

While Lewis was on the phone, Teddy came down with an Army duffel slung over one shoulder. He was shivering hard now. He'd been outside in punishing weather for hours. The shed had almost burned itself out.

Peter asked, "Do you have anyplace to go?"

"This is my house," Teddy said. "I live here."

"Dude, you've got no heat, no front door, no glass in your windows. We'll get you fixed up, but it'll take time. What if those guys come back? For now, we need you someplace safe and warm. Do you have any family nearby?"

Teddy shook his head. "I'll just go with you, I guess."

Lewis put his phone away and looked at Peter. That wasn't going to work. If they were going to have a conversation with Leanne, Teddy couldn't be along for the ride. They'd drop him at a hotel on the way.

They walked out to the Yukon together. Teddy opened the back door and climbed inside. Peter got in the front passenger side and turned on the seat warmers. By the time Lewis had started the engine, Teddy had lain down, pulled the green Mexican blanket over his head, and begun to snore.

"Crap." Lewis got the car turned around and headed down the driveway, fighting the wheel, the heavy vehicle slipping in the ruts.

This was a different version of Lewis. Usually he was cool, calm, and competent, always slightly amused by the world. But now he looked somehow unsteady, a man in a small boat fighting a strong tide.

Peter knew what was on his mind. "You're worried about Dinah and the boys."

"Hell yes I am." Lewis's face was grim. "My name's in those notebooks. Dinah wanted me to get my shit legit so we could live a real life, out in the open. Somebody gets interested in me and looks hard enough, they'll turn up our marriage, get her name. They get that . . ."

He came to the end of the driveway and hit the brakes, the engine throbbing. "What the hell do they want with those notebooks, anyway? Why go to all that trouble?"

"Teddy's stories struck a nerve with somebody," Peter said. "Whoever these guys are, they're clearly not law enforcement, so maybe they're people from your old life. Someone who's been looking for you. Someone you hit, maybe."

Lewis frowned. "Well, if that's who they are, they'll be looking for payback. And they won't care who they have to hurt." His hands clenched the wheel like he wanted to tear it off the steering column. "Teddy wasn't part of the main crew, like Nino and Ray, but he worked with us on plenty of jobs. If he really was writing down everything he could remember, that'd be more than enough to put us on the radar of some real bad people."

"That means they'll probably be after Nino and Ray, too. And whoever else Teddy put down on paper."

Lewis glanced into the back seat at the man snoring under the blanket. He lowered his voice. "Maybe I should have let that motherfucker die back in Bakersfield. Keep your damn mouth shut, that's the first rule."

"Let's take a step back, do some risk assessment," Peter said. "Teddy texted you around eight p.m., right? So whoever these guys are, they've had the notebooks since sometime yesterday evening. They hung around overnight, trying to wait Teddy out, but he stayed hidden. At about eleven this morning, they figured he was dead and hit the road.

But they've still got to actually read the notebooks, to figure out what they have. And they need to get back to Milwaukee before they can do anything."

"Unless they got a second crew waiting."

"Sure," Peter said. "But how would they know where to wait? Even if they're all dialed in, they can't make a move until later tonight. Because Charlie's at school with basketball practice, right? And Miles stays late, too, until Dinah's shift at the hospital ends, and she can pick them up. Both places have half-decent security, and no professional criminal would march into a school or a hospital and abduct somebody. Too many cameras and witnesses. So we have a few hours. It's only three o'clock now."

"That sounds right." Lewis sighed. "Man, I should call Dinah, but with this burner, she's not going to pick up."

"June's used to oddball calls on her work phone. I'll get her up to speed. She can reach out to Dinah."

"But now June's involved. One more person at risk. I can't have that."

Peter smiled kindly. "You know how pissed off she'll be if you shut her out? Trust me, you do not want June Cassidy mad at you."

Lewis scratched his nose. "She's scary enough when she's mad at *you*, Jarhead."

"Just you wait, brother. I'm gonna tell her this whole thing is your fault." Peter took out his phone.

June answered after two rings. "June Cassidy."

"It's me. Got a minute?"

"Absolutely," she said. "Get over here quick, my boyfriend's out of town."

Peter could hear the grin in her voice, could picture the spray of freckles and wicked green eyes. A memory rose from the night before. They'd gone for a late-night run in the cold, then climbed into the shower together, slick with sweat. "It's no use pretending," he said. "I know you're into me."

"I beg your pardon, but I believe it was you who were into me. Several times, in fact."

Peter cleared his throat, glad he hadn't put the phone on speaker. "Uh, I'm here with Lewis. We have a situation. Can you talk?"

He explained what had happened to Teddy. The missing notebooks, what was in them, what could be at risk.

"I'll call Dinah," June said. "Keep me in the loop. If I don't hear from you by four thirty, I'll pick up her and the boys, then find a hotel for the night. We'll use my car and my credit card. Teddy's never heard of me, so the bad guys won't know to look for my name. Piece of cake."

"You're a rock star," Peter said.

"Is Lewis doing okay?"

Peter glanced at his friend, who was staring out the window. "Not really, but we're working the problem."

"The only way out is through," she said. "Stay safe. And keep me posted, or I'll kick your ass. You read me, Marine?"

Peter grinned. "Yes, ma'am. Loud and clear, ma'am." He put the phone away and looked at Lewis. "June sends her love. Can we go now?"

Lewis nodded and hit the gas. The engine roared and the tires spun as the Yukon leaped forward, throwing great clots of snow in its wake.

Peter reached inside the paper bag and peeled the foil from a peanut butter sandwich.

It was frozen solid.

5

LEANNE

The daylight was fading as Leanne Parnell hustled across the parking lot toward her Chevy Malibu, coatless in the winter cold. She shook her hair out of the too-tight ponytail she wore at work, mind focused on the baggie of weed in the center console and whether she needed to stop at the liquor store on her way to meet Mika tonight. But when she saw the big Black guy step out of a dark SUV, she knew somehow that he was there for her.

She opened her mouth and tipped her head to one side, as if she'd just realized she'd forgotten something, then spun on the heel of her smart black pumps to hustle back toward the clinic. But a white man had appeared behind her, tall and bony, phone in his hand, blocking her path. She'd never even heard his footsteps. She turned again. If she could just make it to her car, she could lock the doors and drive. But the Black man was right in front of her now, holding up his open wallet the way cops do, some kind of paper showing through the plastic window.

His face was blank and emotionless. "Leanne Parnell? I'm an investigator with the state police. We need to talk."

She thought about running. The Black guy must have read her mind. He clamped his free hand onto her upper arm, tight as a tourniquet. As the winter wind rose up and cut into her like a scalpel, she wanted a lungful of that good Michigan hydro more than she'd ever wanted anything in her life.

The Black guy said, "We can sit in the car, or we can go to the clinic and sit in the conference room with your supervisor. But I think you'd prefer this conversation stay between us." His deep voice was calm and reasonable, but beneath that was something else, something that scared her.

She wouldn't be in this position if she'd kept up her grades, Leanne thought. If she hadn't had that little coke problem in high school that had brought her GPA down so far her only option was community college. If she hadn't had another slip at Lakeside that kept her from transferring to a real college, which limited her to a third-tier master's program with no available scholarships, just a crapload of loans. She'd set her sights on speech pathology because her advisor told her the money was good and there were plenty of jobs. Like nursing, but without all the messiness of the human body.

By then she'd gotten better at maintaining. Prescription Adderall to get her up, weed to smooth out the speed bumps, the combination enough to keep her floating along like a balloon in a ballroom. Not flying up into the rafters, but not bottomed-out on the floor with the dirty napkins and cigarette butts, either. Just enough lift to tamp down her stepfather's voice in her head and keep her from spiraling down into the pit.

It took her two tries to pass the state exam, and the best job she could get was up here in nowheresville, working five different clinics spread halfway across northern Wisconsin, putting seven hundred miles a week on her car. Rent was cheap, but gas was expensive, and the pay wasn't anywhere near what her advisor had said. Which meant she had trouble making a dent in her student loans until she managed to snag a key to the first clinic's drug locker. Now she had the keys to all five and had almost paid off her degree. Her performance reviews weren't great, but she was going to turn it around, get her life together. Quit using. Get a better job in Chicago. Start dating doctors. Once she got married, she'd spend her days by the pool at the country club, working on her tan. She'd finally have a beautiful life, just like in the magazines.

Meantime, she was making do with whatever men she could find. One was an insurance agent, another a former patient. And Mika, whom she'd met at the bar. Combining sex *and* drugs was the best way to step outside of her whirling thoughts. Which were whirling out of control now, the stolen pill bottle from the drug locker in the bottom of her purse, the illegal bag of pot in the glove box. She stared at the ground, wondering how they'd found her out.

"Leanne." The big Black guy's voice brought her back to herself. He looked at her as if he could see right through her. He had an odd kind of stillness, she thought. Very focused. Very scary.

But she'd handled police before. So she swung her long blond hair and gave him the smile that she used on the guy at the drug-testing facility when she needed to fool the test with another girl's pee. "All right," she said. "You win." Then shook off the Black guy's hand and walked toward the dark SUV.

He opened the back door, held out a hand to help her in, then gave her time to scoot across to the far side before climbing in after her. The white guy sat in the front passenger seat, half-turned so he could see her.

She felt cold and exposed in her thin blouse and short skirt. She shouldn't have left her ugly old coat in the car. She wished again that she had that dope, just one hit to calm her nerves. But she didn't, so she clutched her purse on her lap to keep her hands from shaking. "What's this about?"

"You look cold." The white guy reached over and turned the key in the ignition. Warm air began to flow from the vents. "Don't be afraid," he said. "We just want to talk."

Not cops, she thought. Too rough-looking. And too polite. The cops she'd met never gave a damn how she felt.

But these two had said they were cops. Which meant they were the other thing.

She shivered, thinking of Mika. What had he gotten her into?

She fumbled in her purse, but the Black guy plucked the whole thing from her hands with no apparent effort. She never could have run from him, she realized now. He passed her bag over the seatback to the white guy, who held it open with one big fist, finding and removing the police-grade pepper spray she kept clipped to the upper pocket. It looked so small in his big hand. Then he reached back in and found the white plastic bottle, tipped it to read the label. Oxycodone.

"That's *mine*," she said. "Give it *back*." Mika would give her twenty bucks for a 40 mg pill, and there were two hundred in the bottle.

The Black guy didn't seem to hear her. "You're sleeping with a friend of ours," he said. "Teddy Wilson."

Now she was confused. "What does that have to do with anything?"

The Black guy's stillness had only gotten deeper. "You're a speech pathologist. When Teddy was your patient, you suggested he keep a journal, write down his memories."

"Uh, yeah." She almost rolled her eyes but didn't. "That's my job."

The Black guy said, "When you see Teddy now, sometimes he tells you what he remembers. Problem is, that's private information, Leanne. Dangerous information."

She blinked at him. He kept talking. "We're not after you, Leanne. We want the people you told about Teddy."

She felt her heart thudding in her chest. This wasn't about pills she was wholesaling to Mika. This was about Teddy's crazy stories. She hadn't even believed him, not really, but she did now. And she'd figured out who the Black man was.

"You're him," she said. "The boss."

A sound came out of him, a growl from deep in his chest. His face looked like it was carved out of dark ice. When he spoke, his voice might have come from the bottom of the deepest, coldest lake in the world. "Who'd you tell, Leanne? And where can I find him?"

It was Wednesday, her night to meet Mika. She cleared her throat, having trouble getting the words out. "If I say, what happens to me?"

"Not a thing, Leanne." This from the white guy, his voice surprisingly gentle. "You have our word. We'll have to keep you with us until we get hold of him, but you'll be safe. When it's done, we'll drop you at your car. You'll never see us again."

She turned to the Black guy, whose name she now knew was Lewis, looking for verification.

He gave her a crooked smile and said, "Long as we get what we need."

6

PETER

Peter sat in the passenger seat of Leanne's blue Malibu while she gunned it up the middle of Highway 70 between high banks of snow, chasing her headlights down the center line. He kept his pistol ready in his hand, although he knew he wouldn't need it. His fastened seat belt, on the other hand, might come in handy any minute.

When Leanne had opened her car door, the first thing she did was pull on a tattered cloth coat and wrap it tightly around herself like a suit of armor. Then she took a little glass pipe from the center console, her hands shaking as she raised the flame to the bowl. She took a huge hit, holding the smoke inside as if her life depended on it, then two more. Peter had to put his window down to clear the air. The front of the Malibu was tidy enough, but the rear footwells were knee-deep in gas station coffee cups and food wrappers. Four air fresheners hung from the mirror, but beneath the perfume of fake vanilla, the pungent funk of weed went deep.

Now she had the pipe tucked between her legs as she drove, the lighter ready in her hand. She'd reached for a pint of Smirnoff in the glove box, but Peter had told her no. Now he was thinking maybe he should allow it. The vodka might slow her down a little. With the Oxy and a prescription bottle of Adderall in her purse, Leanne Parnell was a one-woman pharmacopeia, clearly not in control of her life, let alone the car she was driving.

She glanced at Peter now. "Teddy's stories. Are they true?"

"I've never heard them," Peter said. "I didn't know those guys back then."

No matter what Leanne had heard, however bad the stories might be, Peter figured the true tales would be worse. He'd never seen Lewis the way he'd looked sitting beside Leanne in the Yukon. Cold down to the bone.

But Peter knew Lewis well enough to know what lay beneath that cold, hard surface.

Lewis was afraid.

He was behind them now in the Yukon, with her purse and phone and wallet and pills, staying well back in case Leanne wrecked the car, speeding stoned down the dark and snowy road.

They were headed to a little resort outside of Eagle River. Peter said, "Why don't you meet Mika at your place?"

She gave him a flat look, only slightly blurry. "Nobody goes to my place. That's just for me." She fumbled a hand into the center console and came up with a dented pack of Marlboro Reds. The car drifted into the wrong lane as she began to fish for a cigarette.

"Don't," Peter said. "Eyes on the road or I'll put you in the trunk."

He didn't know if he could actually do that to this scared, stoned blonde with her dark roots showing. He reminded himself of Teddy's trashed house, with the shed on fire and Teddy curled up beneath the tree in the killing cold.

Leanne got the Malibu back on track, her face clenched tight. "I need a cigarette. I'm jumping out of my skin."

"When we get there." There was enough smoke in the car already. "Tell me about Mika. What's his last name?"

"I don't know, I can't pronounce it," she said. "He's Albanian. The first time we met, he told me he was a traveling salesman. Although with that big Mercedes van, I knew it couldn't be true."

"So what *does* he do?"

"He drives the van up from Chicago once a week, fills it with untaxed cigarettes from some Indian guy he knows, then drives them back to Chicago. He supplies these gas stations, they buy everything he can get. Nobody pays the tax and everybody makes money."

"He told you this from the outset?"

"God, no. He opened the van once to grab his bag and I saw all the boxes in the back. I knew right away he was a crook." She shot Peter a look. "No offense."

Peter smiled. "None taken. Is that Oxy in your purse part of his regular pickup, or is that a side thing?"

She shook her head. "That's a side thing. Just between me and Mika."

"So he's not on his own," Peter said. "He works for somebody else."

"Well, he's not the boss. He wouldn't drive all the way up here every week if he was."

"Maybe he just likes seeing you," Peter said.

She shrugged as if dismissing the idea, but a half smile played on her lips. She was beginning to relax, even a little glad to be able to tell somebody all of this. Then she seemed to remember that two strange men had kidnapped her and the smile disappeared.

"What's going to happen to Mika?" she asked.

"Same as you," Peter said. "He tells us what we need to know and we all go on our way." It might work out that way, so it wasn't technically a lie.

She was quiet a moment. "Did somebody do something to Teddy?"

Took her long enough to ask, Peter thought. "Four men went to his place in the woods. They killed his dogs and wrecked his house, tried to burn it down. Came close to killing him."

She stared out the windshield. "Mika wouldn't do that."

Peter kept his eyes on her face. "Somebody sure as hell did. What did you tell Mika about Teddy?"

"Just a few of his stories," she said. "It was something to talk about, you know, after. Mika was a crook, I thought he'd be interested."

Peter shook his head. "Like shop talk with the nurses in the break room."

She threw both hands in the air. "*Exactly* like that." So glad Peter understood.

"The difference is, sharing Teddy's stories can get people killed."

"But how was *I* supposed to know that? I mean, Teddy told *me* the same stories."

"Teddy had a brain injury," Peter said. "He thought he was talking to his speech therapist. Who he happened to be sleeping with. He was showing off. You know he really likes you, right? He trusted you. And you told your friend Mika, who probably sold Teddy out to some very bad people."

"I never meant for that to happen." Her face crumpled and tears began to roll down her cheeks. She put her foot on the brake and brought the Malibu to a sliding stop in the middle of the darkened road. "I really need another hit on that pipe."

Peter reached over and put the car in park. "Open your door."

As she did, Lewis rolled up beside them with his window down. "What's the problem?"

But Leanne had already snatched up the pipe. Both men watched as she sparked the lighter and filled her hungry lungs with hot smoke, the pain etched deep in her face.

She took a second hit, then handed Peter the pipe and fumbled a Marlboro with trembling fingers. When she got it lit, she leaned back in her seat and looked at Peter. "Mika's got family in Chicago," she said. "His cousins. That's who it would be."

Peter nodded. It was a start.

Soon enough, Mika would give them names and addresses and everything else they needed.

Fifteen minutes later, with Peter now driving, they pulled over at the turnoff to the North Lake Resort. Lewis called from the Yukon. "She got a text from our boy. He's in cabin seven."

"Lucky seven," Peter said. "You want to get in there first to set up?"

"Ten minutes." The Yukon rumbled past them and disappeared into the darkness.

The resort was really just a sprawling bar-restaurant on a frozen lake with an ancient concrete dock. In the summer it would be a non-stop party, but on a Wednesday night in February, the parking lot was empty but for a few pickups parked close to the door and a half-dozen snowmobiles lined up beside the packed trail that would run from lake to lake, bar to bar.

To the left was a poorly plowed road that ran behind a row of widely spaced cabins lined up in the dark evergreens, facing the shore. Number seven was the same as the others, a small clapboard shack that looked like it was being eaten by snowdrifts. Unshoveled steps rose to the back stoop. A black Mercedes Sprinter was parked at a wide spot on the road, with the passenger side closest to the building and a two-wheel U-Haul car trailer attached to the hitch.

The neighboring cabins were lightless, carless. Peter saw no sign of

Lewis or the Yukon. He pulled over behind the van and leaned forward to adjust the Browning, which dug into his left hip. "What's with the trailer?"

"I don't know," Leanne said. "That's new." She looked at him, her hands knotted in her lap. "What do we do now?"

He eyeballed the cabin through her window, wondering if he'd seen movement at the curtains. "Does he come out to meet you?"

"Oh, no," she said. "I just grab my stuff and head inside. Then, you know, we party. He always has good stuff."

"Okay." Peter reached into the back seat for a small overnight bag and put it on her lap. She didn't move. "Time to go, Leanne."

"What are you going to do?" Her voice was small and quiet.

"It'll be okay." He turned off the engine and put the keys in his pocket. "We're just going to talk. But if things get loud and you're scared, run to the bathroom. If there's a bathtub, get in and stay low. You'll be safe there." If somebody pulled the trigger, a cast-iron tub might protect her from a stray bullet.

She took a shaky breath. He could see the panic rising on her face. Peter wasn't crazy about bringing her along, either, but he couldn't take her keys and leave her in the car, not in this weather. So he reached across her and pushed her door open. The bitter cold blew in. "I won't let anything happen to you," he said. "Just this one last thing and you're done. But now you have to move. You have to help make up for what happened to Teddy."

She put one leg out, then the other, and pulled herself to her feet. Either she was braver than Peter thought, or she was medicated into a trance. It didn't matter which.

As she walked toward the cabin, the back door opened and a man stepped out. He was slim with thick black hair and held his right hand behind his hip. His breath plumed out when he spoke. "Who is that with you, Leanne?"

"Mika," she called, "I can explain."

His right hand edged out from behind his body. It was bulbous and fat, holding something. A gun.

Peter rose from the Malibu, shuffling left to aim the Browning above the roof of the car, but he was too slow. A shadow rose beside the steps, grabbed Mika's right wrist, and twisted the gun from his grasp, toppling him face-first into the deep snow. Lewis leaped and landed on the floundering form as if from a great height. There was a flurry of movement, the fisted pistol rising and falling. Then Lewis stood up and Mika lay still and half-buried in white.

Lewis tucked the gun into a jacket pocket, then bent and slung the inert Mika over one shoulder, mounted the steps, and disappeared into the cabin.

Leanne hadn't moved. Peter came up behind her and caught her arm to escort her toward the door. "You see? Nothing to it."

7

eter stood behind Leanne in the entryway, watching as Lewis dropped Mika on the floor with a thump. The carpet at the center of the cabin was covered with a ten-foot square of translucent plastic sheeting, rough-edged where it had been cut from a larger roll. The shabby slipcovered couch, small table, and two wooden chairs had been shoved to one side to make room. On the table was a claw hammer, a roll of duct tape, a bottle of Absolut, and a stack of thin towels gone gray from washing.

Lewis knelt to empty the Albanian's pockets, tossing away wallet, keys, phone, and a folding knife. Mika's maroon button-down shirt was torn and damp, his dress pants caked with snow. One shiny leather shoe was missing. The exposed sock had a hole in the heel. With the plastic laid out on the floor, Peter was having trouble feeling sympathetic.

Leanne was stuck in place, her overnight bag clutched to her chest and one hand to her mouth. Peter hoped she hadn't figured out her lover's plan for her. He pointed to the table with two wooden chairs and gave her a gentle push. "Take a seat."

She scuttled over to sit in the farthest chair, tight against the wall. The cabin was a single room with a king-size bed at one end and a modest kitchenette and bathroom door at the other. The couch and table had filled the space in the middle. The air smelled like fried fish and the windows were white with frost. A wall heater ticked feebly, unable to keep up with the arctic blast outside.

A pretty lousy love nest, Peter thought. Even without the murder setup.

Mika stirred on the floor and Lewis rose to his feet, graceful as a cat. The Albanian sat up, put a hand to the back of his head, and glared up at Lewis. He was in his early twenties, with deep-set eyes under a prominent brow. The mottled purple shadow of a bruise was already emerging along the side of his face. His thick hair was stiff with product and had retained its position combed straight back from the low forehead.

Now he sneered at Lewis. "You're in a lot of trouble, pal." He had a broad Chicago accent overlaying a trace of Eastern Europe. "You got any idea who I'm connected to?"

"No." Lewis regarded him calmly, his face expressionless. "Tell me their names."

The Albanian saw Leanne at the table, still clutching her bag. He began to stand. If he was scared or in pain, he had it locked down. "You brought these guys? Bitch, I'm gonna hurt you bad."

Leanne flinched. Lewis leaned in, cold as ice, and slapped the Albanian across the face. It was left-handed with minimal windup, but still hard enough to crank the younger man's head to the side and knock him back to his knees. "Pay attention, Mika. This isn't about her, it's about you. And whether you survive the night."

Mika shook his head to get past the blow, eyes narrowed, cheek turning red. "Fuck you."

Peter leaned against the wall with the Browning hanging from his fist. He had to admire the young Albanian's attitude. Despite being outnumbered, getting his ass kicked, and now kneeling on a big sheet of plastic, he still refused to back down. It wasn't going to help him, but it was impressive.

Lewis slapped him again, this time with his dominant right, putting more into it. Despite the open hand, the enormous force spun the other man's shoulders around and put him on the floor. Lewis stared down at him. "Mika. Were you at Teddy Wilson's house this morning? You one of the guys tried to burn it down?"

Punch-drunk now, Mika fought his way back to one knee, blinking. "You're a dead man. You just don't know it yet."

Lewis took Mika's gun from his pocket, a cheap automatic with electrician's tape wrapping the grips, and held it down along his leg. Behind him, Leanne made a high, panicked noise and scrambled past the kitchenette and into the bathroom, overnight bag tight in her arms. The door slammed behind her.

Lewis didn't even seem to notice. The intensity crackled off him as if he'd been dipped in liquid nitrogen. He stared at Mika like he could poke a hole in him with his eyes. "Who'd you tell about Teddy? Who was there?"

"Wait." Climbing unsteadily to his feet, Mika stumbled back against the couch. "You're him, aren't you?"

Lewis press-checked the slide to make sure there was a round in the chamber. "I want names, who you told about Teddy. Or I'll put a bullet in your ankle." He showed Mika his teeth. "Blow it to pieces, won't never be right again."

Mika's calves hit the edge of the couch and he tipped backward onto it, hands up as if he could hold back a bullet, eyes wide as he stared at the Black man. "Holy crap. You're him. You're Lewis."

"Last chance." Lewis pointed the pistol, his face cold and dark. "Who'd you tell?"

Mika's veneer of toughness began to slip. He pulled up his legs as if the water was rising. "I can't. They'll kill me."

"Imagine what I'll do." Lewis pressed the trigger. *BANG.*

The gunshot was loud in the closed room. The base of the couch gave off a puff of dust between Mika's raised legs. A yelp came from the bathroom. Lewis frowned, took the gun in both hands, and aimed with care. "Hold still, asshole."

Peter wasn't sure if he'd really do it. Mika, on the other hand, had zero doubts and was frantically trying to figure out how to hide his ankles. "Okay, wait, it's my older cousin, Zef. He's in Chicago, pulling jobs. I heard the stories from Leanne and passed them on, that's all I did, I swear it."

Peter put out a hand to stop Lewis and pushed off the wall. "Why tell anyone at all? They're just stories, some guy talking shit."

Mika looked at Peter for the first time, eyebrows climbing. "Are you kidding? A semitrailer full of dope burned up in New Jersey? A cartel hit in Miami? My cousin's told those stories since I was a kid. It's the Ghost Killers."

"Ghost Killers?" Peter glanced at Lewis, who shook his head as if shaking off a gnat.

Mika kept talking, the floodgates open. "A real heavy crew. Big scores, serious takedowns. Made a lot of enemies, but nobody ever knew who they were. I mean, you start asking around, a lot of people heard stories. Maybe they were real, maybe not. But Leanne had names and places. Lewis and Nino and Ray. Houston and Miami and Bakersfield. She said there were notebooks, the guy wrote everything down."

Peter said, "What does your cousin want with the notebooks?"

"I don't know. I'm the youngest. Zef doesn't tell me anything."

"What about Leanne?"

Mika's eyes dropped down to the plastic sheet, then slid over to the hammer and duct tape on the table. "He just told me, you know, take care of the girl. Make her disappear."

That's what the car trailer was for, Peter thought. Mika'd planned to put the Malibu on it, take it back to Chicago with him. Probably with Leanne's body in the trunk. "And you were okay with that?"

Mika raised his chin. "You don't say no to Zef."

Lewis spoke now. "Tell me about him. What's he into?"

"You name it, he's into it. He's not afraid of anybody or anything. You hear about that social club in Cicero, maybe fifteen months ago?"

Peter had read about it in the paper. A social club was like a private bar, members only. This one was a Mafia hangout. The Friday night after Thanksgiving, the place was packed with soldiers from the Chicago Outfit, some kind of celebration. Four men had gone into the place with ski masks and assault rifles. Four against forty. They'd killed the capo and six of his guys, including his two top lieutenants. Then they cleaned out the register and took guns, watches, wallets, and rings off every man there. It was a decapitation of the Chicago family, and a warning to everyone else. They'd left behind an Albanian flag on the pole out front.

"That was Zef."

Peter shook his head. "And you told this asshole where Teddy lives." He walked to the bedside table and opened the drawer. Beside a faded maroon Gideon Bible lay a cheap ballpoint and pad. He handed the pen and paper to Mika. "Who does your cousin run with and where do we find them? Write it down, names and addresses, where they live and where they hang out."

Mika put his hands up like a traffic cop. "I'm not doing that. If he finds out, he'll kill me. Plus he's my cousin, my family."

Lewis pointed the gun toward Mika's crotch and pulled the trigger. *BANG*. A geyser of dust rose from a hole in the couch cushion between his legs. Mika jumped halfway to the ceiling.

"You don't say no to us, either," Lewis said. "You still got a chance to live. Now write, or I start putting holes in you for real."

Mika grabbed the pen and pad and started writing. "I don't know addresses. I need my phone, everything's in there."

Peter scooped it off the floor, an expensive, state-of-the-art device. That simple fact told Peter that Mika wasn't a real player. If he was, he'd have a burner. "What's the code?"

Mika gave him an offended look and sat forward on the couch. "That's my *Samsung*, man. Give it here." As if some things were sacred, and they were all on your phone.

Lewis looked at Peter. "Pass me that claw hammer. You hold him down."

With his feet already under him, Mika came off the couch in a hurry, lips peeled back, both hands reaching for the gun. Lewis had time to turn to take the impact on his shoulder, but the Albanian, although slimmer, already had a grip on the weapon. He held on like a terrier as Lewis spun around, trying for leverage. Lewis was bigger, but Mika's desperation made him strong, his body bent like a bow in the effort to take control of the pistol.

The barrel swung toward Peter. Browning raised, he danced sideways to get out of the line of fire. Lewis and Mika continued their waltz. Peter didn't want to shoot Mika without getting answers first, and he didn't want to hit Lewis by accident. He reversed the Browning in his fist and closed on the pair, looking for an opening to shut this thing down.

BANG. BANG BANG.

Mika had gotten a finger on the trigger, or a finger on Lewis's. Peter's ears rang. He didn't know if anyone was hit. He was behind the Albanian now, but Mika was hunched up, protecting his neck and head. Peter swung the Browning, but only managed to find the bunched muscles of the smaller man's shoulders. It wasn't enough. Mika didn't relent. He just tucked himself closer to the gun, mouth open as if to bite Lewis on the forearm.

Lewis and Mika kept turning. Peter reached inside and got his free hand on the collar of the Albanian's shirt. He swung the Browning again, a hammer at a nail, and landed a blow with the magazine baseplate at the back of the other man's skull, feeling the impact all the way up his arm.

The Albanian sagged slightly and stopped turning, but kept his grip on the gun. "Hit him again," Lewis said. Peter swung a second time, putting everything he had into it. The crack of metal against bone sounded like two pool balls colliding.

Mika groaned softly as his legs buckled. Lewis pulled the pistol free and let him fall. When he hit the plastic sheet, Lewis stepped back and kicked him hard in the side of the head.

Mika curled up reflexively. His scalp was bleeding freely. Lewis went to kick him again, but Peter put out a hand. "We still need those names."

"Motherfucker." Lewis straightened up, breathing hard. "You hit?"

"I don't know." Peter checked himself. With all the adrenaline, sometimes you didn't feel it. "I don't think so. You?"

Lewis shook his head. "He never got the barrel around."

Peter glanced over his shoulder. The fridge had a bullet hole in it. He turned for a better look. Two more dark dots marked the drywall over the sink.

On the other side of that wall was the bathroom.

8

Peter went to the bathroom door. "Leanne?" He tried the knob, but it was locked. "Leanne, open the door. Everything's under control out here."

There was no answer.

He put his ear to the hollow particleboard. Nothing. He took a tight grip on the cheap knob and twisted hard. He felt a soft snap as the pin gave way and the knob turned freely.

But the door only opened an inch. Her overnight bag was behind it, wedged against the toilet. It was a tiny bathroom. He put his shoulder to the door, but it didn't move. "Leanne, help me out here."

No answer. Just a soft sound he couldn't quite identify.

He stepped away and leaned back on one leg and kicked out hard at the lower door hinge. The material was thin and soft. The screws gave way. He couldn't reach the upper hinge with his foot, but now he could get his hand into the gap along the jamb. He grabbed the inner edge of the door and pushed up and out, levering it away. He was still wearing his winter coat. Sweat popped on his forehead as the upper hinge began to bend. Then the particleboard tore away and the hinge came free.

He pulled the door out of the bathroom and let it fall behind him, then stepped into the small lavatory. Leanne lay curled up in the bathtub, just like he'd told her. But the tub wasn't heavy cast iron, it was cheap fiberglass, and the bullet had passed right through.

There was an oblong hole high on one cheekbone. From the red mess behind her, Peter knew without looking that the back of her head was gone.

The other round had cracked the shower's mixing valve. The soft sound came from the cold water that sprayed from the torn metal into the bloody tub, running pink down the drain.

One more member of the legion of dead who would come to Peter in his dreams.

Behind him, he heard Lewis's voice, low but insistent, asking questions.

Peter closed Leanne's eyes, then took down the shower curtain and laid it over her body. He wasn't worried about anyone hearing the gunshots. The neighboring cabins were vacant. Nobody else was close enough to notice.

The sound of retching pulled him back to the main room. Mika lay on his side like a hurt dog, emptying his stomach onto the translucent plastic sheeting. "What'd you do to him?" Peter asked.

Mika's face was pale, and a thin clear liquid seeped from his ear. The smell of vomit was strong. Lewis raised his hands as if in surrender. "Nothing. Dude just started puking."

But Peter already knew the reason. They'd hit Mika in the head three times, very hard. Peter had seen enough Marines with brain injuries to know the worst symptoms. At best, they'd given the man a serious concussion, his brain banging against the inside of his skull like pudding shaken in a cup. At worst, Peter might as well have stuck his gun into Mika's ribs and pulled the trigger.

"We can't just leave him here." Peter knelt beside Mika. He'd stopped throwing up, but now he was convulsing. A seizure was a bad sign. His eyes were rolled back in his head, but Peter could see the mismatched pupils, one huge, the other a pinprick. "We should get him to a hospital."

"Closest trauma center is at least an hour's drive, maybe more with the snow, and all they'll do is airlift him downstate. You think he's going to live through that?"

"We call 911. The chopper'll come direct from Wausau, land in the parking lot in thirty minutes."

"The county sheriff will get here first, and we got a dead girl in the bathtub. How you think that's gonna play out? You see any way we don't end up in handcuffs?" Lewis gestured at the plastic sheet laid out on the floor. "Man was ready to kill Leanne with a hammer, remember? You really want to put your freedom on the line for him? Not to mention lose any shot at tracking down the assholes who took Teddy's notebooks?"

Peter knew Lewis was right, but that didn't mean he had to like it.

The seizure ended and Mika went limp. Peter rolled him onto his side in case he started vomiting again. "Hey, Mika." He didn't respond. His breathing was rapid and shallow. "I think he's unconscious." Peter had done more than his share of battlefield first aid, but he was no corpsman. All he knew was that the man's brain was probably bleeding or swelling or both. Either way, seizures meant that the pressure was building inside his skull. When it pinched off the blood flow to his brain, he'd be dead.

"It ain't your fault, Jarhead. None of this is. Dude wrote his own death sentence when he went for the gun."

"I told Leanne to shelter in the tub," Peter said. "If she'd stayed at the table, she'd still be alive."

Lewis leaned against the kitchenette counter and tapped the pad of paper furiously against his leg. The top sheet was dark with his neat block handwriting. He didn't look at Peter. "Go home," he said. "Take the Yukon. This ain't your problem."

"The hell it's not." Peter stood. His voice was loud and his face felt hot. "I told Leanne I'd protect her."

Lewis shook his head. "I'm the one let him get hold of the gun. You go. I'll deal with it."

Peter scowled at him. "Cousin Zef and his crew have the notebooks, with names and places. Who knows what else Teddy wrote down? I'm not leaving you to face that alone."

"This ain't helping people can't help themselves, Peter. This's the bad old days, come back to bite. It's my mess, I'll clean it up."

Peter put his hands on his hips. "So you think I'm going to go home and tell Dinah you're out there on your own while I sit around and drink beer? Is that who you think I am?"

Lewis pulled in a long, slow breath, then let it out, finally meeting Peter's eyes. "No, brother. I know who you are, and that ain't it."

Peter looked down at Mika. Blood was congealing in his hair, and more fluid had leaked from his ear. Then he realized the man's chest wasn't moving. He bent and pressed his fingers to Mika's carotid. No pulse.

Peter straightened up and rubbed his eyes. The adrenaline crash was catching up to him. His heart was still pounding too hard. The taste of copper had gone sour in his mouth.

He'd killed men before, from a distance and close up. More times than he could count. But he'd never gotten used to it. He didn't want to. He wanted to stay human. And for that, when you took a life, you needed to feel it.

He glanced around at the small, cheap room, the sagging bed, the dead man on the floor on a sheet of plastic, the broken bathroom door, the dead woman in the tub. "Was it always this bad, back in the old days?"

Lewis wouldn't look at him. "Mostly it was worse."

"You were in it for ten years. Why'd you stay with it for so long?"

Lewis gave Peter a slow shrug. "I liked the money, and I liked handing out the punishment. You get good at something, you stick with it. Even if it did take a lot of whiskey to wash it away at the end of the day. Besides, I didn't have nothing better to step toward, you know?"

"Until Dinah."

Lewis nodded and let out a long breath. "And those boys."

While Lewis went through Mika's phone, Peter wrapped Leanne's body in the shower curtain and carried her out to the Malibu. It was not lost on Peter that he was basically carrying out Mika's plan. Then he rinsed the blood from the ruined bathtub and wiped down everything they'd touched. The bullet holes and other damage would get enough attention from the cabin's owners. No need to add homicide to the list of crimes.

Besides, if Leanne was discovered dead, the police would quickly find the video from the entrance to the clinic where she worked. Peter and Lewis had known the cameras were there and kept their backs to the lenses, but there was no reason to give the police any leads to follow. It was better to let Leanne simply vanish. A missing person wasn't a criminal case. The longer it took someone to look at the security feed, the better the chance it would be overwritten by the next week's footage, or the week after that.

"I don't get it," Peter said. "Why would the Albanians need to kill her? Who was she going to tell? What did she even know?"

"Your mistake is expecting this to make sense. Guys like these, they don't make decisions like you and me." Lewis handed Peter his notepad, with several more pages filled, then went to the bed and pulled off the green patterned spread. "You take the Yukon. It's just past the last cabin, keys on the floor. I'll clean up here, take the Malibu, and catch up with you downstate. Can you get those notes to June, see what she can find out about our Albanians?"

"Sure." Peter set the Malibu keys on the table as Lewis began to straighten out the body on the plastic.

He closed the door behind him and the cold hit him hard. He zipped up his coat and walked faster, his boots crunching on the snow. He was tired, but he didn't want to sleep. He knew when he closed his eyes, he'd see both Leanne and Mika.

And this was just the beginning.

Something told him it was going to get a lot worse before it was over.

9

LEWIS

Lewis had been an island, once. For a long time, ever since his auntie died when he was fifteen and left him all alone.

Coming up on the street, Lewis had learned about toughness, never showing weakness or fear. He'd become who he needed to be for that time and place. He'd survived with a kind of grim joy, but as he got older and started thinking about things, he came to understand that survival wasn't a life. You can only clean your guns so many times.

He'd only ever wanted to be capable, to be good at something. To have a job and a house and a car. As a kid in that neighborhood, he hadn't known many people like that. Adult life had been a mystery. His auntie had kept him fed, mostly, and he supposed she'd loved him, in her way. But nobody had taught him anything about how to live, least of all how to be a man. He'd had to figure all that out for himself.

The Army got him started by teaching him to cultivate his

self-discipline. When so much is out of your control, you learn to control yourself and your reactions to the chaos of combat. Whenever possible, he made his bunk in the morning, he brushed his teeth, he did the sit-ups and push-ups and ran the miles that kept his body strong and his mind clear. He learned the weapons and tactics that would keep him alive. He learned to be ready. Most of all, he learned that his tenacity and capacity for sheer effort would overcome most of the challenges that were thrown at him.

When he got back home, he took what he'd learned in the sandbox and made himself a simple set of rules for his new line of work.

You never tell people what you really do for a living. Everybody in the crew gets an equal share. You never do a job in the town where you live. You only go after people the law can't get. You take the dope out of circulation. You don't harm the innocent. You only kill people who are trying to kill you. If they put their hands up, you don't pull the trigger, otherwise it's just plain murder. You take care of your people. And you stick to the rules, even when it costs you.

Especially when it costs you.

It was ugly work. The rules helped him sleep at night.

It was too easy to backslide, though. He'd broken every rule at least once. Sometimes he'd done it for reasons he thought were sound at the time, but most often it happened in moments of anger, fear, or pain. Breaking a rule had *never* worked out for the best. The shame and regret that came with those failures threatened to consume him.

But he'd learned from those experiences, too. He'd learned that a life without rules was a life of savagery. It meant falling into the abyss of rage and hatred and greed, without meaning or hope. A life without rules was no life at all.

Over time, he got better at staring down his fear and anger, and turning them into ambition and action.

He'd had a lot of success over the years. He'd made a life on his own terms.

But he'd never had love.

He had the guys, of course, Nino and Ray. Those friendships were about being strong and capable and reliable, about not letting your partners down. That was one kind of love, he knew, but it wasn't the kind he meant.

Real love was when he'd fallen for Dinah as a boy of sixteen, and thought he'd lost her for good. When he'd found her again as a man, because Peter had brought her back into his life. It only reinforced the lesson he'd learned all those years ago.

Love was dangerous.

Love made you vulnerable.

Love was giving another person the means and opportunity to destroy you beyond all repair and hoping they wouldn't.

And what he felt for those boys? It was even worse than loving Dinah. In an instant, without his knowledge or permission, they'd become a part of him, vital organs held hostage outside his body, unprotected and exposed to all the pain and beauty of the world.

He loved them, ached for them, with a ferocious intensity that terrified him. He wanted to be everything those boys needed, everything he'd never gotten for himself. He wanted to be the kind of father that their own father would have been, if he'd lived. When eleven-year-old Miles leaned into him while they stood together in the kitchen making spaghetti, or when fifteen-year-old Charlie stepped inside a fist bump after a ball game to stand chest to chest and wrap his long arms around Lewis's shoulders? He felt that precious contact in his bones.

Like the worst kind of cancer.

Or some crazy comic book radiation that gave you superpowers.

He still couldn't quite believe that Dinah and the boys had allowed him into their home, into their hearts. He hadn't known he was even capable of giving that kind of love, or receiving it. After all those years of being alone, of holding himself apart, he realized he'd been scared of failing some test he hadn't even known existed.

He was still scared of that, most days.

Then Dinah, this strong, proud, gorgeous, zero-tolerance-for-bullshit Black woman with a spine like a steel bar, would see something in his face, some glimmer of that pain. And she'd bend herself toward him, eyes wide open, put her lips softly against his, and stare right into him with the force of the sun, her light and heat filling him up from the inside.

I know you, Lewis, she would say. You're a good man, whether you believe it or not.

In those moments, Lewis was both lost and found.

Aw, hell, he'd think. What's a motherfucker supposed to do with a woman like that?

He could come up with only one answer. Try like hell to act like the man she thought him to be. A different man than he'd been before. The man he *wanted* to be. For himself, for her, for those beautiful boys.

Now, with two bodies in the trunk and the snow coming down harder, Lewis felt himself failing. Slipping backward in time, losing ground to the worst version of himself.

A man who wanted vengeance rather than justice.

He made a point to keep his speed down. He didn't know the lay of the land up here, which towns would pull you over for a DWB, Driving While Black. A traffic stop was the last thing he needed.

He wished he had the Yukon. The plowing was still hit or miss, and the Malibu wasn't built for this slop. More than that, he wished Peter was riding shotgun. The jarhead's ability to keep a map in his head was especially useful at times like this, navigating narrow roads through endless trees in the bottomless dark. Plus it just felt good to have the man beside him. Lewis knew a lot of people, but he'd never met anyone he could count on like Peter Ash.

That was another kind of love. Like the brother he'd never had.

But it wasn't right to have the jarhead there, deep inside these empty woods. Lewis would carry this weight alone, looking for the right place to unload. Somewhere out of sight, where another driver wouldn't happen along and see the Malibu pulled over and stop to help. Someplace he wouldn't get the car stuck in the snow. The kind of place where the bodies wouldn't get found for a long time. It helped to stay calm, examine the options, plan ahead. That was the secret to surviving this life he'd chosen. The life he'd thought he'd left behind.

But you couldn't plan for everything. The contents of the trunk proved that. So did Teddy Wilson's notebooks. Lewis's neck and shoulders were cranked tight, his jaw aching from his clenched teeth, just thinking of what might happen to Dinah and the boys.

It was different in the bad old days. Lewis and his crew, Nino and Ray and the others, they were the Heavy Lifters, armed and dangerous, serious men taking down major targets. They knew what they'd signed up for, weighed the risks against the rewards. And if things didn't go their way, like maybe somebody got shot in the head? They'd made their choice. Live or die, it was a hell of a ride.

Since then, the Heavy Lifters had gone their separate ways. Lewis had a family now. He'd promised Dinah that those days were behind him.

But just because you're done with the past, it doesn't mean the past is done with you. So Lewis would step back into that life, do what he had to do to keep his family safe and slam the lid on this thing for good.

It helped that the rewards from those days had been substantial, especially the windfall from the first time he met Peter. They could spend whatever was necessary to get it done. Just sipping off the interest was more than he and Dinah would ever need. More than those boys would need when Lewis was gone, even if they had a bunch of kids.

Man, he hoped Charlie and Miles would have a bunch of kids.

He hoped he got to live long enough to meet them.

Up ahead, the roadside widened into a parking area, lumpy but plowed not too long ago, just a few fresh inches making everything look clean and white. There were no other cars.

Lewis pulled over and killed the lights.

10

hrough the windshield, Lewis saw a beaten track that snaked off through a mature hardwood forest, the trunks and limbs decorated with windblown snow. A small brown sign announced a cross-country ski trail. This was the place, he thought. It was pretty.

Until he opened the door and the cold hit him, mother*fucker*. The Malibu dashboard read eighteen below. Who in their right mind would live up here? But Lewis could take the punishment. He zipped his coat, popped the trunk, hefted the rolled green bedspread onto his shoulder, and started walking.

It occurred to him again that maybe Nino had been right, all those years ago. Instead of taking Teddy to the hospital, they should have put him in the ground. It was breaking the rules, but it would have saved Lewis a whole lot of time and money. Would have prevented these two deaths, too, and what Lewis would have to do next. He reminded himself that the option was still open, if Teddy couldn't learn to keep his mouth shut. If he couldn't be counted on to keep the past in the past. Although that would break a rule, too. Maybe the most important one.

Teddy wrote down his memories because he wanted to remember them. The funny thing was, Lewis had the opposite problem. He wanted nothing more than to forget the bad old days, but he couldn't. Each job was burned into his mind. The Russian gangsters in Cleveland. The bikers who shot Teddy in the head.

Of all the jobs they'd done, the one that really stuck with him was outside the Port of New Jersey. They'd taken down some mobsters trading cash for a shipping container full of drugs. As it turned out, somebody brought a twelve-year-old kid to the meet, the son of the boss of the family. What kind of asshole would do that? The boss didn't even go himself. Somebody probably thought he was educating the kid in the business, or just showing him what a big shot his father was. It didn't matter. Lewis didn't even know the kid was there until it was over. He was in the back seat of a car, behind tinted glass.

It didn't protect him, of course.

Lewis tried to tell himself it wasn't his fault. A mobster had brought a child to a drug deal.

Except Lewis was the one who'd planned the job, who'd made it happen.

If Lewis had decided to stay home that night, the kid would still be alive.

So really, who else could possibly be to blame?

With the body on his shoulder, he bypassed the trail and walked directly into the clustered trees, choosing an uphill trajectory that only a fool would follow. The drifted snow rose past his thighs, in places past his hips. Beneath it lay hidden obstacles, fallen branches and rocks that grabbed at his feet and tipped his ankles. He welcomed the wind, knowing it would quickly obscure his tracks.

Ten minutes in, beginning to warm from the work, he found a shallow depression excavated by the roots of a downed maple. He left Mika in the pit and went back for Leanne. She was smaller but somehow harder to carry.

One of the things Lewis had learned in the Army was how to kill people and not give a shit. But now he found that he didn't like leaving Leanne in the snow, wrapped in the clear shower curtain, looking so cold and lonely. None of it was her fault, not really.

So he unrolled Mika from the bedspread, and used his pocketknife to carefully cut away the shower curtain around Leanne's body, then laid her out on the green comforter as best he could, tucking her purse in beside her.

So when she got found, they would know who she was and notify her people.

He folded the remains of the shower curtain and stuck it under his arm, then stood looking down at her for a long moment, wishing, as he sometimes did, that his auntie's churching had stuck with him. If it had, maybe he'd have some words to say over the sad skinny girl who'd been in the wrong place at the wrong time.

But he didn't. All he could do was fold the comforter over her body, as if it might warm her on this cold winter night, and wherever her poor soul might go afterward.

Then he turned and walked away into the darkness without looking back.

He would harden himself and go hunting.

Just like the old days.

He waited until he crossed the county line before plugging the SIM card back into his burner. If someone somehow happened to find the bodies the next day, Lewis didn't want the number to show up on a cell tower near the ski trail. It was just a burner, but he'd learned long ago not to give the law anything for free.

He needed to talk with Nino and Ray. Their names were in those notebooks, too.

He hadn't spoken to Ray since they'd shut down the crew. Ray had a new life in Houston, and contact with Lewis could jeopardize that. The phone rang a few times, then went to voicemail. Lewis wasn't surprised. "Hey, it's me. I know you don't want to hear this, but some old business has come up, something serious. Call me back, please."

Next he called Nino. The call went straight to voicemail, just like it had that morning before they'd gone to find Teddy, and the mailbox was still full. This was fairly typical since Nino had opened his restaurant. Lewis sent a text, knowing Nino wouldn't recognize the burner's number. They had a lot of practice communicating like this. *It's me. Call ASAP, for old times' sake.* No reply came. That wasn't unusual, either.

Lewis didn't like that he couldn't reach them, but he wasn't worried. Like the jarhead and June, Nino and Ray were two of the most capable people he knew.

He had one more call, and he wasn't looking forward to it. He didn't know how Teddy would react.

"Hiya." Teddy was chewing something crunchy. They'd dropped him at a cheap hotel in Crandon, twenty miles from his cabin. His own phone had fallen from his pocket when running from the shooters at his house, and they hadn't managed to find it again. Lewis had given him a spare burner. "How'd it go?"

At least Teddy had remembered their old rules about the phone, Lewis thought. No names, no details. "We got what we needed."

Teddy swallowed noisily. "Was the jarhead right? Did she tell somebody about my notebooks?"

"She did. A guy she knew."

"A guy," Teddy said. "Is she, ah, screwing him?"

"It doesn't matter. The guy's connected to a crew out of Chicago. They have some kind of hard-on for us, from what we did back in the day."

"When you say it doesn't matter, that means she's screwing him."

Lewis cleared his throat. "Look, she said she was real sorry. She didn't know the guy was connected. She never meant for anything bad to happen to you. She'd take it back if she could."

Teddy was silent for a moment. Then he said softly, "She's dead, isn't she?"

Lewis sighed. "It was an accident. We took her to meet the guy, but there was a fight and the gun went off. She got hit by a stray round."

Teddy made a snuffling sound. Lewis realized the big man was crying.

"Dangit, I really liked her. I mean, I never asked her to be my girl-friend or anything, but I really liked her."

"I know," Lewis said. "I'm sorry."

"I mean, she had problems, I know that, but nobody's perfect. I've only got one eye, for gosh sake."

It was hard to imagine the old Teddy, Upstate Wilson, being so kind. Or so honest. Or saying *gosh*.

"Hang on," Teddy said. Lewis heard the click as the phone was set down on a hard surface, followed by a series of loud, wet honks as Teddy blew his nose.

Then he said, "Okay, we're going to Chicago, right? When are you picking me up?"

"Maybe it's better you don't go. How's that hotel? Or maybe you want to stay somewhere else?"

"No, I'm going with you. They killed my dogs. They wrecked my house and took my things. They took my dang notebooks. You know how long it took me to remember all that stuff?"

"You told me you were done with those days. You started over. You became a vegetarian, remember? You even stopped slapping mosquitoes."

"She wouldn't have got hurt if that guy hadn't told somebody. So right now, I'm thinking they're worse than mosquitoes." Lewis heard a rumble in Teddy's voice, a little bit of the old Upstate Wilson coming through. "And it's my fault you're involved, because I told her about the notebooks to begin with. So are you gonna come get me or do I hafta steal a car and chase you down?"

Lewis pulled back onto the road, wondering why he'd thought the outcome would be any different. Teddy had never been much interested in doing what he was told. "Actually, we could use another car, if you can pick one up quick. You sure you remember how?"

"Heck, some things you never forget. I'll meet you in Chicago."

11

PETER

After leaving Lewis, Peter drove south for thirty minutes to get some distance from the resort, then used a secure messaging app to send June a digital photo of the notes Lewis had made during his conversation with Mika. June was a reporter with Public Investigations, a nonprofit group of investigative journalists, and her subscription databases provided access to all kinds of specialized information. Before she'd met Peter, she'd worked the police beat for the *Chicago Tribune*, and still had contacts there, which might be helpful, too.

She'd called him immediately. "Peter, what the hell is this?"

He told her about finding Leanne and what had happened afterward. "We're headed to Chicago. The notes I sent are all we've got to go on right now."

When he finished talking, she was quiet for a moment. He could hear her breathing on the other end of the line.

"This is fucked," she finally said. "You know that, right?"

"I do," he said. "I feel really bad about Leanne. I crossed a line back there, picking her out of that parking lot. But Lewis is my friend. He'd do it for me in a heartbeat. I'm sorry, but that's the way it is."

"Don't be sorry," she said. "Be careful. If you walked away from Lewis and his family, you wouldn't be the man I love. But listen to me now, Marine, and listen good. When it's over? Make sure you get your ass back home to me in one piece. Understood?"

"Yes, ma'am." He felt it well up, his gratitude for her. A frequent feeling. He cleared his throat. "We just need to know who these people are, what we're up against. Can you start digging?"

"Already on it." Behind her voice was the clacking of her fingers on her laptop keyboard. "Dinah and the boys are down at the pool. We're going to order pizza from—"

"Don't tell me where you are." Peter was thinking of the plastic sheeting on the floor, and the hammer on the table. "Just in case."

She started to say something, then stopped. "All right. Stop at home and get your go-bag, please. I'll call you when I have something useful."

Four hours later, he made a quick detour into Milwaukee. The house was dark and silent. His go-bag, a midsized backpack with a carefully considered selection of supplies, was on the floor of the coat closet by the side door. Then he made a stop at Lewis and Dinah's place, three doors down. He had a spare key on his ring, and the combination to one of Lewis's gun safes in his head.

June called him back as he rolled through Chicago's northern suburbs. "Well, the good news is that your guys are certified shit-crusted assholes."

Relatively mild language, for June. When she was well and truly worked up, her vocabulary could make a Marine drill instructor blush. She claimed she'd picked it up working the police beat, but mostly she cursed the way small children sang to themselves, for the sheer unconscious joy of expression.

"And the bad news?"

"They're fucking nuts, Peter. Balls the size of coconuts. It's like the Wild West, what they're doing. That thing about the social club takeover in Cicero, four guys taking on forty mob soldiers? It's true. They killed seven people and got away clean, and apparently it wasn't their first time. Carlo Fratelli, my Chicago PD contact who used to do organized crime, now on a DEA joint task force, said they bragged about it all over town. But he got zero hard evidence, and nobody would testify because the Albanians scare the crap out of everyone. They're worse than the Sicilians in the old days."

"But it was an Outfit club. Didn't the mob go after them?"

"No, because it turns out the Albanians basically wiped out the Outfit's top level of management, which kicked off a distracting succession fight. According to Fratelli, there's talk that an ambitious younger lieutenant actually hired the Albanians for the hit, like a takeover bid."

"They *work* for the Mafia?"

"If they did, it was a one-time deal. A month after the thing in Cicero, they took advantage of the succession war and went into another Outfit nightclub, a high-end after-hours gambling joint. A couple hundred thousand on the tables, Fratelli thinks. Two days later, that same younger lieutenant, maybe as part of the effort to look like a boss, got the Albanians to agree to a meet at a Shell station off I-55. Ostensibly to negotiate a deal, but the Outfit had twenty soldiers waiting. The Albanians got two gas pumps running and hosed the place down, turned it into a standoff, threatening to torch the station and kill everybody, including a dozen bystanders and themselves. In the end, the cops showed up and arrested half the Italians, but your guys managed to slip the noose."

"So that's their thing, hitting clubs?" Peter was trying to figure out why they'd diversify into stealing notebooks from former heisters.

"No, they're opportunists. According to Fratelli, they're mostly drug wholesalers, buying and selling, nothing that requires much in the way of brains or organization. They're just four major-league assholes. And they're all related, which Fratelli says is pretty common with Eastern European groups like this. Zef, his brother Donat, his cousin Lorik, who goes by Larry, and Zef's half brother Kron. They came over from Albania ten years ago. Since then, each has been arrested multiple times. Assault, armed robbery, murder, murder for hire, the list goes on. But not a single case went to trial. Mostly, Fratelli says, because all the witnesses either develop amnesia or disappear entirely."

Oddly, this news made Peter feel better. After all, he might have to shoot one or more of them before the sun came up.

"Anyway," June said, "they're not discreet. I went through their socials and it looks like they live large. Fancy restaurants and expensive cars, including a white Jeep like the one you saw up north. I've mapped the addresses you gave me, which seem to be houses on the northwest side, in and around Portage Park. I'll send you everything, including a good face pic of each one. One last thing—I also looked your guys up on my various databases, but there's very little showing there. The houses and the cars on their socials are all owned by different corporations. So they must have a good lawyer who knows how to do this kind of thing."

"Can you think of why these cowboys would care about Teddy's notebooks?"

"Well, I asked Fratelli about that other thing, the Ghost Killers. He says it's an urban legend, popular in the underworld. According to the stories, the Ghost Killers appear at a criminal enterprise and kill anyone who raises a hand to stop them. They take all the money, destroy any drugs they find, and vanish into the mist. Surgically clean, minimal collateral damage. There's one story about a takedown of some big shots from the Gangster Disciples, and another about a hit on some Mafia types in North Jersey."

"Huh," Peter said.

"Right? Anyway, Fratelli told me that he knew about a couple of crimes like this, professional hits against really big players. When a snitch told him about the Ghost Killers, Fratelli got curious and called some cops in other cities. Turns out that most big departments have seen one or two hits like these. But the timing in each city is years apart, and the targets and methods are all over the map. Fratelli says he can't imagine a criminal group organized enough to do something like this and get away with it. The current thinking is, they're not connected."

"Sounds like good news, I guess."

"That's not all of it," June said. "Part of the mythology is that someone, nobody knows exactly who, has put out a bounty. A quarter-million dollars for information that leads to the capture of the Ghost Killers."

Peter closed his eyes. "Which is why the Albanians went after Teddy's notebooks."

"That's my guess. If Teddy wrote down what he said he did, those notebooks will give them Lewis on a platter."

After they ended the call, Peter's phone vibrated with a series of texts. Mapped addresses, a list of cars and plate numbers, pictures of faces.

He forwarded everything to Lewis.

12

After midnight, Peter sat in the Yukon in an empty lot off Irving Park Road, not far from the Kennedy Expressway, glad for the heated seats as he waited for the others. He'd already memorized the Albanians' cars, the facades of the houses, and a map of the area.

The snow had reached Chicago around noon, then fallen until after supper. Eleven inches, the radio said. The city's traffic, often miserable in the best of weather, had been snarled for hours. Now the roads were empty but for the plow trucks and shift workers who needed the money too badly to call in sick. As the storm continued to the east, the sky cleared and the temperature dropped low enough to kill.

He pulled up the pictures of the Albanian faces again, locking them deeper into his mind so he didn't make a mistake. Zef, Donat, Lorik-who-went-by-Larry, and Kron. They were related by blood, but they didn't look alike. The only features they had in common were dark curly hair and eyes like stones, hard and still and dead.

THE PRICE YOU PAY

Peter remembered the second time he'd met Lewis, when Lewis had said that he and Peter weren't all that different. At the time, Peter wasn't so sure he agreed, but now here he was, preparing to fuck up some Albanian gangsters with a guy named Upstate Wilson.

Life was a slippery slope, he thought. You don't watch your step, it can be a long fall to the bottom.

The Malibu pulled up beside him, Lewis behind the wheel. Two minutes later, a big cream-colored Mercury Marquis rolled into the lot, a nicer version of the old Crown Victoria police sedan. Teddy's moon face shone through the broad windshield.

They stood together behind the Yukon and pulled body armor over their sweatshirts. The wind blew cold and mean, pinching their noses and swirling snow off the surrounding rooftops. Lewis handed out the ordnance Peter had brought, suppressed Browning pistols in custom drop-leg holsters and suppressed Heckler & Koch MP5 submachine guns with retractable stocks. Each man added ammo pouches to the plate carriers and filled them with extra magazines.

The gear was similar to what Peter had used in Iraq, going house to house with a team of Marines in a stack at his back. Peter was the rare platoon commander who'd taken his turn as first man through the door. It made a difference, the fact that he'd put himself on the line with his guys. The platoon became extremely tight, and that made them extremely effective at engaging with and killing the enemy. This was command's rationale for giving them the toughest duty, over and over again. Which probably explained the high incidence of post-traumatic stress with Peter's guys.

This brutal winter weather was totally unlike Iraq, of course. But the feeling was the same, the flutter in his belly and the tightness in his shoulders as he cinched down the straps and checked his weapons. In Iraq, he'd maintained his own gear religiously, breaking down his pistol and M4 carbine before and after every mission. Along with his radio, his weapons were his most important physical tool for both doing his job and staying alive. Peter knew Lewis was similarly fanatical about his own gear, so Peter just made sure he was familiar enough with the equipment to be as effective as possible.

When they were ready, Peter climbed into the Yukon and headed to the first address on the list. Lewis drove the Malibu to the second house, and Teddy took the Mercury to the third. They would look for lights in windows and cars on the street or in the driveway. There were five addresses, all within a few miles of each other. Once they had the lay of the land, they'd take it house by house. Starting, if possible, with Cousin Zef.

The first address was a small brick cape in Old Irving Park with metal security grates over the windows and a four-foot chain-link fence that wrapped the front of the property. Peter didn't see any vehicles from his list parked on the street.

The only visible light was over the front door. He drove around to the alley, finding a one-car garage beside an empty parking slab and a six-foot privacy fence protecting the rear. All the back windows were dark, too. He couldn't see inside the garage.

He left the Yukon idling in the alley and went to the back gate, but found it locked from the inside. So he looked both ways and began to climb the fence, heart pounding, doing his best to be both fast and quiet. It wasn't easy with thirty pounds of armor and ammunition and a submachine gun slung at his back.

When he dropped into the snowy yard, a floodlight went on outside the back door. Peter pulled the HK around, thinking he was screwed and wishing he wasn't alone as he scanned the house for movement.

Nothing happened. Still no lights inside the house. After a few minutes, the floodlight went off. Peter took two steps through the deep snow toward the garage window, and the light went on again. He froze. After a few more minutes, the light went off. Motion sensor. He continued toward the garage, and the light went on a third time. With one eye on the house, he kept moving. The garage window was covered with a security grate, but with cupped hands up against the bars, Peter could see inside. No car.

Good enough. Peter returned to the back fence, where he was able to unlatch the gate and walk through to the Yukon. Inside, he pulled his phone and saw a three-way text from Lewis. *No indications at #2. Nobody home. On to #5.*

Peter replied, *No indications at #1. Nobody home. On to #4.*

He headed down the alley and turned left toward Addison. His phone vibrated again. It was a text from Teddy's burner. *#3 looks like a party.*

Peter could hear the bass thumping from the end of the block, even with his windows up and the Yukon's heat cranked high. In the southeastern corner of Portage Park, it was an unusual street because the homes had driveways to one side, rather than an alley running behind them.

The house was a plain brick bungalow in the middle of a line of similar buildings, with larger brick apartments on the other side of the street. Both curbs were lined with cars. He drove past at normal speed, noting the lights behind crooked blinds, the white Jeep and black-on-black Range Rover in the driveway. He spotted Teddy's Mercury around the next corner and pulled up beside it.

Teddy's round face was intent, the dashboard light showing the puckered scar as a curved shadow in his beard. "That's the same Jeep," he said. "The BMW and Mercedes from the list are on the next block. The plates match."

Lewis was in the passenger seat, face washed out by the streetlight, knuckles white on the grip of the MP5. His knee bounced like a jackhammer. "The Malibu's two blocks north, with the keys on the floor. We'll pull out and you can leave the Yukon here. Then we'll put the Mercury across the driveway and go hit it."

"Okay," Peter said. "What's the plan?"

"Kill everyone but Cousin Zef," Lewis said. "I'll go in the front, you take the driveway to the back to pick up any squirters. Teddy, you're outside with the engine running."

"What do you mean?" Teddy's voice was plaintive. "Those guys shot my dogs. I'm going with you."

Lewis shook his head. "Teddy, you been out of the game too long. And you only got one eye. You stay in the car."

"You can't make me." Teddy put his massive hand on the shift lever. "Let's go."

"Hold on." Peter inched the Yukon forward to keep the car from pulling out. "We're not killing everyone but Zef," he said. "We need them all alive. We need information. Even if we find those notebooks in a tidy little stack, we still need to know who put that bounty on your heads. What if Zef isn't the one who knows?"

Lewis fixed his eyes on Peter, that implacable stare like a hot desert wind. "Then we kill them after."

Peter was used to his friend being so cool he was arctic. This was a different version of the man, wound so tight his spring was about to snap.

"You know I've got your back on this," he said. "But we already killed one person today and got another one killed by accident. Why don't we try not to kill anybody else if we can help it? Anyway, I thought you had rules about this kind of thing."

"These shitbirds *know my name*," Lewis said. "They can use that to find Dinah and the boys. The damn rules don't apply."

Peter kept his voice gentle. "But isn't that the point of having rules? To keep us from becoming like them?"

The muscles flexed in Lewis's jaw, his lips pressed into a thin line. Then he let his breath out slowly through his nose and his face eased slightly.

Peter reached through the open window and took hold of Lewis's heavy shoulder. This was about more than getting the notebooks back. About more than Dinah and the boys, too. It was also about Lewis, who was trying to keep the man he'd been from winning out over the man he was trying to be.

Peter understood the nature of that challenge better than most people. He'd been working on the same thing since he mustered out of the Corps. He tightened his grip on his friend. "I got you, brother."

Lewis closed his eyes. "I know."

"So here's the play," Peter said. "We do it like we did in the sandbox. Go in loud and strong. Keep them alive if we can, so we can get the intel we need. June's contact said the cops would love to hang something on these guys, right? What do you bet there's something incriminating in that house?"

Lewis shook his head. "They'll still know my name."

"We don't even know if they've cracked those notebooks," Peter said. "Let's just see how things evolve, okay? Maybe they won't give us a choice. That'll be on them, not on us."

Lewis nodded.

"Okay," Peter said. "Why don't you take the Yukon and my HK? I'll double-time back to the house, see what I can see. At least we'll have some idea of what we're walking into before we kick down the door." Peter looked past Lewis to Teddy. "You good with that?"

The big man was sulking, his arms folded across his massive chest. "I'm not staying in the car."

"If they'd shot my dogs, I wouldn't want to, either," Peter said. "But if you're going in, we don't want the guy who won't swat a mosquito. We need the old Upstate Wilson. The meat eater. Can you do that?"

Teddy gave him a bright-eyed grin, lips gleaming with saliva. "Oh, yeah."

Peter left the Yukon and pulled his winter coat over the bulky armor and ammo pouches, so if someone drove past, he'd look a little less like an infantryman.

Lewis climbed out of the Mercury and closed the door softly behind him. They stood together in the narrow space between the vehicles. "I'm sorry, brother. It's just—the clock keeps ticking."

"I know what's at stake." Peter kept his voice low. "We need to get in and out before the city wakes up. But we need more than those notebooks. We need to know who put up that bounty."

Lewis nodded again. Peter thumped his fist against his friend's chest, holding his eye for a moment. "Stay cool. I'll text you."

Then he shrugged deeper into his coat and walked toward the thumping music, feeling light and strong and ready.

Headed for a party.

13

The buildings were packed together, separated only by skinny driveways that would have been narrow even for a Model T, which was probably the most common vehicle when these lots were laid out. At least this place didn't have a fence to climb, Peter thought. There was a concrete porch on the left, then a driveway with the white Jeep parked in front of the black Range Rover. The music was so loud it rattled the glass.

The wind picked up again, biting at the tips of his nose and ears. His coat wouldn't zip over the bulky armor, and he felt the warmth from the car ebbing. The cold would make him clumsy and slow his responses, especially his hands. He wore good tactical gloves, but they weren't enough.

There was no landscaping, so the front windows were exposed to the street. Inside, blinds covered the glass, although light crept around the edges. Peter didn't need a passing cruiser to decide he was a Peeping Tom, so he went to the right and walked up the unshoveled driveway of the house next door, trying to look like he belonged. He wasn't worried about the crunch of his boots because of the bad Europop blasting through the walls. It was one in the morning on a weekday. The neighbors must love these guys.

Although apparently nobody had called the cops to complain, which meant the Albanians had scared the block into submission. Or maybe Chicago PD just had better things to do than respond to a noise complaint. Peter hoped they were very busy, somewhere far away.

He came to a side window. These blinds were down, too, but they were cheap and maybe broken, the bottom rail stuck six inches above the sill. Peter leaned in and found a narrow view into the space beyond.

He saw the backs of the heads of two men on a sofa, playing what looked like Red Dead Redemption on an enormous television. Their feet were up on a particleboard coffee table, which was scattered with multiple handguns, a takeout container overflowing with cigarette butts, and a black tray holding a Ziploc bag full of rough white powder, a chef's knife, and a couple of chopped lines on the tray. Definitely a party.

Peter couldn't see the features of the men on the couch, but got a better look at a third guy, stretched out on a leather recliner by the front window, wearing only a pair of red bikini-style underwear. He was hairy, heavily muscled, and smoking a cigarette. Peter recognized the blocky jaw and narrow, crooked nose from the photos June had sent earlier. He was the Albanian called Kron.

A black shotgun with a high-capacity box magazine leaned against the wall within arm's reach. The front door was maybe eight feet to his left. If the bungalow was laid out like most Peter had seen, Kron would also have an unobstructed sight line to the kitchen and the rear entry.

Kron's sight line was blocked, however, by three skinny young girls in skimpy clothes, dancing clumsily in the wide opening to the dining room. Their slack, stoned faces were pockmarked with acne and red around the nostrils. They didn't look much older than fifteen. They would make things more complicated.

He moved to the next window, which had once been a dining room, and saw another man counting bills off a fat pocket roll. From June's photos, Peter knew this was Cousin Zef. He wore only a pair of shiny jeans slung low on his narrow hips. His bare chest was smooth and pale as a vampire's. The only furniture was a built-in china cabinet on the right and a cheap folding table against the outside wall that held a blocky piece of computer equipment and another black shotgun. Zef held the money out to the tallest girl, who wore an acre of eye makeup, badly smeared. As she tucked it into her halter top, Zef put a hand on her shoulder, pushing her into the living room.

Peter kept moving. After the dining room came a small window, too high to see through. He slipped around the corner and found a larger window. It was the kitchen, every horizontal surface packed with empty liquor bottles and takeout containers. A huge spotted cat crouched beside the sink, drinking from the dripping faucet. As he stood watching, it raised its head and hissed at him.

He slipped up the rear stoop and tested the door. Despite a high-end deadbolt, it was unlocked. He peeked inside and saw the back landing, with a closed door to the kitchen and darkened stairs up to the second floor and down to the basement. He eased the door shut, then went back down to the yard and the next window, which was partially covered by a hanging sheet.

It was a bedroom with a bare mattress on the bare floor, a dirty blanket in a tangle, and discarded clothes in a heap beside what looked like a used condom. Super classy. He crossed to the driveway with the Jeep and Range Rover, passed a lit-up glass-block window that was probably for the bathroom, then peeked into a second bedroom. Another bare mattress, but no blanket, and two more used condoms. He was profoundly glad he'd arrived too late to see them in use. A third black shotgun lay on the floor beside the bed, pointed toward the door. Just in case.

He reversed direction and retraced his steps, noting that the second-floor gable windows were dark. Nobody would be asleep up there, not with that music blaring. Back at the living room window, he saw the girls moving toward the front door. He hoped that meant they were leaving.

Which left four guys, at least two of them Albanians, and plenty of weapons. But nothing that looked like the notebooks.

Still, the odds were better than he'd hoped.

He stood in the shadows at the front corner of the house and texted Lewis and Teddy a quick description of the building layout and the people he'd seen. As the girls teetered out the front door on cheap heels, wearing nothing in the killing cold but their hot pants and halter tops, he wondered where their parents were. Or maybe it was their parents' fault.

The girls climbed into a rusty little car parked on the street, fired up the engine, and drove away.

Peter took out his phone. It was almost one thirty in the morning. He texted Lewis. *OK to go.*

Lewis replied immediately. *Coming now.*

14

The big Mercury sedan ghosted into the space at the end of the driveway, blocking in the Albanians' cars. Lewis stepped out and handed Peter his HK. Peter slung his coat across the passenger seat and eased the door shut. They had cheap Bluetooth headsets he'd picked up at a gas station on the way downstate, but the music was too loud for them to work worth a damn. He looked at Lewis and said, "Back door's open. Count of sixty?"

Lewis nodded and headed toward the front porch, taking an orange-handled electric lock pick from his pocket. Teddy followed behind, bouncing on his toes with a wide and toothy grin.

Peter knew how he felt. The adrenaline was in full flow now, burning in his veins like gasoline, lifting him to a higher plane. Was it wrong, how alive this made him feel? The humming tension before a fight, the bright, vivid clarity of the red right now?

Counting down, he ran along the driveway past the Jeep and Rover toward the rear of the house. The magazine pouches bounced on their straps, the armor heavy on his shoulders. He was no longer cold. A glance in the side windows told him that the bedrooms remained unoccupied. From the back, he could see that the kitchen was still empty except for the cat, its head now buried in a takeout container.

He crept up the rear stoop, weapon ready, the taste of copper in his mouth. He eased open the door and stepped into the entryway, listening. Not that he'd be able to hear anything over the electronic synthpop.

He wasn't crazy about going in both doors at the same time without active communication. Generally speaking, it was a good way to get shot by your teammate. Textbook practice was to go in heavy through the front, with a couple guys posted outside the back to scoop up the runners. But they didn't have the manpower for that. To capture the Albanians without killing them, their best chance was to go in hard and fast, and that meant both doors.

He put his hand on the kitchen doorknob. It turned, but the door didn't move. This one had a deadbolt, too, and it was locked. He didn't have a pick and he was running out of time. He felt confident in the volume of the music, so he placed the HK's suppressor to the jamb and pressed the trigger. The shot sounded like a cough in the enclosed space. The door still didn't move. He fired again and this time the door shuddered open an inch as the round blew the deadbolt free of the strike plate. He flipped the selector into burst mode and nudged the door open another few inches, the gun barrel leading the way into the gap, his heart almost leaping from his chest when the spotted cat bolted between his legs and down the basement stairs.

He could see clearly through the kitchen doorway into the front of the house. No Lewis. Maybe the front door had a high-end lock, too, slowing him down. Zef stood in the wide opening between the dining room and living room, his back to Peter, watching the action on the flat-screen. The two men on the couch were focused on their game, but

Kron's eyes were locked on Peter as he rolled sideways out of the re-cliner and grabbed the shotgun.

Peter aimed at his center mass and shouted, "Freeze, hands up," like he was a cop. But the music was too loud for him to be heard from the kitchen. Maybe Kron wouldn't have cared anyway. He hauled the shotgun around and Peter's finger tightened on the trigger. No way he was going to die in this dump while June waited for him at home.

Then Lewis blew through the front door with the HK leveled, mouth open in a shout that never made it past the Europop. Kron was a few steps away, the shotgun coming around fast. Lewis locked onto him and put a suppressed burst into his torso.

Kron must have been high as a kite, because he didn't even seem to notice, raising the shotgun to his hip, zeroing in on Peter. The barrel's bore was a bottomless black hole. With the ten-round magazine, the gun didn't even need to be pumped. If it was loaded with buckshot, Kron would barely need to aim. Three rounds from that range would cut Peter in half.

Before the Albanian found his shot, Peter fired twice and stitched six rounds across his chest. Kron stumbled backward, twisting. As he fell, some reflex or inborn habit made him pull the trigger in a spasm, *BOOM BOOM*. The blast hit the TV, punching fist-sized holes into the screen and turning the picture into a flickering mess.

Teddy stepped past Lewis, huge and grim, the HK looking small in his massive grip as he shouted soundlessly at the two men on the couch, who were reaching for the pistols on the coffee table. Cousin Zef spun on his heel, spotted Peter advancing through the kitchen, and leaped sideways into the dining room for the shotgun on the fold-ing table.

Peter got to him first, smashing the HK's heavy suppressor into the back of Zef's head and knocking him forward to bounce his face off the plastic edge of the table on his way to the ground. A kick to the stomach curled him up and put him out of the fight.

Glancing into the living room, Peter saw the two men on the couch with their hands up. Lewis and Teddy had things under control. Breathing hard, Peter seized Cousin Zef's wrist in a control grip, locked his shoulder, and pulled him scrabbling across the worn hardwood toward the living room. From start to finish, the whole assault had taken less than thirty seconds. The only sound he'd heard, aside from the shotgun blast, was earsplitting French-language Europop.

Peter pointed at the Bluetooth speaker on the TV console. "Turn that off," he shouted, barely able to hear his own voice.

Lewis looked over and Peter saw something register in his face. He dropped Cousin Zef's wrist and began to spin, but Lewis had already raised his weapon and was pulling the trigger. Peter felt the breeze on his neck as the rounds flew past. He finished his pivot and saw a naked man with a shotgun begin to topple like a tree, dead on his feet with three neat round red holes in a tight cluster on his forehead.

Peter hustled over and kicked the shotgun away and looked down at him. It was Lorik, who went by Larry. Where the hell had he come from? Peter looked through a side passage, which led to the bedrooms and bathroom. Then he saw that the man's hair was wet and his body beaded with water. Lorik had been in the shower.

He'd made his choice, just like Kron.

Peter turned back to the living room and saw Lewis and Teddy yelling at the men on the couch, who'd taken the opportunity to reach for their weapons again. Zef stared at Peter as he climbed to his knees.

Peter was losing patience with these morons who didn't know when to stop fighting. The music was still blasting, he couldn't even shout at the guy. So he picked up the shotgun and swung it like a baseball bat, slamming the polymer stock into Zef's side and knocking him back to the floor. Then Peter reversed the weapon and let the Albanian stare into the barrel, which in Peter's experience often had a clarifying effect. As Zef slumped back to the floor, the music abruptly died. Teddy had found the off button.

The room reeked of spent powder and the acrid stink of unwashed men. Peter stepped back to keep one eye on the kitchen. Anyone upstairs gunning for them would have to come through there. "We need to clear the rest of the house."

"First things first," Lewis said. He pulled plastic flex-cuffs from his back pocket and tossed them to the two men on the couch. "Put 'em on, nice and tight."

Peter glanced at them as they slowly complied. He recognized Donat from his chinless face and sharp widow's peak, but June hadn't sent a picture of the second man. He was younger and clearly trying hard not to seem terrified as he looked from Lorik's body to Kron's, crumpled sideways on the hardwood atop a sticky crimson pool that matched his underwear.

When the two on the couch were firmly cuffed, Lewis looked at Teddy. "Clear the building." Teddy nodded and slid past Peter, teeth bared and weapon ready. Lewis stepped over to Zef with that tilted smile. "You figure out who we are yet, motherfucker?"

15

LEWIS

Lewis stared down at Cousin Zef.

He didn't want to be doing this again, kicking down some dude's door with a gun in his hand. He'd thought he was done with those days. But right now he didn't have much choice.

If Zef had read the notebooks, it would complicate things.

Still, Lewis felt the buzz of the action like a quadruple espresso on an empty stomach. He didn't want to admit how much he had missed the rocket-fueled thrill of walking into a criminal's castle and winning the fight. That was one reason he'd stayed in the game for ten long years. It was *fun*.

He knew the crash would come, followed by the black dog of depression and regret. But for the moment, it didn't matter. Lewis and his guys were alive, and the others were dead or captured.

He dropped a set of flex-cuffs next to Cousin Zef and toed him in the ribs with a size twelve combat boot. "You make me put those on you, I guarantee it's gonna hurt."

Zef's face was still as a stone as he sat on his heels, slid his hands though the holes, and cinched the plastic zip-fasteners with his teeth. It wasn't his first time, that was for sure.

Lewis reached down and tugged them tighter. "Stay down or I'll knock you down."

He left Peter to watch the prisoners and went out the front door to check the street. He was sweating, and the winter air felt good. Despite the two shotgun blasts, he heard no sirens, saw no lit windows. They were lucky it was February and not July.

By the time he'd returned to the living room, Peter had collected Kron's shotgun and the pistols from the coffee table and put them on the far side of the recliner, away from the Albanians. Teddy came back through the kitchen with a bright smile, bouncing on his toes like a little kid. "All clear, boss. Basement, too."

On the floor, Kron stirred and gave a soft moan. Teddy frowned down at him, then fired a single round into the man's head.

Lewis looked at Peter. "I guess he didn't have any trouble stepping back into the bad old days."

Peter eyed the bodies. "None of us do."

Cousin Zef was glaring at them. Lewis gave him the checkpoint stare and nudged him again with his boot. "Where are the notebooks? You give me what I came for, we'll walk out that door."

Zef smiled tightly, but there was no humor in it. His eyes were as cold as fish on ice. "If I give you what you want, you will kill me. Kill all of us." His accent was stronger than Mika's, the consonants more pronounced, the vowels coming from the back of the throat.

Lewis frowned. "I'm not like you, Zef. I don't murder people for kicks. I just want the notebooks."

Zef shrugged a shoulder, showing Lewis he wasn't afraid to die. "You will find them anyway. They are in kitchen, in liquor box. Under the table."

Lewis strode into the kitchen and found the box. It had once held bottles of expensive whiskey. He pulled back the folded flaps and saw the hardback spines of a dozen or more large black notebooks. The relief flowed through him like a river.

He carried the box back to the living room and stood with it under his arm. It was lighter than he'd expected. "Now tell me what you were going to do with them."

"Is nothing to do," Zef said. "Is already done."

The relief drained away. "What do you mean?"

Zef smiled, this time with genuine amusement. "I mean you are too late, Mister Ghost Killer. You are shit out of luck." His accent made *shit* sound like *sheet*. "I am dead man, yes? But they are coming for you, too."

Lewis felt the bottom drop out of his stomach. He slung the HK behind him, then pulled a notebook from the box and opened it. It was an empty cover. The pages were gone, cut out with a sharp blade. He shoved the notebook back in the box and pulled out another. It was empty, too. Then another, and another. He dropped the box and stood over the kneeling Albanian, hands shaking with fear and rage. "Where are the pages, Zef?"

"Long gone. Soon they will know everything in your life. Your woman, your children, your friends, your money. They will hunt you like an animal."

"Who will hunt me, Zef? Who paid you to find the notebooks?"

Zef laughed out loud, enjoying Lewis's discomfort. "I do not know. Deal was done online, no names. A big payday for me. I think they want you bad."

Peter cleared his throat. "Hey. Why cut out the pages? Where are they now?"

Cousin Zef ignored him and turned to Teddy. "You are the one from the cabin, yes? The one fucking Mika's slut."

Teddy turned pink. "Leanne wasn't a slut." He took a step forward. "Are you the dickhead who shot my dogs?"

"Aw, does that make you sad?" Zef's voice was mocking. He looked at Lewis. "This one is not real Ghost Killer. I think he is more like pet rabbit. Up at cabin, he ran away."

Teddy took another step toward Zef, the long scar livid on his cheek. "Was it you? Did you kill them?" Lewis threw out his arm to block his path, not that it could have stopped the big man.

Zef said something in Albanian, then spat on the floor and looked back at Teddy, eyes bright. "I didn't kill your dogs, little rabbit. You did. If you came out to face us like a man, they would still be alive."

"Teddy, wait." But Lewis was too late. The big man shoved past and backhanded Zef across the face, knocking him to the floor, then began to kick him.

Lewis grabbed his arm and tried to pull him away, but moving the man was like trying to deadlift a prize-winning steer. All he managed to do was reduce the effectiveness of the kicking. Peter jumped in and grabbed the haul strap on Teddy's armor. Zef shouted in Albanian as he tried to block the blows with his cuffed hands.

Between Lewis and Peter, they somehow managed to yank Teddy back a step. Then Lewis heard a clatter from the living room. The men on the couch.

He dropped Teddy's arm and began to turn. "Peter, behind you."

The older man, Donat, was already recovering from his dive over the recliner to the corner where Peter had tossed the Albanians' weapons. He'd knocked down a lamp and now knelt on the floor, raising a pistol in his cuffed hands.

"Don't move," Lewis shouted, his HK already up and ready, but the man didn't stop.

Lewis pressed the trigger and the HK thumped in his hands. Donat slumped.

Peter was shouting, too, with his weapon aimed at the kid, whose name they didn't know. "Drop it, kid. Don't make me shoot you." The boy crouched wide-eyed and frozen on the sofa with an angular Uzi machine pistol in one hand. The Uzi wasn't aimed at them, but it wasn't exactly pointed away, either. How had they missed an Uzi?

Behind him, Lewis heard a yelp, then a thud. He spun and saw Teddy curled up in the fetal position and Zef on his feet in the dining room opening, pivoting toward the folding table, where the black shotgun lay gleaming.

"Stop right there," Lewis shouted, his gun sight centered between the man's shoulder blades. "Don't do it." But he didn't fire. He still needed the Albanian to find the notebooks. Then Zef had the shotgun in his cuffed hands and was turning toward Lewis.

"Drop the damn gun," Lewis said.

Zef paused, looking sideways at Lewis with a grim smile. "Would you?"

"Tell me where the pages are and I'll let you live," Lewis said. "You keep the bounty and walk away."

The smile widened and Lewis knew Zef didn't believe him. Because Zef had his own way of doing things, and it didn't involve allowing an enemy to live.

Peter kept shouting at the kid in the living room. Lewis watched the muscles flex in Zef's back. He couldn't see the man's hands clearly. Then he heard the cough of Peter's weapon. Reflexively, his eyes flicked away from the Albanian for a fraction of a second, but when he recovered, Zef was twisting hard from the waist, the shotgun barrel coming around fast.

In a hurry, Lewis pulled the trigger twice, shooting for the legs. His aim was off and he put six rounds into Zef's back and side. Zef's momentum kept him turning, but his chest was a mass of red. Then his knees gave way and he fell face-first. When he landed, the shotgun clattered across the floor and Lewis knew he was dead.

He ran to the living room, where Peter now straddled the kid on the couch, the cushion under them soaked crimson, trying to cinch the boy's belt around his upper thigh. The young Albanian's leg was bleeding heavily above the knee. His eyes were wide and his face was pale from pain and blood loss and shock.

"He wouldn't put the gun down." Peter glanced over his shoulder. "Do you have a tourniquet?"

"No." Lewis's stomach was a bottomless pit. He'd failed his family. The notebooks were gone.

Peter returned to his task. "He's going to bleed out if I can't get this tight."

"Everyone else is dead," Lewis said.

Peter frowned, intent on the belt. "All the more reason this guy should live. Maybe he knows something."

Lewis got close to the kid. "Hey. Where are the notebooks? Where the hell are the notebooks?" The kid just looked at him, barely functional and scared to death. Lewis pushed himself away. He couldn't catch his breath. He didn't know what to do next.

He felt a presence looming behind him and whirled with the HK. It was just Teddy, who had climbed to his feet, still clutching his groin. Zef must have kicked him in the balls.

"I'm sorry," Teddy groaned. "I got mad."

"Oh, you got mad?" Lewis said. "He was baiting you, Teddy. Now we've got nothing."

Teddy looked at the floor. "I'm sorry, Lewis. It's all my fault."

Lewis licked his lips. He stomach tightened like a knot. He felt like he was going to throw up. "Go turn this place upside down, Teddy. Get their phones, find a laptop, search the whole house. Find *something*, please."

Teddy hung his head and limped away.

"Lewis," Peter said. "Get in here. Now."

Lewis felt the black dog coming. From the pressure behind his skull, he knew this time it would be bad.

"Let him die," Lewis said.

Peter glared at him. "What would Dinah say about that? He's only a few years older than Charlie, for Christ's sake. I think he was just too scared to actually put the gun down."

"Shit." Lewis went to Donat's body, rolled him onto his back, and stripped off his belt. It was made of nylon webbing, with a sliding infinity buckle that could be cinched down much tighter than the kid's crappy plastic one. He returned to Peter. "Move over, let me get this on him."

16

Lewis figured they might need the Mercury for something later, so he moved it from the foot of the driveway while Peter found the keys to the white Jeep. Then they hollered for Teddy and the three of them used the dirty blanket from the bed to carry the kid outside and load him into the back seat.

Peter opened the driver's door and slid behind the wheel. "There's a hospital twelve blocks away."

Lewis shook his head. "I've got this. It ain't my first time doing a high-speed drop-off. They got too many cameras at hospitals these days. The cops catch your face, you're screwed."

Peter slid out of the car. His calm, steady eyes held Lewis in place for a moment, the jarhead seeing something there that Lewis thought he had locked away. "You okay, brother?"

"No," Lewis said. "Go help Teddy find something we can use."

Then he got in the car and threw it in gear. Locating nearby hospitals was part of his ordinary prep for any job, so he already knew where he was going. A block away, he pulled over and turned to look across the seatback.

The kid was even more pale, and sweating despite the cold. Lewis had taken a bullet more than once, so he knew the pain was bad. Maybe it was just the shock, but the kid was holding it together, not crying or screaming. Better than some grown men Lewis had known.

"You speak any English?"

"Little bit English." His accent was much stronger than Zef's.

Lewis wasn't holding out much hope of being understood, but he needed to tell the kid something. "You're lucky my friend was there. He saved your life. Now here's what's going to happen." Lewis drew his pistol and laid it along the seatback for emphasis. "A year from now, I will find you. If you haven't straightened up, found a job, gotten yourself right, I'll shoot you myself. You understand?"

Eyes wide, the kid nodded.

He gave the kid his checkpoint stare. "Before you get any ideas about revenge, I'm always strapped. So if I spot you walking up on me, ever, you're a dead man. We clear?"

The kid nodded again, more vigorously.

Lewis sighed. He couldn't believe he'd been willing to let the kid die. He wasn't even old enough to need to shave.

He put his gun away, took a baseball hat from the dashboard and pulled it down low, then threw the Jeep into gear.

The emergency entrance was on West Eddy, a covered bay with two parked ambulances and an atrium with stairs for foot traffic. Lewis pulled the Jeep behind the right-hand ambulance and hustled around to the passenger side, keeping his head down. Looking for cameras was the best way for them to capture your face. If they found him, he'd become a person of interest. They'd link the hurt kid to the four dead Albanians. Lewis couldn't afford any of that right now.

He pulled the kid out and put his arm around him and together they made it past the ambo to the outer doors, which opened automatically. Lewis helped the kid into the glassed-in vestibule and leaned him against the wall, then pulled out his knife. The kid shrank away from him.

"No, man, I'm cutting the cuffs." He took hold of the boy's wrists. "So they don't think you're an escaped prisoner." He flicked the blade twice and the plastic fell away. The knife was very sharp.

He bent to scoop up the severed cuffs, but he must have triggered the motion sensors because the inner doors slid open. On the other side was the reception desk and a sturdy-looking woman in blue scrubs, who turned at the movement. "You hurt?"

The kid grabbed Lewis's arm. "Walgreens," he said. "Addy-son."

Lewis looked at him. "I don't understand."

The woman in scrubs came closer. She must have seen the blood, because she shouted over her shoulder. "Got a walk-in, probable GSW. Get me a stretcher right now."

On the far side of the reception area, a uniformed cop started hustling their way, his gun belt bouncing with every stride.

The kid's grip tightened. "Walgreens," he said again. "Addy-son."

Lewis still didn't get it. The cop picked up his pace. "Wait right there," he called. "I just want to talk." Behind him came two people with a stretcher.

Lewis tore himself free and ran.

He left the Jeep two blocks from the Albanians' place, then walked back in the cold, turning over the kid's words in his head. But he couldn't make sense of them. Not just what they meant, but why the kid had even said them. Walgreens? Addy-son?

His nerves were snarling like a buzz saw. He could feel the crash coming now, the black dog's stinking breath hot on his face. Despair and regret and exhaustion rose like floodwaters, threatening to carry him away. He wanted nothing more than to anchor himself in the safe harbor of Dinah's arms and sleep for a week, but knew that would have to wait.

He climbed the house's steps with leaden legs. Inside, someone had opened a couple of windows to help clear the smell of blood and spent powder. It also made it easier to listen for the sound of sirens or the high revs of fast-approaching engines. Lewis knew they should get the hell out, but he needed to find something, anything, that would help him find the notebooks.

He found Peter standing at the folding table beside the blocky piece of computer equipment, which turned out to be a complicated-looking printer. The rest of the table was covered with rows of bloody phones and keys and wallets and rolls of bills. Peter's combat gloves were stained dark from going through dead men's pockets. The Albanians' Uzi and pistols were laid out at the end, and the black shotguns leaned against the wall in the corner.

"What've you got?"

"Not much." Peter also looked exhausted. "Only got one phone unlocked using a face. I checked recent texts and email but didn't find anything. The rest have passwords, so we won't get anything there. But I did find these." He pointed to the top of the built-in china cabinet, where a half-dozen empty FedEx mailing envelopes, with their distinctive purple and orange logo, were scattered. "I think this is why they cut out the pages, to fit them inside."

Lewis picked up an envelope, his stomach sinking. Zef had told him it was already done. "Tell me you found some full ones."

"Not on this floor. Teddy's searching the rest."

There was no reason for Zef to hide them. He hadn't known they were coming. Lewis took his burner from his pocket and pulled up the browser.

"I already did that," Peter said gently. "There are fifteen FedEx drop boxes within a five-mile radius. Within ten miles, it's more like sixty. Even if they dropped the mailers after the last evening pickup, we'd never get to them all before the trucks come in the morning."

Which meant, Lewis thought, that if the mailers were already out the door, they were gone.

"But there's a little good news." Peter pointed to the printer. "Turns out, if you're going to use a twenty-four-hour drop box, you have to prepay and print your own label. So there's probably a laptop around here, too. If we're lucky, we'll find the FedEx website open with the address right there."

Lewis tried to focus on the problem. There was solace in that. "Unless somebody printed from his phone."

"You can do that?"

Lewis sighed. Peter was extremely capable in many areas, but technology was not one of them. Half the time, the jarhead couldn't even find his own cell phone, which drove June nuts. "We need to get the rest of those phones open. I know a guy who can do that. The Albanians had to communicate with their buyer somehow."

"We'll hope for a laptop. I haven't searched the cars yet. Maybe we can pull an address from one of the nav systems. But the house is basically empty. No extra clothes, no food in the fridge."

"It's a party house," Lewis said, "and maybe a place to hide their stash. Teddy's good at finding those hiding places."

"Whatever there is, we'll find it. I figure we clean the place out, take weapons and other valuables, not give the police a reason to think too hard about motive. June's contact told her that Zef hit the Italians a few times, so they're the obvious suspects for a hit like this."

Lewis raised his eyebrows. "Smart. We'll make a heavy lifter out of you yet."

Peter gave him a dark look. "No need."

Lewis knew that look. Peter was feeling the weight of the dead. Lewis was trying hard not to.

To distract himself, he focused on the Uzi. "Where did that come from? I didn't see it when we came through the door."

"Me neither," Peter said. "Under the coffee table?"

Lewis went to the living room. The table's bottom shelf was missing. He looked at the couch. At the near end, plugged into a wall outlet, was a black charger. The other end of the cable lay on the floor.

He moved the table and knelt to peer under the couch. Enough room for an Uzi, for sure. And something else. He reached into the darkness and pulled out a flat black rectangle. A cheap laptop.

He handed it to Peter with the charger. "Find something to put all this junk in. We need to go." His hands were beginning to shake. The black dog was howling now. His stomach wanted to empty itself, but he swallowed it down.

"We should take the printer, too," Peter said. "In case we can't unlock the laptop. June wrote a story last year about the FBI getting into some corporate machines to repeat the last print run. Maybe we can find the mailing address that way."

Teddy came in from the kitchen with a gym bag in one hand, waving a folded paper grocery sack with the other. His round face was bright with glee. "Look what I found inside the furnace. Cash money and two bricks of powder."

"What about those notebook pages?" Peter asked.

Teddy's face fell. "I looked everywhere."

"Okay," Lewis said. "We're gone. Load everything in the Range

Rover except the pistols and the loose dope. We're leaving the Malibu, so we'll need another ride. Time to put these Albanians behind us."

Peter went to the kitchen to find some kind of bag. Teddy took the Rover keys on the table, then put the big printer under one arm and carried the dope and money out the front door. Lewis reminded himself to check the Rover's nav system. The Jeep didn't have one, but the Albanians' two other cars, a BMW and a Mercedes, probably did.

He thought again of the kid he'd taken to the hospital, what he'd said before Lewis had left. Maybe it only sounded like English. Maybe it was Albanian.

He pulled out his burner and opened the browser. He hit the voice button and said, "Walgreens. Addy-son. Translate from Albanian into English."

There was no Albanian translation site on the first page of returns, or the second. But there was a Walgreens on West Addison, a mile away. What was the kid trying to tell him, the closest place to buy medical supplies? The crash was killing his brain. He needed coffee.

Peter came out with a brown paper bag with a yellow smiley face printed on each side, along with the words HAVE A NICE DAY! He started loading stuff into the bag. The last thing was the FedEx mailers from the top of the china cabinet. "You about ready?"

But Lewis was back on his phone, searching Google Maps for FedEx drops.

There it was. The same corner as the Walgreens. No, the same address. He went to the Walgreens site and found it. A FedEx counter inside the store. Three blocks from the hospital where he'd dropped the wounded kid. And it was open twenty-four hours.

He felt a wave of gratitude for what the kid had done, followed by the lift of fresh adrenaline, like gasoline in his veins. The shakes were gone. He held up the phone to Peter in exaltation. "Brother, we're in business."

17

ewis set Leanne's keys in plain sight on the seat of the unlocked and wiped-down Malibu, then got into the Mercury with Teddy for the drive to West Addison. Peter was a block behind them in the black-on-black Rover. June had told Peter the Albanians' vehicles were all owned by shell companies, so the Rover was unlikely to be linked to the dead until the police got inside their social media. Safe to drive for a few hours, anyway. It was three o'clock in the morning.

Teddy had already moved the Yukon a mile farther from the house, loaded with the stuff taken from the Albanians' house, along with the HKs and body armor. Pistols would be enough for this next job, plus submachine guns at a Walgreens might make an enterprising detective curious about a possible connection to a nearby quadruple homicide. The goal was to make this look like a couple of knuckleheads from the neighborhood.

That section of Addison was retail and four-family apartments, handsome brick buildings that had seen better days. The plows had narrowed the streets with a heavy berm of gray snow along the wheels of parked cars. Commuters would be up before the sun to shovel themselves out of their spots, an unavoidable part of winter in the city. But at three in the morning with the wind blowing hard, there were few moving cars and no pedestrians.

They were all riding high again from what they were about to do. Lewis knew from experience that the fresh adrenaline wouldn't last, but they'd talked about it, and quickly agreed to just push through and get it done. They'd rest when it was finished.

Peter was on the phone from the Rover, a three-way call. They all wore the cheap wireless headsets now, the poor man's comm system. "So how are we doing this?"

Lewis glanced at Teddy, who drove leaning forward over the wheel with a wide smile on his moon face. "The big man and I go inside and make it happen. You turn left two blocks before the store and sit tight around the corner, past the alley entrance."

"Two guys to cover a place that size? Not enough. I'm going with you."

Lewis wasn't going to let Peter commit armed robbery against civilians. He was less likely to get shot than when taking down the Albanians, but far more likely to get caught. A drugstore was a hot target and would get a rapid response. There were cameras, inside and out. The clerk would have an alarm button under the counter.

"Sorry," Lewis said. "We need you behind the wheel and out of the camera feed. If we get blocked out by the cops, we'll run to you. If not, we'll pick up the Yukon and meet you on Roosevelt Road in Lawndale, just east of the tracks. There's a place I know, we can dump the Mercury there."

Unfortunately, Peter wasn't stupid. "Don't be an asshole, Lewis."

"Way too late for that, Jarhead." Lewis knew that Peter had come to some kind of peace, or at least a functional coexistence, with his post-traumatic claustrophobia, but a week in jail would really screw that up. Seven to ten in state prison for armed robbery might well kill him.

"What if there's an off-duty cop inside, or a patrol unit nearby? You need a third man."

"Peter," Lewis said. "Please." Bad enough Lewis had gotten Peter involved in this thing. He wasn't going to watch his best friend lose his mind behind bars, one visiting day at a time. "Your left is coming up. Stay on the phone."

"If this goes bad, I'm kicking your ass."

Lewis leaned forward to check the side mirror, relieved to see the black Rover peel away behind them. "Take a number, brother."

A block ahead, the drugstore came up on the left. Like many other Walgreens from the same era, the building had a brick-and-stucco exterior and a large illuminated sign in red script. Beside it was the parking lot Lewis had seen on the map, and the narrow service alley behind. The lot was neatly plowed with three cars in it, two older models and a small white sedan with a red-and-black security company logo on the doors. A modest FedEx sticker was visible on the store's glass entryway.

Lewis bumped Teddy on the shoulder. "Gimme a medium recon route." They rolled down Addison for four more blocks, then cut back in a double loop to check the snowy streets on both sides of the main drag, both men peering out their windows, looking for cruising patrol cars—or, more likely at this hour, cars idling at hydrants while officers napped to the low crackle of their radios.

It was Lewis's favorite time of night. Wide-awake while everyone else was asleep. But with that added hum in his blood that came from knowing he was going to walk into some joint with a gun in his hand, and damn any man to hell who stood in his way.

This feeling was why he hung out with the jarhead, he thought.

Peter had a knack for stepping into other people's problems. Lewis could walk beside him and use these skills, but feel righteous about it.

Unlike what he was doing now.

When Teddy had made a complete loop with no law in sight, he returned to Addison and rumbled toward the Walgreens from the opposite direction, knuckling his bad eye. Lewis knew the prosthetic got itchy when he left it in too long.

Teddy said, "We good to go?"

Lewis checked him over. "Long as you're good, Teddy. I can always walk in there alone."

Teddy's mouth bunched like a fist. "Don't you dare. It's bad enough you have to be here at all. This whole darn thing is my fault."

Lewis didn't insult him by denying it. "Then let's hit it. See if we can get what we need and make it out without getting shot in the face."

Teddy gave him a shy smile. "You know, it didn't turn out so bad. Not that I'd recommend doing it on purpose."

Lewis grinned back at him, then braced himself as Teddy turned hard into the lot, tires slipping only a little on the rock salt and sand spread by the plow truck. He backed into a handicapped space by the door and killed the engine.

They already wore fresh blue nitrile gloves. COVID had faded, but Lewis still had a few N95s in the Yukon. Turned out they came in handy when you wanted to do a little armed robbery. They pulled the masks into place, tugged their winter hats down past their eyebrows, and got out of the car. They carried their suppressed pistols down low along their thighs, where they'd be less easily noticed.

Lewis shouldered into a small black pack. "Some Heavy Lifters we are. Robbing a Walgreens."

Teddy's eyes crinkled up and the mask widened as a grin grew beneath it. "Remind me to pick up some gum while we're in there.

Maybe a Snickers bar." Teddy feeling the joy, both of them juiced up like their afterburners were lit.

Lewis said, "Start the clock."

In his ear, Peter said, "Roger that."

The glass entry door slid open before them like it had been waiting all night for the privilege.

18

Inside, it was a Walgreens, much like all the others. Registers to their right behind low U-shaped shelves designed to channel customers toward the counter while offering magazines and junk food. A young Black security guard in a gray uniform had a hip perched on the counter while talking with the salesclerk, an even younger white woman in a red fleece and ponytail.

The guard saw Lewis and Teddy coming. He tried to shift his weight to his feet as he reached for his weapon, but Teddy was fast and his pistol was already pointed at the guard's forehead. "Hands behind your head. Lady, put your hands up and step back from the counter. If the cops show up, I'm killing you first." Upstate Wilson in the house.

Lewis scanned for the FedEx sign and saw it high on the wall in the back by the photo counter. The grates were down at the pharmacy, so nobody to worry about there. He glided down the wide central lane, scanning the narrow secondary aisles as he passed. There were three cars in the lot, but so far he'd seen only two people.

He caught a flash of movement and turned, gun up. A fat man in a long black coat was half crouched by the cold medicines. Lewis pointed the pistol at him and closed in. "Hands up right now."

The man's eyes were locked on the big black automatic. The rest of him stayed motionless, like a mouse at the baseboard when you turned on the light. "Hands," Lewis said. "Don't make me shoot you."

"Please, no." The man had brown skin with a little chin beard and a Bears pom-pom hat that looked funny over the knee-length black wool dress coat. He held his arms wrapped close around his thick upper torso.

The man wasn't fat, Lewis realized. Under the open coat, he held a black-haired baby to his chest, fast asleep in a padded carrier, tiny pink pajama legs and footies poking out below. While Lewis watched, a pair of tears leaked from the man's eyes and trailed down his cheeks.

Lewis made his voice easy. "You're cool, man. Nobody gonna get hurt. But I'm in a hurry, so you need to step lively, you hear?"

Lewis didn't like the way the streets of North Division came out in his voice when he was on the edge like this. As though everything he'd done since those days, everything he'd learned, somehow didn't count. As though he'd always be that scared child trying to find a way to survive.

The man remained frozen in place. He wasn't going to take his hands away from his child. Lewis liked that about him. So he moved in and grabbed a fistful of coat, then pulled the man out of his protective crouch and hustled him toward the rear of the store. "We're going this way, man." The guy was clumsy as a rusted robot, but he was moving. "You're doing good. Everything gonna be fine. That's a beautiful baby you got there."

The man choked back a sob and clutched the child tighter. His face was smooth, with no scar tissue. His wrists were slender and his hands were slim. Not a fighter. Although, Lewis knew well what a parent was capable of when their child was threatened, and he didn't allow himself to relax.

The photo counter was a waist-high peninsula cluttered with equipment. Behind it was a modest alcove with a wide-format printer on the far wall, open shelves stuffed with shipping supplies and cardboard boxes on the left, and a jumble of larger boxes on the floor to the right in front of a tall gray cabinet with two full-length sliding doors.

"Come here." Lewis pulled the man into the alcove, tucked him into the corner by the big printer, and turned him to face the wall. "Don't move, don't make trouble, and your baby will be fine."

Peter's voice spoke in his ear. "One minute in." It seemed like much longer. It always did.

Lewis scanned the open shelves. He didn't see any mailing envelopes, but did see three plastic tote bins. He tucked his pistol into the small of his back to free up his gun hand, then pulled the bins out to get a better look inside. They just held smaller packages.

He turned to the right to check the boxes on the floor, but again saw no bins or envelopes. One box had a Dell logo, sized for a laptop. It was out in the open, with the logo clearly visible, so obviously they didn't have a protocol for protecting valuables.

He slid open a gray cabinet door. More boxes, but most of these were white with purple and orange lettering. FedEx shipping boxes of various sizes, in no discernable order, maybe the outgoing mail. Still no envelopes, though. He closed the slider and opened the next. Jackpot. Plastic bins with document-sized envelopes. Too many bins, too many envelopes.

He didn't even know where the mailers were going. They wouldn't have the Albanians' return address on them, either. He would look for identical addresses. If each notebook had its own mailer, there would be fourteen of them.

"Two minutes," Peter said.

He pulled the bins out one by one and flipped through the mailers like a file clerk, looking for identical addresses. Fat envelopes, thin envelopes. Who were all these people, sending physical documents? Hadn't they heard of email? Lewis had sold two dozen apartment buildings in the last five years and had signed all the docs electronically.

"Don't you—" Teddy shouted from the front of the store. It came through Lewis's earpiece a half instant later. Then a clatter, maybe a display falling over, hard grunts through the earpiece.

Lewis pulled down another bin and kept flipping. "Big man, you got this?"

Peter's voice. "I'm coming."

"*No*," Lewis said, low and urgent. "We're almost there." Another bin, more mailers. He should have been an accountant. Steady work, low stress. Health insurance.

"Three minutes."

"Son of a *bitch*," Teddy said, then an indistinct crack through the earpiece. Not gunfire, but something else. "Stay down!"

Another bin. He kept his eyes and fingers moving. No, hang on. He backtracked. The last two addresses the same. The next four, too. He dropped them on the floor and pulled down the next bin. All in a row, he found eight more. Each one thick and heavy and headed for a PO box in Indianapolis. The return address was the same Walgreens he was standing in. He dropped them on the floor and knelt beside them.

He found the pull tab on the top mailer and ripped it open. He shook the papers halfway out and thumbed the edges like a deck of cards. Angular handwriting slanted across the unlined pages. People and places jumped out at him, names he knew.

He'd found them. The relief was like a cool breeze on a hot day. He jammed the papers back into the envelope, then peeled off the backpack and stuffed all fourteen mailers inside. He went through the previous bin, then the one before, looking for strays and finding none. He pulled the last bin from the cabinet, found nothing. He had everything.

"Four minutes."

"Guys, I got 'em. We're good to go." He got his gun in his hand and shouldered the pack, feeling the weight of all that paper. "Moving to the front. Everything okay up there?"

"All good," Teddy said. "For me, anyway."

Lewis went to the man with the baby and turned him away from the corner. The man wouldn't look at him. Tears streaked his cheeks. "Give me your phone." The man didn't move. Lewis patted the man's coat pockets, found the device, and held it up. "This will be in the trash can outside." He put his hand on the man's shoulder. "You're okay. Your baby's okay. You were never in any danger." The man still wouldn't look at him.

This was the difference between who he used to be and who he was now, Lewis thought. The old Lewis wouldn't have cared. The new Lewis couldn't help himself.

"Stay here and count to a thousand. Then eat something, get your blood sugar up while you're waiting for the cops."

He thumbed open his knife and cut the line to the phone receiver, then headed toward the register, where Teddy frowned down at the security guard. The young man sat on the floor with his arm bent at a nasty angle, bleeding from a cut on his forehead, face contorted with pain. Metal shelves had fallen from a candy rack and empty calories lay scattered everywhere. Teddy said, "He figured out I had a bad eye and tried to take advantage."

"His mistake." Lewis slipped behind the counter with his knife out. The young woman in the red fleece shrank away from him, trying to make herself as small as possible. "You're okay, miss." Lewis reached past her and cut the cords to two more landline receivers. Then he raised his hip and slipped across the counter.

Teddy patted the pocket of his greasy green parka. "I got their phones and his gun."

"Put 'em in the trash outside," Lewis said. "We're gone."

Outside, the cold air felt good. There was no sound of sirens. The waste can was half-full and it would take the broken-armed security guard a few minutes to wrestle off the heavy lid. Lewis and his people would have more than enough time to get themselves lost in the city. He resisted the urge to peel off the hat and mask, knowing there might be stoplight cameras that could look through the windshield. He unslung the heavy backpack and climbed into the big Mercury.

Teddy fired up the engine and eased out of the parking spot and into the alley, where they ghosted away into the frozen Chicago darkness. Lewis clutched the backpack to his chest like an angel who'd reclaimed a lost soul.

Finally, he could *breathe* again.

19

Lewis's spot in Lawndale turned out to be a lonely railroad siding, hidden between the high walls of a scrap yard and an industrial warehouse. Lewis took bolt cutters from the Yukon to remove the padlock on a chain-link gate, then led them through. Teddy stopped to close the gate behind them.

It was all about speed now, getting themselves clean and clear. Patrol cars would soon be actively searching for the Mercury, because they'd have pictures of it from the Walgreens parking lot cameras. Chicago was a sprawling town, with a lot of ground to cover, but the police could get lucky like anyone else.

They transferred the Albanians' printer and the backpack full of notebook pages from the Mercury to the Yukon. They pulled the SIM cards from their burners and cracked them with their thumbnails, then put the phones into a plastic bag and stomped them into a plastic ruin. Peter had already sent June a text, telling her they were successful and safe. June would pass the word to Dinah.

It was almost four a.m. Removing all possible trace evidence from the vehicle would take hours they didn't have, and with modern technology it was hard to know if you'd actually done the job. The most efficient way to eliminate fingerprints and DNA was with fire. On the way from Addison Street, Peter had bought a two-gallon gas can at a twenty-four-hour station and filled it at the pump. Chicago was a good town for all-night places.

Lewis took the bricks of dope from the gym bag, cut open the plastic wrap, and set them on the van's vinyl seats. Then he soaked the entire cabin in gas, threw a lit matchbook through the open window, and danced away with the grin of a naughty child as the fumes ignited with a *whomp*.

The superheated air pushed Peter back a step and he felt the grin matched on his own face. From the right distance, a firebomb always felt like a warm summer day. They stood side by side in the snow, three tired and dirty men, and watched the flames rise, riding the last of the adrenaline, rapt with the spectacle of destruction.

Peter kept flashing back to the Albanians, watching Kron bring the shotgun around in slow motion, Lorik raising it to his shoulder. Peter had been faster, and the others had died. Everybody had died except the kid. At least Peter had managed that much.

He thought again about what Lewis's life must have been like in the bad old days. He wondered if it was like Peter's own long war, which he remembered with a mix of pride and shame. He wasn't surprised that Lewis didn't like to talk about it. Aside from June, Peter only really talked about the war with others who'd been there.

He wondered who Lewis talked to.

Or if he kept it all inside, the way Peter used to.

"We should go," Lewis said. "We meet at my place. You know the address, Teddy?"

"I used to," Teddy said. "I mean, I wrote it down. But now I need it again."

"You wrote it down?" Lewis stared at him, eyes gone cold as ice despite the heat of the burning van. "My home address? Where Dinah and the boys live? In your motherfucking *notebooks*?"

"Well, yeah. I put their names, too, plus Nino and Ray, 'cause you know I can't hardly remember anything unless I write it down. Not Nino's or Ray's addresses, though. I don't know where they live. I don't even know their last names."

The muscles jumped and popped on Lewis's face. Reflected flames from the burning car flickered darkly on his skin. His hand drifted down toward the pistol on his hip. "Teddy, I swear to God . . ."

Teddy looked genuinely puzzled. "Why are you mad? Don't you have an address book?"

Lewis's voice rose. "Yeah, you dumb shit, but it's in code. Not written down in plain English with all my thoughts and feelings and every crime I ever did in my entire fucking life. So if by some chance I get rolled up by the law, my friends don't all get rolled up, too."

"Lewis." Peter bumped him with his elbow. "We're good. We got the notebooks."

Teddy looked at his feet. "I'm sorry, Lewis. I'll fix it."

Lewis let out a breath. "It's already fixed," he said. "Why don't you get a hotel room and catch some sleep. Drop that parka in a dumpster, it's got blood on it. Then pick up a new phone, leave a message at Shorty's, and let us know how to reach you."

There was no way Lewis would let Teddy know where he lived now.

"I can do that." Teddy kicked at the crusted snow, then looked back at Lewis. "So when do I get my notebooks back?"

"You don't." Lewis's voice cut like an axe. "I can't have that crap out in the world."

The big man frowned. "They're my notebooks. I worked hard to remember what's on those pages. I want them back. Besides, it's over."

Lewis gave Teddy that icy stare again. "Don't be stupid. This ain't over. Whoever put that bounty on our heads, those guys are still out there, looking for us. Now they know those notebooks exist. Maybe they know some of what's in 'em. So I need to know what's in 'em, too, see how bad our exposure is. Maybe it'll help us figure out who's behind all this."

Teddy set his mouth, his prosthetic eye gleaming in the firelight. "You're not reading my notebooks. They're private." He stepped toward the Yukon, loose and easy. In the greasy green parka, he looked enormous. "Tell you what, Lewis. I'll read 'em again myself. Then I'll tell you what you need to know." He reached for the passenger door.

Peter didn't even see Lewis move. Suddenly, a black automatic was in his right hand, the round suppressor jammed up tight under the bigger man's chin, Lewis's left hand clenched tight on the front of the parka. His face was cold and hard. "I like you, Teddy. I helped bring you back from the dead, remember? Twice, if you count yesterday. But don't make me choose between you and my family. 'Cause I'll send you straight to hell without thinking twice."

Teddy's hands floated up and his knees bent slightly. "So that's how it is." Anything childlike in him was gone. Upstate Wilson was back all the way. Maybe he'd never been gone. He stared hard at Lewis, no doubt running scenarios in his head, how to slip the pistol and take it for himself.

Peter couldn't believe this shit. "Hey." He used his command voice. "*Hey!*"

Neither man looked at him, but Peter knew he had at least part of their attention. He moved closer and eyeballed each man, conjuring up his inner drill sergeant, trying to pretend there wasn't a loaded gun between them with a finger hard on the trigger.

"You're being dickheads, both of you. Lewis, all Teddy wants is his own stuff back. Teddy, we get what you were trying to do with the notebooks, but you told stories you should have kept to yourself. This whole thing really is your own damn fault. And we just lit a fire that will lead all the cops in the world right to us. So go ahead, fuck each other up."

He looked from one man to the other. Both were breathing hard, unconsciously oxygenating for the fight. But Teddy no longer leaned into Lewis's clenched fist, and Lewis's finger had slackened on the trigger.

"Here's how it's going to go," Peter said. "*I'm* taking the notebooks. If I need to read them, I'll read them. But I'll keep my mouth shut about it. And when this is over, Teddy, you'll get them back. That's a promise." He leaned in close and put a hand on each man's shoulder. "Can you guys live with that?"

Teddy dropped his hands and straightened his knees. He wouldn't look at Peter or Lewis. "I'm sorry." Just like that, Upstate Wilson was gone again.

Lewis let go of Teddy's parka and made the pistol disappear.

Peter stepped back and watched the two men shake hands, then turn away from each other.

But some things, Peter knew, you can't undo.

Like putting a pistol to a man's head.

Or putting another man's family in harm's way.

One minute later, the black-on-black Rover bumped across the snowy gravel toward the road. When it had vanished into the early-morning darkness, Lewis said, "You know I'm gonna read those notebooks anyway."

"No," Peter said, "you're not. Why do you think Teddy got all worked up about it? There's things he doesn't want anyone to know in those pages. Things he's ashamed of doing, maybe ashamed of even thinking."

Lewis looked away. "Hell, we all got that."

"So you know how he feels. Plus what if he wrote about his sex life?"

Lewis snorted. "Heard enough about that already."

"So I'm protecting you," Peter said. "Taking one for the team."

"No, you're gonna study those parts," Lewis said. "Try to up your sorry-ass game."

Peter grinned. "Yeah, that's what I need. Sex tips from Upstate Wilson."

Lewis shook his head and blew out a long breath. His shoulders sagged. "You know this ain't over," he said. "Whoever those guys are put that bounty on my head, they're still out there."

"Agreed," Peter said. "There's something else we're missing here. We need to regroup, find a way to get inside those phones, that laptop. I don't have those skills, and I don't think June does, either."

"I know a guy, back in town. My man Robert. We can hit his house on the way."

Lewis always knew a guy. "Okay," Peter said. "Tomorrow, we'll start looking. But today, Dinah and the boys are safe. So right now, we're going home."

Lewis closed his eyes and rubbed them with his thumbs. "Home sounds pretty good." Peter had never seen him look this tired before.

Behind them, the Mercury's paint caught fire. The windshield glass had already cracked and sagged and soon would melt.

"I'm driving," Peter said. "I've had more sleep than you."

He expected a fight, but Lewis just tossed him the keys. "There's a forest preserve swamp off 41, north of the city. We'll dump the HKs there. I never keep a weapon with a body on it."

As they drove away, the sedan's tires were just beginning to burn.

20

STREYLING

Ninety minutes before, a middle-aged man with long legs, sharp features, and a receding hairline had crouched in the back seat of a dented Nissan Sentra, watching as the outdated beige sedan with Wisconsin plates pulled out of the driveway, followed by a big black Range Rover.

His name was Jay Streyling, although it was no longer the name he used, not since it had become a liability many years ago.

He'd selected the Sentra because it was in the shadow between streetlights on the opposite side from the address he'd been given. The fact that it was unlocked was a bonus. His loaner vehicle was two blocks away, and he'd have preferred to sit in warmth, but that wasn't how this game was played. In the intense cold, the exhaust plume would have looked like a signal flare. Even with the engine off, an unfamiliar vehicle might arouse too much interest. Unfortunately, his loaner was too far away to allow him to follow the sedan and Rover.

He'd only been scouting the bungalow for a few minutes, waiting on some local talent, when a Black guy in combat armor under a winter coat walked up the street and into the house looking like his dog had died. A few minutes later, the front door opened and he came out looking like his dog had somehow come back to life. Two similarly equipped white guys had loaded some stuff into the back of the Rover. The tall white guy had climbed into the Rover and the extra-large white guy had joined the Black guy in the sedan, then they all drove away.

The Rover was black-on-black with severely tinted windows, a favorite of affluent thugs everywhere. The sedan was an odd companion, reminding Streyling of a motor pool car from his formative years. Except those never had bumper stickers, and they were almost always tan, blue, or black. Also, that model was at least ten years too old to still be in the field. Like Streyling, when the motor pool cars got up in years, their service was terminated. They were dumped into an auction lot, then driven hard by the highest bidder until all remaining utility was wrung out of them.

Streyling, however, planned to make a fresh start before that happened to him. Every American had the right to reinvent himself in the manner of his own choosing, that was his philosophy. A person never knew what opportunities might present themselves to an alert and prepared mind. Despite the oath he had taken several lifetimes ago, not to mention the rigors of his present employment, Streyling's allegiance had only ever been to himself.

After noting the license plate numbers in his phone, he took a monocular from his shoulder bag and glassed the house. He quickly noted several small round holes in the panes of the front windows. Streyling had seen holes like that before. He'd made some himself.

He unfolded himself from the back of the Sentra and stepped into the street. He was dressed for the Boston steakhouse he'd been pulled away from eight hours before, in a gray topcoat and dark pants. The Chicago wind blew through them as though he wore nothing at all. He told himself not to feel the cold. He was very good at not feeling uncomfortable things. He'd had decades of practice. It had become his nature.

As he walked up the driveway to the front steps, he pulled on thin leather gloves, then took a Glock pistol from the pocket of his coat. He didn't need to rack the slide because he always kept a round in the chamber.

This was not the plan. The plan was to meet the local talent on-site, then let them capture the Albanians while he sat comfortably in his heated car. That accomplished, Streyling would ask the questions to get what he needed, and when he was done, the local talent would make sure the Albanians were permanently out of the picture. His employer had paid good money for valuable information, after all. It was only prudent to ensure that information wouldn't be resold to another party.

But plans were not reality. The armored men were gone, the local talent was still thirty minutes out, and Streyling had questions now. What had happened inside that house? Why had the men packed up and left in the middle of the night? Why was the house still lit up like broad daylight?

When he peered through the front door and saw the dead bodies in the living room, all his questions were answered. The armored men were not the men he'd come to interrogate. The armored men had come for the same purpose as Streyling. Somehow, they'd gotten here first.

So who were the armored men?

Streyling didn't know for certain, but he had a hunch.

He was fairly certain he'd just seen the Ghost Killers in the flesh.

Mindful not to step in any blood, he worked his way through the house, examining everything but finding nothing. The armored men had taken anything of interest or value. What they'd left behind were four bodies and a very red spot on the couch where, Streyling concluded, a badly injured man had been.

None of the armored men had seemed injured to Streyling, at least not to the degree suggested by the saturated cushions. He spent a few extra minutes trying to re-create the sequence of events and, by extension, get inside the minds of the men who had pulled the trigger. Then he returned to the Sentra, retrieved his shoulder bag from the back seat, and walked two blocks to his car. It was a tan Dodge Durango left for him at airport parking, with the keys atop the rear right tire as promised. The Glock had been in the glove box with two spare magazines. Like the full tank of gas, the pistol was a courtesy, and not expected back.

His employer's business was small but effective, as well as extremely well-funded and well-connected. With reliable contacts in many major cities, almost any imaginable service was available, if you could meet the price. His employer's reputation for ruthlessness, due in part to Streyling's influence, helped encourage this kind of cooperation. The cultivation of fear was crucial in this industry. Either you were the eater or the eaten, and Streyling was quite clear which of those he wanted to be.

His employer's operation was run primarily through hired attorneys and private bankers. There were many who were not scrupulous about the nature of the work they performed, as long as the pay was high enough. Streyling felt much the same himself, as did the Israeli hacker who had traced an email back to this street address in Chicago. The now-dead information sellers were moderately sophisticated in their use of technology, but not remotely sophisticated enough to fool the Israeli specialist.

Because he'd been in a rush to catch the last flight out, Streyling hadn't time to go home and pack a suitcase. But he had everything he needed in his shoulder bag, which was always by his side. The contents would appear innocuous at first glance. The electronic devices appeared to be the kinds of things that any business traveler carried, although one of the cables was actually a homemade garrote, and one of the chargers had been custom-made to conceal a ceramic blade. Streyling did a fair amount of flying, and he didn't like to be without a weapon. Nobody would find the hidden compartment in the bag's false bottom, with identification and credit cards in four different names.

All of it was replaceable, with the exception of a small notebook filled with contact information written in a code of his own design. In his work, Streyling had a wide range of duties. It was amazing what you could accomplish when you knew the right person to call.

Although, for his employer, this was a different kind of project. A passion project that took precedence over everything. Streyling didn't have access to the numbers—despite his years of service, he was kept in the dark on most things—but he was certain the resources consumed would have been enormous. Privately, he thought the whole thing was an emotional boondoggle, a colossal waste of time and money. The hook had been baited for years. Now, in complete defiance of his expectations, there was a fish on the line.

Streyling had convinced his employer to allow him to take the lead. He had hunted men before, in his former life. When he had things under control, he would make a call. His employer would get the desired result, and Streyling would get paid.

Now he was on the freeway, headed north across frozen farmland with the sky not yet beginning to brighten in the east. He'd reached out to his employer with an update and was surprised to learn a new address for the target, ninety miles north.

He'd sent the local talent home.

For the Ghost Killers, Streyling wanted men he was certain were competent.

They would take the first available flight out this morning.

It would put them in Milwaukee around noon.

Ready to go to work.

21

PETER

The streetlights had just gone off when Peter pulled up at a modest brick house on 72nd, across from Enderis Park. His mouth tasted like dirty socks and his skin itched all over. The first time he was deployed, he'd lived rough for months on minimal sleep, but it hadn't improved his aim or the clarity of his thinking. He was looking forward to a shower and some sack time.

In the passenger seat, Lewis blinked his eyes open. Peter didn't know if he'd slept, but he'd sat with his seat tipped back, still and silent as the dead, for the whole ninety-minute ride back from Chicago.

Peter said, "I've been thinking about logistics. I still don't get how the Albanians made their deal so fast. They leave Teddy's at eleven in the morning, get the notebooks home by six, and by midnight the pages are ready to ship to Indianapolis? How would that happen so quickly? For a quarter-million dollars, doesn't the buyer need to vet the content somehow? Plus how do they know they'll actually get the pages? And the sellers, how do they know they'll actually get paid?"

"I've been wondering that, too," Lewis said. "Only thing I can figure is, Zef started reading on the way home. Once he knew what he had, he could start negotiations, send photos of a couple of pages to show good faith. All he'd need was a few details that the buyer would believe to be accurate. He'd hold back anything useful to make sure he got paid. Hopefully, when we get into those phones, we can get some idea of how that went down, what information got sent. Not to mention who those damn buyers are."

He reached for the brown paper bag, dumped out the remaining peanut butter sandwiches, then popped open the glove compartment and took out a plastic box of bleach wipes.

"I never figured you for a wet-wipe guy," Peter said.

Lewis shook his head. "That boy Miles is a walking disaster. Last week he spilled a whole milkshake into these cupholders here. Wipes wouldn't make a dent. I had to use the wet vac."

Peter smiled. He found a perverse amount of enjoyment watching Lewis, the most dangerous man he'd ever met, navigate the mundane challenges of domestic life.

Lewis turned in his seat and retrieved Cousin Zef's laptop from the back. He opened the lid and began to wipe the machine clean. "Maybe you'd start on those phones," he said. "I don't want to bring a dead man's blood into Robert's house. Get 'em out of their cases, that's where it collects."

When the phones were scrubbed down, Lewis dropped them into the paper bag with the laptop and got out of the car. "Just be a minute."

"Take the Albanians' printer, too." It was in the back of the Yukon.

"No need," Lewis said. "We got the notebooks."

Peter watched as Lewis rang the bell. The door was a thick slab of varnished oak with a high window of frosted glass. A minute later, a little girl opened it. She was five or six, hair in pigtails, her skin dark against the cream-colored polo shirt of a school uniform. When she saw Lewis, she jumped forward and wrapped her arms around him.

A slim man in a neat black suit appeared behind the girl, a broad smile on his face. He and Lewis embraced, then Lewis held out the paper bag. The slim man opened the top to glance inside, then nodded. After a moment, they bumped fists and Lewis walked back to the car. "He'll bring them by the house around one."

"That's your hacker? In the suit? With the daughter?"

"Three daughters, actually. Robert runs a consulting business with his wife. White hat security intrusions, stress tests for corporate systems. Known him since he was a kid. Does me a favor every once in a while."

Ten minutes later, Peter pulled up in front of his house and got out of the car. "I'm making breakfast if you want some. I can bring it to your place."

Lewis climbed behind the wheel. "Thanks. I'd like that."

Peter dropped his go-bag at the side door, toed off his boots, and walked upstairs. In the bathroom, he stripped off his jacket and shirt, then stepped out of the rest of his clothes. When the water was as hot as he could stand it, he stepped into the spray, the many old scars standing out white on his heat-reddened skin, his bony, muscled frame gleaming like welded girders in the rain.

He soaped himself twice, brushed his teeth, and scrubbed his hair until his scalp hurt. Then he turned the shower to full cold, yelping aloud as his sore muscles seized up, then sighing as their ache finally began to ease.

Dressed, he went downstairs to the kitchen. As always, the house felt empty without June at the little round table, talking on the phone or banging away at her laptop, chasing down whatever story she was working. She had an office upstairs, but she liked to be in the middle of things. He glanced at the clock on the stove, counting the hours until she got home.

He dumped some bulk chorizo in a cast-iron skillet with a generous handful of chopped frozen tater tots, let them cook for a few minutes, then added onions and mushrooms. He wasn't particularly proud of the tater tot move, but he was hungry, and it was easy.

He scrambled a half-dozen eggs with a fork, then poured them into the softened vegetables with some grated cheese and stirred gently with a spatula until the eggs were just set. He divided the mixture between two large wheat tortillas, hot from the oven, and after a generous shake of Cholula hot sauce, rolled them into burritos, wrapped them in foil, and walked them to Lewis's place, three doors down. The weather had warmed to twenty degrees, and although still below freezing, it felt almost like spring in comparison to the subzero temperatures they'd been dealing with.

He found Lewis in his gun room.

The house was a hundred and twenty years old with a basement foundation made of quarried stone blocks, eighteen inches thick. The gun room took up more than half of that space, well lit and orderly with a pair of long workbenches, tall metal storage cabinets, and two large gun safes. Peter had the combination to one of them, but he'd never seen the second one open.

All but one of the windows had been replaced by glass block for security. The remaining window, in the boiler room, had a removable security grate bolted to the inside. It wasn't a bad neighborhood, but the worst neighborhood in town was only a five-minute drive.

He found Lewis wearing faded black jeans and an N.W.A sweatshirt, loading the blood-spattered body armor into an ancient gas-fired incinerator that vented into the chimney. The incinerator hadn't been legal since the seventies, but that was small potatoes compared to what they'd done in the last twenty-four hours.

Peter added the paper bag with his own bloody clothes. Lewis peeled off his nitrile gloves and threw them on top of the burning pile, then pushed the cover back into place. "In fifteen minutes, that armor won't even be ashes," he said. "I saved the ceramic plates for spares. Work clothes are already gone. Money and wallets, too."

"You burned the money?" Peter handed over a burrito. "That's not like you."

"I know, right?" Lewis tore open the foil and took a neat bite, then dabbed his lips with a folded paper towel from a roll on the work-bench. "Back in the day, I'd run the bills through the washer a couple times, get most the blood out of it. But now I wash my kids' clothes in that machine, you know? So out it goes. This wasn't never about the money, anyway."

Peter started on his own burrito. It was rich and hot. "What's next?"

Lewis pointed to the shotguns leaning in the corner. "One last chore."

They finished the meal, then perched on high stools and broke down the guns for cleaning. Eventually they would talk through last night's killings the way they had talked through everything else they'd done together, good and bad, but neither man was ready yet. They'd need twelve hours' sleep first, and a bottle of good bourbon, and, if possible, a bonfire in the woods. For the moment, though, it was enough to be sitting together in silence with that familiar and comforting work, the soft scrape of the bore brush, the smell of solvent and oil.

When the weapons were ready for service again, they loaded them into the safe and Lewis spun the wheel. It was almost nine in the morning.

Upstairs, Lewis went to check his email and investments in his second-floor office. Peter poured himself a cup of coffee in the kitchen, then sat on the couch in the attached family room, beside a life-sized cardboard cutout of Michael B. Jordan, the actor, wearing a bright blue suit. Dinah had told June, after watching *Black Panther* on television with the boys, that the actor was "too delicious to play the villain," so June had bought the cutout as a joke.

Peter dug through the backpack with Teddy's notebooks until he found the envelope with the earliest dates. Teddy's handwriting wasn't good and the words just swam on the paper. He finished his coffee, but it seemed to have no effect. He kicked off his boots and stretched out on the couch. He wasn't exactly tired, but his eyes felt like they'd been wrapped in sandpaper and his head ached with a slow, steady throb. Part of it was the lack of sleep, but most was the adrenaline debt his body owed.

Lewis, on the other hand, returned to the kitchen still seeming to burn with the same intensity as the incinerator. Peter closed his eyes and listened to the water running in the sink, the spritz of a spray bottle, the sounds of his friend scrubbing the already-spotless countertops.

Peter had witnessed this ritual before. When the granite and steel gleamed, Lewis would move to the bathrooms. Then he'd tidy the house, taking extra time in the boys' rooms, picking up clothes, making beds, straightening their desks. After that would come the roar of a very expensive vacuum cleaner, taking away all dirt, leaving behind neat parallel lines in the carpets.

Making everything ready for his family to come home.

June and Dinah and the boys were due home around one.

22

PETER

Peter woke to a very large dog climbing onto the couch and licking his face. "Agh." He covered up. "Mingus, off." The animal ignored him and tried to nose past his forearms and keep slurping. A hundred and fifty pounds of untrainable mutt.

When he finally managed to push the beast away, he saw Miles standing by Peter's feet, a sweet and dreamy eleven-year-old who hadn't quite hit puberty, looking at him very seriously. "Uncle Peter, it's lunchtime. Why are you sleeping? Are you sick?"

The cardboard cutout of Michael B. Jordan smiled down at Peter from the end of the couch. The mailing envelopes leaned against the coffee table. Peter was glad he'd tucked the notebook pages back inside. He didn't want Miles to get curious.

"Just feeling lazy, I guess. How was the water park?" When he'd called June after coming home, she'd told Peter that they'd gone to the Wisconsin Dells.

"Great!" Miles grinned. "I went on all the slides a hundred times. Charlie did, too."

Peter looked at Miles's fifteen-year-old brother, leaning into the open fridge, looking for something to power his ferocious metabolism. Charlie was not yet the size of Big Jimmy Johnson, his biological father, but he was well on his way. "You have fun, Charlie?"

"I mean, it was okay, I guess." He flashed Peter a hundred-watt smile as he opened a gallon of milk, letting Peter know that he wasn't so teenage-cool that he couldn't enjoy the water park with his little brother. When his school and sports schedule allowed, Charlie would put in a Saturday on a house project with Peter, learning the fine art of old-house renovation. Those were Peter's favorite workdays.

Voices floated from the entryway, then June walked in. She sat beside Peter on the couch and leaned over for a kiss. Her lips were soft. Peter wrapped his arms around her and held her close, drinking in her familiar yet always intoxicating scent.

Her voice low, she said, "How was it?"

"We got what we went for, and we made it out in one piece. That's all that matters. Where's Dinah?"

June glanced over at Miles and Charlie, both now in the kitchen, sparring over the last donut. "Upstairs with Lewis, getting changed for work." She sighed, then looked at the stack of mailers. Peter knew she wanted to get her hands on them. "She's pretty stressed-out about this. A lot more than when Lewis goes to help you with something."

"The stakes are a lot higher on this one," Peter said.

June nodded. "You're heading out again?"

"We need to find the people who offered the bounty. Whoever they are, they started this thing, and I don't think they're going to lose interest after getting so close yesterday. Plus Lewis doesn't want this hanging over his head, and I don't blame him. I could use more of your help figuring that out once Lewis's tech guy gets into their phones and laptop."

"Anything you need, Marine." She wiggled her body against his. "*I need a shower. Want to scrub my back?*"

"Yes, ma'am." Part of him began to salute.

Her wicked smile told him she felt it. She bit his ear. "Then you better get your ass back home on the double."

In the front of the house, the doorbell rang.

Mingus barked and ran for the door. Without making a conscious decision, Peter dumped June against the back cushions and leaped off the couch, reaching for the .357 Lewis kept in the side table drawer.

Sprawled on the couch, June raised her eyebrows as Peter stood with the pistol in his hand. "Are you expecting somebody?"

"Actually, yes." His heart was pounding. "The guy with the phones." But that didn't explain why he'd picked up the gun. He told himself it was just a hangover from what they'd done in Chicago.

Mingus barked again. Peter slipped into the living room and peeked through the curtain. He saw the slim Black man from the house across from Enderis Park, wearing a puffy gray parka with an elegant computer bag hung over his shoulder. A sleek Audi sedan was parked up the street.

Peter stuck the revolver into the back of his pants, pulled his fleece down to cover it, shoved Mingus out of the way, then unlocked and opened the door. "You must be Robert. I'm Peter, a friend of Lewis."

They shook hands. "Nice to meet you." Robert's was thin but strong, with the long fingers of a concert pianist. He tipped his head to the side, examining Peter like a curious bird. "Are you the same Peter who helped Dinah with that problem a few years back?"

Peter stepped back to let Robert inside. "Lewis told you about that?"

Robert smiled. "I've known Lewis since I was nine years old."

Through the open doorway, Peter checked the street. The only vehicle he didn't know was a tan Dodge Durango parked at the far end of the block by the brick four-family. It was always harder to keep track of the renters' cars. He closed and locked the door. "Can I get you some coffee?"

Dinah appeared at the top of the stairs, dressed for her upcoming shift at the ICU. "Robert, how lovely to see you." Even in purple scrubs, with her long neck and straight back, she looked somehow regal.

Lewis followed her down the stairs. "My man. Thanks for making the trip."

Dinah sent the boys up to their rooms with the dog, and the adults gathered around the big kitchen island. Robert hung his parka across the back of a chair, took the electronics from his bag, and laid them out on the polished granite, one by one, in a precise line.

"I unlocked each device and set them to airplane mode. I reset the passwords to today's date. The phones were clean, no viruses or spyware or other hidden apps."

He removed the laptop last and tapped the lid with a manicured fingernail. "This machine is a different story. It was infected with a worm at the root level. This is not script-kiddie stuff. It's complex and sophisticated, incorporating ideas and elements from multiple sources, including Russian-allied Killnet and Israel's Unit 8200."

Lewis frowned. "Russians and Israelis? Working together?"

"Oh, no," Robert said. "This would likely be a private contractor, repurposing captured code. It's quite common when powerful tools find their way onto the black market."

"Like after the NSA leaks a few years back," Peter said.

Robert nodded. "Exactly. But the skills on display are at a much higher level than usual. It's quite idiosyncratic. Whoever it is, he's showing off."

Aside from Robert, June was the most computer-savvy of the group. "Did you learn how he injected the worm, and when?"

"I did," Robert said. "It was embedded in an email yesterday, triggered when the email was opened. That's a very high-end skill. The email also contained a link to a newer file-sharing service called Elevate."

June looked at Peter. "The fact that it arrived yesterday is probably not a coincidence."

"A coincidence to what?" Robert asked. "What are you trying to determine?"

"Something was stolen," Peter said. "Lewis and I got it back, but now we're trying to figure out who sponsored the theft."

Robert said, "The sender used a VPN, a virtual private network, as well as a proxy server. The signal was bounced across the world to at least a dozen different anonymous servers, and likely many more. If you're interested in the details, I've emailed Lewis a full report. Finding the sender will almost certainly be impossible through technical means."

June smiled. "What about nontechnical means?"

Robert tipped his head to the side again, the curious bird now examining June with interest. "Social engineering can be a powerful tool. The laptop is still infected, so the sender wouldn't know what we know. If you like, we can reopen that line of communication. Perhaps embed a worm of our own."

Lewis said, "What was the rest of the email's content?"

Robert pulled a sheaf of paper from his bag and set in front of Lewis. "I printed out the complete chain. I didn't want you to accidentally infect your own system via Wi-Fi, just by opening the laptop."

Lewis looked down at the top sheet, his voice cold and dry. "The subject line is 'The Ghost Killers.'"

"Here we go," Peter said.

Dinah said, "I don't understand. Who are the Ghost Killers?"

Lewis cleared his throat, not looking at her. "Apparently that's what some people called my old crew, me and Nino and Ray."

Robert said, "Skip to the last page. There's an attachment."

Lewis flipped through to the end. "What is it?"

"It's an Elevate folder, highly compressed, used to convey large or sensitive files. The folder contains material totaling almost three giga-bytes. I hope you don't mind, but I took a look."

Lewis stared at him. "And?"

"There are fourteen PDFs," Robert said. "Each PDF contains more than two hundred scanned images of handwritten pages."

Peter glanced at the Albanians' printer, on the floor in the corner. The printer that was too nice to just run off address labels. It was also a scanner. With a sheet feeder on top.

"That's how the Albanians did the deal so fast," he said. "And why they cut the pages out of the covers, so they could use the sheet feeder to run them through the scanner faster. Once the buyer verified the material, Cousin Zef sent everything electronically. Mailing the phys-ical pages was just the last step."

Lewis looked like he was going to be sick.

Upstairs, Mingus started barking again.

Dinah put her hand on his arm. "Lewis, talk to me, please."

Lewis waved at the mailers by the couch. His voice sounded like it came from very far away. "The actual pages don't matter. They never did. By the time we got there, Teddy's diaries were already gone. Loose in the world for anyone to read." When he turned to Dinah, Peter could see what it cost him. But Lewis had never shied away from the difficult things. "Whoever these people are, they know where we live. They know about you, and they know about the boys."

Dinah stiffened, her face gone tight. June looked at Peter. He nodded.

Robert said, "I'm so very sorry. Please tell me how I can help."

"You've been very helpful already," June said. "We'll definitely want to go back on these guys, but first we need to regroup. We'll be in touch."

Mingus barked louder. Peter heard the clatter of toenails on the hardwood steps, then more barking at the front door. The dog had a profound dislike for every postal worker and delivery person who appeared on the block, which meant there was often a lot of barking.

Lewis sat silently, looking at Dinah. She'd closed her eyes, processing this news. June cleared her throat. "Robert, what do we owe you for today?"

He glanced at Lewis, then back to June. "Not a thing. The debt runs in the other direction." He picked up his shoulder bag. "I'll let myself out."

Peter looked at the clock. It was one thirty. Time to get moving. They could load up and be gone in thirty minutes.

Miles wandered into the kitchen. "Dad? I saw some men from my window upstairs. They came up from the ravine, and now they're outside the back fence. Their coats say 'Police' on the front."

23

They all turned to look through the wall of windows.

The backyard was a rectangle with six-foot fences on the sides and a four-foot fence at the rear, to maximize views of the wooded ravine falling steeply down to the Milwaukee River below. There was a gate beside the house, but it was iced in and wouldn't open.

In the far corner, a man with an automatic rifle swung himself over the short fence, where recently planted cedars partially hid him from view. Two more men already crept carefully through the snow-covered landscaping toward the house. All three wore ski masks and body armor with POLICE in large white letters on the front. Weapons up and ready, forty feet and closing.

"Why are the police here, Lewis?" Robert's eyes were wide. "I thought you were done with that life. I can't get caught up in this."

They all stood staring at the approaching policemen. Something about them didn't look right, but Peter couldn't put his finger on it.

Until June said, "I thought the police didn't use silenced weapons." "Some do," Lewis said. "But none of 'em carry Russian guns."

Peter realized he'd also noted the distinctive curve of the rifle's magazine that made the AK-47 and its variants recognizable from a distance. The men outside weren't cops, they were assassins. *"Everybody down."*

They all dropped to the floor. Dinah grabbed up Miles in her arms and hauled him behind the shelter of the kitchen island. June was right behind them, pulling Robert with her. Peter had the .357 in his hand.

Peter heard the tinkle of breaking glass. He looked left and saw the Michael B. Jordan cutout fly backward with three holes in his cardboard chest. Peter locked eyes with Lewis, who nodded. They didn't have a choice. They would fight to protect the people they loved.

Moving in a crouch, Lewis reached up and slapped the switch that lowered the electronic blinds over the windows. As they hummed down, he scrambled over to the small pantry and came back with his 10-gauge.

Peter slipped past Dinah to the wall beside the back door, a glass slider. He reached over to close the slatted blinds that hung between the panes. "There'll be more men at the front," he said. "Mingus," he called. "Mingus, come!"

From the entryway, the barking became truly ferocious.

"Dinah," June said. "We should go to the basement. Where's Charlie?"

Dinah didn't respond. She sat with her back against the stove, eyes wide, Miles wrapped tight in her arms.

"Dinah." June spoke more loudly. "Where's Charlie?"

Dinah blinked, then her eyes snapped into focus. "Upstairs," she said. "You take Miles." The basement door was in the kitchen, right beside the pantry. She pushed him toward it and raised her voice into a shout. "Charlie, come downstairs, right now!"

Peter looked at June. "You can get into the gun safe?"

"I know the combination." June had discovered an interest in fire-arms several years ago, after an unpleasant man had drugged her and held her captive. She and Lewis often went to the range together, and she was familiar with his vast inventory, although she preferred a .22 for target shooting. She pushed poor Robert, who looked scared but strangely composed, after Miles. "Mingus, leave it! Mingus, come!"

Dinah shouted again, louder still. "Charles Parker Johnson, get your butt downstairs now! This is not a drill!" Not for the first time, Peter thought that Dinah would have made a very good Marine.

The dog kept barking, which made communication difficult. Also, Charlie liked his headphones. Dinah shook her head, irritated, and ran into the living room toward the stairs to the second floor. Lewis went after her. "I'll take the front."

Peter didn't like any of it. The Colt Python was a fine weapon, but six rounds and a four-inch barrel was no match for three AKs. Al-though, if he got lucky, those Teflon-coated magnum rounds might make a hole in that armor. If he got close enough, he didn't even need to do that. He was all too aware of the vulnerable places that armor didn't cover.

He heard Dinah's wood-soled work clogs take the steps two at a time. Lewis called, "I've got three more at the sidewalk. They've blocked in our vehicles with a big pickup." Then came the *chunk chunk chunk* of rifle rounds hitting metal. "They're firing into our engine blocks, both the Yukon and the Subaru. We're not getting out that way."

Peter thumbed the hammer on the .357. He stood beside the glass slider with his back against the outside wall. The other side was stone. The slider was the only door at the rear of the house and the obvious entry point, unless they were going to climb through the windows. But that would be slow, so they'd try the door first.

He could see Lewis in a similar position at the front, but he wasn't looking at Peter. He was looking up the stairs, as if willing Dinah and Charlie to appear.

June knelt at the open basement door, her face fierce. "Mingus, you fucking shithead, get the hell over here."

The barking finally stopped and Mingus trotted into the kitchen. His tongue hung out sideways across his teeth in a doggy grin. June shoved him down the steps, then followed. Miles and Robert were already out of sight. Behind her, the door swung shut.

Peter reached over and gently unlocked the glass slider. No reason to make these guys decide to find another way inside. He glanced at Lewis, who was looking up the stairs with a finger to his lips. Dinah appeared as if floating, her clogs in one hand, Charlie at her heels holding an aluminum baseball bat in both hands like he meant to use it.

As they stepped from the landing to the entryway tile, the rear sliding door silently opened an inch.

Peter dropped into a crouch and waved Dinah forward as if he could pull her along by force of will. Lewis nodded at Peter, his face tight with concern, then returned his focus to the front door. Dinah was coming fast down the hall, Charlie right behind her. Peter looked back at the slider as it crept open three more inches.

Dinah and Charlie cleared the entrance to the kitchen and turned toward the basement door. Dinah stopped to push Charlie ahead of her. Peter heard Charlie's sneakers on the steps and the creak of the basement door closing as the fat muzzle of a suppressor eased into the slider's opening. Then the barrel, then the curved magazine. The shooter was right outside, listening carefully.

Peter thought of the operator's mantra: slow means smooth, and smooth means fast. But he was tired of waiting.

From his crouch, in a single, smooth motion, he reached through the opening, jammed the pistol's muzzle hard against the upper thigh of the man standing on the other side, and pulled the trigger.

BOOM. The pistol recoiled hard and Peter used the force to pull his arm back, retreating behind the shelter of the wall. Ears ringing, he smiled grimly, knowing the attacker was out of the fight and probably busy bleeding to death from a ruined femoral artery. One down, five to go.

The glass shattered in the slider, the slatted blinds crumpling, way too late for the rounds to find him. The wall trembled against his back and he knew the other two shooters were firing at the stone outside. Frustrated, undisciplined, wasting ammunition. Knock yourselves out, guys.

From the front he heard the roar of the 10-gauge, once, twice, three times. Lewis on the offensive, loaded with double-ought buckshot, the shortened barrel sending a nice wide pattern with a good chance of doing damage.

Then the front door slammed shut, followed by the crack of AK rounds punching through the thick, hard oak. Lewis shouted, "Two down over here. You okay?"

Peter's ears were ringing. "I'm just great, Lewis."

"You call that a positive attitude, motherfucker?"

Peter smiled. He didn't need to ask how many shells Lewis had left. The shotgun had a five-round tube and Lewis always kept one in the chamber, so three remained. The Python was down to five rounds. Aside from the kitchen knives and the serrated folding blade in his pocket, all the other weapons were in the basement with June, Dinah, Robert, and the boys.

Both sides had lost the element of surprise. The odds had improved, but Peter and Lewis were still outnumbered, outgunned, and unarmored. Next time, the attackers would come from someplace unexpected.

He found the switch for the powered blinds and raised them up a few inches, then peered across the granite countertop. There, in two windows, a pair of black shadows in the gap, no more than fifteen feet away. He braced the Python on the counter, lined up the sights on the first shadow, let out his breath, and pressed the trigger, *BOOM*, then quickly lined up on the second, *BOOM*.

Both shadows dropped, more glass fell. Peter didn't know if he'd hurt them or not. Then a gun barrel rose up and poked through the spiderwebbed pane and sprayed the room blindly. Peter hunkered be-hind the island again, glad the back side was shelves packed with thick cookbooks, protecting him with all that paper. Next time he'd sand-wich in some steel plate. If there was a next time.

At least he'd convinced the shooters that the windows were a bad idea. He heard the shattered sliding door roll open with a grinding noise from the glass in the track. As he turned, he saw a second gun barrel clear the threshold, sweeping back and forth aggressively as the gunman looked for a target. Before the shooter could advance, Peter scooted toward the opening, reached out with his free hand, grabbed the hot rifle barrel behind the fat suppressor, and yanked hard.

Unprepared and connected to his weapon by a strap, the shooter lurched forward over the body of his fallen comrade. As the shooter shifted his weight to pull back, Peter put the Python to the armored man's Kevlar side panel and pressed the trigger. *BOOM*.

The gunman lurched sideways as the power of the magnum round tore through his chest. He tried frantically to free his rifle from Peter's grip. He was already mortally wounded, but his body hadn't figured it out. The rifle fired four times on semiauto, *POP POP POP POP*, the rounds flying past Peter and into the gas stove behind him. Weaker now, the man kept fighting, but Peter held him close. The smell of sweat and blood and spent powder filled his nose. The other man's eyes glared at him through the holes in the ski mask. Peter growled, "Who sent you?"

But it was too late for answers. The other man's knees buckled and he fell, pulling the AK with him. Four down, maybe five. Peter shoved the Python into the back of his pants, then unclipped the rifle's strap at the barrel and pulled the weapon free. The man had landed on the back steps, face-first on top of his extra ammunition. Because Peter didn't know where the third shooter was, he wasn't about to step outside to roll the body.

"Hey, Lewis!" He refastened the loose strap and slung the rifle around his shoulder. The ringing in his ears was worse.

"I lost my guy," Lewis called back. "You see him?"

"No," Peter said. "But I got an AK. Two shooters down here, maybe another wounded."

Lewis threw the deadbolt on the heavy door and hustled toward Peter. At the kitchen, he pivoted left and stopped with the shotgun ranging across the ruined room and his back to the basement door. He was breathing hard. "We saw six, right? You think there's more?"

"We'll find out." Peter was breathing hard, too, riding the rush of adrenaline. He leaned across the fallen shooter and did a fast peek out the open slider. "Nobody in the backyard." He couldn't help looking at the dead men. He was glad they wore ski masks so he couldn't see their faces. The snow beneath them was dark with blood. "They must be at the side of the house. Or they're already gone."

"The truck they came in was still there a minute ago," Lewis said. "How you want to do this?"

"I'll go out the back and work my way around. You stay here and guard the basement. If you see any strangers in those side windows, pull the trigger."

Lewis nodded, then rolled his shoulders to loosen them. His face thrummed with tension, and also a kind of ferocious joy. Peter knew how he felt.

Then he heard a faint metallic *clunk* from the entryway. He turned with the AK raised but saw only the shot-up oak door easing shut. "I thought you locked the front."

Lewis frowned. "I did."

Peter ran. Nobody in the front stairwell, nobody in the living room. The door was unlatched. He stood to one side of the door, then opened it a crack and looked through the gap.

He saw a tall, skinny blond guy in a black dress coat, somehow already on the far side of the white picket fence, walking backward on the snowy sidewalk. When the blond beanpole saw Peter, he raised a pistol and fired one-handed. The porch post splintered, then a round hit the stone siding, sending chips flying like shrapnel.

Partially shielded by the door framing, Peter aimed the AK at center mass with his finger tight on the trigger. "Stop right there," he shouted, using his command voice.

Even with the ugly AK pointed right at him, the man in the topcoat didn't flinch, and he didn't stop. He had a leather strap across his chest, some kind of bag slung behind him. Still walking backward, he fired again. The chrome deadbolt chimed dully by Peter's hip and the door swung inward a few more inches from the force of the round.

Peter had the beanpole in his sights, but he couldn't pull the trigger. The thick stone exterior of Lewis's house could stop rifle rounds, but the house behind his attacker was clad with wood. The AK's heavy caliber would punch right through it, and probably the house behind it, too. Peter knew the people living there. They had little kids at home.

The beanpole seemed to read Peter's hesitation. He stopped fifty feet away and took aim. Peter didn't like it, the calm deliberation, the two-handed stance. He ducked out of the opening and immediately felt the thud of impact as the pistol rounds tore up the doorjamb.

God, he was tired of getting shot at. All the fun had gone right out of it.

"Lewis, you see anybody?"

"Not yet."

He could shoot the beanpole in the calves or ankles. Firing low, the only collateral damage would be the concrete foundation of the house behind him, and his rounds were unlikely to penetrate. He'd never hit that small target under fire with the unfamiliar AK, but the shotgun's wider pattern would do the trick. "Lewis, bring that ten-gauge," he called. "This guy looks like management. If I can get him low, maybe he'll talk to us."

"Oh, he'll talk to us." Lewis appeared at the end of the hall, hugging the wall to stay out of sight behind the half-open door, then tossed Peter the shotgun.

He caught it one-handed, then pitched the AK to Lewis, shouldered the shotgun, and leaned out, looking for a target.

The beanpole wasn't on the sidewalk. Two dead men lay in the snow where Lewis had shot them. Movement to the right drew Peter's eye as two men in black body armor broke from the corner of Lewis's house and ran for the street, one of them limping badly. But they weren't an immediate threat. Plus the shotgun had only three shells remaining and Peter wanted the blond guy in the topcoat.

He was faster than he looked, because he was already across the road and two doors up, opening the rear hatch of a tan Dodge Durango. The same car Peter had seen up the street by the apartment building earlier.

The guy had been scouting the damn house.

But now the frozen gray plow berm hid his lower legs. Above the berm, Peter still didn't have a safe shot. He could fire through the berm but wasn't likely to hit what he couldn't see.

The two runners high-stepped through the snow, headed for the

Durango. "Stop right there," Peter shouted. His finger was tight on the trigger. The runners looked over their shoulders but kept moving. The beanpole ignored him and reached into the Durango's cargo bay. Peter badly wanted to fire, but he still had no safe shot. He wasn't willing to harm an innocent to stop a bad guy. He'd done enough of that in Iraq and Afghanistan.

As the runners closed in, the beanpole pulled out something long and slender and black, and raised it to rest atop his shoulder. The tip was bulbous and pointed. The back end flared like the bell of a trumpet.

Oh, shit, Peter thought.

Where the hell did the guy get a rocket-propelled grenade?

24

G o!" Peter turned and pushed Lewis back toward the kitchen. He'd fired his share of RPGs in the Marines and had a great deal of respect for the weapon. Originally designed to crack the armor in tanks, they were also used to destroy enemy strongholds from a distance. There was no catching a rocket-propelled grenade, no deflecting it, no outrunning it. All you could do was try to get behind something solid. Fast.

They sprinted down the hall and through the kitchen to the sliding door, where they both dove over the downed shooters with their arms outstretched like Olympic swimmers from the starting block.

Still airborne, Peter heard the hard *crump* and *whoosh* of propellant, then a much louder blast as the warhead detonated somewhere in the front of the house. His foot jerked like somebody'd kicked him in the sole of his boot. He landed hard as the blast wave hit like a hundred hands pressing on his skin. A half moment later, a wall of heat passed overhead.

It was nice in the snow. Cool, restful. He wanted to lie there forever. But that was a bad idea. "Get up, Marine," he said. His voice was strange and tinny in his ears. He realized from the pain in his chest that he'd landed partly on the shotgun.

Again came the *crump* of ignition and the *whoosh* of propellant. He flattened himself into the snow once more. The warhead went off much closer this time, maybe inside the house. It sounded like a lightning strike. The blast wave was worse, but when it was over, he managed to get his feet under him. This crap had to stop. "Lewis, we need to move."

Lewis rolled over and got his knees under him, blinking. "Yeah."

"Go get your family." Peter pawed the shotgun free of the snow and lurched for the frozen gate at the far side of the house, feeling like his limbs were not entirely connected to his body. Somehow he made it over the top of the gate, then shuffled along the snowy narrow walkway toward the street, picking up speed as he went, hoping to catch the guy reloading his rocket launcher.

Instead he saw the tan Dodge accelerating away from him. The two shooters were gone, he assumed in the Durango. He raised the shotgun as the Dodge reached the end of the block. It took the corner without slowing. The rear tires slid on the winter-slick pavement and the car fishtailed, the rear end slamming into the plow berm on the far side of the road.

Beyond the berm was a thick stand of trees and a brick pumping station. The car had slewed around, and now Peter could see the windshield from a forty-five-degree angle, but he couldn't see the driver, just the reflection of a cloud-darkened sky. He pressed the trigger anyway and felt the kick against his shoulder. The windshield showed a rip the size of two fists, but the car hadn't stopped. He racked the slide and aimed for the engine compartment and fired again. But the car was moving too fast and he just blew a cluster of holes in the back door. The driver gunned the engine and the vehicle straightened out, and then it was gone.

He heard a sharp crack to his left and turned. Lewis's front entryway was now a splintered opening the size of a delivery truck. The cracking sound was the second story beginning to buckle downward. Orange flames flickered inside. The house was old and the wood frame was dry as tinder. If the fire trucks didn't get there quickly, it would burn to the foundation.

June was still in the basement. Along with almost everyone else Peter cared about.

He sprinted into the jagged rupture, shouting their names.

The stairway structure was somehow still intact, probably because he'd rebuilt it when they'd added on for Dinah's new kitchen. Lewis stood at the door, shouting for his wife and pulling at the knob with no result. The frame had settled just enough to pinch the door in place.

It was old pine with three panels. Peter reversed the heavy shotgun and slammed the butt into the upper panel, popping one corner loose of the ancient molding that held it in place. Another strike and the panel popped inward and fell down the basement stairs. He peered through the hole but saw only black.

His ears were still ringing, but he could hear new cracks like gunshots as the second floor continued to sag. The RPG must have hit the center column that carried the new overhead beams. Now there was nothing holding them up but good intentions. It would all come down soon.

Lewis seemed to understand Peter's objective. He reversed the AK and attacked the door's center rail. With that gone, they could kick out the other panels and free everyone from the basement. But the pine was hard old-growth wood, and the tenon holding the rail in place was too sturdy. Peter alternated blows with Lewis, trying to stay focused while his mind screamed at him to get out of the house. He could feel the heat of the growing fire on the back of his legs. One of the shots must have severed a gas line.

With a tearing sound, the ceiling dropped three feet, drywall peeling free to land on the furniture and carpet. They weren't getting anywhere with the center rail. The door was stuck. Peter grabbed Lewis's arm and pointed at the gap they'd already made. "We go down," he shouted. "Get everybody out a basement window."

Lewis glanced behind them at the ruined great room. "You go. Take them out the boiler room. I'm right behind you."

"No." Peter's fist tightened on Lewis's shirt. "You're coming with me."

"The notebooks," Lewis said. "The laptop."

He pulled his arm free and scrambled over to the couch. At that part of the house, the ceiling was only four feet from the floor. Peter shoehorned himself through the hole in the door but waited and watched as Lewis pulled aside fallen drywall, searching for the backpack with the FedEx mailers. When he found it, he returned to the kitchen island, where he dumped the cheap laptop and phones into the pack's open compartment, then passed it through the hole.

Peter took the bag and headed down into the darkness as Lewis climbed through behind him. They'd killed six people to get those notebooks, and four more to keep them. They'd better be worth it.

June met them at the bottom with a pistol in her hand. She wrapped her other arm around Peter's neck and pulled him close, her lips soft at his ear. Somehow the words penetrated the ringing, faint but clear and warmed by her breath. "Thank fucking God."

He pulled her aside to make room for Lewis. "We have to get out of here. The house is coming down."

Lewis led them to the gun room. Robert was crouched under one of the heavy worktables and Dinah knelt under the other, with Miles clutched close and Mingus's collar held hard in her fist. Charlie stood wearing another armored vest, an Albanian shotgun in his hand, eyes raised to the exposed subfloor overhead.

Peter was desperately glad Charlie hadn't needed to pull the trigger. He thumped the boy on the shoulder and pointed to the boiler room door. "Get that window open. Break it if you have to."

More loud cracks told Peter the collapse was coming. The basement framing would probably hold unless the whole second floor gave way at once.

Lewis looked at Dinah, his face intent, his emotions shut down so he could function. "We gotta go." She put out her hand and he pulled her to her feet. "Follow Charlie," he said. "I'm right behind you, after I grab a few things."

One wide gun safe stood open, the neatly organized contents containing enough firepower for a squad of Marines. Peter took a box of shells for the 10-gauge. Lewis punched a combination into the other safe's keypad, then spun the wheel and pulled the door open. He removed two plain blue backpacks and a brown leather duffel, then began methodically taking banded stacks of bills from a shelf and loading them into the duffel. When he added a spare laptop, then handed Peter two burner phones and pocketed a third, it occurred to Peter that his friend was still set up for the bad old days, ready to run and gun at a minute's notice.

The duffel full, Lewis shouldered one blue backpack and tucked the duffel under one arm. Peter had the shotgun and the backpack with the notebooks and Albanian computer. June hoisted the second blue backpack and led the way.

The boiler room was cold. Charlie had the security grate unlatched and the ancient wood window hinged up and hooked to the ceiling. He'd also found a stepladder and leaned it against the stone foundation wall. Dinah held the dog's collar with one hand and Miles with the other. Peter realized that Miles didn't have any shoes. Nobody had a coat. It was well below freezing outside. For the moment he was warmed only by his adrenaline, and that wouldn't last.

The window opening was small, so Peter took off the backpack and handed it to Charlie, then climbed the ladder and peeked outside. No bad guys, but he could hear the first faint sound of sirens.

It was maybe eight feet to the neighbor's house, four feet to a row of evergreens planted for privacy and now overgrown. He set the shotgun outside and crawled out after it. The wind bit his face, his bare hands aching in the deep, drifted snow. Charlie handed out the bags and another shotgun, then climbed out with Miles right behind him, grinning like a madman from the excitement, oblivious to his bare and frozen feet.

Dinah came next in her scrubs and work clogs, then June, then Robert with his laptop bag, turning his head alertly as if to gauge the distance of the sirens. Mingus scrambled up and out trailing a clothesline leash, followed by Lewis, his face weary as he pulled Miles onto his back. "Robert, I never meant for you to get caught up in this."

Robert licked his lips. "I can't be here, Lewis."

"Of course not." Lewis pointed toward the street. "Your car's that way. You should be gone before the cops get here."

Robert looked at his feet. "You did a lot for me, back in the day. I still got that first library card you took me to get, pretending to be my older brother."

Lewis grabbed the back of Robert's neck and pulled him close. "Long as I'm alive, you'll always be my brother." Then he pushed him away. "Go on, now. Take care of those girls."

When Robert was gone, Peter said, "We should stay for the cops. Everything we did was self-defense. Find a good lawyer, it all goes away."

Lewis shook his head. "We stay, everything here becomes evidence. There ain't no statute of limitations on what I done. Me and Nino and Ray and Teddy, we'd all go to jail for a long time. Get an ambitious prosecutor, maybe Dinah does, too."

"I'll take the bags and make them disappear," Peter said. "You can handle the cops. You got away with it for ten years. What evidence can they possibly find?"

"I don't know and I don't want to know. Anyway, you're forgetting the most important thing. Somebody wants my head on a pike. Wants *all* of us now. Talking to the cops only makes us easier to find. After what happened today, you think he's gonna stop trying?"

Peter knew the answer to that. "Okay," he said. "Let's regroup at my place."

Lewis flicked his eyes at Miles. "Too close. Plus the cops will talk to the neighbors. They'll know we're tight, the six of us. They won't wait for a warrant to kick down your door."

The sirens were louder now, rising on the wind. "Then where the hell are we going?"

Lewis's face was gray with exhaustion and loss. He opened his mouth, but nothing came out.

"Follow me." Peter led them to the back corner of the house. It groaned like a dying thing. He thought of the kitchen cabinets that he and Lewis had built for Dinah. The new windows they'd installed, the strong new framing, the crisp drywall that replaced the old cracked plaster. The hours of care and effort spent making the house a home.

He hopped the fence into the yard, headed toward the river. The two shooters lay sprawled where they had fallen, their blood dark against the white snow. Behind him, he heard Lewis say, "Don't look, Miles. Charlie, don't look."

But he was too late.

The boys had already seen way too much.

Walking single file through the deep snow, they angled down the steep-sided ravine until they found the narrow trail that ran along the river. The beanpole's Dodge had gone south, so they headed north. The compacted snow on the path had melted and refrozen dozens of times, and the footing was treacherous. Everyone had trouble staying upright except for Mingus, who had slipped his clothesline leash and ran ahead, nose sniffing for trouble.

Dinah and the boys had taken refuge in a basement while a gunfight raged above them, had nearly been blown up twice, and now their home was destroyed. They were strong people, and holding it together, but for how long? The burner had no signal at the bottom of the ravine, so Peter started climbing again, hitting redial. One foot was cold and wet. The impact he'd felt on his boot was shrapnel lodging in the Vibram sole. He'd pulled out the metal, but now snowmelt was seeping in. It was a lot better than a hole in his foot.

Finally, his call connected. After the third ring, a low voice said, "Shorty's."

"Walter, it's Peter."

Silence. Walter was a former Navy man who ran the corner bar Lewis once used as his unofficial office. Walter wasn't much for talking.

"I'm with Lewis," Peter said. "Did anyone leave a message for him, a phone number?"

A pause. "If somebody left a message, it's for Lewis. If he wants to hear it, put him on."

Lewis was forty yards away at the front of the column, carrying Miles on his back. "He's got his hands full. Come on, Walter, how long have you known me? The guy who left the message would be a big ugly white dude with a scar on his face."

Another pause. "There's a guy looks just like that sitting right here. Drinking his fourth can of Old Style."

"Thank you. His name is Teddy. Tell him to bring the Rover and meet us on Humboldt, just south of Capital, east side of the street before the turn lane." A set of stone steps climbed from the ravine to the road right there.

Walter must have cupped his hand over the receiver, because Peter couldn't hear the conversation on the other end. Then Walter came back on.

"Dude says give him an hour. He just ordered a pizza."

"Walter. Somebody just put two RPGs into Lewis's house. Tell Teddy to get his ass in gear right now."

This time, there was no pause at all. "Roger that. Ass in gear."

By the time Peter tucked the phone in his pocket, he'd reached the area below his house. He climbed through the drifts to his sheltered yard, glad to be out of sight of the first responders shouting in the street, then slipped through the back door to retrieve his own go-bag and June's work backpack. If they were going to find the people behind this, they would need all the tools of her profession.

His kitchen felt warm and safe and clean. He looked around for a moment, fixing the details in his mind. He knew he might never see it again.

On his way out the back door, he tucked a pair of June's winter boots into his bag, thinking of Miles's bare feet. Then he grabbed six random coats off the hooks, stuffed them under one arm, and headed outside, leaving the door unlocked so the cops wouldn't have to break it down. Then he dropped down into the trees and hustled to catch up with the others.

When they made it to the top of the stone steps, the black-on-black Rover was waiting.

25

A mile and a half to the south and west, Streyling parked the battered Durango on a side street, then dropped the empty magazine from his Glock and popped in a new one with the heel of his hand.

Ricky stared at him from the passenger seat, still breathing hard from the frantic escape. "What the hell was that? You said they were thieves, not trained operators."

It was true, Streyling thought, the Ghost Killers were significantly more skilled than he'd expected. His team had always proved capable before, but that didn't excuse their failure. "I counted six of you and only two of them. Plus a couple of women and kids." He racked the pistol's slide and pointed the gun at Ricky.

Ricky scrambled to bring his rifle around. Streyling shot him in the head twice, then quickly shifted his aim to the back seat and put four more bullets into Gutierrez, who was already wounded in the hip. The acrid funk of spent powder filled the car, along with the iron tang of blood. Streyling had always liked that combination.

It wasn't just his team's inability to deliver that had guaranteed their deaths. He couldn't have taken Gutierrez to the hospital, because the police investigated every gunshot wound, and they'd soon connect him to the attack at the house. Gutierrez knew too much. And Ricky would have fought the decision, so he had to go, too. On the plus side, with the entire team dead, Streyling would be in full control of the narrative. His employer was a formidable person, and Streyling needed every advantage he could get.

There was something happening here, he thought. Something unexpected. He wasn't sure what it was, not yet. But it contained an opportunity of some kind, he knew that much.

He got out of the car, opened the gallon of paint thinner he'd bought at a hardware store that morning, and splashed it around the vehicle. Then he popped a road flare and tossed it through the shattered window. The fire would turn the car into another invisible burned-out junker for the city to tow when the snow melted. He'd already seen several like it in that neighborhood. If the bodies actually got noticed, the blaze would also slow their identification.

Brushing the broken glass off his topcoat, he walked into the frigid afternoon with his bag over his shoulder and the RPG launcher under his arm. He'd find a place to drop it soon enough.

It wouldn't matter if the police managed to link the Durango or the men to the violence he'd just commissioned. The contact who'd provided the car had assured him that it was registered to a person who didn't exist. The men were off their employer's books, with no threads leading back to anyone.

Streyling had sterilized the vehicle regardless. A true professional didn't cut corners. That way, when things went to hell, and he was running hard and fast, he had the comfort of knowing he'd left nothing in his wake that might catch up to him.

That no-strings policy applied to the rest of his life as well. He'd been recruited out of Penn by both the FBI and the CIA. The FBI culture was to follow the rules, black-and-white thinking powered by moral certainty. The CIA was all about gaining leverage and information by any means necessary. Streyling had always been drawn to the gray areas.

He'd spent twenty-five years doing journeyman intelligence work at hardship postings in backwater countries. He had always known that every relationship was about seeking advantage, so the cultivation and manipulation of assets had come naturally to him. Government pay was a joke, however, especially compared to the risks required to do the job. He quickly learned to supplement his income and enhance his lifestyle with a variety of entrepreneurial endeavors. After all, the Agency had spared no expense to teach him to lie, cheat, and steal. It would be a shame not to use those skills on his own behalf.

When they recalled him from Kinshasa ahead of his scheduled rotation, he realized his extracurricular activities had been discovered and simply walked away. He was certain he hadn't failed the polygraph, because he'd been beating the box since his first day on the job. It might have been the female asset he'd been sleeping with, or a routine account audit, or the nosy new chief of station taking an interest, but it didn't matter. Streyling was ready to live by his own rules.

Although, the problem of long-term solvency remained an issue. He should have set aside enough funds to retire, but he'd never been good at restraining his appetites.

After several blocks of walking, he turned down a rutted alley and spotted a six-foot wooden fence that looked fairly new. Directly behind it was a dense, snowy tangle of bushes. Being careful with his shoulder bag, which was heavier than it had been an hour ago, he dropped the RPG tube over the top of the fence, where it wouldn't be discovered until the bushes were pruned or the fence was replaced, which might well be never.

When the Durango had fishtailed and he'd seen the tall man with the shotgun aiming right at him, he'd ducked below the dashboard and mashed the gas pedal to the floor. He drove blind for a solid city block, sideswiping several cars, before he felt safe enough to stick his head up so he could steer. He could still see the wolfish face staring coldly at him over the barrel of the gun.

The Ghost Killers had eliminated four experienced men—call it six, Streyling thought—and had almost managed to take him out, too. Streyling wasn't wearing body armor, and he had a highly developed sense of self-preservation, which was why he'd walked away instead of engaging them in the kitchen. He assumed they had gone down the ravine. It's what Streyling would have done. He'd seen the map. They could pop up anywhere along a five-mile stretch of river.

The rewards for success on this project were significant. His employer had promised him ten million dollars for the capture of the Ghost Killers, in addition to a ten percent finder's fee on any assets discovered. Failing capture, he would receive two million, as long as he recorded a video of their deaths for his employer's personal satisfaction.

Failure was a different matter. His employer would be quite unhappy with the news he had to deliver. The penalty for poor performance could be severe, though no more than usual in this industry. He'd been climbing into the lion's cage his entire career, so the normal course of business wasn't the problem.

This passion project, however, was different. Through a great deal of research spanning several years, Streyling had finally been able to discern the reason behind it. But it still seemed like a distraction, the whole thing driven entirely by emotion, including a kind of free-floating rage that was deeply concerning. As if the death of the Ghost Killers would be pursued regardless of the cost.

To Streyling, it seemed self-evident that, for his employer in pursuit of this goal, Streyling's own death was an acceptable loss. This was not, in fact, acceptable to Streyling, but he couldn't simply walk away from this job. Aside from the fact that he still didn't have enough money set aside to live as he would like, there were other consequences that he preferred not to think about, the ruthlessness of his employer chief among them.

Which explained Streyling's reluctance to check in with the office.

He called the virtual number and waited for it to cycle through the elaborate international routing and redirect to whatever new phone his employer was using that day.

Then she was there. "Mr. Streyling, perfect timing. I hope you have good news."

His employer's voice was a rich contralto, full of warmth. She was, Streyling thought, the smartest woman he had ever met. The smartest person, in fact, except for Streyling himself.

Although they spoke frequently, he had only met her in person three times in his seven years of employment. She had always worn a suit, black or blue with a faint chalk stripe, probably silk and definitely bespoke, with the blouse buttoned to the neck and the cut of the jacket and pants quite severe. The suit had probably cost more than Streyling spent on clothes in an entire year, and he liked to spend money on clothes. The overall impression was of money, power, and repressed sexuality.

Each time they met, her personal security team had searched him for weapons and other devices. Either she didn't trust Streyling or she didn't trust anyone. Although he had to admit it was the logical choice for a person in her position, her attitude made it much more difficult for Streyling to manipulate conditions to his advantage. Which was, of course, the point.

Her distant and imperious manner left no doubt as to who was the employer and who was the employee. Early on, Streyling decided to lean into this with a show of deference, expecting her manner to change as his accomplishments on her behalf added up. He was disappointed. Early on, he had tried to learn more about her personal life, beginning with the reason behind her desire to capture the Ghost Killers, but after divining that elusive little nugget, there was little else to learn. She appeared to have no lovers, no friends. Only employees and clients and an abiding interest in her passion project.

In his experience, her self-control was utterly complete, until, without warning, an entirely different woman appeared. Her elegant poise vanished completely, replaced by a sudden mad violence, as if a savage creature in a bespoke suit had been released from a cage.

He had seen this occur in person only once, but he knew that it had happened a number of times. Certainly the stories got out, along with the videos, the things she was capable of, the utter lack of squeamishness. The videos were actually Streyling's idea. They only served to enhance her reputation. Another thing she'd never given him credit for.

Now, with all of this at the forefront of his mind, he stopped walking and closed his eyes so he could focus on the conversation and insert a deference into his voice that he did not feel. Streyling had always been a good actor.

"I'm sorry, ma'am, the news is not good. I went to the address with the team and observed two of the three men I saw in Chicago, along with two women and two boys. Unfortunately, they spotted us before we were in place, and dug in. Despite being significantly overmatched, they managed to eliminate our people entirely."

"All six."

"Yes, ma'am."

"Despite being, as you say, significantly overmatched."

Streyling wasn't fooled by the mild tone of voice. His employer only showed what she wanted others to see. "Yes, ma'am."

"That is . . . improbable. And unfortunate." Not concerned about the six men who had died, but the loss of useful resources and the costs that would result.

"Yes, ma'am. Please remember, the Ghost Killers are a very experienced crew with, as you know, ten years of high-level hits on hard targets. Not that this is relevant, but they very nearly killed me as well. Despite the fact that I put two RPG rounds into the house."

"Did you at least manage to injure one of them?"

"Not that I know of, ma'am."

"And where are they now?"

"I don't know. I'm sorry. I was under fire and my vehicle was compromised. I managed to extract two wounded members of the team, but they died from their injuries. I believe the Ghost Killers are no longer at the house, and are on foot."

"You believe."

"Yes. I do not have direct observation of this, but they would not have remained. I managed to do significant damage to the house. My men put high-velocity rounds into the engine blocks of their vehicles. There are four dead on the premises. These are career criminals. They would not want to stay to face the police."

He heard her heels clicking on a hard floor, then the change in ambient sound that meant she'd walked outside, although judging by the hush of the traffic, she was on a very high floor. He had no idea where she called home, if indeed there was such a place. Each time they had met, it was in a different city, and always in a luxury high-rise apartment. Although the apartments had been nearly empty of furnishings at the time. He had no idea what that meant. Maybe it didn't mean anything.

He heard the piezoelectric pop of her platinum lighter, then a sharp inhalation. She held the smoke in her lungs for longer than he would have thought possible. Her exhalation was like a sigh.

"You're a disappointment."

"Yes, ma'am. I'm sorry, ma'am."

"I hope you don't think you're my only option."

He imagined her sharpening a long blade. He'd never seen her do that, but somehow the image was vivid in his mind. It was the videos. He shook his head to clear it.

"No, ma'am. But I have seen three of them with my own eyes. I've witnessed their capabilities firsthand. This gives me a significant advantage over another hunter."

She pulled in smoke again. Even though the call was routed through a dozen different jurisdictions, the sound was clear enough to hear the hot crackle of burning paper. "I won't remind you of your position," she said. "Tell me you have a plan to find them."

He cleared his throat. "I do, ma'am. Ari is working on locations for the other names, family connections, other points of leverage. I have the notebook scans to mine for further information. Let me put some things in motion. I'll call you back with details by the end of the day."

"Make sure you do." She severed the connection without another word.

He opened his eyes and started walking again, one hand cradling his shoulder bag protectively. The cold was acute.

After fifteen frozen minutes, he passed a small lumberyard and hardware store, then opened the door to a coffee shop. The decor was retro-industrial, and the air smelled like the coffee beans they were roasting on the far side of the counter. Streyling didn't care about any of that. He just wanted to get warm and find a power outlet.

He bought a drip coffee, paid cash, and found a seat. From his bag, he removed the laptop and charger he'd taken from the home office on the second floor of the house he'd just destroyed.

The lock screen showed a photo of four Black people, two adults and two children. The man would be the one the notebooks called Lewis. The photo would be helpful.

The woman and children were obviously another path to take, another way to gain leverage. In Streyling's mind, violence was never a moral measurement, but rather a series of calculations made to achieve a desired end. To gain advantage, Streyling had always used every means necessary.

From a zippered pocket of his coat, he took the new thumb drive he'd gotten from Ari, their Israeli hacker, and plugged it into the laptop's socket. Then he leaned back and sipped his coffee, imagining what secrets the machine might hold, and let the intrusion software do its magic.

He wasn't going to tell his employer about the laptop, at least not yet.

Depending on what he found, he might not tell her at all.

26

A very large man in a green parka hunched behind the steering wheel like a circus bear taught to drive. He turned and waved cheerfully as they piled into the Range Rover, showing a livid pink scar where his beard didn't grow. "Hi, everyone, I'm Teddy."

As if he were their fucking tour guide, June thought.

She was still sweating despite the cold of the ravine, her heart beating too fast in her chest. She knew she was in shock. It wasn't her first experience under gunfire.

She'd never enjoyed it. But she'd always survived it.

She planned to keep surviving. No matter what.

The mad scramble to the basement kept replaying in her head. The crippling fear. The noise and pressure waves of the two explosions. The ominous groans as the house began to fall in on itself. The relief at seeing Peter come down the stairs. The dread on Dinah's face as she looked from Charlie to Miles and back, afraid for their lives.

She was still reaching for her seat belt when Peter said, "Go, Teddy.

Take a left at the light." The big SUV leaped forward and rolled through a yellow, picking up speed.

The Rover seemed new, but it smelled like armpit and cigarettes. Peter was in the passenger seat, head turning like a slow metronome as he scanned ahead and to their left, searching half the world for signs of danger. Lewis sat behind Teddy, his head turning to the back and the right, searching the other half of the world. As if he and Peter were following a plan they had never discussed. As if each had known in advance what the other would do.

She envied them their clarity of purpose. They were focused on the external threats. They were men. More than that, they were warriors, it was how they were wired.

But the guy who'd blown up the house wasn't the only threat. This little group of refugees needed to take care of each other, too. Otherwise they'd fracture and fall apart. Which would only make it harder to face the forces trying to kill them. Caring for each other was the only way they'd stay strong enough to survive. And they were all hurting.

June sat behind Peter, leaning forward slightly so she could reach past the door pillar and rest her hand on his broad shoulder, grateful for the solidity she found there. His head kept turning, searching for threats, but he put his hand on hers, and she felt the elemental reassurance of human touch. The boys were unusually silent in the third seat, with Mingus crouched over them, growling soft and low. Dinah was sandwiched between June and Lewis.

June patted Dinah's leg, then turned to look behind her at the boys. Charlie stared straight ahead, his eyes wide. Miles had both arms wrapped around the enormous dog, his face buried in the animal's heavy ruff. She thought about what Peter had learned over the years, dealing with his post-traumatic stress, that the best way to normalize a traumatic experience was to talk about it.

But Dinah wasn't talking, so June started the conversation. "That was pretty scary back there," she said. "How are you boys feeling?"

"I'm good," Charlie said. But he didn't look good. He looked like he'd stood too close to the crumbling lip of a cliff and peered over the edge. June knew the feeling. Her stomach was in knots, too. For a few minutes back there, she'd thought she was going to throw up.

"How about you, Miles? It's okay to be scared, you know."

Miles didn't answer. He just shook his head and wrapped his arms tighter around the growling dog.

Dinah stared straight ahead, her profile elegant and composed. There was always something regal in her bearing that June had always envied. But now her posture, usually gracefully erect, was stiff as stone. It was the only visible indication that she was upset. "None of us are okay," she said. "But we'll get through this."

Even sitting three to a row, June noticed, Dinah and Lewis sat without touching. She realized she hadn't heard them speak to each other since they started the hike down the ravine. "Dinah, talk to me."

But Dinah still wouldn't look at her. "What is there to say?" Her voice was icy. "Aside from the obvious, about armed men attacking our home, then blowing it to smithereens?"

She'd converted her fear into anger, June thought. It was a protective mechanism. June had done it herself. Long-term, it rarely helped. What helped was taking action. Finding the people behind this.

Lewis didn't respond to Dinah. Because his default expression was that tilted smile, she often thought of Lewis as someone who was amused by the world. Sometimes the smile was barely visible, other times it was broad and warm. Often, especially when he was with his family, it was genuine. When he was under stress, he wore it like a shield.

But now the smile was gone. Instead, every muscle in his face and neck was rigid, the architecture as clear and visible as a medical cadaver with the skin removed. As if some critical part of him had been stretched so thin it was ready to break.

"Teddy, turn left at the light," he said. "Then get on 43 and head south past downtown."

"On it." Teddy took the corner fast. They all held on to something, pulled by the force of the turn. Dinah shifted sideways to press against June, maintaining the space between her and Lewis. At the on-ramp, Teddy accelerated strongly, checking the side mirror as the powerful car slipped smoothly into the stream of traffic.

"Where are we going?" Charlie asked.

Dinah said, "Not now, Charlie."

"But what's going on? Who were those men? Why did they attack us?"

"Charlie." Dinah's voice had an edge to it.

Lewis cleared his throat. "We're going to an airfield south of town. June's been there."

June remembered. Last spring, when she and Lewis had needed to get to South Dakota in a hurry, he'd called in a favor from a guy with a small plane. She'd wondered who he was texting by the river, and now she knew.

"Then what?" Charlie said.

Peter turned in his seat. "We need to get you and Miles someplace safe with June and your mom." He glanced at Lewis. "I was thinking about my parents, up by Lake Superior."

"That would be great," Lewis said. "No connection to me or mine. You think your folks'd be okay with that?"

"I'll call to make sure, but I know they'll want to help."

Charlie made a face. "You're sending us away? Why can't we stay with you?"

"Peter and I." Lewis stopped for a moment. "We have to find out who sent those people today, and why."

"And kill them," Charlie said. "Like you and Peter killed the men at the house."

It wasn't an accusation, just a statement of fact.

Nobody spoke for a moment.

Lewis closed his eyes. June wondered what the boy knew about his stepfather. Clearly he had absorbed something over the last few years.

Lewis finally spoke. "Yes, Charlie. If we have to. To keep you and your brother and your mother safe."

Then Miles, his voice muffled by the dog's fur, said, "I really liked that house."

"Me too." Dinah's voice still had that edge.

Lewis closed his eyes again. "Dinah."

"Not here." The edge now sharp enough to cut.

"Dinah," he said again. "We need to talk about this."

"Not now," she said. "Later." The angle of her head pointing at the boys in the back seat.

"All right. But soon. We have decisions to make."

"Not you," she said. "Me. *I* decide." Then she closed her mouth, her lips pressed tightly together, forming a thin, hard line.

June knew that she and Peter would always be okay. They'd worked too hard at it, knew each other too well, had been through too much together to ever let each other go.

She'd thought the same about Lewis and Dinah. Their bond had seemed unbreakable. But now she wasn't so sure.

They drove the rest of the way in uncomfortable silence, the frozen landscape scrolling past on the other side of the window glass.

27

I t wasn't an airfield so much as a runway with a few modest buildings scattered on both sides. The painted metal hangars were faded,
their low-sloped roofs blanketed with snow. The entrance was right
off the interstate frontage road. There was no sign.

At least the runway was plowed, June thought.

Lewis directed Teddy past a long row of derelict buildings, then
into a small gravel parking area behind a hangar that was larger and
better kept than the others.

"Teddy, you stay with the car and keep an eye out. Everyone else,
let's go." Lewis pulled bags from the back of the Rover, then led the
way to a plain steel door set like an afterthought into the wide rear
hangar wall. June got the dog back on his leash, noticing as she did
that Peter took up the rear, walking backward to eyeball the road.
He'd removed a pistol from his kit and carried it down along the side
of his leg. His other hand held a phone to his ear. "Dad, it's me."

His dad built custom homes in northern Wisconsin. Peter's mom was an artist and art professor. Peter was an only child, but his parents' home had been an unofficial halfway house for abused and neglected kids. Pregnant fourteen-year-olds whose mothers had kicked them out of the house. Half-starved toddlers with cigarette burns on their arms. Every social worker and church official in three counties knew the Ash family would take in a child without hesitation. For the occasions when the bad parents decided they wanted their abused kids back, Peter's dad kept a 20-gauge by the back door and a deer rifle in the closet. Peter's mom was on a first-name basis with every cop in the district and had the sheriff's dispatcher on her speed dial.

Inside, the hangar interior was cavernous and mostly empty. The rear wall had a line of rolling mechanic's toolboxes and other airplane maintenance equipment. In the front corner, stairs led up to a modest second-floor enclosed area, she assumed an office or apartment. Beneath it was a short line of cabinets with a sink, microwave, and minifridge, then an oddball furniture setup including a well-worn couch and a couple of lawn chairs, the whole thing kept above freezing by a glowing heat panel in the ceiling.

The space seemed even larger with the huge hangar door raised, framing the gray aircraft just outside on the concrete apron with the flat, snowy expanse beyond. The plane was ungainly, but oddly sleek and graceful, even standing still. It was a Twin Otter, June remembered from the enthusiastic explanation of the pilot the previous spring. The two engines idled with a high mechanical whine, and the cabin door was open with the step unfolded.

June turned to Peter, tall and rawboned in the cold, still standing at the open man door with one eye on the parking lot and the other on the plane. Over the noise, she said, "I'm not going to your parents' with Dinah and the boys. I'm staying with you."

He gave her that wolfish grin that always made her want to start peeling off his clothes. "That's exactly what my dad told me you'd say."

The pilot appeared in the plane's doorway. He wore a brown bomber jacket and ball cap, his gray hair in a ponytail behind. He looked at Lewis, who raised a finger as if to say, *Give me a minute.*

Then Lewis pulled his family into a cluster, with June and Peter standing just outside the circle. "I'm sorry about this, boys. It's all my fault. I'll get it solved as fast as I can. But you'll have fun up there. Peter's parents are really great."

Miles said, "How long will it be?"

Lewis didn't look at Dinah. "Maybe a week," he said. "Maybe a month. Maybe longer. You should settle in. Think of it as an adventure."

Charlie shook his head. "I want to go with you. My dad was a Marine. You taught me how to shoot. I can run ten miles, do a hundred push-ups. I want to help."

"I appreciate that," Lewis said, "and I respect it. But you're fifteen, Charlie. You're not a soldier, and this is not a game for beginners. I'm not going to sugarcoat this. Whoever's behind this, they're very bad people and they want me dead. Me and everyone else I love. That includes you and your brother and your mother. I can't have you at risk."

"But why would somebody want to kill you? Tell me that, at least."

Lewis took a breath and let it out. "It's about my life before I knew you and your brother," he said. "I did some things I'm not real proud of. We can talk about it when you're older. But right now, I need you to suck it up. Your job is to look after your mother and your brother. They need you."

Charlie's jaw flexed, but he nodded. "Okay."

Miles sniffled, softly crying. Lewis opened his arms and pulled them both in. "I'm sorry," he said again. "You boys are everything to me. I love you both more than I can ever put into words." He held them close for a long moment in the cold. Then he let them go. "I'll see you soon."

Dinah gently pushed them toward the plane. "Go on," she said. "Take Mingus. Be careful of the propeller. I'll be there in a minute."

When they'd climbed the steps to the plane, she turned to face Lewis. June took Peter's arm and began to back away. This was a private conversation.

Dinah held out a finger. "No, you two stay. You need to hear this, too." She dipped her chin at the blue backpacks at Lewis's feet. In the frigid hangar, wearing her nurse's scrubs, she held herself as stiff as a statue. "What's in the bags, Lewis?"

He looked down at them. "A change of clothes for you and the boys, all current sizes. Legal documents and credit cards in our new names. Fifty grand in cash, prepaid phones. Everything we need to start over."

Her eyebrows rose with her voice. "You're telling me you *planned* for this, Lewis? For a bunch of killers to blow up our house? I thought you'd gotten out of that life. I thought everything was different."

"I am out. Things are different." His shoulders were hunched and tight. "The bags are an insurance policy, for a worst-case scenario."

At the airplane, June saw the boys' faces in two round windows, watching the conversation.

"That's not what 'out of that life' means," Dinah said. "'Out' means it's over. Done with. Nothing coming back to threaten my boys. But now I realize that you'll never be out, not the way I thought."

Lewis's face had turned gray and pinched, as if something essential had evaporated from within. He took a ragged breath.

"I understand. Let me get you safe and set up again. A new life. Then you won't ever have to see me again."

"Oh, no," she said. "You're not getting off that easy." And she stepped right up to him and thumped him hard on the sternum with her fist.

June could hear the sound from four feet away. She could

practically feel the force of it herself, the physical and mental fortitude of an ICU nurse long accustomed to holding life and death in her hands.

Lewis retreated a step. Dinah advanced. "Lewis, you need to *fix this.*" She punctuated her words with a second thump, harder than the first. Lewis retreated again. Dinah went after him, her face alive with anger. "I want my *life back.*" Another thump. Lewis retreated and Dinah advanced, punctuating her words with her fist. Backing him up, step after step. "I want *those boys.*" Thump. "To have *their* lives back." Thump. "*With you in it.*"

Lewis stopped retreating. Dinah's fist pounded him harder with every word. "You *damn* fool. *Do. You. Understand. Me.*"

They were both breathing hard, something powerful passing between them, a current of strange electricity, the force of their connection. As if Dinah and Lewis were the only two people in the hangar, or on the planet. June and Peter might as well have been on the moon.

"Yes, ma'am." Lewis cleared his throat. "I understand. I don't want to lose you."

"Then you better get right, and act right. You hearing me, Lewis?"

"Yes, ma'am. Loud and clear." Lewis stepped closer and put a big hand on the curve of her hip. The tension in his face had eased. "I'll call you tonight, okay? Better yet, call me when you land."

She pushed him back and his hand fell away. "You still don't get it. Here's how it's going to be. I'm not getting on that plane. I'm staying with you."

Lewis looked hollow-eyed and nauseous, like he'd just been sucker-punched in the stomach. "Dinah, please. This is more dangerous than you know."

She glared at him. "I know June is staying. So I am, too. If one of you idiots gets shot, you'll need a good nurse."

Without another word, she lifted the blue bags by their grab handles and carried them up the steps and into the plane. Through the windows, they watched her move down the aisle and hug the boys. After a long moment, she emerged with empty hands.

The pilot followed her out and walked over to Lewis. He wore a pirate mustache and sideburns, his face deeply seamed from sun and wind. He named a figure. "You'll make the transfer?"

"Soon as you're airborne."

"I always did like that about you. Lock up when you go."

They shook hands and the pilot climbed into the plane and pulled up the steps behind him. The boy's faces were framed like ancient photographs in the small, round windows.

Then the engines roared and the twin propellers turned until they became a blur. The airplane rolled forward to the runway and turned to face into the wind. The engines became louder still. June put her hands over her ears. The plane began to accelerate. They all walked forward to watch, Dinah's hand up as if she could somehow reach out and call back the passengers within. The front wheel left the blacktop. Then the rear wheels lifted and the plane was off the ground, suspended between earth and sky. It rose higher, then higher still, until it disappeared into the clouds.

June shivered, and not from the cold.

She looked at Peter, then Lewis, then Dinah.

Trying to shake the sudden feeling that one of them wouldn't live to see the boys again.

28

A s the sound of the airplane faded, they all looked at each other in silence.

Peter rubbed his eyes. It was after three. The adrenaline was long gone and the exhaustion had sunk deep into his bones. "Before we do anything else, do you suppose there's any coffee in this place?"

"Best idea I've heard all day." Lewis hit a red button on the wall and the enormous hangar door began to drop down. He walked to the little furniture arrangement under the radiant heat panels and stared wearily at a tarnished twelve-cup Bialetti espresso maker on a hot plate beside a high-end Mahlkönig grinder. "Anybody know how to work this thing?"

It was the kind of quirky coffee setup that only a true fanatic would embrace. Peter bent to examine the Mahlkönig and saw that the hopper was already loaded with beans. "I got this. You want to text Teddy and see if he wants a cup?" He turned on the grinder and watched the grounds fall into the container. The heat from the overhead panels felt good on his shoulders. "Hey, did you ever reach Nino or Ray? We might need a few more bodies on this."

Lewis shook his head and dropped onto the couch. "I tried again on the way down here. The bartender at Nino's place said he was busy in the kitchen, so I left a message. I did the same for Ray at the community center in Houston. It's nice to know they're both alive, at least. But I don't think they're going to be much help."

Dinah eyed the couch dubiously, the foam stuffing bulging from the torn seams, then took a seat on a folding lawn chair. Peter wondered if she regretted her decision to stay. It wasn't glamorous, what they did. Mostly it was ugly.

June paced back and forth. "We're on the defensive now," she said, "which is where they want us. But we need to go on the offense. We need a plan of attack. Do we know anything about the guys who came after us today?"

"Not much," Lewis said. "It wasn't a few dudes hired off the street, though. Those guys looked like pros. Organized, equipped, and trained."

Peter unscrewed the espresso maker and filled the bottom section with cold water. "Maybe ex-military, or former law enforcement." He tipped the coffee grounds into the funnel and tamped them down. "Did you ever go after a crew like that? Maybe they're coming back at you now."

Lewis shook his head. "Most of our targets were homeboys and white trash who came up the hard way, built themselves into a power. Bikers, white supremacists, all kinds of gangbangers. But they might have upped their game since then, found themselves some shooters back from the war. You get your ass shot at for Uncle Sam, get a taste for that adrenaline, you don't exactly want to go work at McDonald's."

Peter reassembled the espresso maker and set it on the hot plate.

"They had matching outfits, those vests with police patches. Does that tell us anything?"

"Anybody can buy a vest and slap on a Velcro patch," Lewis said. "We did it ourselves, back in the day. Police, FBI, DEA."

"They'll have a war chest, whoever they are," June said. "They already spent a quarter million just for information."

Peter took a carton of milk from the minifridge and gave it the sniff test, then half filled the paper cups he'd set out. "What if they hired it out? Found somebody with military connections, maybe from Northern Mexico, or a dirty military contractor with an off-books team of killers?"

"They'd have to do it in a hurry," Lewis said. "The Albanians didn't know what they had until, what, two days ago? They didn't put the notebooks in the mail until last night."

"That's true of anyone." Peter set the cups in the microwave, waiting for the espresso. The hot plate glowed red. "They had to get seven guys to your house, with armor and serious weapons, inside of eighteen hours."

"Those assault rifles didn't fly commercial," June said. "Maybe these guys are local. Or within a fourteen-hour drive, say."

"Draw a circle on a map, that's everything from New York to Oklahoma City to the Black Hills," Lewis said. "That don't exactly narrow things down. Plus a lot of these motherfuckers, the Crips, the Salvatruchas, La Eme, have people in two dozen cities. It might be some boss in L.A. who calls the branch office in Chicago."

"So it could be anyone," Peter said. "Any group you hit over ten years."

"Yeah," Lewis said. "But June's right, it will be somebody with deep pockets. Somebody with the technical know-how to issue an open bounty on the dark web." He frowned. The espresso maker began to hiss as the steam pressure built. "Somebody big."

They looked at each other, none of them liking that last conclusion.

June took a breath and let it out. "Okay. That gives us an organizing principle, something to look for when we go through Teddy's notebooks. There's got to be something useful in those pages."

"I wouldn't count on it," Peter said. "The bad guys used those notebooks to find Lewis, but Teddy made it easy. There might not be anything there to help us find the bad guys."

Dinah raised her chin. "I'll read them."

"No," Lewis said. "Definitely not."

She gave him a frosty stare. "We already had this conversation, Lewis. You are in no position to make demands of me."

"Dinah, there will be things in those notebooks—"

"*Lewis.*" Her voice was sharp enough to shut his mouth, but not entirely unkind. She got up from the lawn chair and sat herself down beside him on the ratty old couch. "It can't be any worse than what I've been imagining for the last five years." She put her hand on his face and leaned in. "Come on, baby. The truth will set you free."

Then the door banged open and Teddy bounded into the hangar, his breath steaming from the cold. "Hey, what'd I miss?"

The espresso maker gurgled loudly and the rich smell of coffee filled the space.

Peter reached over to the microwave and hit start.

When they all held a cup of the rich, bitter brew, June said, "I'll dig through the Albanians' phones and laptop, search their email and whatever messaging apps they use, see what bread crumbs they might have left behind. But the clock is ticking on those phones. The police will find the Albanians soon, if they haven't already. They won't have any problem getting court permission to access their accounts, find their locations."

Peter nodded. "It's time to get rid of the Rover, too," he said. "If you found it on Cousin Zef's social media, the cops can, too. We don't need to get pulled over because they got the dealer to turn on the GPS locator, or we got caught on some state trooper's plate scanner."

Teddy was frowning. "But I *like* the Rover."

"It was always temporary," Lewis said. "No loose ends, remember?"

"Now," June said, "the Albanian laptop. If we want to try Robert's idea of sending malware back up the email chain, we'll need a new guy. I know someone in Chicago, but he's not like Robert. He's a black hat hacker, strictly highest bidder. Unless you've got someone else, Lewis?"

Lewis shook his head. "Just Robert." He frowned. "I should message him, make sure he's okay. Which reminds me, I gotta pay the pilot." He leaned over, opened the leather duffel he'd packed in his basement, and removed the backup laptop he'd taken from the safe.

June made a note. "Next, the FedEx mailers headed to Indianapolis. You know anybody mad at you there?"

Lewis shrugged. "I've never even been to Indianapolis."

"Those were next-day envelopes," Peter said. "Because they got dropped off too late for the last pickup, they'd probably arrive first thing tomorrow. We could go sit on the location, see who shows up. That's, what, a four-hour drive?"

"Not worth the effort," June said. "I checked that address, it's a mailbox place. People will be going in and out of there with packages all day long. You can't look for someone carrying fourteen mailers, either, because you guys intercepted them."

"What if we send them some new mailers?" Peter asked. "Go back to that same Walgreens in Chicago and send off fourteen envelopes full of blank paper. Mark the envelopes with red tape or something, to make them easier to identify."

"No," Dinah said. "We should put a GPS tag inside one of the mailers. Then we won't need to see them to follow them." June raised her eyebrows at her friend. Dinah smiled shyly. "I put tags in the boys' backpacks, in case they get forgotten at school, or the boys go somewhere they shouldn't." Then she looked away, blinking. No doubt thinking of where the boys were headed now.

June patted Dinah's arm. "And that's how we'll send our malware back up the email chain. We send the new tracking numbers, with our virus embedded in the link."

"See, this is why you're the brains of the outfit," Peter said.

She tapped the side of her head. "And don't you forget it, boyo."

Lewis stared at the laptop screen. "What the hell? How is that possible?"

Dinah leaned over to look. "What's the matter?"

He shook his head. "It's empty."

"What's empty?"

"The money market account. There's nothing in it."

His fingers flew across the keyboard and touch pad.

"The investment accounts, too. Two dozen, across five brokerages. They're all empty." He looked up at Peter, who suddenly could imagine Lewis as a child. "The money's all gone."

29

W hat," June said. "Everything?"

Lewis nodded. He looked smaller, somehow, as if all the muscle he'd built over the years had vanished in a heartbeat.

"Your regular laptop," Peter said. "That must be what that guy took from your house before he pulled out that rocket launcher. I thought you said Robert beefed up your cybersecurity."

"He did." Lewis was standing now, shoulders hunched, back bent. "The laptop and the accounts. Randomly generated passwords, two-factor identification via email, the works. But they hacked my email, too. They took it all."

June thought about what he'd done for that money. What it represented now. Peace. A new life. Security for his family. All gone.

Dinah stepped up to Lewis and put her arms around him.

He said, "I'm sorry, Dinah."

"Don't be sorry," she said. "You and I are all we need. But can we keep going? Can we still find those people?"

Lewis leaned into her. June watched his face as he gathered himself with conscious effort. His shoulders dropped and his back straightened as he rebuilt himself from that scared, feral child he had been into the strong, capable man he had become.

Then he looked down at the leather duffel. "There's four hundred in the bag," he said. "We have multiple credit cards with high limits. That's more than enough to get us started."

Then he gave them all that tilted smile.

"Hell, it's only money, right? We can always get more." The smile widened to show his teeth. "Plus we know who took it. That beanpole motherfucker who blew up our house."

Teddy rubbed his hands together. His glass eye gleamed, and the curved scar was a livid line through his beard. "So," he said. "Back to work, huh?"

They got off the freeway south of Kenosha, just past the Mars Cheese Castle. Lewis directed Teddy a mile west to a well-graded gravel road, where a large metal pole barn stood hidden inside a dense cluster of pine trees. The rattle and whine of power tools seeped through the rusting walls. A small sign read DON BENTLEY'S TEXAS MOTORS.

The sliding door opened just wide enough for a man to slip out, shading his eyes with his hand. He wore the wide, bushy mustache of an eighties porn star and a comb-over blown the wrong way by the wind. Lewis shook his head at the sight of him. "Bentley's so damn crooked he can't even pee straight. But he's got good inventory, and his guys can chop a vehicle to parts in an hour flat."

Teddy put a sorrowful hand on the Rover's elegant dashboard. "This is no place for a beauty like you to end up."

By four o'clock, June stood in the last of the daylight and watched Peter reverse a late-model Acura SUV from the pole barn. He stopped the car beside her and got out, leaving the engine running. June handed him the stack of Albanian phones from Robert's computer bag, which she'd gone through on the drive down. "I'm done with these."

"Anything useful?"

She shook her head. "Personal use only. A little too personal, actually."

The Albanians had used their phones to pay their bills, play games, text their friends, and try to get laid. She'd found a disturbing number of naked selfies and dick pics. There are some things in life you can't unsee, and extra-hairy Albanian junk was definitely one of them.

"If there's an electronic trail," she said, "it will have to come from the laptop. That reminds me, can we take Teddy? He might come in handy with that hacker."

"When he's done saying goodbye to the Range Rover." Teddy was still behind the wheel, mourning the loss. Peter bent to kiss her. "You'll be careful, right?"

She grabbed the neck of his shirt and pulled him close, feeling his smile against hers. His lips were the only thing about him that were soft. She felt that wobble in her knees. Why did he always smell like clean sweat and sawdust? It seemed unfair. "You be careful, too, okay? I'll see you at the hotel."

Peter went off to help Lewis and Teddy transfer their things from the Rover to a beefy blue four-door pickup, and June called out to Dinah, who stood at the border of the snow-covered field, arms wrapped around herself, watching the sun slip past the edge of the horizon. "Time to go."

Dinah walked over to the Acura's passenger side, her expression clouded. She had the backpack with the notebook pages over one shoulder, and June could see the weight of it in her posture.

June opened the driver's door, but Dinah just stood there, looking back at the shrinking sliver of sun.

June said, "Having second thoughts?"

"I don't know if I can do this."

"You don't have to, Dinah. You can take this car and drive north. Six hours from now, you'll be safe with your boys. Nobody would blame you."

Dinah looked at her across the top of the SUV. It was getting colder. Their breath turned white in the winter air. "I talked a big game, back at the airfield, telling Lewis how it was going to be. But what happened at our house scared the daylights out of me. I'm not like you, June. I'm not fearless."

June gave her a sympathetic smile. "I get scared like anybody else. Fear is useful. It makes you pay attention. But you can't let it keep you from doing something that you know is important."

"It's more than that," Dinah said. "I'm always trying to get Lewis to share more of himself, right? I want to know him better. But what if I see something in him, or see him *do* something, that I don't *want* to see?"

"That's a risk," June said. "Not to mention we might get shot at again. One of us might take a bullet. But what you said before, about the truth setting you free? You were talking about Lewis, but maybe that applies to you, too. You want to know all of him, right? I can tell you this much, reading those notebooks won't get you there. Getting in this car, being a part of ending this little nightmare? It's the only way to do that."

"That's why you go with them, isn't it? So you can know Peter, really know him."

"That's one reason," June said. "The other is, I love him. My being there makes it marginally less likely that he gets hurt or killed."

"But how do you handle it? I mean, how are you okay after what happened today?"

June raised a shoulder. "I'm not. But it's also not the first time somebody tried to kill me. It's not even the fourth or fifth time. At a certain point I decided not to let it own me. I mean, you only live once, right? So I've learned some ways to deal with it. Peter taught me some breathing exercises, and a few forms of meditation. Lewis taught me to shoot."

"But you must like it, at least a little. You keep coming back for more."

"I guess I do." June smiled wider. "It makes me feel alive. Maybe it's how I'm wired. Or maybe the pain and fear are just the price you pay for doing the right thing. Because the right thing is never the easy choice. It's almost always the hardest one."

"Being an ICU nurse can be like that. You see a lot of ruined bodies. A lot of pain, a lot of blood. A lot of death. It affects you. If it doesn't, you're a monster. But you do your job anyway. Trying to make things better." She looked back at the crimson horizon and let out a long breath. "Okay." Then she opened the door and got in the car.

Peter arrived with Teddy. "You're with the ladies. Like a guard dog, you understand? They point, you bite."

"Sure." Teddy eyed the car. "Can I drive?"

June scowled at him. "Hell no. I'm tired of being a passenger."

Teddy hung back. She was pretty sure she scared him a little. She didn't mind that at all. She slapped the roof of the car. "Come on, Teddy. Back seat, move your ass."

Peter gave her that wolfish smile. He was well aware that patience was not her middle name.

When Teddy climbed into the rear, the whole vehicle sank several inches. June took her seat. Peter bent to kiss her through the window, then stepped away. Dinah already had her seat belt fastened and the backpack of notebook pages at her feet. She lifted her hand to Lewis, who was transferring the long guns to the pickup. He saw her and put his hand to his heart. She put her fingers to her lips and blew him a kiss.

June put the car into gear. "You ready?"

Dinah gave her a wobbly smile. "No," she said. "Let's go anyway."

"Atta girl." June hit the gas and spun all four tires on the gravel. The Acura took off like a spooked horse, slewing sideways in the snow, narrowly missing a large pine before straightening out and flying toward the road.

Sprawled sideways across the back seat, Teddy called out, "I don't feel safe."

"You're *not* safe," June shouted with a wild grin. "Cancer, tornadoes, whatever. We're all gonna die someday."

Dinah grabbed the oh-shit handle and held on tight. "You're crazy, you know that?"

But as June made the turn toward the freeway, a small smile crept onto Dinah's face.

30

The Acura was fast and tight, with a radar detector hardwired under the dash. That might have been June's favorite feature. On the freeway, it beeped almost continuously because Wisconsin state troopers had set their usual series of speed traps approaching the border. Dinah had already gone through some of Teddy's notebook pages. Now she pulled out a stack and went back to her reading.

After they crossed into Illinois, traffic moved faster and June could go ninety without attracting attention. She glanced in the rearview and saw Teddy curled up asleep on the back seat. She tapped Dinah on the leg and said softly, "Are you finding anything useful in there?"

"I hope so." Dinah kept her voice low, too. "Once you skim over all the sections about his bowel movements and sexual fantasies."

"Ew," June said.

Dinah shrugged. "I deal with more disgusting things at work every day of the week. Plus I have two boys, who are sweet but also fairly disgusting in their own way. Teddy's basically a twelve-year-old horndog."

"But also an armed robber. And a killer."

"Yes, that's in here, too. For a guy with a traumatic brain injury, he's recovered a lot of details. But there's no order to it. He's basically just writing stuff down as it comes to him. Who knows if there's anything in here that will help? I'm trying to build a chronology, figure out which memories and events go together. It's going to take a while."

"You'd make a good reporter," June said. "Sifting through mounds of possibly useless data is a big part of my job."

"Well, when you and that hacker get that laptop figured out, we'll work on these together." Dinah held up the notes she'd made on the back sides of Teddy's pages. "So far the list of—he calls them targets—ranges from bikers in Bakersfield to Jamaicans in Queens, the Dixie Mafia in New Orleans, MS-13 in Phoenix. Miami, Dallas, Chicago, Cleveland. I'm only three mailers in, and the list keeps growing."

June wasn't sure how to ask this, so she just asked. "Are you learning anything new about Lewis?"

"Actually, Teddy writes about Lewis a lot. But his take isn't what I thought it would be. It turns out that Lewis had strict rules about who he'd go after. Not street-level dealers, but their bosses. People who Lewis knew had been bad for a long time, who'd gotten away with doing violent things."

June thought of her conversation with Peter about the Albanians. How the fact that several of them had been arrested for murder, then released when the witnesses disappeared, had made both her and Peter feel better about what would likely happen.

Dinah said, "Lewis also had rules about how they did the work, what Teddy calls rules of engagement. Rules about when you can shoot somebody, and when you can't."

"Like in war," June said. "Even in combat, you can't kill whoever you want."

"Teddy says, at the time, he didn't like it. He thought they should just go in shooting and kill everyone. The rule was, if somebody put their hands up, they got to live. But it didn't usually work out that way. Most of the other guys were armed. And most were actively trying to kill Lewis and the guys."

"So a lot of people got killed." But that wasn't quite right, she thought. "Lewis and Teddy and Nino and Ray killed a lot of people."

"Yes," Dinah said. "It's complicated, right? Maybe it's okay to kill somebody who's trying to kill you. But you're the one who kicked down their door to begin with. And you were almost certain they would pick up a gun. So is that self-defense? Or is it murder?"

"I'm not a lawyer," June said, "but I'm pretty sure it's not self-defense if it happens while committing armed robbery. I think it's first-degree murder."

"So Lewis is a murderer," Dinah said.

June nodded. Legally, Peter was, too. Maybe that's why it was important to know their targets were bad people.

"But Teddy also wrote that he feels differently about Lewis's rules now. He said the rules were what made them different from the gangsters. The rules kept them from turning into animals. Do you think that's true?"

"I don't know," June said. "I think you should ask Lewis."

"Teddy also says that Lewis was a kind of genius. Because the life span of a thief going after drug dealers was about six months. Lewis ran the crew for ten years, they always made money, and none of them died."

June's phone rang. She fished it from her bag and checked the screen. She'd put Peter's and Lewis's burners into her contacts, but this number came up as blocked. "Hello?"

"Hey, June, it's Carlo Fratelli." Her contact on the Chicago cops. "Got a minute?"

She glanced at Dinah. "Actually, Carlo, I don't. I'm in the middle of something."

"It'll only take a minute, I swear. Just a couple quick questions. We talked the other day about those Albanian thugs, you remember? I'm curious, what was your interest there?"

"I told you yesterday. Background information for a story I was looking into, but it hasn't gone anywhere yet."

"Really," he said. "Background. What's the story?"

She didn't like the way this was going. She remembered again why she always tried to tell the truth to her police sources, especially veteran detectives. They were really good at catching people in lies. It was essentially what they did for a living. But she was in too far now.

"It was about immigrants who are criminals. But I dug up the numbers on that, and it turns out that, statistically, immigrants are actually much more law-abiding than American citizens. So maybe that's my angle, if I can sell my editor on it."

"That shouldn't be hard, you're pretty persuasive." It didn't sound like a compliment. "One last question, June. Where are you now?"

"I'm on the freeway, taking a laptop to my computer guy." At least that much was *kind* of true, she thought.

"Huh. I thought maybe you were coming to see me. To tell me the actual truth about why you asked about those Albanians." His voice rose. "Because I'm looking at them right now, and I tell you, they're pretty damn dead. So I'm going to need you to drop whatever you're doing and get your butt down here before I call the Wisconsin state troopers and tell them to pick you up and put you in a very small room for a very long time."

31

June's heart raced. She automatically glanced in her rearview for flashing lights.

But Fratelli wouldn't know where she was. Because she worked as an investigative reporter, and because past stories had involved both whistleblowers and people who had threatened her safety, her phone was highly modified with, among other things, a custom proxy server that spoofed her GPS data to conceal her location. The NSA could find her without trying too hard, but the Chicago police probably didn't have the resources, even with a court order.

"If you want to buy me dinner, Carlo, all you have to do is ask. I can make it down to see you next week." She rolled her eyes at Dinah.

"Lady, this is not a joke," he said. "It's also about more than four dead Albanians whose own mothers probably won't miss them. Because, as I was standing here looking at day-old bodies, which I gotta say don't exactly smell like roses, a colleague told me about something he'd seen on the news. A similar assault on a house in Milwaukee, military-grade weapons, high body count, and it happened just a few hours ago."

"Hey, I read about that, too," she said. "Crazy stuff."

He seemed to ignore her, although she was sure he registered her comment. "So, I reached out to the Milwaukee cop who caught the case, a guy named Hecht. He told me his incident was actually the reverse of what happened to the Albanians. In Chicago, two, maybe three people went into a house with military weapons and killed four heavily armed gangsters. In Milwaukee, four guys in tactical gear attacked a house using military weapons, but this time it was the attackers who died. Plus Hecht found two more bodies, wearing the same kind of gear, dead in a burned-out car, for a total of six. The family that lived in that house has disappeared, and the building is a total wreck. To me, that smells like retaliation."

"Really? Why would you think the two incidents were connected? Aside from the kind of weapons you say were used, which as you know can be found on half the street corners and suburban basements in America."

"Because one, you asked me a bunch of questions about the Albanians last night, and now they're dead. And two, when I mentioned your name to Detective Hecht, the lead on that Milwaukee thing, he told me that your Subaru was parked right in front of the house, shot full of holes."

She'd forgotten about the Subaru. That was going to open up a whole can of worms. "Wait, somebody shot up my car? Damn, I just paid it off."

Fratelli wasn't buying it. "Cut the crap, June. I know the two incidents are connected because the connection is you. I've read your stuff. You have a history of finding yourself in the middle of big stories. But now you're telling me you don't know anything about this."

"I live on that block, Carlo. Sometimes I park on the street. All I know is that my car wouldn't start today, so I borrowed a friend's." This was also technically true. The car wouldn't start because somebody shot it full of holes. "Seriously, you're barking up the wrong tree. Didn't you tell me the Chicago mob was gunning for the Albanians? Coincidences do happen."

"Not to me they don't. When the Milwaukee uniforms canvass your neighbors, they're going to learn a lot more about you and the people who lived in the house. And here's another thing. Hecht ran the title on that house. The owner is an anonymous corporation out of the Maldive Islands, wherever the hell that is."

"That's news to me," she said.

"Really? Because the house you're apparently living in is owned by a different anonymous corporation, also out of the Maldives. So don't talk to me about coincidences."

"I'm a renter. Maybe the same landlord owns both houses and he doesn't want the government to find out." She told herself he really didn't have anything. "Listen, let me ask you a question. In that Milwaukee thing, did anyone else get hurt? Any neighbors or pedestrians or anyone?"

His tone softened slightly. "That's the first thing you've said today that tells me you haven't become a total piece of crap." He sighed. "No, nobody else got hurt. A couple of the houses on the street took damage, but no people."

Now he was doing that older-brother thing, his voice full of warmth. It even sounded genuine.

He said, "We've known each other a long time, you and I. We did each other a lot of good, back in the day, because you were always on the right side of things. I think that's still true. You're a crusader, like me. So let me give you some advice, friend to friend. You're in trouble, lady. You need to get ahead of this. Go talk to Hecht and tell him what you know. Then come talk to me. Whatever you're into, I can help you get out from under."

He wasn't wrong, June thought. But he didn't know about Peter and Lewis and Dinah and the boys. They were all in this too deep to start talking to the cops now.

"Well, I haven't heard from the Milwaukee police. And I'm pretty sure the dead Albanians aren't yours to investigate. Because you're on that DEA task force, right? So really, you're just another interested party. And I've got a lot of work yet to do today, so I think I'll let you go."

"June, wait," he said. "Please." He was quiet a moment. When he spoke, his voice was low and intent. "If you're involved with these people, you're playing a real dangerous game."

She didn't allow herself to call him a condescending prick. "It's not a game, Carlo. And I'm not playing."

"June, they had assault rifles. They had a rocket launcher, for God's sake. These are serious people."

"I appreciate your concern, Carlo. I really do. But I'm pretty fucking serious myself."

Then she ended the call.

Dinah said, "That didn't sound good."

"It wasn't. Give me a sec." June found the number for Peter's burner and made the call.

He answered it on the third ring. "Are you there already?"

"No," she said. "I just got off the phone with Fratelli, my source in the Chicago PD. He called because the cops found the Albanians. He also made a connection between that and what happened at Lewis and Dinah's house."

"Because you asked him about the Albanians?"

"Yeah, and because my car's parked out front of Lewis and Dinah's place, full of bullet holes. Plus my address of record is three doors up. So now he thinks I know something. He wants me to go talk to the cops."

"But he doesn't have anything."

"Not that he was willing to share with me. But I'm sure my fingerprints are all over that house."

"Me too. Let's cross that bridge when we come to it. You've stonewalled the police before. And you're a journalist, which gives you a kind of special status, right?"

"Theoretically. Until a judge orders me to reveal my sources and I don't have any. I told him I was looking into a story about immigrants who are criminals, but I'm not."

"You're always looking into a dozen different stories," Peter said. "Most of them don't turn into features. That's the way the job works. You just say somebody put a bug in your ear, and you made a phone call."

"I guess." She let out her breath in a slow stream. "I really don't want to talk to the Milwaukee cops."

"Have they called you?"

"No."

"So why would you initiate a conversation with them? You have a demanding job. You're traveling for work. They can't expect you to cancel a trip because your car got shot up."

"They'll think I'm not cooperating."

"You don't have anything to add to the investigation. You weren't there. You were working. That's all you have to say."

"Until they find my fingerprints and show up at our door."

Peter sighed. "I wasn't going to tell you this, but when Lewis was getting new documents for his family, he got a few sets for you and me, too. They're in my go-bag. Worst case, if this gets ugly, we can drop out and start over as new people."

"I don't *want* to be a new person," she said. "I have a byline, a professional reputation, a *career*. I was nominated for a damn Pulitzer, remember?"

"Juniper, it won't come to that," he said. "We're going to find these guys, right? Then we'll figure a way to hang this whole thing around their nasty little necks."

"You're motherfucking *right* we are."

"That's the June Cassidy I know and love. Go meet your hacker. I'll see you at the hotel."

"Oh, wait," she said. "Fratelli did say something that struck me. He mentioned the rocket launcher."

"What about it?"

"Well, you can't buy a rocket launcher just anywhere, right? If you were a bad guy, where would you get one?"

"That's an excellent question." She heard the smile grow in his voice. "If only we knew a semiretired career criminal who's also kind of a weapons nut."

"That's what I was thinking. Maybe he knows a guy."

"He knows a lot of guys," Peter said. "We'll send off those fake mailers and get right on it."

Hopefully, the GPS tag would lead them right to the bad guy's physical location, June thought. Her Chicago hacker would try to get them inside their enemy's electronic systems, which June well knew could provide a wealth of information. And Lewis would try to find the guy who had provided the rocket launcher to the man in the topcoat, so hopefully they could backtrace him that way.

So they had three real ways to find these shitbirds.

At least one of them had to work, right?

32

June's hacker lived in the South Loop in an Art Deco building that had seen better days.

The lobby had once been elegant, with an ornate tile floor and high oak wainscoting, but the tile was patched with cement in places, the wainscoting worn by a century's trailing fingers. An ancient clock ticked on the wall, showing six o'clock. The only gesture to modernity was a trio of security cameras in the upper corners, their slim wires trailing across the uneven plaster ceiling.

A white guy with broken veins in his nose stood behind a narrow reception podium by the entry door. He was in his fifties, roughly the size and shape of a refrigerator, and handsome in a grizzled ex-cop kind of way. He wore a shabby blue blazer that covered a bulge at his hip. According to his name tag, his name was Sean.

"May I help you folks?" He smiled politely, but his eyes were on Teddy, who shambled in behind June.

June stepped to the podium and returned the smile. "Hi. I'm here for Hiram Goetz in 23C. Will you call up for me?"

Sean frowned at the phone console on the wall behind him. "He expecting you?"

"No," June said. "But I know he'll see me."

"Mr. Goetz doesn't see anyone."

"Why don't I call myself?"

"He won't answer. Anyway, it's an old building. You can't even leave a message, it's just a speaker on the wall. I don't think he can even hear it."

"Trust me, he can hear it." June was pretty sure Hiram would have modified the intercom to make sure he didn't miss anything. "I promise you, he'll want to talk to me. I have a job for him." She gave him her conspiratorial reporter's smile that said they were all in this together, and wasn't the world strange?

Sean finally sighed and handed her the receiver, then punched in the number. From memory, she noticed. It rang six times in her ear, and then the line went silent except for a faint hiss.

"Hiram, it's June Cassidy. I'm downstairs. I have a project you might be interested in, something even better than last time. But I should warn you that it might be more than you want to take on. The last guy who worked on this almost got killed."

The doorman stepped away, as if he'd rather not hear. June listened to the hiss. Hiram was thinking about it, she was pretty sure.

She let him think a minute, then another. Finally she said, "Okay, you're not interested. I get it, you're coasting toward retirement. I don't blame you. As you get older, it gets harder to stay current. I'll call Zhang."

The voice on the other end was abrupt, like the croak of a frog. "I don't do face-to-face anymore."

"Unfortunately, this is a face-to-face job," she said. "I have a laptop with a dirty worm. I need you to go back on the people who infected it."

Again, the hiss.

"The worm," he said. "What's the provenance?"

"I'm told it has elements from Killnet and Unit 8200. Very sophisticated."

Another pause, longer this time. Through the hiss came a dry, fricative rasp. A palm passed across facial stubble, or fingernails on skin.

"Who's that with you?"

She smiled up at the closest ceiling-mounted camera. Hiram Goetz had hacked the building's security system. Or maybe he'd had it installed. "Interested parties," she said. "They'll keep their mouths shut."

"They can wait in the lobby. Face-to-face with you is bad enough."

"They're not official anything, Hiram. They'll keep their hands in their pockets. We'll be gone before you know it."

Another long hiss. "It'll cost you twenty."

"I'm on a reporter's budget," she said. "How about ten? If it runs into tomorrow, we'll talk."

There was a rhythmic creaking sound that took her a moment to recognize as a laugh. "You came to me, girly. Cost is twenty. Buys you twenty hours and I keep the worm. Try to go cheap on me and the price doubles."

She waited a few seconds and chewed on her lip for the camera, as if she were thinking about it. "Okay. But no upcharges, Hiram. Twenty is twenty."

While the receiver hissed, she put her hand on her hip and stared up at the dark unblinking lens. Sean shifted behind his podium. Her workbag was heavy on her shoulder.

Finally he spoke. "Come on up. And tell the sergeant to send my packages with you."

The elevator was small and slow, the brass turned green with age. There was no camera that June could see, although with Hiram's skills, that didn't mean there was no camera.

"He looks like a nice old man, but he's not. Don't touch anything, don't say anything. Try not to look directly at him. He used to work for the government, until they put him in prison. Now he works freelance, black bag stuff."

Dinah looked at the illuminated floor numbers, rising. "Maybe I should wait in the lobby, like he said."

June gave her a tight smile. "I'd rather you didn't."

Teddy's arms were loaded with brown boxes stacked in tiers like a wedding cake. "Peter said I'm supposed to be the guard dog. That means Dinah can wait downstairs."

June reached out and put her finger on the stop elevator button. The car lurched to a halt, bouncing on its cables for a moment. "She won't be safer downstairs. The doorman is on Hiram's payroll. Better to stick to the plan and not change things up on him."

Dinah took that in. "How is it you know a person like this?"

"His name is an open secret in certain circles. Corporate guys, finance guys, anyone looking for an edge and willing to pay for it. I ran into him on a story, maybe a decade ago. He asked me to keep his name out of it and I agreed. So sometimes he takes my calls."

"Why won't he just take the money and not do anything?"

"Hiram's entire existence is transactional. If he gets what he wants, we get what we want. Also, he's curious. He probably only agreed to see us because of the worm that Robert found."

Dinah looked at the control panel. "This is my life now?"

"It's just a moment in time." June took her finger off the button and the elevator began to rise again. "Before you know it, everything will be back to normal."

But she wasn't very convincing, even to herself.

33

The door to 23C was dark oak with worn varnish, just like the other three units on the floor.

They didn't even have to knock. June saw a shadow fall away from the peephole lens, then heard the hard clack of a deadbolt being thrown back.

Then she heard another clack. Then another, and another, continuing until June had counted seven sets of heavy hardware released. This wasn't a positive development, she thought. The last time she'd been to the apartment, there had been only three locks.

At last, the door swung partway open and a man stood half-hidden behind it.

He was small and narrow and his head seemed too large for his body. Colorless hair combed straight back over prominent ears, a cartilaginous beak of a nose, and small dark eyes staring at them from deep inside a complicated network of wrinkles and folds. This was her fourth time seeing him in ten years. He'd always seemed old, but never seemed to get any older. He wore the same clothes each time, too, threadbare khaki pants and faded blue sneakers and a brown cardigan sweater unraveling at the sleeves.

"You took too long to get here, girly."

"We needed a minute to talk in the elevator," she said. "I had to tell them your rules."

He considered that a moment. On the wall just inside the door, she could see an ancient intercom panel hanging from the plaster by its wires. Newer wires joined it to a separate green circuit board and a small white plastic box with the Bluetooth logo embossed on the surface.

"Okay," he finally said, and held out his hand. "Half now, half when it's done."

June unslung her bag and removed a stack of hundreds she'd gotten from Lewis, then walked forward and put it in his palm. "That's ten."

He riffled the stack with his thumb as if he could count the bills at speed. For all she knew, he could. Then he put the money in the pocket of his cardigan and backed away into the unlit entry hall. "Clock starts now. Close the door behind you."

June followed, with Teddy close at her heels and Dinah lagging behind.

The entryway light came on abruptly. Goetz stood ten feet away carrying a weird-looking weapon pointed in their direction. It was angular, with a homemade look, and the enormous bore had at least a dozen separate holes, each large enough to fit her index finger. "Hiram, you don't need to do this."

"Fifteen projectiles in a dispersed grouping," Goetz said. "Animal tranquilizer. Designed it myself. You'll be out before you hit the ground. Pretty bad hangover, too."

June glanced behind her and saw the array of splintered scars in the back of the door. He'd fired the weapon before.

Goetz nodded at a large secure mailbox mounted to the wall, the kind designed for luxury homes, with a drop slot on top and a keyed compartment at the bottom. "Weapons in the bin. Nice and slow."

June shook her head. "Not a great start, Hiram." She pulled open her workbag so he could see the .22 inside, then let the gun fall into the metal box. Teddy made a sour face, fished a gigantic pistol out of the pocket of his parka with two fingers, then did the same.

Goetz looked at Dinah. She shook her head. "I'm a nurse," she said. "I don't do guns."

"Open your coat and lift your shirt and turn around."

Dinah did as he asked.

Goetz grunted his assent, then turned and walked into the next room with the tranquilizer gun.

It had been a grand apartment once. A wide bank of windows, ten-foot ceilings with elaborate plaster moldings, parquet floors in an elegant pattern. Now the floors were stained and the moldings cracked and the walls hadn't been painted in a long time. The furniture was spare and shabby, a dusty old couch and two cheap club chairs arranged on a thin area rug. On the ceiling above the rug, someone had screwed a large piece of sheet metal that looked like it had been beaten with a hammer. Only the windows were clean, displaying the bright towers of downtown Chicago and toy cars moving on toy streets twenty-three floors below, rush hour in miniature.

Goetz walked through open French doors into what would have been the formal dining room. Now it held two eight-foot high-end computer desks in the center of the room, with a single expensive office chair between them. The front desk held multiple keyboards and an enormous array of monitors connected by tangled wires to a tall black server rack in the corner, each server with a pair of bright green indicator lights. The back desk held a row of tin cans filled with hand tools, along with a strange assortment of mechanical devices in various

stages of assembly or repair, whose purpose she couldn't begin to identify. She was reminded how much she preferred dealing with Hiram
from the distance of an internet connection.

Goetz hung the tranquilizer gun from a bicycle hook screwed into
the wall and crooked his fingers at June. "Give it to me."

She opened her bag and removed the laptop. "The password is today's date."

"And the worm?"

June took the thumb drive from her pocket. "This is code only. But
it's still active on the laptop, so be careful what you connect to."

"And what is it you want me to do?"

"The worm arrived embedded in an email and took over the machine. I want to do the same thing back to the original sender,
take over *their* system, and harvest everything we can. I should have
the email content, a FedEx tracking number, in a half hour or so.
If you can change this worm so it won't get recognized, great. If
you need to use something different, that's fine, too. But I want to
know everything possible about whoever is on the other end of that
email."

Behind the desk, Goetz pointed at Teddy. "You, meat puppet." He
pointed a long bony finger at one of the club chairs just inside the living room. "Sit there." Then he pointed at the faded couch. "You two
girls take the sofa."

Teddy looked at June. When she shrugged, he plopped into the
chair. When June and Dinah settled on the couch, a small dust
cloud rose.

Goetz plugged the thumb drive into a dongle and hit a few keys.
On a central screen, orange text glowed on a black background. He
leaned closer to examine it. "Interesting."

As he got to work, Dinah sat in silence, fingers twining nervously
in her lap. Teddy had his eyes closed. The only sounds were the hum

of the electronics and the rapid rattle of Hiram's fingers on the keyboard. June fought the flutter of her eyelids. If she fell asleep in this mausoleum, she might never wake up.

Forty minutes later, her phone vibrated in her pocket. It was a text from Peter with the FedEx tracking number. She said, "Hiram, I have the link. Let me know when you're ready."

"Ready now." He rattled off a string of nonsense letters, a Gmail address. She confirmed it and sent the link. She heard his fingers on the keys. "Got it. Come type the text." He stepped away from the desk, taking the tranquilizer gun with him, making room for her.

He'd been using his own system to design the hack, but all his other screens were dark now, and he'd opened the Albanian laptop because she'd send the Trojan horse email from there. She realized with a jolt that he already had the Ghost Killers email chain up, with the new link embedded in a reply. Of course he would discover where the worm had originated, she thought. Had he also read the entire email chain? Copied the fourteen notebook PDFs? Would he know about the bounty on the Ghost Killers? She hoped not. There was nothing she could do about it now.

Goetz disappeared into the kitchen. She scrolled up to the earlier emails to get a feel for the Albanian's writing style, then scrolled down again and began to type. *Apologies but problem with FedEx last night. Here is new tracking number. Expect package tomorrow.*

That was enough explanation, she thought. Let the other side wonder what had happened. She stepped back. "All done."

Goetz returned with the gun under his arm, carrying a tall glass filled with ice, a can of Red Bull, and a bottle of Polish vodka frosted with cold. "Hit send."

He watched her click, then he waved her away from the desk. When she was clear, he hung the strange weapon back on its hook and sank into the expensive office chair, dwarfed by the high leather back.

"Now we wait for him to open the email." He held up the Red Bull. "You want?"

She'd rather drink turpentine, she thought. Nor would she ingest anything in that apartment she hadn't brought in herself. "No, thank you."

He mixed his cocktail and took a sip, examining her from head to toe. "This is a different kind of thing for you," he said. "You're not reporting a story. You're hacking back at somebody."

She shrugged. "Somebody came after some friends of mine. Now I'm going after him."

"Listen to you, girly. Like a real gangster."

She showed him a toothy smile. "Tell me about the worm."

"Impressive," he said grudgingly. "But not elegant. Also overkill, like swatting a fly with an atom bomb. Some elements never were used. Some elements I'll have to study, run simulations, to see what they actually do."

"What about the source," June said. "Any idea who made it?"

He shrugged. "Could be anyone, from anywhere. There are many, many smart people coming into this now. All he needs is a laptop and an internet connection."

"Could it be corporate?" Robert had said it might be a rogue security contractor.

Goetz shook his head. "He's bragging, with all the Killnet and 8200 code fragments. Like a poet quoting other poets, telling us how smart he is. That's not corporate. That's a guy like me."

She studied his face. "Was it you?"

His wrinkles revealed nothing. "I don't remember."

His workstation pinged. He stood up and reached for his keyboard. "I'm in their system." The center screen lit up, orange letters spooling down through black. "Hm."

"What?"

"Something's not right." He pulled his keyboard closer and hit a few keys, then reached for the mouse.

Now the laptop came to life. He glanced at it. "Oh. That's not good."

June came back to the desk. "Let me see." He didn't move from his keyboard. She elbowed him over a step, making room for herself, but she was still closer to him than she wanted to be. He smelled sharp and astringent, like witch hazel, but layered over something else, something less pleasant.

On the laptop, there was a reply to her email.

Dinah must have read her face. "June?"

"You don't want to know."

"June, tell me." Dinah's voice was calm, but firm.

She read aloud from the screen. "'Nice try. I already know everything about you. I'm not going to stop coming until I have video of you dying.'"

34

On the center screen, the orange text continued to scroll. Goetz was typing furiously on his own keyboard, managing something on his servers. "Turn that thing off," he said. "You're done, girly."

"No, I'm not." June put her hands on the laptop and hit reply. *Who are you?*

The response came back immediately.

I work for your enemy.

You're just the help? Who's your boss?

A serious player. The last person you want coming after your small-time crew.

She looked at Goetz, who was still working his keyboard. "Are you getting anywhere?"

"Not yet, but I will. Kill that machine now."

"Thirty seconds." She turned back to the laptop, typing, *Why is he our enemy?*

Another quick response. *You'll find out when you meet. You will not enjoy the experience.*

June tried to channel the personality of a Ghost Killer. *You're over-confident. The Albanians are dead.* She remembered what Fratelli had told her. *In Milwaukee, between the house and the burned car, you lost six people. We almost got the seventh. But we have lost nobody.*

But the house is totaled. You're on the run.

How would he know that? she wondered. All the attackers were dead except the man with the rocket launcher who took the laptop. Maybe that's who she was talking to. He would be a field man, though, not the hacker.

Did you get the glass out of your topcoat? It was a guess. But the reply told her that she was right.

The six dead were contract employees. Your enemy has many more. But you have lost all your money.

This confirmed what she'd been thinking. The enemy was a big player, and he'd hired out the hit. That would be useful in narrowing their search.

She sent back the laughing-so-hard-I'm-crying emoji. *We have more than enough to find you and your boss. What do you think will happen when we do?*

She waited, but there was no answer. Beside her, Goetz muttered to himself. His fingers flew across the keys. He had two more monitors lit now, each filled with orange text that scrolled upward relentlessly.

June hit reply again. *There is a way out for you. Keep the money you stole from us. Consider it a finder's fee. All we need is the name and address of your employer.*

The reply came. *Why would I bargain? I have you where I want you.*

"He doesn't know where we are," Dinah said. She'd gotten off the couch and come to read over June's shoulder. "Does he?"

"He's bluffing." June tried to mouse to the reply button, but the pointer wouldn't move. She realized she was sweating. Had the room gotten warmer? "Hiram, you're running proxy servers, right? Tell me he can't get our physical location."

"No." A pause. "Probably not. I told you, kill that machine." Goetz pulled another keyboard toward him and the remaining three monitors came to life. The orange text was scrolling there, too, faster by the second. Goetz shook his head, lips moving silently.

"Should we leave?" Dinah asked.

The Albanian's laptop screen flared white for a half second, then a popping sound came from somewhere inside it. Dinah backed away as June slammed the lid closed. The machine was scorching hot to the touch. She pulled the power cord and stepped away from the desk. The air in the apartment smelled strange. She heard a faint humming noise, as if standing near a wasp's nest. "Hiram."

"What?" He was glued to his screens.

"Hiram, something's happening."

When he looked up, she saw the smell register on his face. He said something in a language she didn't recognize. At that moment, he didn't look like a nice old man at all.

The noise grew louder. In the corner, a thin gray plume began to rise from the server tower. On his screens, the orange text was a blur.

He pushed past her toward the servers. On the six-foot bank of machines, all the lights had turned red. As he pulled the plugs from the wall sockets, the smoke darkened and the stench of burning plastic filled the room.

He ran to the kitchen and returned wearing a pair of oven mitts with a red fire extinguisher under his arm. He pulled the rack away from the wall, then shucked the mitts and triggered the extinguisher and hosed down the backs of the servers. A white-yellow cloud spread into the apartment.

He glared at June. "What are you waiting for, girly? Open some windows."

She worked her way from the dining room into the living room, turning the cranks. The sashes swung open only a few inches, some kind of safety feature, but clean winter air began to fill the apartment.

"Hiram, what just happened?"

He pointed the extinguisher's nozzle at her. "I got no idea how, but somebody just fried most of my hardware. So my price just went up."

She heard a growl. Teddy put his hands on the arms of the chair as if to rise. The scar was a livid gap in his beard.

Goetz angled back toward the safety of his desks. "Don't get up, meat puppet. I'm warning you."

Teddy's glass eye gleamed. "What are you going to do, old man?"

Goetz gave him a ghastly smile, thin white lips and crooked brown teeth. "There's a device in the frame of that chair, custom-made. Compressed air, plastic pellets. Like a shotgun, but quieter. You triggered the pressure plate when you sat. If you try to get up, you're going to get the equivalent of twelve-gauge buckshot right up your ass. If you manage to live, you'll shit into a bag for the rest of your life."

"Teddy, don't move." From her position by the living room windows, June could see the mailbox with her .22 inside, but it was no help to her now. Goetz was five feet from his tranquilizer gun, hanging on the wall. "Hiram, we had an agreement, remember? Twenty is twenty."

"That was before," Goetz said. "Now it's two hundred. But if you don't want to pay me, I know who will. I read that email chain. I bet you're worth a lot more than two hundred to them. We'll just sit tight until they show up."

"I thought they couldn't get our location," June said.

Goetz raised a shoulder. "I saw something in the code."

His expertise was so far beyond June's knowledge that she had no idea if that was even possible. She thought he was lying, but there was no way to know. If he wasn't, they were fucked.

She glanced at Dinah, backed against the kitchen wall, not far from Goetz. She was shaking her head, as if that alone could stop what was happening.

Teddy began to lean slowly to the left, a faraway look in his eyes as he raised his right butt cheek slightly. Then he slid his right hand beneath it, palm down, feeling around for something. The pressure plate.

When his gaze sharpened, June knew he'd found it. She reminded herself that Teddy had been a safecracker and alarm specialist in the days before he'd gotten shot in the head, when everybody knew him as Upstate Wilson.

"Stop moving, you idiot." Behind his desk, Goetz couldn't take his eyes off Teddy. "You're going to make a mess."

June began to ease across the living room toward Goetz.

Teddy lowered himself gently down on the back of his hand, then leaned to the right and repeated the process. Now he sat on the backs of both hands. Then he pressed his body upward so that only his hands touched the chair. He stared right at Goetz, lips peeled back from his teeth.

Transfixed, Goetz reached absently for the tranquilizer gun. June took longer steps, trying not to seem to hurry.

Teddy tipped forward, all his weight balanced on his hands, round face pink with effort. Then he let himself fall forward and, as his torso cleared the seat, he shoved his hands outward toward the arms of the chair.

June heard a hard pop followed by a sound like a dozen hammers striking steel. That explained the metal plate screwed into the ceiling. On his feet, Teddy rose to his full height, grimacing. "Dangit," he said. Behind him, the seat of the chair had opened like a torn flower.

Teddy shook one hand in the air, as if trying to remove something unpleasant. Fat droplets of blood painted the dirty walls.

Goetz turned abruptly and grabbed the strange weapon. June was three steps away. Before she got there, Goetz got the fat barrel up and leveled at her chest. It was the diameter of a gallon of milk. "Everybody stop." His pupils were black.

June hit the brakes, her hands rising of their own accord, then risked a quick glance over her shoulder at Teddy. "Don't move." Both of them staring at Goetz and trying not to look at Dinah.

She still stood beside Goetz's desk. Silently, she took two steps forward, snatched up the Albanian's laptop, then brought it around and smacked it hard into the back of Goetz's head.

He yelped and dropped his strange weapon, then scrambled under the desk to reclaim it. When he got there, Teddy was waiting, bleeding hand held protectively to his chest, the other reaching down to grab Goetz by one skinny ankle and hoist the old man high into the air and away from the gun.

Goetz made a strangled cry and pinwheeled his arms. Ignoring him, Teddy walked to the largest living room window and tried to open it farther, but it was already cranked as far as it would go.

He took a grip on the outer edge of the sash with his bloody hand and pushed. With a cracking sound, the hardware gave way and the window swung wide. The cold winter wind rushed in. Smiling grimly, Teddy pushed Goetz through the opening and held him aloft, twenty-three floors above the pavement.

"You dickhead," Teddy said. "You were going to sell us out."

35

What the heck is the matter with you?" Teddy gave Goetz a vigorous shake. "What kind of freak puts a homemade shotgun inside a chair to shoot somebody up the poop chute?"

Dangling upside down over empty space, limbs flailing, Goetz grabbed for the window opening, but couldn't keep his grip. Teddy held him high, arm fully outstretched, with zero apparent effort.

June wanted to scream, but she forced herself to take a long, slow breath instead. She needed to be fully functional until they got out of the apartment. "Teddy," she said.

He kept talking, wired on pain and blood. "A messed-up guy, that's who." He shook Goetz harder. The banded stack of hundreds, half of June's payment for Goetz's services, escaped from the pocket of his cardigan and fell into the night air.

Goetz croaked, "They fried my gear. Somebody's gotta pay for that."

"Not our fault the other side beat you like a rented mule." Teddy shook him again, talking all the while. "You should have quit while you were behind. Instead, you threatened to *sell us out.*"

"Teddy," Dinah said from her hands and knees on the floor. "I found your finger. If we hurry, we can get to the hospital and they'll reattach it."

The big man stared at Goetz. "How about if I drop him and then we go to the hospital?"

"If you drop him," Dinah said calmly, "I won't help keep your finger alive on the way."

June was impressed with Dinah. All those years working in the ICU had obviously made her cool under pressure. June was still trying to dial down her heart rate.

"Maybe I don't care about the finger," Teddy said. "Maybe I'd rather hear him scream all the way down. Maybe I want to hear the *splat.*"

June thought about grabbing Teddy but knew she'd never be able to control the giant man.

Dinah stood up. She had something cupped in her palm. "Teddy, what was Lewis's rule, back in the day? You can only kill them if they're trying to kill you."

"But he *did* try to kill me, with that dang chair." Teddy held out the injured hand. The index finger was severed messily at the second joint. Blood ran down to his elbow and dripped onto the floor. "He came pretty dang close, too."

"But he didn't succeed," Dinah said. "And he's not trying to kill you now, right? Rules are rules, Teddy."

"Besides," June added, "if you drop him, somebody will notice. The police will come in a hurry. The doorman has my name and the lobby cameras have our faces. Your blood and fingerprints are all over this apartment."

Teddy glared at Goetz. "If I bring you back in, then what? All is forgiven? Cross your heart and hope to die? I don't think so." He turned to June, his eyes hard. "He knows your name. He knows how to reach the other side. He was inside the Albanian's laptop. What else does he know?" He sighed. "I'm the guard dog, remember?"

Then he opened his hand.

Hiram Goetz fell without a sound.

Until he landed.

Then he did make a kind of a *splat*.

June heard it from twenty-three floors away.

She gathered up her thumb drive and the dead Albanian laptop and stuffed them in her bag. "Don't touch anything else. We need to haul ass." She was trying not to think about their failure. The reverse hack, and now the fake FedEx package with the tracker, both useless. The only progress they'd made was learning that Lewis's enemy had hired out the hit team and planned to hire another. Only the need to keep moving kept her from lapsing into shock.

Dinah was already in the kitchen, rattling ice cubes into a container, then banging through cabinets. "I need to wrap that hand. Then we should clean up this mess. Maybe we can make it look like a suicide."

She emerged wearing yellow dish gloves, carrying a metal travel mug, a roll of paper towels, a bottle of Clorox cleaning spray, and a white plastic garbage bag. The ICU nurse seeing what needed to be done and getting to work.

Teddy stood at the window, injured finger held to his chest, looking down at what lay below. The chest of his parka was covered with his own blood. "I'm sorry."

"You should have thought of that before you dropped him," June said.

Teddy turned toward her, his face plaintive. "You think I didn't? He threatened to sell us to the people trying to kill us. I couldn't let him walk away."

While June wished things had ended differently, she couldn't argue with his logic.

Dinah tugged at Teddy's wounded hand, pulling it toward her. "What's done is done." She wiped the blood off his arm and folded a swath of paper towel into a makeshift bandage.

June took the Clorox and sprayed the damaged window, then wiped away the blood and fingerprints with a paper towel. She hoped the cleaner had enough bleach to scramble any DNA she missed.

Dinah finished the rough bandage, holding it in place with a rubber band, and began to wipe Teddy's blood spatter from the chair and walls. Then the three of them teamed up to clean the floor and any other surfaces they might have touched, working their way toward the door. The used paper towels went into the trash bag to take with them.

In the entryway, June used a key from a desk drawer to unlock the security box where they'd put their guns. "You were great back there, Dinah."

Dinah gave her a look. "I didn't have a choice."

"Sure you did," June said. "You could have frozen up."

"Oh, please," Dinah said. "I wouldn't last long in the ICU if I did that."

June stuffed the pistols in her bag and swiped a paper towel across the box's smooth metal surface before peeking through the peephole to scan the lobby. "All clear. Let's go." She used the same paper towel to turn the knob.

Dinah slipped past, carrying the trash bag and the metal travel mug. Inside the mug was a bed of ice with Teddy's severed finger on top. "We should take the stairs. There must be a back door, right? Maybe we can bypass that doorman." Dinah was definitely getting the hang of this, June thought.

"Hang on a sec." Teddy vanished into the apartment for a moment, then returned carrying the tranquilizer gun and a plastic bag full of spare darts. The boyish grin was back. "Can I have this?"

36

PETER

After a stop at Best Buy, they'd returned to the Walgreens on Addison just after six. For obvious reasons, Peter was the one who had gone inside. A second security guard was the only evidence that Lewis and Teddy had robbed the place just a few hours ago.

He'd taped a Jiobit Smart Tag to the narrow bottom of a standard FedEx box, then built a false cardboard bottom over the GPS device. It wouldn't fool an active search or a frequency reader, but it was good enough to pass a casual inspection. After dropping two reams of blank printer paper into the box, he'd used more clear tape to reinforce the outside. Then he filled out the address label by hand at the FedEx counter, paid cash for next-day shipping, and headed for the South Side.

June had called with a progress report as they passed the tail end of the CSX intermodal yard. The clanging of the train cars sounded clearly in the closed truck. She'd sounded dispirited. Peter understood why. Not only had her hacker failed to do what she'd hoped, he was dead, and it was now clear that the person at the other end of the email knew the Albanians were dead, too. The fake FedEx package was obviously a ploy, and Lewis's enemy wouldn't be retrieving it. Which meant the GPS tracker was useless.

They weren't exactly making progress on this thing. He hoped June and Dinah would find something useful in the notebooks. Although he wasn't holding his breath.

Now they were in Grand Crossing, on the South Side, with Lewis behind the wheel. The neighborhood was narrow streets lined with brick bungalows and modest apartment buildings, working-class and poor, mostly Black. The modest commercial blocks had metal grates over the windows. Park's Beauty Supply, J and J liquor, Southtown Subs. At least a quarter of the storefronts were boarded up.

Lewis pointed down Prairie Avenue. "Al Capone's house is a couple blocks that way. It's a museum now."

"You spend a lot of time down here?"

Lewis shook his head. "Just to see Philly Maurice." The gun dealer. They passed a muffler shop, an accountant's office.

"Working with Nino and Ray," Lewis said, "we brought home a lot of hardware I didn't want to keep. I didn't know the ballistic history, or whether the serial number was on a list somewhere. Maurice bought and sold, decent prices, always had a real good inventory."

Lewis drove like he did everything, with a clean efficiency that seemed effortless. Somehow he never ended up at a red light. His head turned relentlessly, examining parking lots and side streets.

"Funny, this always seemed like a prosperous place, at least compared to where I came up. Not as many burned-out businesses or vacant lots. But the neighborhood's a lot bigger. Maybe a lot harder to find your way out of."

"This isn't just a nostalgia drive," Peter said. "You're looking for something."

Lewis flashed him a tilted smile. "Maurice drove a bright yellow Hummer, back in the day. Loved that beast. Haven't seen the man for five years, but I'm thinking he's still got it, or something like it. He had a few places he used to go on this strip. Baba's Steak and Lemonade, Roy's Soul Food."

"A yellow Hummer's not exactly low-profile."

Lewis snorted. "Philly Maurice never was the low-pro type. But he's real smart, and real careful. Got to be both to stay alive in his business. When I first met him, he was bringing clean guns up from down south, selling to bangers and thugs like me. Maybe eight years ago, he started buying wholesale, Chinese-made AKs and Type 92 pistols, direct from the manufacturer. Later, he added war surplus from the Balkans. Whole shipping containers brought through the Port of Chicago. Markup something like a thousand percent. That's when he started making real money. We thought about moving on him, back in the day, but he was a real hard target."

"And you're sure this is the guy?"

"Philly Maurice is the only dude within a sixteen-hour drive of my house can get his hands on a rocket launcher." He glanced at Peter. "Did you get a good enough look to see what kind it was?"

Peter thought back to the man in the topcoat, the tube on his shoulder. A diamond-shaped warhead and a flared exhaust at the back. "It was an RPG-7, I'm sure of it." He'd seen enough of them to know. He'd even fired a few himself. "Why are we driving around? You can't just call this guy, set a place to meet?"

Lewis shook his head. "Maurice was always hard to reach. He changed phones every few days, the new number only given out to regulars. I've been gone too long to get back in that loop."

"But he'll remember you?"

"Philly Maurice remembers everything. The man's an elephant."

They passed Baba's Steak and Lemonade, and a few blocks later, Roy's Soul Food. No Hummer. Then, as they approached Garvey's Jamaican Getaway, Lewis took his foot off the gas. "Speak of the devil."

Peter hadn't seen a Hummer in years. This one was canary yellow. Despite the gray slop on the streets, it looked like somebody had just detailed it with a toothbrush. The way it was parked, it took up four spaces in the lot.

Lewis turned down the side street and put the pickup at the curb. "Better bring your pistol. Philly Maurice won't take you seriously if you ain't heeled." He flashed the tilted smile again. "Thing about talking to a gun dealer, it's always a real polite conversation. Because you know everybody a bad motherfucker and everybody strapped."

Lewis had some extra street in his voice, Peter thought. Usually it came and went, Lewis intentionally dialing it up or down to make a point, or maybe just to amuse himself. But this seemed different. Something about the neighborhood, or Philly Maurice, taking Lewis back in time.

Garvey's Jamaican Getaway was a plain rectangular building, its roof thick with snow. Someone had painted palm trees on the side without windows. The awning on the front was striped in the colors of the Jamaican flag. An enormous Black man stood by the door and watched them approach from across the parking lot, one hand already reaching inside his heavy black parka.

"Hey, Junior," Lewis said. "The man still giving you the shit work, I see."

Junior eyed Lewis suspiciously. The reaching hand went still, having found what it sought. "I know you?"

"Used to," Lewis said. "How's that sweet Brenda? Beautiful as ever?"

Junior's face softened, a smile creeping across his lips. "Turned nine last week. We had a unicorn piñata." He nodded to himself. "Yeah, I remember you. Been a long time."

"Too long." Lewis reached for the door handle. "Making up for it now."

"Hold up. I know he ain't expecting you. Might want to wait until tomorrow. The man's in a mood."

"We cool," Lewis said. "Won't take but a minute."

He pushed open the door and walked inside, with Peter hustling to keep up.

The restaurant was warm and less than half full, which Peter supposed wasn't unusual at this late hour in a working-class neighborhood.

The side walls were decorated with murals of tropical beaches. Pans clattered in the open kitchen and the air smelled of jerk chicken spices and fried plantains. Peter's stomach rumbled. Maybe they could get something to go.

In the far corner, three Black men sat with their backs to a long table. The first was small with an angry pout and a shotgun across his lap. The second was medium-sized with a pushed-in face and an Uzi on a sling under his bomber jacket. The third was large with dead eyes and a heavy chrome revolver on the empty chair beside him. Like the three bears, Peter thought, if the story had been written by Chester Himes.

On the far side of the table, two young women, both Black, as slim and stunning as supermodels, chattered brightly in dresses so tight you could count their freckles. Between them sat a trim Black man, maybe sixty, with a well-groomed beard and dreadlocks flecked with gray, wearing a brown leather car coat buttoned to the neck even as he forked food into his mouth. Beside his plate was an enormous pearl-handled Desert Eagle and an inexpensive cell phone.

Nobody else in the group was eating. If the restaurant's other diners saw the weapons on conspicuous display, they pretended not to.

Before Peter and Lewis had advanced a half-dozen steps, the little guy with the shotgun, still seated, raised his weapon to his shoulder. The big man stood, his revolver like a toy in his hand. The medium-sized one said, "Maurice."

The women stopped talking abruptly. The trim, bearded man looked up, still chewing, and examined the newcomers curiously. Something about him reminded Peter of Lewis. The same sense of stillness, of coiled potential energy waiting to be released.

Then Peter corrected himself. Not waiting for release, he thought, but eager. Like a pit bull straining at a chain.

Unhurried, Maurice finished chewing, then swallowed, then ran a thick pink tongue over bright white teeth, eyes on Lewis the whole time. The three men were silent, but Peter was certain they'd already spotted the pistol on his hip and the big black automatic in Lewis's shoulder holster. Their weapons might as well have been back in the truck, for all the good they would do in this moment.

Finally Philly Maurice wiped his lips with a napkin and said, "It's been a minute, youngblood. Where you been keeping yourself?"

"Here and there," Lewis said.

The older man's phone buzzed on the table. His gaze dropped to the screen, then returned to Lewis. "Second-story man, as I recall. And a collector. You're the one wanted that 28 Navy. Among other things."

"Among other things. That's why I'm here."

Maurice shook his head. "I used to know you, but I don't know you anymore, if you catch my meaning. Especially when you just walk up on me like this."

"I'm not looking to buy or sell," Lewis said. "Just a quick conversation."

"Hell, youngblood, we doing that right now." Maurice smiled. The supermodels laughed gaily. The gunmen didn't even twitch.

Lewis smiled politely. "A quick and private conversation."

Maurice picked up his fork and took another bite, talking with his mouth full. "Well, that sounds like business, and I don't do business at suppertime. In fact, after the day I had today, I don't think I'll do business with you at all."

Lewis tipped his head slightly to one side, the way he did when something had caught his attention. "You know, I had a day my-self. Why I came to see you. Maybe we talk a little, help each other out."

Somehow, it was the wrong thing to say. Maurice's mouth bunched in distaste. "That's enough. Get them out."

The man with the shotgun stood and aimed his weapon at them.

Lewis frowned. "We known each other a long time, Maurice. Won't hurt to listen."

Maurice pointed at the door. "Out," he said. "And if you see them again, kill them."

The big man took a step toward them, his revolver rising.

Peter looked at Lewis with the unspoken question of whether they should make a move. Lewis shook his head and Peter was glad. The other men were prepared, success was nowhere near guaranteed, and the restaurant was full of innocents.

Together, they turned and walked away.

Crossing the parking lot, the winter wind cut through Peter's clothes, but it felt good after the overheated restaurant. "That went well. You still think he's the guy who supplied the rocket launcher?"

"I know he is." Lewis spat into the dirty snow. "And somebody already talked to him."

"The cops?"

"Be my guess. You see that face? Now he thinks I'm a snitch, maybe wearing a wire." Lewis sighed. "So much for the easy way."

"What's the hard way?" They turned the corner and headed for the truck.

"It won't be pretty." Lewis hit the key fob and the running lights flashed. "We're gonna need Nino and Ray."

"I thought they hadn't called you back."

"They haven't."

37

STREYLING

Streyling was on the Amtrak to Chicago, looking through the ransacked Ghost Killer laptop, trying to find an angle that Ari Mueller had missed, but he was having trouble focusing on the details.

He was still angry with the little Israeli for taking over the laptop in the coffee shop, fifteen seconds after Streyling had plugged in the Israeli's thumb drive.

When the keyboard and mouse stopped responding to his touch, Streyling had called him. "Just get me in. I'll take care of the rest."

"I'm already past the firewall," Ari replied. "But the boss told me not to give you access until I'm done. 'Cause I got the *skills*, yo."

Ari was such a child, Streyling thought. When he fell into that fake rapper slang, he always reminded Streyling of the owner of a falafel place he'd once frequented in Lebanon, who seemed to have had learned his entire English vocabulary from watching gangster rap videos. Streyling had borrowed a great deal of money from him to pay off a gambling debt in Cyprus. The falafel shop was gone now. To avoid repayment, Streyling had told a member of Hamas that the owner was an American spy. The shop had been blown up with the owner inside. By an RPG, incidentally.

The laptop screen had flickered and flashed, Streyling reduced to a bystander as Ari's intrusion package bypassed the fingerprint lock and the supposedly unbreakable password manager to find the details for five different investment brokerages. That done, Streyling had watched as Ari slipped into five different email servers to get the security verification code for each brokerage, then methodically drained the balances into a series of numbered accounts overseas.

Streyling's eyes widened at the size of the balances. The Ghost Killers had been more successful than anyone had ever imagined.

"Ten percent of that goes to me, Ari. Let me know when you need the account and routing numbers."

"Those aren't my orders, yo. Everything goes to da boss. If you don't like it, take it up with her."

Despite his annoyance, Streyling was impressed at Ari's cyber mastery over the laptop, including the way he had detected the worm in the reply email from the people pretending to be the dead Albanians. Not only had he managed to disarm it, he'd then triggered a remote malfunction that had somehow fried their equipment. It reminded Streyling of the successful Israeli attack on Iran's centrifuges using the Stuxnet virus.

From what Streyling had gleaned, the Israeli had actually begun his career with Israel's elite Unit 8200, so the Stuxnet comparison might be correct. Then he'd bounced over to a private security contractor, where he'd run a small off-books electronic intrusion section, before their mutual employer had plucked him away. Ari Mueller seemed to think that made him special.

Either he didn't know enough to be appropriately fearful, or he somehow believed he was too valuable to be at risk. To Streyling, Ari was like one of those yappy little dogs that some women kept. You thought they were harmless, until you stopped paying attention. That's when they sunk their sharp little teeth into you.

Although it wouldn't happen to Streyling. He was always paying attention.

For example, if Ari *was* in fact too valuable to be at risk, that was useful information. Streyling's mind was always searching for the next opportunity. He needed to figure out how to get his ten percent.

Money had always flowed through his hands like water. He liked the high life, casinos in Monte Carlo and Macau, expensive toys, expensive hotels, expensive women. He'd always lived for today because he might not have a tomorrow.

Somehow, though, he'd kept on living. Despite his many lucrative side hustles, by the time the Agency had uncovered his transgressions, Streyling found himself in a great deal of debt. He'd taken out markers from half a dozen lenders, people who were neither understanding nor sympathetic. While he worked for the Agency, their ability to collect was hampered. Once those ties were severed, however, hard men had come calling.

This was how his employer had gotten Streyling to work for her. When she'd bought his markers, she had also bought his life. In theory, he was working off his debt. In reality, the interest she charged made that impossible. She basically gave him an allowance. Which made him a kind of indentured servant, a slave with an invisible chain.

He couldn't just walk away. Even if she couldn't find him herself, which was unlikely, she could easily resell his debt to far more unpleasant people who would truly leave no stone unturned. If he survived capture, he might well see himself in a far worse condition of servitude.

Still, he had been counting on the Ghost Killer payments to get himself free. The ten-million-dollar bounty would get him clear, with enough left over to live a relatively frugal life. But he didn't want to be frugal. He wanted the good life. Whether he captured the Ghost Killers or not, the promised ten percent would not only clear his debts, but let him live very well for the rest of his life.

Although, he was beginning to doubt that she would actually pay him what he was owed. The fact was, she treated him like chattel. She'd never acknowledged the value he had brought to the organization, the many millions of dollars his ideas and actions had produced. It was his idea to start removing her competition from the board, and his tactics that had made it happen. Under his leadership, using the off-books teams as muscle, they had wiped out entire firms, harvesting the clients and resulting fees as the spoils of war. Streyling wasn't allowed access to the numbers, but he was certain that his actions had doubled or tripled the size of her business, and the resulting profits.

The bottom line was, she owed him. That was all there was to it.

He had finally managed to focus on the Ghost Killer laptop, wondering if there was anything in the password manager that he could use, when his phone rang.

It was her. "Ari managed to narrow the server's location down to eight square blocks. Downtown Chicago, north of the river."

"Those are tall buildings," he said. "Tens of thousands of people live and work in that footprint."

"Correct," she said. "But the only person I'm aware of with those skills in that physical footprint is a man named Hiram Goetz."

He didn't know the name, but he didn't need to. "By the time I get there, they'll be long gone."

"I'm aware of that. The question is this: If the Ghost Killers know Goetz, who else might they know in Chicago?"

Then he understood. The man who had provided Streyling with the

Durango when he first flew into town. The same man who'd provided the ordnance a few hours later. "You think they'll reach out to him?"

"It's possible," she said. "If they do, you'll be there."

"I need more men," he said.

"You'll have them."

He had told himself not to bring this up, but the words were out of his mouth before he knew it. "What about my finder's fee? That's a lot of money I put in your accounts."

"I'm holding it for you," she said. "I wouldn't want to diminish your enthusiasm for the job at hand. Besides, with your history, you'd probably just piss it away, right?"

He closed his eyes. "And the new FedEx package? From the Ghost Killers email, with the tracking number?"

"It can't be anything good," she said. "Have it destroyed."

She hung up, and Streyling looked out the window at the vast switching yard that served the downtown station, thinking about the package. He wouldn't destroy it, not yet. It might prove useful.

When he arrived in Chicago, he found a replacement car, a faded red Explorer with the keys atop the front tire, waiting in a parking structure near Union Station. He'd called ahead from Milwaukee. Once he was in the driver's seat, he sent the same man a text. *Car acceptable. Need to meet ASAP. Location?*

No answer.

After a minute, he sent another text. *My employer asked you to provide every courtesy. We have business to conduct.*

Finally he got a reply, an address and a name. *Garvey's Jamaican Getaway.*

38

I t was well past dark when Streyling saw the painted palm trees and striped awning. He put the car across the street where he could see the entrance, watching customers filter out in twos and threes. He figured the man must like restaurants. When they first met, less than thirty-six hours ago, he was having breakfast at a soul food place three blocks down.

After a half hour with nothing unusual, he walked across the parking lot. At the door was the same enormous Black man standing guard, stuck out in the cold while everybody else ate and drank in warmth and comfort. Streyling gave the name he was known under. "He's expecting me."

The guard took his phone out of his giant puffy coat. "White dude from the other day's out here, says he's got a meet." He listened for a moment, then put the phone away and stepped out of Streyling's way.

The restaurant was almost empty. Aside from a man waiting behind the bar and an elderly woman working a mop in the open kitchen, the only other people were gathered in the far corner of the dining area. Three armed goons stared at Streyling with open hostility as he walked toward them. Behind a long table, Philly Maurice sat with a bottle of Red Stripe, watching two gorgeous girls in skin-tight dresses dance to loud frantic music that Streyling didn't recognize or like, although he liked the look of the girls very much. He was the only white man in the room, although with his many years in Africa, this was nothing new. A very large pistol lay on the table beside a cheap cell phone, and a haze of fragrant smoke hovered against the ceiling.

Streyling stopped outside the perimeter and raised his voice over the music. "I only need a minute, Maurice. I'm looking for a man named Lewis, a serious man. Do you know him?"

Maurice didn't move his eyes from the girls. His face gave nothing away. "I know a lot of people."

"This Lewis is a heister, runs a heavy crew. Smart, disciplined, good at his job." Streyling knew better than to look at the dancers. When this thing was all over and he was a wealthy man, he could buy as many girls as he wanted. "May I sit?"

Maurice turned to regard Streyling dispassionately. "No, you may not." Although he was perhaps ten years older than Streyling, he was one of those men that age did not diminish, but only made more substantial. He made a gesture at the man behind the bar and the music dropped. "What's your interest in this cat?"

"That's not relevant to this discussion," Streyling said. "Have you seen him?"

"Not relevant?" Maurice picked up the very large pistol and turned it in his hand. "Right now, I'm the one decides what's relevant." The three shooters each took a step back from Streyling. The girls stopped dancing.

Maurice kept talking, his tone measured and even. "For a guy I barely know, you been asking a lot. Couple days ago, you ask me to provide a car and some muscle. Your money spends like anybody else, plus you're connected to somebody serious, so I'm happy to do business. Until you find me the next morning and make the ask for some serious boom-boom, shit I do not sell in my own backyard and for good reason. You tell me the hardware's going cross-country, you'll double my rate, and by the way, remember what happened to the last guy pissed off your boss, I mean the whole slap and tickle. So I say okay, one time only, and you never heard of me. But right now I got the law breathing down my neck about a certain item got used ninety miles away in *Milwaukee*, they say practically has my initials on it. And here you are asking about some two-bit heister and telling me it ain't fucking relevant?"

"Trust me, Maurice, you really don't want to know."

"Trust you? All I heard from you so far is lies. I spent four hours downtown with very expensive lawyers, talking to the damn FBI. They're promising full immunity. They want a name, or they're going to make my life very difficult. Thing is, I only got one name to give them, and it's yours."

In the last thirty years, Streyling had spent thousands of hours in the company of men like Philly Maurice. Local warlords, tribal leaders, the heads of various religious or revolutionary or criminal factions, surrounded by dead-eyed killers, some of them no more than children. Each man convinced of his own sovereignty and importance, ready and willing to put Streyling's head on a stake. Working with them required patience and deference, especially in front of their own people. But sometimes you needed to remind them who they were dealing with.

"You know who I speak for," he said. "Right now she barely knows your name. You want me to get her on the phone for this? I can call her right now."

Maurice pulled his head back like a turtle into his shell. "I ain't that dumb."

Streyling let his voice rise. "Dumb enough, if you think there's any daylight between her and me. This is personal for her. So we both expect you to keep your mouth shut with law enforcement and provide us with your full cooperation." He softened his tone. "Besides, I'm sure that item will never be traced to you in any way that can be used in court. The police know nothing, and they never will."

He walked past the shooters to the table, pulled out a chair and sat. "Now," he said. "A hard case named Lewis. Do you know him?"

Maurice set the pistol down carefully. "I do. He was here tonight, with a white boy."

"Tonight? How long ago?"

"Not long. I was finishing my supper."

Streyling wondered if he'd seen them earlier, walking out of the restaurant. Unfortunately, he'd been too far away to see faces. "What did he want?"

"A conversation."

"What did you talk about?"

"Some low-rent thief I ain't seen in five years? Not a damn thing."

"Did he leave a phone number?"

"Hell no. I ran him out of here."

"I have a feeling he'll be back." Streyling put his elbows on the table and leaned forward. "When he does, here's what'll happen."

39

LEWIS

nvolving Nino and Ray wasn't a choice Lewis took lightly.

After Lewis shut down the Heavy Lifters, Ray had returned home to Houston and changed his life. He'd found God and started a community center in Greenspoint, the neighborhood where he'd grown up. He'd made it clear he wanted a clean break and hadn't spoken to Lewis since the day he left, although Lewis had sniffed around enough to get a sense of the work Ray was doing. He felt bad about just showing up, but if Ray wasn't going to return a phone call, Lewis didn't have another option.

Nino, on the other hand, wasn't the type to get religion. Between Nino and Ray, Nino was the one Lewis had to keep on a leash. A born killer, Nino had never liked being hamstrung by Lewis's rules, but he'd stuck to them because the crew made good money. Now he ran a white-tablecloth joint in Minneapolis, wearing a suit and tie every night and glad-handing with local big shots. Lewis had never been able to reconcile the old Nino with this new version, but it was possible he'd missed something. Maybe Nino was a born restaurateur, too. Maybe that was why he was ignoring Lewis's texts.

There were no commercial flights until the next day. Lewis called his friend the pilot, who was quick to point out that Lewis still hadn't paid for ferrying the boys up north. But when Lewis promised him forty thousand in cash to meet at Midway's private terminal, he was happy to fuel up and get airborne.

Lewis dropped the jarhead at the Intercontinental, where he would join June and Dinah in sifting through the notebook pages, then headed south toward the airport. He was frustrated with the failure of the computer worm and the now-useless GPS tracker in the FedEx package. It seemed like his enemy knew everything about Lewis, but after a day and a night of digging, Lewis had learned almost nothing about the other side.

Aside from the notebooks, the only remaining available avenue was finding some kind of leverage against Philly Maurice, so he'd tell them whom he'd sold that rocket launcher to. Even if Teddy managed to get his finger reattached, he wouldn't be at full functionality. Peter was hugely capable, but one man wasn't enough. Lewis needed his old crew back together.

The Twin Otter was efficient and agile, but not exactly fast. The pilot also owned an older but well-maintained Gulfstream that burned through fuel but had greater speed and range. By nine thirty, Lewis was on the ground in Houston, behind the wheel of a rented Chevy with the windows down and the humid gulf air soft on his skin.

The Greenspoint Youth and Family Center was in a former church school off Greens Road, surrounded by vast apartment complexes. The center's website said it was open from 6:00 a.m. to 10:00 p.m. every day, providing everything from early day care to after-school and evening programs, along with a social worker's office and a small free clinic three days a week. The same kind of services Ray's family had needed when he was a kid.

Lewis walked through the front door, where he found an older man behind a waist-high counter that had once probably served the school secretary.

"I'm looking for Ray. You know where can I find him?"

The man was thick in the chest and shoulders with scar tissue around his eyes and a ragged half-moon out of the top of one ear. He gave Lewis a pleasant smile and passed a pen and a large manila envelope across the counter. "We have a no-weapons policy. You don't want to put it in your car, you can leave it with me. No questions asked, pick it up on your way out."

Somehow, the man had known about the holstered pistol in the small of Lewis's back, under his untucked shirt. "And if I say no?"

"Up to you, but Ray won't be happy. This time of night, we also have a few off-duty officers here, playing ball with the kids. We want to keep this a safe space."

Lewis was in a hurry, and he didn't need a hassle with the police. He also knew Ray would be a tough sell even without pissing him off. So he wrote his name on the envelope, dropped the gun inside, and passed it back across the counter.

The deskman tucked it into a drawer, then pointed down the hall. "Last room on the right. If he's not there, try the gym through the double doors."

Lewis thanked him and started walking. The cinder-block walls were recently painted a cheerful pastel orange. The linoleum floor was scarred, but bright with polish. Lewis could still smell the cleaning solution. It smelled like lemons. Not like his own childhood at all.

The office door was open. A lean Black man sat behind a worn metal desk, working at a laptop. His tight black T-shirt showed the overdeveloped physique of a boxer. On a side wall was a picture of Black Jesus, halo and all. A dented four-drawer file cabinet stood in one corner and a packed bookshelf in the other. Lewis knocked on the doorframe.

"Yes?" Ray looked up, then frowned. "Crap. What do you want?"

"You never returned my calls."

"Got nothing to say to you, Lewis."

"You didn't even listen to my messages?"

"Those days are over," Ray said. "I've moved on. I'm doing this now."

"I know. And I respect that, Ray, I do. I stepped away from the life when you did. But here's how it is." Lewis walked into the room and closed the door behind him. "Some people are coming after me because of something we did in the bad old days. They already tried once. Came pretty close, managed to blow up my house in the process. Then they somehow cleaned out all my goddamn bank accounts."

"Don't blaspheme," Ray said. "And if you need money, I don't have any. I put it all into this place."

"I don't need money, Ray. I need your help. I got no idea who these people are or why they're after me. They're not going to stop until I'm dead."

Ray spread his hands. "What can I say, Lewis. You reap what you sow."

"I know it," Lewis said. "I brought this on myself, I'm real clear on that. And you don't owe me a thing. I want to be clear on that, too. But we worked together almost ten years, side by side. Fought together, bled together, almost died together a couple times. If you come in on this, I'm the one'll owe the debt, a big one. But here's the kicker.

It's not just me they're after, it's the whole crew. Once they punch my ticket, they'll come for you, if they're not coming already. They've got your name, and they seem to have money and manpower to burn."

Ray's face remained impassive, but the muscles bunched in his arms and shoulders, straining the thin fabric of his shirt.

"They sent seven guys to my house," Lewis said. "Trained shooters with full-auto rifles and a rocket launcher." He tipped his head toward the door. "You think one guy behind a counter will stop them? You got kids here all day, old ladies taking yoga classes. Who else will get hurt while they're looking for you?"

Ray leaned back in his chair and rubbed his eyes. "See, this is why I didn't call you back, man. I don't want this in my life."

"I don't want it, either, Ray. But it's here. We got to deal with it. You don't have to pull a trigger, I can do that. I need your eyes and your mind. I need the Heavy Lifters. We always got it done before, right?"

Ray sighed and looked over at the Black Jesus on the wall. "I'm not saying yes. But who else are you talking to?"

"Nino's next. Peter's been in it since the start. You remember the jarhead, right?"

"How could I forget? He nearly ruptured my left nut with that groin strike."

"That's on me, brother. I'm the one told you and Nino to take him down." Lewis and Peter hadn't started out as friends. "I didn't count on him being faster than the two of you put together."

"Least I actually made contact," Ray said. "Nino didn't even get a hand on him. But I can work with him."

"I've got Teddy Wilson, too. They came after him first."

"Upstate Wilson? You still carrying water for that one-eyed redneck?"

Lewis shrugged. "He ain't so bad since he got shot in the head."

Ray rubbed his jaw, giving Lewis a long look. "You're different. Something happened to you."

Lewis waved it away. "Nothing happened, man. Teddy just ain't got nobody else."

"Lot of people ain't got nobody else," Ray said. "Difference is, you didn't used to care. So, what changed?" A small smile crept across his face. "You're still keeping time with that woman, aren't you? Jimmy's widow, the nurse."

Lewis sighed. "Her name's Dinah. We got married. I adopted her boys."

Ray's smile grew, then fell away. "They were in the house, weren't they? Your family, when the shooters showed up."

Lewis nodded.

"You could have led with that, you know. We'd have got here a lot faster."

Lewis raised a shoulder. "I wanted you to decide on the merits."

Ray snorted. "Shit, Lewis got kids? I got to see that." Unlocking a drawer, he pulled out a pistol and a half-empty pint of Wild Turkey and dropped them into a messenger bag. "Give me five to pick up a change of clothes on our way out."

"You're staying here at the center?"

Ray closed the laptop and came around the desk. His feet were bare and calloused from years of working the heavy bag. "I told you, I put all my cash into this place. Every year, it costs two hundred large to keep the doors open. Even with grants, I can't afford to pay that and my own rent, too. Besides, I'm here all the time anyway."

"You know," Lewis said, "we get lucky, there might be some money in this."

Ray walked through the doorway, leaving it open behind him as they walked together down the hall. "I'm glad you brought that up," he said. "Same split as before, right?"

40

They found Nino after midnight, wearing a dirty apron over pleated suit pants, washing wineglasses behind the long mahogany bar in his place in Linden Hills. The front door was locked, but Lewis could see him through the window. Opening the lock only took Lewis a moment.

"We're closed," Nino called out from behind the bar, head down, focused on the slop sink.

Ray put a foot on the brass rail and leaned against the bar's polished top. "I'll have a fuzzy navel. And an appletini for my friend here."

Nino looked up, grinning. "Holy shit. What are you two doing here?"

"In the neighborhood," Lewis said. "How's business?"

"Don't get me started. Hey, what are you drinking? And don't give me any of that fuzzy navel appletini crap."

"Beer," Lewis said. "The good stuff. Hamm's, Old Style, like that."

"Everyone's a comedian." Nino shed the apron, set out napkins and heavy tumblers, then grabbed a bottle of eighteen-year-old Macallan from the top shelf and poured generously. He raised his glass. "Here's to crime."

They drank, thumped their glasses down, and Nino poured again, leaving the bottle on the bar. "Seriously, what are you guys doing here?"

"Answer my question first," Lewis said. "How's business?"

"Are we telling the truth here?" Nino swirled the scotch in his glass. "You thought it was hard taking down dopers, you should try running a restaurant. You know what decent meat costs these days? And you can't just point a gun at the vendor to get him to deliver what you need. No, he wants a sweetener, a fucking tip, just to show up with your order. Same with the fish guy, the liquor guy. Everybody's got their hand out except the person you really want to kick back to, the goddamn health inspector."

"Don't blaspheme," Ray said. "Please."

Nino looked at him. "Seriously?"

"Yeah," Ray said. "Seriously."

Nino shrugged. "Okay." He downed his scotch. "Anyway, the pandemic almost put me out of business. My investors are screaming to get paid, but we're still nowhere close to breaking even. I can't go back to them for more, so I keep dipping into my nest egg, which is getting smaller by the minute. Which is why I'm here washing dishes at midnight, because I can't afford to pay the bartender to close up." He held up his hands. "I know, I should have started smaller, maybe pizza or something, but I've been dreaming about a fine-dining place for years. The menu, the cocktails, even the light fixtures." He made a face. "The reality is, I work sixteen hours a day and I'm still losing money, got no time for the gym, and I'm seriously stressed, so I eat."

Nino put a hand on his belly. He'd always been built like a beer keg, but now the look was more pronounced. He glared at them.

"Don't say it. I got fat. My therapist says I'm sublimating my unconscious urges with food."

"You're seeing a shrink?" Lewis was worried about another Teddy situation, although Nino had never been the sentimental type.

"Don't worry, I told her I'm a retired pot dealer. All she cared about was if I could score her a quarter ounce at cost, for 'therapeutic purposes.'" He rolled his eyes. "Long story short, if you're here to ask if I want to go back to work, the answer is yes. Maybe I can lose the stress, drop a few pounds."

Lewis explained the situation. "This is really about saving our asses. There might not be any money in it."

Nino poured himself another drink, leaving the cork out of the bottle. "I don't care about the dough. I just gotta get out of this straight life. It's killing me."

The late flight back to Chicago was uneventful, and they made it to the Intercontinental by two thirty in the morning. Lewis knew the manager, who had given them two suites without putting any names into the computer.

Lewis handed Nino and Ray their key cards. "You're sharing with Teddy."

Ray said, "Bad enough we got to work with that redneck, now we got to bunk with him, too?" Lewis had told them about the notebooks.

"I'm with Ray," Nino said. "Upstate broke the first rule, keep your mouth shut. How can we trust him now? I think we should just finish what those bikers started and put him out of our misery."

"Quit complaining," Lewis said. "Teddy's part of the crew. Meet me back at the truck at five a.m. and we'll get to work." He'd left the four-door pickup in a self-parking structure a few blocks away, not wanting the vehicle's plates on the hotel's cameras or valet records.

He let himself into the suite. The bedroom doors were closed, but Dinah had left a note taped to theirs. In her orderly nurse's script, she'd written, *Teddy lost the finger. Also I spoke to the boys. Supper was T-bones and tater tots. Stanley took them out on snowshoes through the woods afterwards. Charlie said it was cool and Miles told me he's never coming home.* Then a smiley face and a big heart with an arrow through it.

Lewis felt something ease in his chest. Not just the boys, but Dinah, too. If he managed to stay alive and do what he had to do, everything would be okay. Even if he died while keeping them safe, he figured that was okay, too.

He went to the minibar and upended a pair of tiny bottles of Bushmills into a glass, then turned and saw the stacks of Teddy's notebook pages neatly laid out atop the credenza. The bright edges of sticky notes bristled out from the sides. June and Dinah were making progress.

He didn't want to look at the pages himself. He didn't need to. He could remember each job like it was yesterday. He'd been thinking about them, one by one, since the conversation in the hangar. Wondering what he might glean from his memory to help June and Dinah find the people who were after them.

He took his drink to the dining table, and was confronted with another pile of paper there. June and Dinah's notes on their reading. He closed his eyes and other memories began to rise unbidden.

Lewis didn't believe in the concept of trauma. For other people, sure, but not for him. If trauma was real for Lewis, his entire childhood would have been one long traumatic experience. He would have been useless, a puddle on the ground. Instead he'd found a purpose.

As a boy, he had watched his parents' lives fall apart. At the time, he didn't know anything about crack cocaine, how it hijacked the limbic system and turned the mind into a machine for craving. All he knew was that, with each passing month, their arguments grew louder and their bodies grew thinner, his father's sturdy frame and his mother's rich curves wasting away until they'd reduced themselves to little more than walking skeletons.

At a certain point, they must have lost their jobs, because the tiny house began to empty itself of their things, his mother claiming they didn't need the table and chairs, or the couch, or the pots and pans. They sat on the floor and smoked that shit, then paced the rooms like crazy people, shouting at each other, until they went out to the corner boys for more shit to smoke. Whenever Lewis tried to talk to them, they turned away.

Until the day came in late fall when he arrived home from school and they were gone. The house was empty except for a pile of blankets on the carpet in his room. He realized it had been empty for a long time. Even when they'd been there.

It was cold inside and his stomach rumbled with hunger. He wrapped himself in a blanket and hoisted himself up onto the kitchen counter to look through the cabinets. There was nothing inside but a half bag of rice and another of dried beans, and he couldn't make either one without a pan.

He carried the uncooked food to the neighbor's house and knocked on the door. She was a round dark-skinned woman with a brightly printed head wrap and a soft, drifty air. She cut and styled hair in her kitchen, and maybe did something else, too, men and women coming and going at all hours. But she always had a smile for Lewis.

He held out the bags of rice and beans wordlessly. She looked at him in the tattered blanket, ashy skin and nappy hair, sneakers coming apart at the seams. Then she stepped to one side and held the door open for him.

He didn't want to go in. It felt like the end of something.

Just until they come back, she said.

Even though they both knew that wasn't going to happen. Lewis nodded and slipped inside like a thief in the night. He was eight years old.

Carefully, Lewis folded up that memory and tucked it away into that compartment in his mind where he held such things. It was a painful memory, but also important, like the headwaters of a river from which all water flowed. It was the source of his sorrow and anger, but also the source of his strength, his motivation.

I will not be like them.

Instead he had become something else. Self-educated, capable, dangerous. Maybe it wasn't the right thing, but it was what was available to him. And it helped him channel his anger into action. A way to pay back those responsible.

He didn't think about his parents often. They hadn't been good parents. Hell, they'd barely been parents at all. But he thought about those corner boys every day, how they kept selling his parents the shit that was killing them. It took Lewis a few years, but he finally got his revenge. It felt so good, he'd made a life out of it, punishing others, and making a little money, too.

It gave him purpose, and a sense of control, especially after his auntie died and he was on the street for good at fifteen.

He looked down at June and Dinah's notes again. This time, he sat at the table and began to read. The warehouse in Phoenix. The cargo ship coming up the canal into the Port of Houston. The tractor-trailer in North Jersey, packed full of product and burned to the chassis. The farmhouse outside of Williston, North Dakota, with naked girls handcuffed to bed frames in every room.

For whatever reason, the law hadn't done the job, so somebody else had to step up. Somehow, it had fallen to Lewis. He wasn't ashamed of what he'd done, but some days, it weighed on him. He'd close his eyes and be back in Queens, strangling that Jamaican with a lamp cord, or stalking through that Cleveland freight yard, shooting Russians in the head.

Paging through June and Dinah's notes, though, was different. To see them written out like this, rather than clanging around in his mind like a ricochet inside a church bell, gave them a kind of order. He could see them more clearly.

Maybe, he thought, Teddy had been onto something with those notebooks.

He found himself sitting at the table with a pen in his hand. At the entry about the Phoenix warehouse, he wrote a few words in the margin. At the entry about the cargo ship, he wrote a few more, then more still. Filling in the gaps in Teddy's memories with details from his own.

He went to the next entry, and the next. When he looked up again, it was after three. He set the untouched glass of Bushmills back on the minibar and got the coffeemaker going instead. He wasn't going to sleep anyway, not now. His memory was better than Teddy's, so he might as well make himself useful. Help June and Dinah find the people behind all this. Teddy had only been on half the jobs they pulled, anyway.

He opened a credenza drawer and found a stack of hotel stationery.

When the coffee was ready, he picked up the pen again and began in earnest.

41

PETER

In Garfield Park, a distressed neighborhood on the South Side where a third of the buildings had been torn down and the rest needed a lot of love, the crew sat in four battered older rentals that they'd chosen for their ability to blend into the city. They were carefully parked on the streets around an imposing old stone apartment building, four stories tall. Waist-high parapet walls surrounded the flat roof. Heavy metal security grates protected every window and door. The only thing missing was a moat, and possibly a vat of boiling oil.

The yellow Hummer was parked right out front, with a black Armada close behind.

The plan for the day was to snatch Philly Maurice off the street without getting killed in the process. If they could get the gun dealer away from his guys, he might be willing to admit to selling a rocket launcher, maybe even tell who he'd sold it to. The FedEx mailer had been a bust, and so was June's hacker. Which meant Maurice was their last chance to find Lewis's enemy.

They'd started at five a.m., picking up the rentals from an off-brand place near Midway airport, then checking a half-dozen buildings where Lewis knew Maurice had stayed in the past. It wasn't yet eight o'clock. The sky was a cold blue, and the wind blew in hard gusts that rattled the hood of Peter's rented Taurus and rocked the traffic lights mounted on the tall, arched streetlights. All five men were wearing earbuds on a five-way call, although Teddy rode with Lewis because his injured hand made it difficult to drive and shoot at the same time. Each man wore armor, which was uncomfortable in the small rentals, and had an assortment of different hats and scarves they'd picked up at a corner store to change their silhouettes and help them escape the shooters' notice.

Peter was parked a block to the west, where the morning sun would turn his windshield into a mirror. It was the only reason he felt even remotely comfortable watching through large binoculars as Philly Maurice and his men walked out of the building and climbed into their vehicles. Two carried shotguns and a third had some kind of assault rifle. Their heads turned left to right as they walked, scanning the street for any signs of a threat. These were dangerous and capable men.

"They're on the move," Peter said. "Maurice is in the back of the Hummer, with Junior driving and another shooter up front. The other two are in the Armada. Three long guns visible, probably more in the vehicles. Turning south on Keeler."

"Got 'em," Nino said.

A moment later, his beige Corolla slid past, a block behind the Hummer. Peter left his spot to circle the block in pursuit, passing Lewis and Teddy in a black Ford Escape, hustling to catch up to Nino.

The Marines had trained Peter in many disciplines, but tailing somebody undetected was not one of them. The Heavy Lifters, on the other hand, were clearly experts.

Under Lewis's direction, the four-car follow was a complex maneuver, at once intensely choreographed, like a ballet, and highly improvised, like jazz. The team rotated every few minutes, the close follow car falling back or peeling away to be replaced a block or two later by a waiting second car, while the third and fourth cars hustled up side streets, staying out of sight and getting into position for the next change. The winter's heavy snow had narrowed the roads, slowing traffic and reducing available parking, which made the process even more challenging.

The whole thing had to appear organic and inevitable, despite constant adjustments for delivery and transit vehicles, road construction, and traffic lights, not to mention the unanticipated turns the target would make on his way to wherever it was he was going. So there was a lot of chatter on the headsets while they coordinated.

Peter asked, "How'd you guys learn how to do this, anyway?"

"Black man with a library card," Lewis said. "Amazing what you can find out for free."

"Seriously?"

"And a lot of practice," Nino added. "Learning from our screwups."

"In the old days, we'd build what the spooks call a pattern of life," Lewis said. "When the target left home, where he went during the day, what kind of hours he kept. See who he met, maybe follow them, too, build out the network, one person at a time. Sometimes it took a week or two, sometimes three or four. But we don't need that today. We just need a place to grab Maurice and get him alone. Have a little chat about the guy who bought that rocket launcher."

The first step was to plant another Jiobit GPS tracker on the Hummer, to make it easier to follow. They'd have done it when they first spotted the vehicles at the apartment building, but Maurice already had a couple of guys on the street, watching the vehicles.

The convoy zigzagged over to Pulaski and continued south over the Stevenson Expressway. The neighborhood had once been mostly Polish and other Eastern European immigrants, but now seemed to be leaning Latino, with Mexican restaurants every few blocks. Peter tried not to drool as he passed.

Waiting at a light, his phone pinged. He lifted it from the console, expecting a text from June. Instead, it was a notification from the app linked to the GPS device in their failed decoy package, one of several notifications generated in the last twelve hours. Apparently the app was designed to let the user know when the signal disappeared from satellite tracking, and again when it reappeared. He figured the package had been in some kind of metal cargo container that interfered with the connection. He pulled up the map to check the current location.

"Looks like our FedEx package made it to the mailbox store in Indy," he said.

Lewis snorted. "Too bad nobody's going to pick it up."

At West 71st, the Hummer turned east and drove all the way to Grand Crossing, where the convoy pulled up in front of a West Indian restaurant on Cottage Grove. Everyone piled out of the cars and went inside, except for Junior, who stood at the entrance, as he had done the night before, with a view of the vehicles parked on the street. He held a pump shotgun down along one leg.

"Looks like someone's a little on edge," Lewis said. "You ready, Ray?" They'd already decided Ray would plant the device because Maurice's crew had already seen Lewis and Peter, Teddy was down a finger, and Nino was too fat to outrun anybody.

"Walking now," Ray said. "Rental's two blocks north, in case the big dude eats me."

Peter had already driven past and parked at a convenient hydrant down the street, where he could keep eyes on both the Hummer and Junior at the restaurant door. "Still looks good here," he said.

"See if you can keep the Hummer between you and Junior," Lewis said. "Don't put the tracker in the wheel well, it's too easy to find. Better to get low and reach under the chassis and find some metal for that magnet. But make it quick. Junior's big, but he ain't stupid. When you're done, just walk on nice and slow."

"Do I tell you how to do your job?" Ray asked.

Now he appeared in Peter's rearview. He'd rounded his back, making himself look older. It was too cold for anyone to be out for a leisurely stroll, so Ray had put on a kind of loose-jointed shamble, as if he'd just had his first few drinks of the day.

Peter watched as Ray cut across to the Hummer, bent his knees as if suddenly dizzy, and braced himself against the yellow side panel. One hand dipped down and slipped under the vehicle's frame, and the other pushed him upright. Then he started walking again, the shamble having devolved significantly as the imaginary whiskey took hold.

Junior lifted his hand and called out to him.

"Dude's waving me over." Ray's earbud was still in, although his voice was muffled from the hat pulled down to hide it. "Telling me to come here."

"Just wave back," Lewis said calmly. "Be friendly, but keep moving. Nino, you circle back and pick him up around the corner."

Ray waved lazily and walked on. "He's a big one, ain't he?"

Junior waved harder, his insistent bass rising through Peter's half-open window, and began to raise the shotgun. "Ray, he's coming after you."

Ray half turned, half stumbled, then caught himself and waved Junior off, a drunk old man just wanting to be out of the cold. Then he shuffled away, nice and easy, pausing only to hock noisily and spit, take a full ten seconds to hitch up his pants, then keep lurching forward. Behind him, Junior had stopped to watch, shotgun over one shoulder, shaking his head.

"You're clear," Peter said. "Nice work."

Now they just had to find a place to bushwhack Maurice.

Unfortunately, it was the job of Maurice's shooters to prevent that from happening.

42

After breakfast, the convoy headed south on Cottage Grove. The wind had picked up, blowing so hard that snow rose from parked cars, causing momentary whiteouts on a cloudless day.

With the new GPS tracker now live on Peter's phone, they could be much looser in their follow, hang back two or three blocks and not worry so much about Maurice getting away from them. What really mattered was seeing the places he went, what his guys did when he stopped. Looking for the opportunity.

The Hummer stopped a few minutes at Cricket Wireless, Junior coming out with a plastic shopping bag, then again at a Cafe Express, Junior fetching a cardboard tray loaded with white cups. The gun dealer Philly Maurice, out running errands with his posse of killers.

"I forgot how boring this is," Nino said.

"Like the Army," Ray said. "Weeks of tedium punctuated by a few moments of terror."

"When we grab this guy," Nino said, "I'd like to find a suitcase full of Benjamins in the back of his rig."

"Listen to you," Lewis said. "Like you never left the game."

"Beats gettin' yelled at by some jerkoff thinks his veal piccata was overcooked."

The convoy stopped for gas on the corner of 95th Street. Lewis said, "Is it just me or has that white Kia hatchback been hanging around for a while?"

"I was just gonna ask the same thing," Nino said, "but about this dark blue Chevy Cruze."

"Maybe we're not the only ones out here," Peter said.

"Worth a look," Lewis said. "Let's loosen up our follow, stay well outside these two cars, see what we can see."

The blue Chevy and the white Kia were definitely hanging around. In fact, they were doing what the Heavy Lifters had been doing, running a circle route around Maurice's little convoy, stopping when he stopped, starting when he started up again. Peter also identified a third car, a tan Toyota Highlander.

None of them wanted to risk too close a look, but by the time the entourage turned south on Michigan, they'd seen enough to know that each car carried two men, four of them with beards, two with darker skin, all of them wearing winter hats pulled low.

"Look like cops to me," Nino said.

"They do have that vibe," Lewis said. "Maurice as much as told us he got pulled in yesterday."

"Want me to dart 'em?" Teddy asked. "We could put 'em in the trunk and take 'em somewhere quiet, ask a few questions."

"Enough with the dart gun." Lewis was still sharing a car with the big man. "Stop fooling with that thing or you'll knock us both out by accident."

"They've got decent technique," Ray said. "If the GPS hadn't let us loosen up the tail, they'd have made us for sure."

"Doesn't mean they're cops," Lewis said. "Maurice always paid for top talent."

"Why would he add another layer of protection?" Peter asked. "He didn't seem to see us as a threat yesterday."

"Maybe he's got a gun deal coming up," Lewis said. "You'd want more muscle if you were doing a big transaction."

"Then why all the white guys?" Nino asked. "Everybody else in his crew is Black. We almost never saw mixed crews back in the day."

"Maybe it's progress," Peter offered. "The brotherhood of man, joined together for a common purpose."

"They don't look like bangers to me," Ray said. "For one thing, they wouldn't drive such crappy cars. I'm with Nino. I think they're cops."

"Does that mean we can't dart 'em?" Teddy asked.

"Don't make me take that gun away from you," Lewis warned.

"Just keep doing what we're doing," Peter said. "It'll all make sense eventually."

As the convoy headed into Roseland, Peter found himself glancing over his shoulder and checking his mirrors more often than necessary. It took him a few minutes to recognize the faint tingling on the back of his neck. It was a feeling he'd learned to trust, the feeling that he was being watched, because it had saved his life more than once. The feeling came and went, but try as he might, he never did see anyone suspicious.

The Hummer made stops at a funeral parlor, then an accounting service, and then a deli to pick up what was probably a lunch order, while the double layer of cars orbited around him like satellites. Roseland was another distressed area, and traffic was almost nonexistent in the middle of the day, which made the follow much more dangerous.

In truth, it didn't matter whether the new guys were cops or killers. Either way, the Heavy Lifters couldn't make their move yet. They needed to remain undetected. So they stayed well back and leaned heavily on the GPS. Peter had his phone plugged in and the app on full-time, so he didn't have to log in every ten minutes.

When it pinged him again, he didn't quite understand the notification. Then he realized it was the other tracker, inside the FedEx package. The satellite had lost the signal again. He wanted to turn off the tracker, or at least disable the notifications, but he wasn't going to take the time to figure it out while tailing Maurice.

By twelve thirty, it was Peter's turn for the follow, so he was four blocks back, two blocks behind the Highlander, when the blue dot marking Maurice's GPS stopped again. There was only one other car in sight, and it was in the oncoming lane. The rest of the crew was driving along the streets to each side. "You guys should peel off," Peter said. "There's zero traffic here and I'm sticking out like a sore thumb as it is."

He pulled over and checked a map on his phone. It looked like Maurice was in front of a small church, a Christian offshoot Peter had never heard of. Across the street was a string of vacant lots. He told the others the address and waited for twenty minutes, but the blue dot didn't move. "Okay, I'm going to do a pass, see what's up."

He pulled out, turned the corner, and drove down a parallel street, just another guy trying to get from A to B. At the street before the church, he turned again, avoiding the actual block while still getting a decent view at the stop sign.

The church turned out to be a converted storefront, with a separate entrance to what looked like offices above. The Hummer and Armada were parked in front, with nobody visible inside. At a loading zone by the storefront entrance, four old ladies in black cloth coats were getting out of a dented blue minivan. The rest of the nearby buildings looked vacant or abandoned.

"This isn't the place to hit him," Peter said. "They're either in or above a church."

"What about our mystery guests?" Lewis asked.

"The Kia's across the street. The Highlander and Cruze are parked a block north and south. All three occupied, engines on. I don't know how we're going to do this with those guys hanging around." Peter crossed the street and kept driving, looking to put some distance between him and the building.

In his mirror, a vehicle appeared, a block and a half behind. "Is that one of you on my tail? I'm on 106th east of Michigan, passing Indiana." The tingle was back.

"Not me," Lewis said. "I'm on Wabash, five blocks out."

"Me neither," Ray said. "I'm on Prairie."

"I'm west of you on 107th," Nino said.

Peter lifted his foot from the gas and let the rental lose velocity without braking. In his mirror, the car grew larger as it closed. He couldn't tell the make or model. It was gray or tan or maybe light blue. He took the Browning from its holster and put it between his legs, then dropped his side windows. If he shot through the glass, he'd be a lot less accurate.

Coasting forward, he kept his eyes on the rearview, so he saw the moment the car stopped gaining on him, and began to drop back.

"Hey, guys?" Peter put his foot back on the gas and picked up speed again. "I think I found my tail. Circle back and let's hit this guy."

"On my way," Lewis said. The others echoed agreement.

But by the time they arrived, the car was nowhere to be found. Peter had watched his mirrors vigilantly, but he hadn't seen the car turn or pull over.

It had simply vanished.

43

JUNE

J une ordered lunch from room service, then checked her cell. Since breakfast, she'd had three new voicemails from Carlo Fratelli, asking her to call him back.

She didn't. Instead, she stood at the table with a cold cup of coffee and scrolled through the joint document she and Dinah had spent the last five hours putting together.

It was a lot of information. With Lewis's additions to their notes on Teddy's pages, June now had to research a hundred and twelve separate jobs, taking place over ten years. And even with Lewis's contribution, they knew almost nothing about any given job. They had the date, the name and type of group targeted, the city or county, the amount of money taken, and the number of dead. It was enough data to allow them to pinpoint the event for online research, but not enough to tell them who might remain as players behind the scenes, or what their motives might be.

Basically, June thought, they were looking for a needle in a haystack.

When they'd woken that morning, Dinah had gone to buy spare clothes and a second laptop and June had typed up their many ad hoc handwritten notes. As fast as June was on the keyboard, it still took her over three hours.

From her email conversation with Topcoat Man, she felt fairly certain that the Milwaukee shooters were hired mercenaries. According to Lewis, this would be very expensive, probably the same amount as the quarter-million dollars already spent on the information bounty. This fact, along with the fact of the mercenaries themselves, allowed her to begin to narrow down the field of bad guys.

She began to work her way through her list, highlighting some entries and crossing out others. Smaller, street-level groups, like bikers, white-power morons, and individual gangbanger chapters, were unlikely to have the deep pockets required to hire out the hit. Even the more serious urban or regional powers, like the Latin Kings and the Gangster Disciples, would be the same. Also, she realized, both types of groups probably wouldn't hire it out for another reason, too. Internally, hiring out the hit would be seen as a sign of weakness. Pride would demand that they do the job in-house and make sure Lewis knew who was twisting the knife.

It could certainly be the leadership of a big national gang, someone like MS-13, 18th Street, and La Eme. These would be old-school bangers who had survived by being both hardened killers and smart, strategic, long-term thinkers. From Lewis's notes, June knew he had targeted the national leadership of several of these and been very successful. Plus there was the Italian Mafia. He'd taken on at least one of the big East Coast families that she knew of.

Alternately, Lewis seemed to have a minor side interest in financial criminals. Because they were mostly stealing over the telephone or internet, running pump-and-dump stock schemes or targeting retirees' bank accounts, they weren't street-level tough guys, which meant they were less likely to go after Lewis themselves. Also, they'd actually be more likely to have the funding to hire out the hit.

Last but not least, June knew that Lewis's crew had hit several cartel-level targets. In June's mind, the Mexican cartels were excellent suspects, as they had essentially unlimited finances, as well as access to military-trained assassins. Many of their killers had actually started out in the Mexican Army.

She felt even more strongly about these three categories after her experience at Hiram Goetz's place, seeing firsthand the technological know-how that could knock out both Goetz's worm and his computers. These were smart people with serious resources.

The good news was that this way of thinking reduced a hundred and twelve events to just sixteen separate criminal groups.

The bad news was that they still had to research sixteen events across a dozen states and ten years of elapsed time.

With June beginning at the bottom of the list and Dinah starting from the top, they went to work.

After typing the city, the name of the criminal group, and the date into the search bar, it wasn't difficult to figure out which news item June should read. A midnight shootout in a San Antonio residence had killed eight members of the Sureños, a subgroup of the notoriously violent Gulf Cartel.

June opened the shared document and began to add to her notes.

Follow-up articles mentioned that three of the eight were American citizens who had previously been in prison for a variety of offenses, including assault, extortion, attempted murder, and murder, and were mentioned by the police as prominent members of the prison-based Mexican Mafia. The other five men were Mexican nationals currently wanted for similar offenses across the border in Tamaulipas, three of those known to the DEA as high-ranking members of the Gulf Cartel. Two survivors, both under the age of sixteen, were found handcuffed to the water main. No money or guns were found, but a large quantity of heroin and cocaine appeared to have been dumped into the gravel yard and hosed into the desert soil. Authorities assumed the attack was gang-related and were following every lead.

June wrote down every name for further research.

Her next search led to a group of bottom-feeders in Seattle, running what authorities later called a stock fraud operation. They were held by masked gunmen for thirty hours while the contents of their overseas accounts were transferred to unknown parties. Before leaving, the gunmen had methodically broken the fraudsters' fingers and wrists with the edge of a laptop computer, then stripped them naked and, using the grifters' own phones, posted a large number of embarrassing photos online. Alerted by an anonymous phone call, law enforcement arrived to find the men handcuffed to their desks, with evidence of the stock scheme on an open laptop and a two-kilo brick of high-purity cocaine in a file cabinet. Taken together, it was more than enough to convict all seven men.

June wrote down their names. Any one of them might have learned a few things in prison.

Next, she read about a dozen men found dead in an unused freight yard outside the Port of New Jersey. Accompanying the first news article was a photograph of two large SUVs, each riddled with more than a hundred bullet holes, and a semi tractor-trailer that was burned to the chassis. Forensic testing of the remains indicated that the trailer had been loaded with heroin, cocaine, and methamphetamine. Law enforcement suspected a drug deal gone bad, although they had no explanation for why the drugs were destroyed.

A follow-up reported that six of the dead were Bosnian veterans of the war in the former Yugoslavia, two of whom had been indicted in absentia as war criminals by the International Criminal Court in The Hague. The other six were known to police as members of the North Jersey mob, three of whom had done state time in Trenton. The youngest, found dead in the back of a bullet-ridden vehicle, was Noah Salvati, the twelve-year-old son of Gino Salvati, the North Jersey underboss.

June got very excited by this last bit of news. The dead son of a Mafia boss was an actual motive for revenge on the Ghost Killers. Then she ran a search on the father and discovered that he'd died in a car accident a year later. According to the article about the death, Salvati was survived by his much younger wife. The North Jersey mob, already on the decline, was further reduced by a crippling series of indictments after the accident. The Bosnians were more active, but only in Europe. Still, she wrote down the names and went to the next search.

Fifteen members of the Russian Mafiya killed in a Cleveland industrial yard, half a mile from the arena where the Cavaliers played.

In L.A., a shootout between two groups of Chinese nationals, known to be competitors in the profitable business of human smuggling.

Three longtime leaders of the Gangster Disciples killed in a large home in an affluent suburb of Chicago.

Five members of an identity theft ring found naked and handcuffed together around a dead tree outside of Bangor, Maine, at the height of mosquito season.

The list went on and on.

Carlo Fratelli left three more voicemails that afternoon. The FBI was taking over the investigation into the shootings at Lewis and

Dinah's place. Evidence teams were on the hunt. June's name had come up in connection with a suspicious death at a Chicago high-rise. Fratelli needed to talk to her.

She didn't call him back.

It was well past seven by the time June and Dinah finished this first pass. With all sixteen jobs taken together, it was a little overwhelming.

She thought about Lewis, sitting alone in the darkened hotel suite last night, adding to their notes. She wondered how he thought about the things he'd done. How he'd thought about them while doing them.

Peter talked about Lewis as a man with a code, and June had seen it in practice many times. There was something beautiful about its simplicity. You keep your promises, even when it costs you. You support your friends, no matter the danger. Like the time he got shot in Denver saving Peter's ass. Or the time he showed up in Seattle just in time to save her and Peter both.

Oddly, the killing didn't bother her. She could tell by her research, these dead were not innocent men. June had known what Lewis was when she met him, the same way she'd known what Peter was. The aura of contained violence came off both men like faint smoke from a banked ember, just waiting to burst into flame. Maybe she should have been scared by that, and by the things she'd seen both men do. But she wasn't. In their company, she felt protected. Safe.

Peter had been in combat for most of his two tours in the Marines. She'd never asked how many people he'd killed over there. But she knew they'd sent his unit where the fighting was the most intense, time and time again, and she figured he'd taken at least as many lives as Lewis had, if not more. Peter had complicated feelings about his time in the Marines, but whether right or wrong, those killings had been sanctioned by the government. He'd been fighting a war.

Reading through these news articles, she realized that Lewis had been fighting a war, too, even after leaving the Army. But it was a different kind of war. An entirely personal one. With no government sanction or support. In fact, the government had been actively hunting him.

He'd taken money from these gangsters, it was true, but she knew he didn't do the work for the money. Maybe that had been an excuse at first, but not later. No, Lewis made the money to finance weapons and hotel rooms and vehicles, to pay his guys, so he could keep doing the work. Which was to remove bad people from the world by putting himself in their way, and killing everyone who tried to kill him first.

It struck her as a hard and lonely life.

She was glad he'd gotten out. She was glad he had Dinah and the boys.

After dinner, June and Dinah sat together and began to review their much-enlarged shared document. It had grown to several dozen pages, filled with names and places and other details, including links to every web page they'd looked at. But nothing that felt like a lead.

Dinah threw up her hands, obviously of the same opinion. "So what do we do next?"

"We start looking into these groups," June said. "See who's still in business. See who's strong enough to hit back." Hopefully that information would narrow things further. After that, she'd start to research all the people involved, living and dead. It could be hundreds of names. It would be a monumental task.

This was more difficult than finding a needle in a haystack, she thought. It was finding a needle in a whole farm's worth of haystacks.

And maybe the needle wasn't even there. Maybe it had never been there. June sighed. What on earth had made her hope she could figure out who the enemy was simply by looking at Teddy's notebooks?

She pushed down her own sense of hopelessness. It wouldn't help her, and it definitely wouldn't help Dinah. "We'll find them," she said. "We just keep digging."

Dinah said, "Would it help if you talked to your friend with the Chicago police?"

"Who, Fratelli? He's not my friend, Dinah. He wants my head on a platter."

June really hoped Peter and Lewis had better luck getting Maurice alone for a conversation.

44

Maurice stayed at the storefront church until after two p.m. The Heavy Lifters were still no closer to figuring out how to snatch him without getting either shot or arrested.

Like the rest of the crew, Peter had a wide-mouth Gatorade bottle to relieve his bladder and a sackful of gas station snacks, but he was craving a steak burrito and a very large cup of coffee. He'd never make it as Sam Spade at this rate.

His phone pinged, but the notification wasn't for the Hummer. "Hey, Lewis." They were back on the five-way call. "Looks like our FedEx package reappeared in Indy, then disappeared again."

"Where'd it go?"

"Nowhere," Peter said. "Both times, it was still at the mailbox store."

"It probably got thrown in a dumpster," Lewis said. "Or somebody found the tracker and stomped it."

Either way, Peter thought, the result was the same.

"Listen, I got an idea," Teddy said. "Why don't we take down one of those watcher cars and ask those boys some questions?"

"You just want to use your dart gun," Ray said.

"Well, yeah. But does that make it a bad idea?"

"Not to me," Nino said. "I'm tired of sitting on my ass."

Peter said, "You know they're in radio contact, right? Just like us. We hit that Highlander, the others will come running."

"Is that so wrong? C'mon," Teddy said, "it'll be fun."

"Take out the watchers, then go after Maurice?" Nino asked. "I've heard worse plans."

"Unless they're cops," Lewis said. "You swat one, a hundred more show up in a hurry real quick. Then we're all screwed." And so were Dinah, June, and the boys.

Maurice's blue dot began to blink, which meant the Hummer was in motion and ended the debate. After a minute, the watchers pulled out and the Heavy Lifters fell back into the rhythm of the four-car follow, orbiting the caravan, heads on a swivel.

Maurice turned west, switching from main drags to side streets and back again, always shifting north. But unlike earlier in the day, there were no stops, just a slow amble through the city with the three mystery watchers ranged around him. Peter thought they might be returning to the stone apartment building in Garfield Park, where they'd picked up the Hummer that morning.

"Hey, Jarhead," Ray asked. "How's your tingle?"

"Nothing right now." At the moment, Peter was the close follow, two blocks behind the Highlander. "If it comes back, I'll let you know."

As the blue dot passed Afro Joe's Coffee & Tea in Beverly, it paused at an intersection. Assuming Maurice had hit a traffic light, Peter took his foot off the gas and zoomed in on the map. After a moment, the blue dot appeared to simply reverse course. "Heads up," Peter said. "He's pulled a U-turn and is coming back our way."

"No sudden moves," Lewis said. "He's trying to flush us."

"Maybe he's got someplace special to go," Ray said.

"Or he just forgot to drop off his laundry," added Nino.

The yellow Hummer appeared in the opposite lane, headed toward him. Peter scratched his nose to hide his face as it powered past him at speed, two beefy tires over the center line. He saw Junior out of the corner of his eye, facing forward calmly like this day was no different from any other. The rear side windows were tinted dark, so Peter couldn't tell who might be eyeballing him. The Armada followed close behind, the shooter at the wheel focused on the Hummer.

Peter kept driving. A block later, he passed the Highlander with two hard-looking men in it. They didn't seem to notice him, either. In his rearview, he watched them disappear into traffic. He kept expecting the tingle to return, but it didn't. "Now what?"

But Maurice wasn't done with his evasive maneuvers. Behind Peter, the blue dot took an abrupt left to power down an alley, then cut right for two blocks, found another alley, and followed it. He gave the others the play-by-play. "Who's he trying to lose, us or the other guys?"

"Be interesting to find out," Lewis said. "Time to get after him again. But keep it loose."

The blue dot took another right onto Cicero. Peter imagined the big Hummer bouncing on its springs, suspension sinking on the turn. On the little screen, the dot seemed to accelerate. Peter's elderly Ford Taurus was no rocket, but how hard could it be to keep pace with a Hummer? He checked his rearview and hit the gas.

"Not too close," Lewis said. "We know where he is. We'll narrow the gap when he's done trying to lose us."

"Unless he swaps cars before we get there," Ray said.

"Risk we have to take," Lewis said. "Keep an eye on that GPS, Peter. If he stops, let us know."

"Roger that." The blue dot maintained course. "He's still headed north. Maybe he's done dodging." Peter turned to run parallel on Pulaski, maybe eight blocks east and a quarter mile behind.

But he couldn't stop checking his mirror. Something wasn't right. "Guys, I've got that feeling again. Anybody else?" They all said no.

"I can't pinpoint anybody. Either he's really good or I'm just paranoid. Is this worth chasing?"

"Even the paranoid have enemies," Lewis said. "If he's there, let's take him down."

"Hot dang," Teddy crowed.

Peter slowed and cut back over to Cicero, giving the others time to get set. He was a half mile behind the Hummer. The street was busy, but it was still early afternoon, ninety minutes before commuter traffic would clog things up. He still couldn't pick out his tail. He took his pistol from its holster again and held it between his legs. "Whenever you're ready."

"In position," Lewis said. "Go right at the light, nice and easy."

Peter made the move, checking his mirrors as he did, counting seven cars behind him, including Nino halfway back and Lewis at the tail end with Teddy in the shotgun seat. He locked the makes, models, and colors in his memory. The tingle was still there. "Anything?"

"Too soon," Lewis said. "Take the next left."

Peter turned again. He hadn't left the driver's seat since he'd picked up the Ford that morning, so he was confident there was no electronic surveillance. Which meant his tail would need to keep good eyes on him or Peter would disappear.

Of the seven cars behind him, four turned with him. Lewis and

Nino stayed in the mix, which meant three possibles. Unless there was more than one tail car, in which case they could be rotating the follow, just like the Heavy Lifters had been doing. Peter didn't like that idea.

"Go right," Lewis said. "Second light."

The zigzag route was still plausible as a shortcut. It wouldn't necessarily spook his follower. But it was also less likely that any of the drivers behind him would be taking the same route.

Peter made the right onto Pulaski and drove past a string of fast-food joints, where he lost one possible to McDonald's. Two remained, plus Nino and Lewis.

"Moment of truth," Lewis said. "Turn into this next lot and drive through to the far end."

It was a row of retail, anchored by a Jewel-Osco. The big parking lot was half full. He eased into the turn and coasted forward. Only one of the cars turned in behind him. He dropped the window, made sure the doors were unlocked, and took the pistol in his left hand.

In the rearview, he saw the first car stop in a loading zone at the pharmacy entrance, with Nino directly behind it. Nino said, "We got a girl with a kid. I don't think they're bad guys."

"What about the second car?"

Ray had been hanging back. "It kept going. Driver didn't even look at you."

Peter cranked the wheel and tucked the Ford into a thicket of parked cars. The tingle was gone. "So much for that."

"Where's the Hummer?" Lewis asked.

Peter looked at his phone. "Still headed north on Cicero. More than a mile out."

Lewis pulled up behind him. "Well, let's go get the man."

45

They gunned back to Cicero, rolling north in a hurry, Lewis in the lead, while Peter kept one eye on his phone. "We're gaining on him."

They were a half mile back when the blue dot diverted to Irving Park Road and got on 90/94 westbound. They had to drive aggressively to catch up, occasionally passing slower cars in the breakdown lane, but this wasn't uncommon on Chicago-area freeways, so they didn't stand out too badly. The dot stayed with 90 at the interchange, and Peter did the play-by-play through the transfer to 190. "That's the spur for O'Hare."

They saw the big yellow Hummer up ahead as it slowed for the three-lane tollgate, the bulk of the huge airport rising on the other side. The Armada was on its bumper, and the three mystery followers were spaced out around them.

"If he's getting on a plane, we're screwed," Nino grumbled. "There will be cops at departures for sure, and too much traffic for a quick exit."

But Maurice didn't go to departures. Instead, the whole rolling carnival got off at Mannheim Road with a dozen other cars.

"Hang back," Lewis said, so they eased up and let some traffic get between them as the Hummer and its followers pulled ahead. They all took the very next exit, marked RENTAL RETURNS and ECONOMY PARKING LOT F, which turned out to be a large five-story structure. It was also the start of the elevated airport train that carried travelers from the external parking lots to the five O'Hare terminals.

They didn't have much time to decide. Mannheim was a divided four-lane, so they couldn't just make a U-turn. Ray asked, "Is there another entrance to this place?"

"Yeah, up ahead," Lewis said. "Nino, you're the only guy they haven't seen, so you follow them inside. With those spiral access ramps, you're going to have to stay right on that Armada to see what floor they're on. Keep a visual and talk us through it. Everybody else, the next right will take us to another entrance to the complex. Once Nino tells us the floor, we head up."

"Are we going to take him?" Teddy sounded eager.

"If the mystery followers peel off, we just might. Or if Maurice and his boys head towards the terminal train. They won't take weapons into the airport proper."

"I've got the Armada," Nino said. "It's already on the ramp. But I don't see our followers. They might have gone into the rental car return. Do you see them on your side?"

"Just getting there now." Lewis was still ahead of Peter and Ray. They'd all accelerated hard to get to the next turnoff on the far side of the structure. "I don't see them, either. Doesn't look like there's ramp access here. You have to take a feeder road past the train station and loop back around to where we came in. There's also a small surface lot on the right."

Peter was ten car lengths back with a map open on his phone. The parking complex was a crowded maze of tangled one-ways, a surveillance nightmare. "Lewis, you follow the feeder all the way around. I'll come behind you and hang at the station." He glanced at his rearview to see Ray make the turn from the street. "Ray, can you check the lot?"

"On it," Ray said.

"I'm climbing the ramp," Nino said. The sound of squealing tires came through the connection. "I can see the Hummer. They're getting off on level four."

"I just passed the Kia," Lewis said. "It's in the left lane, waiting by the station entrance."

Ray said, "I've got the Highlander. He's in a handicapped spot, with line of sight to the entrance and exit. I'm going to park like I'm waiting for someone to come out of the train station."

"I see the Cruze," Lewis said. "He's ahead of me, pulled to the side of the road, watching the exit on this side. I'm going to have to pass him and loop back."

"This is a mess," Peter said. "We need more cars." He came to the station and coasted past the Kia without looking at it. At the end of the drop-off area, there was a turnaround that would let him double back to the station. As he took it, his phone pinged.

The tracker app was telling him the Hummer had vanished. "The parking garage is screwing with the GPS signal. Nino, do you have eyes on?"

"I got him," Nino said. "They're stopped in the middle of the aisle, guys getting out of both cars. But they're on the east side, away from the train station. So I don't know what the hell they're doing."

"I'm thirty seconds from the ramp," Lewis said. "Should I come up?"

"I don't know," Nino said. "The big guy went to a parked car and got in. But the Hummer and Armada are still in the middle of the aisle. I don't see any suitcases."

Peter asked, "Are there any open spots nearby?"

"None I can see," Nino said. "This floor is packed. Okay, now he's backing out. It's a silver Chrysler 300."

Peter said, "I think Ray was right earlier. They're not getting on a plane, they're changing vehicles."

Nino groaned. "Surveillance evasion part two. Yep, now Maurice is getting into the Chrysler with the big guy, and the Hummer's going back into that same spot. And it looks like the two shooters are trading the Armada for a tan Tahoe."

"Wherever he's going," Ray said, "he really doesn't want company."

"That's the genius of the yellow Hummer," Lewis said. "It's so obvious that you can't imagine Philly Maurice in anything else. Without it, he's invisible."

"I think we have to let this play out," Peter said. "See where he goes now that he thinks he's clean."

"I agree," Lewis said.

"Me too," Teddy said sadly.

"No GPS," Peter said. "It won't be easy."

"Speak for yourself," Nino said. "We did this work for years without all that fancy tech."

Maurice and his people headed down the spiral ramp on the far side of the structure. Nino reported that Junior was driving the Chrysler with Maurice visible in the passenger seat. All three shooters had relocated to the Tahoe.

The Cruze must have seen Maurice, too, because the Highlander left the parking lot for the feeder road in a hurry, passing Peter at the train station. The Kia rolled out after it. Lewis, who'd been dawdling by the rental car drop-off, was a hundred yards behind. "They've had a good look at each of us now," he said. "Time to up our game."

The Chrysler got back on Mannheim Road, pulling its tail along behind it, merging onto I-90 east, and returning the way it'd come, heading deeper into the city.

It wasn't yet dark, but the freeway was clogged with traffic. The mystery followers were very good, Peter had to admit. Even in rush hour, they were always in motion around the Chrysler, pulling ahead, falling back. Slightly outside their orbit, the Heavy Lifters were doing the same thing. It was much more difficult without the GPS, and the silver sedan was a lot harder to see from a distance than the big yellow Hummer. Which was the whole point of Maurice swapping cars, of course. The tan Tahoe was tall enough to stand above most of the traffic, which helped.

"Maybe the other guys are feds," Nino said. "ATF or something. They think Maurice is doing a deal tonight and they're going to roll him up."

"Bad luck for us if they do," Lewis said. "We really need that little chat."

Behind the Chrysler, the Tahoe flashed its lights and eased through the traffic toward the far right lane. A half mile later, it took the exit for Irving Park Road. The Chrysler powered on alone.

"I have a question." Peter was still thinking about the tingle. "There were four of us behind Maurice on our way to the airport, right? So why did the guy keep picking me to follow?"

"When we find him," Ray said, "we'll ask him."

"Unless he was a figment of your imagination," Nino said.

But Peter knew the guy was real. And still back there somewhere, even if Peter couldn't feel it.

A few miles later, Maurice got off at Kimball and headed south into Avondale. The mystery followers had plenty of time to get behind him, and so did Peter and the others.

On the surface streets, rush hour was even worse. The slower speed and frequent traffic lights added to the challenge, making it more difficult to rotate positions in the heavy flow.

Another problem was that Junior turned out to be a very good driver, now that he didn't have to keep the shooters in tow. He had an eye for reading the traffic, finding the hole and slipping through, somehow always moving ahead faster than everyone else. The Chrysler was a big, heavy sedan, but it must have seemed like a sports car compared to the Hummer.

So it wasn't too surprising when Junior punched the gas and flew through a yellow as it turned red, leaving his close follow, the Highlander, stuck on the bumper of a stopped delivery truck, and Peter three cars behind it. "Ray, he's loose."

"I've got him." Ray was already on the next block.

"Stay close," Lewis said. "He's slick."

The Cruze was also stuck, one car up in the left lane. "Junior's dropped two followers. Anybody have the Kia?"

"Behind you, four cars back," Lewis said.

"Wait," Peter said. "He lost *all* of them?" Something didn't smell right. "How did Junior lose all three? They're better than that. Even in this traffic, they should have had a car in front of him."

"We can't all have my level of natural talent," Nino said. He was on a side street, leapfrogging ahead.

The light turned green. The delivery truck was slow to get moving. Peter found a hole in the right-turn lane and goosed it through the intersection, passing the Highlander and leaving the Cruze behind. Why weren't *they* making these moves?

Then he felt the faint tingle return to the back of his neck. And he knew.

"It's a setup," he said. "They're drawing us in. Clearing the path to Maurice. And when we try to take him, they'll hit us. All at the same time."

There was silence over the phone line.

"Motherfucker." Lewis's tilted grin came through his voice. "The jarhead do earn his keep, don't he?"

"Finally!" Teddy shouted. "Do I get to use my dart gun?"

46

I t had taken some negotiation, Streyling thought, to get Philly Maurice to agree to serve as bait for the Ghost Killers. It wasn't enough that his employer had connected Maurice to her sales contacts in China several years before. But then, Streyling had offered up some buyers in Africa. Revolutionaries. High-volume sales, and outside U.S. jurisdiction. Maurice wouldn't be just a gun dealer anymore. He'd be an international arms dealer.

Now Streyling sat in the faded red Explorer, his windows down and engine off, tucked into a doorless garage three blocks from the Keeler Avenue house.

He had the Ghost Killer laptop out again, chasing down the details in the password manager. All the accounts seemed to be in the wife's name. Two different credit cards, two local bank accounts, with only a couple grand in each. He'd spent hours looking at transactions going back at least a year, but none of them showed any activity that added useful information.

The energy bill was in her name, too, along with the internet and various streaming services. At the bottom of the alphabetical list, he found an account for her cellular service. Because the wife probably didn't want to spend her life using a cheap disposable phone. When he logged in, however, he found not one phone number, but three. If the Ghost Killers didn't show tonight, that intel was worth a follow-up.

His guys had seen a few vehicles earlier in the night, but there'd been nothing notable for hours. It was almost four thirty in the morning and colder than a Norwegian's idea of hell. The forecast called for more snow. He checked his watch. Three more minutes until the next radio check-in.

Deployment was a tactical decision, so he'd let the unit leader make that call. Four men were close and in concealed positions, two on the street and two in the alley. Many of the buildings in the area had been torn down, including the houses on either side of Maurice's, leaving good sight lines and few remaining residents to report suspicious activity, which was helpful. The remaining two men were circling like sharks in a vehicle the Ghost Killers had never seen, a beater Caprice that Maurice had dug up somewhere. Maurice's gun monkeys were in a stolen Kia a dozen blocks away, just in case. The streets were empty, which would make the Ghost Killers easy to spot.

Streyling had worked with this unit before, and the guys were very capable. They would do the heavy work, put the targets in cuffs if possible, and Streyling would come in at the end. One of the team was a decent field medic, so he could patch up any nonlethal injuries. If any of the Ghost Killers were mortally wounded, Streyling would get his employer on a video call so she could tell the man why he was dying, and watch it happen in real time. Then she'd fly in and do the honors with the survivors herself.

Still, having seen firsthand what the Ghost Killers could do, he would have liked more guys. Budget wasn't the problem, it was manpower. His employer ran a lean, highly mobile operation. Her nineman personal team traveled with her everywhere, but she would never put her own security at risk by putting them in the field. Because she needed a kill team only once or twice a year, she used a small private military contractor that ran two black units. The first had been wiped out in Milwaukee. The second was set up around the Keeler house now. Apparently, the contractor had only so many people who'd kill a man for a paycheck and cover it up with no questions asked.

Streyling still didn't understand why it was so hard to find trained mercenaries. The hazard pay and survivor benefits were excellent. Unfortunately, in his experience, ex-military were mostly overgrown Boy Scouts who wanted to be reassured they were working for the right side.

As if there were such a thing, Streyling thought. As if their previous career in government service hadn't made that abundantly clear.

There was only one side. Your own.

The Boy Scouts would learn that, eventually.

Stifling a yawn, Streyling closed the laptop and slouched deeper into the cracked plastic seat. The fourth can of energy drink tasted like industrial waste, and his back ached from sitting in the car all day and night. He'd been certain the Ghost Killers would have come long before now. Had he misjudged them?

"This is One." The unit leader's voice was quiet in the darkness. "Status check." He was a former Ranger with a drinking problem, a common occupational hazard. As far as Streyling had determined, it had never interfered with his work.

"This is Two, clear here."

Somebody softly cleared his throat. "Three, all good."

"This is Four. Colder'n hell." He was a wiseass from Alabama who liked to run his mouth.

"Five and Six, nice and toasty." The mobile team in the heated Caprice.

"Screw you, Barry."

"Shut it, both of you," One said. "Next check in fifteen. Otherwise stay off comms unless you see something."

They all sounded as tired as Streyling felt. Earlier in the night, they'd been switched on and ready to go. But they'd been working long hours, had slept in shifts in their cars the night before. It took a toll. You could burn the candle for only so long. Maurice had finally stopped texting for updates. There were enough radios for only Streyling and the six-man unit. Maurice's gun monkeys were supposed to be standing by their phones, but they were probably snoring in their stolen Kia, if they hadn't just given up and gone home.

In his ear, Streyling heard a quick burst of static, or what he thought might be static, then a shout, then a kind of mumble. Then silence.

"This is One. Say again, I repeat, say again."

No response.

Streyling straightened up and pulled a short-barreled AR onto his lap as the Ranger said, "Check in, people."

"Two, clear."

"Three, clear."

"Four, clear."

Silence.

"Five, Six. Status check." More silence. "Crap. Hold position. They're coming."

Streyling told himself that he'd expected some losses. He picked up his phone and texted an update to Maurice, Junior, and the gun monkeys.

Five minutes passed. Ten minutes. The wind blew cold through his open window. Streyling strained to hear over the sound of his own heartbeat. Along with the rifle on his lap, he had a fresh Glock on the passenger seat and extra mags for both weapons, all courtesy of Maurice.

Fifteen minutes now. He really needed to piss.

Over the radio came a cluster of soft pops, followed by a grunt. Someone said, "What the hell?"

"Talk to me, people." The leader's voice was low and calm.

"This is Two. I got nothing."

"Three. Same. Who the hell are these guys?"

Four was silent. He'd been set up behind a cluster of garbage cans beside the concrete stoop at the front of an abandoned house, across the street and two doors down from Maurice.

"Four? Deon, report."

Streyling heard a rustle of cloth, the scrape of a boot. Then another group of faint pops. "You have got to be kidding me." The Ranger, at normal volume, sounding annoyed. Then a hard thud as something hit the man's earpiece, or the earpiece hit the ground. He was three doors down in the other direction.

"This is Two. One, status check. Repeat, status check."

No answer. Two's position was in the shadow between a garage and a side fence directly behind the house, with a view of the backyard and the alley. Streyling could hear the man hyperventilating over the radio.

"Three, status check."

Three was inside a ruined shed on the far side of the alley, with a view up and down the lane. "Man, we are screwed." He was from Brooklyn and sounded it. "We gotta get outta here." They both knew they were next.

"Good idea." A new voice came over the radio, liquid and dark and intimate in their ears. "You walk away, you live. You got my word on that. Otherwise you'll get a triple-tap up the tailpipe, and that's a real bad way to die."

Streyling felt the adrenaline hit like he'd just mainlined cocaine. A primitive response. Something about that voice, the Ghost Killer speaking right in his ear. He hadn't been prepared. His heart clattered in his chest. He told himself not to be afraid. The voice didn't know where he was. They'd never seen him, he'd made certain of that.

Obviously Two felt the same way, because he gave a little yelp, then swore.

Three said, "Whaddaya think, Jamal?"

"Hell, I don't know."

"Tick tock," said the dark voice. "Live or die, up to you."

"Screw it, I'm coming out," Three said.

"Wait for me, we'll go together." Footsteps crunched in the snow.

Then came two sets of soft pops in rapid succession. Unlike the others, neither man spoke a word. There was just a single rough cough and a long gurgle that faded, slowly, to silence.

The dark voice spoke again. "I know there's somebody else on this channel. A blond beanpole likes to use a rocket launcher, be my guess. I can hear you breathing, motherfucker. Enjoy that while you can. Because I am your enemy, and I am coming."

Streyling's heart rate spiked again, making him clumsy as he fumbled with his radio. He finally managed to turn off the mic, then started up the Explorer and inched out of the garage, careful to keep the engine noise down as he got the hell away from that place. Maurice's life wasn't worth Streyling's own. Nobody's was.

After three city blocks, he came to the Caprice, still in drive, one front tire nudging gently against the curb. The passenger window was shattered. But there was nobody inside. There weren't even any bullet holes in the car. It was like the two men had vanished into thin air.

Attempting to regain control over his breathing, Streyling reminded himself that the Ghost Killers still had no idea where he was. They definitely didn't know his real name. Even Maurice didn't know his real name. Which was a good thing, because soon enough Maurice would tell them anything they wanted to know. Although Maurice didn't know much about Streyling's employer, either, certainly not enough to help them actually find her.

The Ghost Killers would keep hunting, though, he was certain of that. Was taking them down even possible, given their capabilities? Streyling had already tried twice, and the second time the Ghost Killers had taken out his entire unit. His guys hadn't fired a single shot.

But his employer wouldn't relent, either. Her resources were essentially endless. She would keep sending him after them. Streyling's death seemed inevitable.

He remembered the dark voice's advice over the radio. *Walk away and live.* Now would be a good time, he thought. Although, without his finder's fee, he didn't have anywhere near enough funds to make that work. He'd have to disappear into the third world, completely off-grid. Not Costa Rica, either. He'd end up in a hut on the beach in East Africa. And he'd need plastic surgery.

His employer would be livid. It would be a double betrayal, his failure followed by his defection. She'd move heaven and earth to find him. Spare no expense. He knew what happened when things got personal for her. A hut on the Bone Coast wasn't remote enough. He thought of the videos, and his heart thudded louder in his chest.

Then he had an epiphany. Suddenly, the opportunity he had sensed several days earlier became clear as day. If he could engineer the right circumstances, all manner of interesting things might happen.

His missing finder's fee was only a fraction of what she'd taken from the Ghost Killers. Not to mention what she had in her own coffers, thanks largely to Streyling's uncompensated efforts. What if he could harvest it all?

His heartbeat began to slow as he considered the possibilities.

47

PETER

They'd started with Maurice's shooters, napping in their idling car in a McDonald's parking lot, surrounded by a faint aura of pot smoke. Lewis shook his head at the lack of discipline. Definitely not a fair fight.

Next came the two men in the Caprice, who were running a perimeter route around Maurice's place. The men probably thought their path was random, but it wasn't, because they were apparently trying to stay between three and five blocks out. So over eight hours, they ended up slow-driving the same streets, over and over.

The most challenging part for Peter was timing the move from behind the four-door pickup. His job was to break out the passenger-side window with a brick so Teddy could open up with Hiram's dart gun, gripping the barrel with his gauze-wrapped hand. The darts didn't have the power to penetrate the glass and still do their job the way a bullet did.

The blunderbuss had three fire settings, just like a combat rifle.

Single-shot, a pattern of five, and the whole fifteen. For the stoned shooters, a single shot each was enough. For the two guys in the Caprice, even with their body armor, five darts did the trick. All they needed was one injection point in the arm or neck or thigh. The stuff worked so fast, the targets barely had time to wonder what happened before they were out.

Neither of them was the blond beanpole who'd put two RPG rounds into Lewis and Dinah's house. Somehow Peter didn't think the beanpole was the kind to lead from the front.

So Peter had removed their radios and earpieces, dragged the men from the car, zip-tied their wrists and legs, and dropped them into the trunk to sleep it off. They were dressed for the weather. Spooned together like lovers, they'd be fine for a few hours.

The four solo sentinels were more difficult, because they knew what was coming. But Lewis had tipped the scale in the crew's favor by letting his guys take a nice long nap, waiting until almost five in the morning to take action. Despite the other side's evident training, the long night and intense cold diminished their focus and slowed their reaction time. For the next two sentinels, Lewis and Ray got a chance to fire the dart gun. Teddy had taken out the last two with a pair of quick five-dart salvos, as Peter and Nino provided backup with their own pistols. None of these were the blond beanpole, either.

Peter was glad Teddy had found that bag of spare darts at Hiram's place. They'd needed to be quick and quiet. He really didn't want to get into a rolling gunfight in a residential neighborhood. He'd seen more than enough civilian casualties overseas.

Plus if Maurice wasn't feeling talkative, Peter wanted to be able to ask the operators a few questions. Like, who they were working for, and what the Heavy Lifters had done to earn this kind of attention.

Nino had argued for killing them after getting some answers. "Leaving them alive will only make it harder for us next time."

"That ain't us," Lewis said.

Nino had just shaken his head as if he'd known in advance how that conversation would end.

Which left the house itself, with Junior and Maurice locked inside. But that was a whole separate set of challenges.

Because twelve hours earlier, Ray had followed the silver Chrysler to the curb out front. Junior got out with his pistol in his hand, eyeballing the neighbors, while Maurice bent to embrace two little girls who'd sprinted from the front stoop under the watchful eye of a plump woman in a turquoise tracksuit.

"Oh, shit," Ray said. "Looks like Philly Maurice got himself a baby momma."

For Peter, this was not a welcome development. "What kind of leverage would these people have to get the man to put his family at risk?"

"Money," Lewis replied. "Money always comes first for men like Maurice."

"Did they think it would make the target more attractive to us?"

"No," Lewis said. "More vulnerable."

"Well, we can't shoot our way in now," Ray said.

"Absolutely not," Peter said.

Lewis said, "Leave it to me."

The house was a long, narrow rectangle, two stories tall. The outside was bright with floodlights, but the interior was dark. Peter stood to the right of the front door, with Lewis on the left. Nino and Ray guarded the back. Teddy was waiting in the four-door pickup with the engine running.

Lewis held one of the phones he'd taken from the shooters in the Kia. He'd used their sleeping faces or fingers to unlock them, then changed the passwords so he could get back in easily.

Junior's number was easy to find. Lewis had typed out the text in advance. "This is Lewis. You're the only man still standing between me and Maurice. If you want to live, step out front, slow and easy."

After a moment, the door opened slowly and soundlessly. Junior stood in the gap, looking at Lewis, then stepped through and eased the door shut behind him. He wore a black sweatshirt with something heavy in the kangaroo pocket. He looked even larger at that atavistic hour.

Peter didn't even see Lewis move, but suddenly he had a gun to the big man's chest, finger tight on the trigger. "Hands, Junior."

The big man tensed, but his hands didn't rise.

"I don't want little Brenda to lose her daddy." Lewis's voice was soft. "That's a hurt no child deserves."

Junior turned to look at Peter, then regarded the two men crumpled in the snow across the street.

"If you looking for help, ain't nobody left," Lewis said. "'Cept that tall, skinny white man who set this whole thing up, and he's in the wind."

"How do you know 'bout him?"

"He sent a bunch of shooters to my house when my family was there."

Junior nodded, his face impassive. "Sounds about right." With a slow, careful thumb and forefinger, he reached inside his sweatshirt pocket and removed a plain black pistol. Peter took it from his hand. It was a workman's tool, simple and reliable. Junior never took his eyes off Lewis. "You best be a man of your word."

Lewis put his own gun away. "I got no beef with you. I just want Maurice and that white man."

"Far as I know, Maurice's upstairs with a gun in his hand. You know there's kids up in there, right?"

Lewis nodded. "We're not animals. We won't harm a child." Then he smiled, teeth bright in his dark face. "Can't make no promises about Philly Maurice, though. What happens inside is up to him."

The big man sighed. "Okay, what I gotta do?"

"Nothing," Lewis said. "I'm just gonna zip-tie you and tape your mouth."

"If you don't plan on killing Maurice, you better shoot me, too. I mean for real, someplace good. If I ain't bleeding bad, Maurice'll smoke me himself."

Lewis frowned. "He expect you to die for him?"

"He expect me to *protect* him," Junior said. "'Cause I said I would. Dyin' just what happen if I don't do my job."

"Then why are you out here with us?" Peter asked.

"Maurice put those little girls at risk," Junior said. "The man don't care 'bout nothing or nobody but himself. I knew it before, but it ain't the same as seeing it like this."

Peter said, "What if he dies tonight? You take over?"

Junior shook his head. "I ain't got the stomach for it. But unless you're real sure about killing Maurice, you better shoot me anyway."

"I got something less permanent." Lewis showed him a tranquilizer dart. They had only two left. "But before I stick you, I got questions."

Junior eyed the slim cylinder with the needle on one end and the red puffball on the other. "Fire away."

"That tall, skinny white man. Can you give me a name, anything about him?"

"Jason Langley. He met Maurice at Garvey's, the same night as you. He works for some big shot, that's all I got. But Maurice will know."

Lewis nodded. "Okay. Now, what's the layout inside?"

48

I t took their last two darts to knock Junior out, and Peter and Lewis working together to ease the big man's bulk down to the cement stoop. Then Lewis eased the door open and slipped into the darkness. Peter followed and pulled the door shut behind him, although not as silently as he would have liked.

The interior was just as Junior had described. They crept through the front room, boots soft on a Persian rug, and into the dining room with dark wood furniture and a large oil painting of Mother Mary with the Christ child in her arms. Ahead was a large white kitchen that gleamed in the night glow of the city. To the side, stairs led up to the second floor and down to the basement.

Junior had described the upstairs, too. The large back bedroom where Maurice sometimes stayed with the woman, the two bathrooms, the front bedroom for the twins. He'd also told them that Tonya, the woman, wasn't much to look at, but a real good cook. The whole building had been gutted and rebuilt, so the house would be warm and the floors wouldn't squeak. Only the stairs were original, steep and winding, with a gracefully curved rail polished smooth by generations of human hands.

They were nearing the bottom when a hoarse voice floated down the stairwell. "Junior, that you?"

Peter ducked back around to approach from the kitchen, and Lewis sidestepped behind the concealment of the dining room wall, then poked his head around the corner. "You best come down here, Maurice."

"Shit," Maurice muttered. "Junior gave me up." Then, louder, "You want me, you gonna have to come get me."

The Heavy Lifters were still on the five-way call, so the other guys could hear Peter and Lewis, and maybe some of Maurice. "Junior's down for the count," Lewis said. "We just want to talk. Don't nobody else have to get hurt."

The response was a long volley of automatic weapons fire down the stairs. The noise was deafening. Peter ducked behind the fridge, hoping for cover. The floorboards splintered and the drywall puffed dust with every impact. Maurice couldn't have seen them, so he must have leaned over the top and sprayed until the magazine was empty. If the woman and children had been sleeping before, they weren't now.

When the gun went dry, Lewis said, "You really want a gunfight with your family up there?" Telling the rest of the crew that they were unhurt.

"What choice I got?"

Peter was just glad it wasn't a grenade. He leaned into the dining room and made a rolling motion with his finger, telling Lewis to keep Maurice talking. Lewis nodded and Peter hustled past the massive marble-topped kitchen island and looped back toward the line of stairs on the opposite wall. If he could get a sense of where Maurice was from his voice, he might somehow take the man down while Lewis distracted him.

They needed him alive. They'd used the last of Teddy's darts. Even if they hadn't, the weapon wouldn't shoot through walls. Maurice's assault rifle didn't have that limitation.

But Lewis had obviously already considered that. "Hell, Maurice, we can talk right like this. Some people coming after me, I just want to know who they are. Let's start with that narrow-ass motherfucker you sold that rocket launcher to. Jason Langley, right? Who's he work for?"

"You don't know nothing, do you, boy? Langley ain't even his real name. I knew you weren't what he said. You're just a low-rent thief."

"Yet here I am, Maurice. Up in your house with my crew. Your soldiers are down, every last one of them, and that Langley dude up and ran away. So whatever payday he promised you, it ain't coming. But I can offer you something. Your life. Just tell me what I need to know and we're gone."

"My life?" Maurice gave a bitter laugh. "If I give you what I know, my life ain't worth a damn thing. She'll cut me up like a side of beef."

She? Lewis and Peter looked at each other. Peter let his rifle hang from its sling and took out his phone to text June. Despite the hour, he knew she'd be awake and worried. *All good here. Any women on your bad-guy list?*

June must have had the phone in her hand, because she replied immediately. *Lotta widows and orphans. You need to be more specific.*

Peter gave up on the stealth approach. He called out, "This woman. Why does she want the Ghost Killers so badly?"

Maurice sighed. "I heard they killed her son. Boy was like twelve or something."

Lewis grunted as if he'd been stabbed in the gut. "I remember," he said. "New Jersey, nine or ten years ago. The father was a mobster. But who's the mother? I never heard of her."

Maurice didn't answer.

Peter texted June. *Try Jersey. A child was killed.* He imagined her at the laptop, fingers flying. A dead child made a pretty good motive. And maybe the woman had been more than a wife and mother. Maybe she'd been the brains behind the husband. And smart enough to stay off the radar.

It took less than a minute for June to reply.

Peter looked at the name, but it didn't mean anything to him. Then he looked at Lewis, but pitched his voice to carry up the stairs. "Mallory Kane."

Silence. Then Maurice said, "I'm dead. We're all dead."

"Don't have to go that way," Lewis replied. "She won't hurt nobody when I'm done with her. You can help."

"Are you kidding? You have no idea what she is, the resources she's got."

"Tell me," Lewis said. "Start with Langley. What's his real name?"

The sigh filtered down from the second floor. "Streyling. Jay Streyling. Used to be CIA. My lawyer's investigator ran his prints and found a bent Army major with an Agency connect who let him glance at the man's file. Dude was on the ground in three separate revolutions, was gonna get busted for selling information to both sides in two of them. That'll tell you something about who she's got on her payroll."

As he texted the information to June, Peter said, "We'll need you to reach out to him."

Maurice snorted. "If his guys are down, he's long gone and his phone's in pieces. He's real good at looking after himself."

"The woman, then. Kane. Where do we find her?"

The old steps creaked above them. Maurice shifting his weight, or maybe moving closer. Behind it, Peter heard the soft sound of a woman sobbing.

"You think I got her home address? Woman barely knew I existed when this thing started. If she wanted something, I heard from Streyling. He always had a fresh video of some dude who crossed her getting cut up with a machete. Not pretty. Now the same thing gonna happen to me."

Again the creak of old wood. Peter put his phone away and readied his rifle, his finger on the trigger. He was standing on a striped cotton area rug. He swiped it against the wall with his boot so he didn't slip.

Maurice kept talking. "All I can say is, she washes money, facilitates deals, trades favors. She got me a connect to a Chinaman runs a gun factory in Qingdao, let me start selling volume. Cost me a shipping container full of RPGs sent to Manzanillo, prob'ly get used against the Mexican Army and the DEA. God only knows what she gets done for the real heavy hitters."

Another creak, softer this time. The sobbing continued. Peter didn't want to imagine the woman upstairs, holding tight to her girls, praying her heart out.

He peeked around the corner and saw bony brown feet and ankles at the wall side of the stair, where the frame was least likely to make noise. One foot reached down for the next tread. Two more steps and Maurice could kneel and get a good angle to empty his rifle into the first floor.

Peter looked at Lewis and pointed at the stairway.

Lewis nodded. His rifle was already at his shoulder. "Let me ask you something, Maurice. If I left this house right now, would you come after me?"

"You kidding? I'd take my family and run like hell."

Lewis made a sour face. Peter was thinking the same thing. Philly

Maurice wouldn't be coming down the stairs if that was his plan. Men like him didn't make it up the food chain by running away.

The bare feet took another step. Above the ankles were dark purple pajamas. Peter saw the barrel of an automatic rifle, the iron sight like a fang at the end.

Enough. Peter scooped up the area rug. It was maybe four by six.

The purple knees bent as Maurice began another careful step. The iron sight began to rise and seek. Immediately, Peter flung the rug at Maurice's ankles as if fishing with a net. Maurice's upper foot tangled. The lower foot landed on the rug and slid out from under him. He began to fall backward. The rifle slewed sideways as he tried to catch himself.

Peter leaped forward and grabbed the hot barrel and tore the weapon from Maurice's grasp, then quickly reversed it and slammed the butt into the older man's belly. When Maurice curled reflexively around his stomach, Peter grabbed an ankle and pulled him thumping down the rest of the stairs. All dignity gone, but alive.

Lewis was there with his gun pointed at Maurice's face. "Now let's have this conversation again, Maurice. If I let you live, you won't go thinking I'm weak, right?"

The older man didn't answer. His face was stony and cold, almost as if he were already dead. Probably the right attitude when you were an arms dealer, Peter thought. Maurice had lasted a lot longer than most in his profession.

"Okay, let's review," Lewis said. "I got all your soldiers down for the count. Not dead, mind you, but out cold. I got your family upstairs, your woman and two little girls. I can wipe you out, Maurice, every person you know and love. Like you never even existed. Burn this fine house to the ground. That what you want?"

"You know it ain't," Maurice said. "What I gotta do?"

"I want your word you're not gonna carry a beef over this," Lewis said. "You don't come looking for me, you don't send somebody else after me, you don't even think about me. You forget I exist. Because I just proved that I can take you out any time I want. But it don't got to be that way. Far as I'm concerned, you told me what I needed to know, so in my mind, we're good." He flashed that tilted smile. "So let me ask you. Are we good, Maurice? I got your word on that?"

Maurice made a face like he'd just licked a lemon. "Long as I don't have to like it. But I guess you do got my word. No beef from me or my people."

"And your word is good, Maurice?"

Maurice nodded and let out a long, slow breath. "You know it is, youngblood. Else I'd have been dead long ago."

"One more thing," Peter said. "Give us your phone. You've been talking to Streyling on it, right? Maybe we can use it to find him."

Maurice reached into the purple pajamas and pulled out a cheap phone. "Passcode's the address of this house." Then he glanced at the screen. "Shee-it." He handed it to Peter.

The screen showed a pair of texts with no name attached.

The first was just a phone number, with an area code Peter didn't recognize.

The second was a single sentence.

Lewis, we need to talk.

49

I t could only be Streyling, Peter thought. "Are you going to call him?"

In response, Lewis pulled out his own phone and disconnected himself from the five-way call. Then he plugged in the new number and put it on speaker.

It rang more than a dozen times with strange pauses along the way that told Peter the call was being bounced across the world a half-dozen times. Finally, someone answered. "Yes."

"Is this Jason Langley? Or should I say Jay Streyling, formerly of the CIA?"

There was a pause on the other end of the connection, maybe Streyling processing that they actually knew his real name. Then he cleared his throat. "You must be Lewis. I appreciate the call after everything between us." The voice was educated, with a slight New England accent.

"Everything between us? You make it sound like you didn't try to kill my wife and children."

"Unfortunately, my employer was quite insistent on that point," Streyling said. "But perhaps we can put that behind us. I have a proposal for you."

Lewis laughed, low and dark and without humor. "You got some balls, I'll give you that. Maurice was very talkative. Now I know who you are, and your boss. Mallory Kane."

"But you don't know *where* she is," Streyling said. "Nobody does, by design. She has her own jet and rotates between several dozen luxury properties located all over the world. None of them in her name, of course. But I can put you in a room with her in three days' time."

Lewis looked at Peter. "Interesting. And what would you want for this information?"

"First," Streyling said, "a finder's fee, twenty percent of your take. Second, my life, guaranteed free and clear of any future threat from you or your people. And third, Mallory Kane's death. If she remains alive, she will never stop looking for either of us."

As if Streyling viewed himself as a victim, Peter thought.

"Number three's easy," Lewis said. "For that finder's fee, you're gonna have to tell me where she is before I can deliver. What makes you think I'll live up to my end?"

"I read some of the notebooks," Streyling said. "Your friend seems to think you're a man of some integrity. Under other circumstances, I believe you and I would get along very well."

"Unlikely," Lewis said. "Right now, the idea of not killing you might be a deal-breaker. But I'll think on it."

"Don't think too long," Streyling said. "The window of opportunity is small and you'll need time to get to the location and prepare. If you miss Mallory now, you'll lose her for good. Also I should mention one other point. When she learns what happened this morning, that a second team has been lost, she will be deeply upset. The only men available to her now are her own bodyguards, who stay with her wherever she goes. But she will never stop hunting you."

"How will she hunt me if she's run out of men?"

"Mallory is deeply connected in the criminal world. She brokers favors, makes introductions. Once she realizes the depth of my failure this morning, and how it limits her options, she will distribute your notebooks to her contacts. Because of your past accomplishments, there will be a dozen interested parties, all competing for the privilege of killing you and your people. She won't even need to offer a fee."

"But who's gonna tell her about this morning's loss?"

"I will," Streyling said. "Because she already knew we were making another run at you. And she would learn the truth anyway. She has eyes and ears everywhere."

"How do I know you're not playing me," Lewis said. "Delivering me to her instead of the other way around."

"Obviously, I'm doing both," Streyling said. "But you will know in advance, and she will not. Whether you survive the encounter will be up to you. Also, because of my failures in the last few days, she'll include my name with yours when she distributes the notebooks. We need each other, Lewis. You're the only one who can take down Mallory Kane. I'm the only one who can put her in your hands."

Lewis rubbed his jaw. "How do I reach you?"

"Same number. But remember, the window is closing." Then Streyling was gone.

Lewis put the phone away and looked at Peter. "What do you think?"

"I think we need to get the hell out of here."

Lewis nodded and took a pair of flex-cuffs from his pocket. "Give me your hands, Maurice. To keep you from doing something you'll regret. Your sweetheart can cut you free once we're gone."

—————

On the front stoop, Peter said, "I can't believe you let him live."

Lewis frowned. "Me neither. I just hope I don't regret it."

They walked down to the street, where Nino and Ray stood watch by the four-door pickup, their breath steaming in the cold. It was just before six. But dawn wouldn't come for another hour or so.

Lewis said, "Where's Teddy?"

"Went for a walk," Ray said.

Nino was grinning. "With a cinder block."

Lewis reconnected his phone to the five-way call. "Teddy, what the hell are you doing?"

There was a grunt, then a wet snap like someone stepping on a green stick. "Just taking care of a few things," the big man said.

"Redneck, we gotta go."

"Hey, do you remember what Nino said, that we should kill these guys because otherwise they'd give us trouble later?"

Lewis closed his eyes. "Teddy—"

"Don't worry, I'm not doing *that*," Teddy said. "I'm a Buddhist, remember? But I was thinking Nino was probably right about later." Another grunt, another wet snap. "So I'm taking out their knees. Because otherwise we'd just end up shooting them tomorrow or the next day, right? So really, I'm saving their lives."

Peter looked at Lewis. "The man's not wrong."

Lewis shook his head with a sigh. "Mother*fucker.*"

"I knew you'd see it my way," Teddy said. "Although I was wondering, should I do their elbows, too?"

50

MALLORY KANE

I n the vast high-rise apartment, oblivious to the exquisite views of the park and city spread out below, Mallory Kane paced back and forth across the polished parquet floor, thinking.

She didn't live in this apartment any more than she lived in any of the other luxury homes she had access to. They were just investments, safe and fungible assets, easily concealed parking spaces for a modest fraction of her clients' money. Mallory's name wasn't on any of the paperwork, but she knew all the concierges and caretakers, kept them well-oiled so she and her security team could come and go as she pleased.

None of the apartments were furnished more than absolutely necessary. Truly furnishing even one of them, beyond inflatable beds, folding chairs, and a couple of couches for the security team, would imply a hope for a kind of permanence that she did not allow herself to have. She had no life of her own. She had a business, which provided the funding necessary for her own protection and survival, as well as the pursuit of the mission that had dominated her thoughts, day and night, for almost a decade.

She hadn't set out to be a monster.

But to get closer to her goal, she had done monstrous things, and learned to live with them.

She blamed her husband, Gino.

He had only become the head of the North Jersey family because everyone above him had died or gotten indicted. He was brutal and paranoid and not very smart. She'd married him young because her father, a minor New York underboss, had forced her to, as a way to strengthen his alliance with North Jersey. Because Mallory was a woman, her desires were irrelevant. Because of her face and figure, she'd been used as a pawn since she was fourteen. Still, she'd found meaning in becoming a mother, and in pursuing her education. She'd gotten an MBA and law degree while her son, Noah, was in elementary school. She'd been planning to leave Gino for the last three years.

Her husband was the one who'd sent Noah to a midnight exchange with John Ricci, his second-in-command. For his education, her husband said, explaining the decision later. A big moment for the family. But he didn't have the balls to tell her ahead of time, or to go to the meet himself. She'd thought Noah was spending the night at his cousin's house.

He was a quiet boy, bright and unathletic and late to maturity. At twelve, his voice still hadn't changed. He was an endless source of frustration to his father, who didn't understand why Noah spent so much time reading. Her most fervent hope was that he would escape the family business for a career in medicine or science or law.

He didn't.

Every day, she thought of him in the back of that car, still wearing his school uniform, watching the exchange through tinted windows. When the first shots came out of the darkness and hit the car, he would have been terrified. She wondered if he'd tried to run, or if he'd been too scared, or too hurt to try. She hoped he died quickly, rather than suffering. She could never know any of those things, because she wasn't there.

Unsurprisingly, her husband wasn't man enough to blame himself for Noah's death. Mallory blamed him enough for both of them. Every night after that night, she dreamed about Noah, sometimes as a quiet little boy in her arms, other times as the young man he'd never had the chance to become. She woke every morning feeling as though she were drowning. She thought about taking her own life, but couldn't imagine doing that while her husband still walked the earth.

On the Merritt Parkway, a year to the day after Noah's death, she put a gun to her husband's head and pulled the trigger, simple as that. The cruise control was set at eighty. When she was sure her husband was gone, she pulled the wheel sharply to the right and let the car leap off the road, down the embankment, and into the trees.

Against her wishes, the airbags saved her life, but they couldn't stop the car from catching fire. Trapped in her seat, she could smell her clothes begin to burn, then her skin. She'd been ready to die, had thought it was the only way to cope with Noah's loss. But her pain-racked body had other ideas. Somehow it forced her crumpled door open and crawled out of the car.

As if it wasn't ready to let Noah go just yet.

In the burn unit, flayed nerves screaming in pain, she realized that she had survived because she wasn't finished with her revenge.

Her husband had put Noah in that parking lot, but he hadn't pulled the trigger.

She would find the people who had orchestrated the massacre.

She would make them pay in kind.

So they would feel pain like hers. Only worse. Much worse.

Only then would she be free of it.

———

When the police interviewed her in the hospital, she said that the shot had come from another car. The bullet was never found, so there was no connection to the gun she had used. She knew the police could see her anger and despair bubbling up like a fountain. They didn't want to believe her. But she had learned a lot in her time as a Mafia wife. She stuck to her story. After all, she was the only witness. The car had rolled several times, shattering the windows, and her husband had burned in the fire, so there was no physical evidence to contradict her. Anyway, what kind of lunatic would shoot her husband while he was driving and she was in the passenger seat?

She was still in the burn unit waiting for a skin graft when her father came to her with papers to sign. He was taking over North Jersey. She would get to keep the house and receive a monthly allowance.

She objected, but again it was hopeless. She was only a woman, after all, and no longer a mother or a wife, which seemed to be the only respectable roles for a female in their world. She was also thirty-five, and now disfigured from the chest down, so her value was further reduced to almost nothing.

Her anger was incandescent. Without a real income, how could she pursue her son's killers? Not to mention pay her medical expenses, which were sky-high. Finally out of the hospital, with scar tissue from her clavicles to her thighs, she put on an open-necked blouse, made up her face, and went to her father to ask for a meeting with New York. Her advanced education had taught her a few things about moving money around. The five families were not what they had been, but they still had plenty of cash coming in. She reminded them that the FBI had gotten Capone on tax charges, not racketeering.

Grudgingly, New York gave her a hundred thousand to move. It was a tiny fraction of what they had taken away. But she smiled and said thank you and made it happen. Two weeks later, she handed them a statement from a numbered account in the Bahamas, less her percentage, which her dad had told her was half of what her competition was charging.

The next time, New York gave her a million.

After that, ten million.

She was on her way.

With money coming in, she hired a security firm to look into what happened in that North Jersey parking lot. It was six months before she learned about the Ghost Killers. It took another year to disprove other possibilities. That was when she found an Israeli hacker to post a series of notices on the dark web. A reward for information. And the security firm kept looking.

But it all cost a great deal of money. She was always aware that what New York gave her, they could take away. If she was to be free to get her revenge, the only solution was to be independent. So she went to Miami, introduced herself to a lawyer she had read about in the paper, and set about making new friends.

At her first client meeting, she realized she'd made a serious mistake. Of the three Colombians, two had the sun-dark skin and blunt-fingered hands of laborers. Dressed in cheap windbreakers and baggy pants, they walked around her rented office and took things off the shelves as if they owned them. The third man, in a pressed linen suit, looked more refined, but his mindset was no different. Despite his heavy accent, his position was clear. She would wash their money and not take a cut. He looked her up and down with an appraiser's eye. "An' if you don', chica, things will be very bad for you."

She felt a tremor inside that began in her stomach and spread outward, infecting her limbs. She turned to the Miami lawyer, who had come for the meeting. His shrug told her he had always known how this would go. He would get a finder's fee for selling her out, she thought, or maybe even get a piece of the money for himself. A piece of *her*.

She had a bodyguard, an older guy she knew from Jersey, but he stayed in the corner, eyes down. He wasn't going to risk his life for her. The tremor began to warm her from the inside. Her burn scars felt fresh and hot beneath her clothes. She wasn't afraid. She was furious.

Apparently, none of these men thought a well-dressed woman could possibly be a threat. Like her husband and father, they thought of her as an object to be used as they wished. But she was not that woman any longer. She had killed her husband without a second thought. She would survive this, too. She knew what she had to do, who she had to become.

So she took a pistol from a drawer and walked around her desk, pulling the trigger until the gun was empty. The three Colombians lay dead, along with the Miami lawyer. Her stunned bodyguard hadn't moved a muscle.

Riding the wave of rage, she took his gun and put a last round into each of their chests.

She'd heard enough stories from her husband to know how to send a message. She drove to a hardware store, bought a machete, and chopped off the dead men's heads.

She'd thought it would be difficult.

It wasn't.

All she had to do was pretend they were the men who had killed her son.

To act that directly, hands-on, felt like setting something free inside of her. The bodyguard disposed of the rest of the corpses, but she wrapped the heads in plastic herself and messengered them to the oceanfront home of the cartel man who ran Florida, along with a note that read, *There seems to be a misunderstanding. My fee is fair, but nonnegotiable.*

Looking back, that was the moment her idea of getting retribution for Noah became more than just an idea that got her out of bed in the morning. It became real, something she could do herself. Something she *would* do. No matter what it took to make it happen.

But first she needed to protect herself from this life she had stepped into. She contracted for a personal security team the next day. But that level of security was expensive. If she wanted to stay safe and also pursue the Ghost Killers, she needed to grow her business. Taking the Miami lawyer's business was just the first step. She hired Ari, the Israeli hacker, to research her competition and her potential clients, as well as perform some high-level intrusions. He also created custom software to automate her unique methods of moving money.

Not long after that, Jay Streyling came her way. His experience made him useful as a fixer and a lieutenant, but he was clearly out of his depth when it came to the strategic complexities of the business itself. This was why, she was certain, he'd spent his entire government career in dirt-road countries. In addition, he suffered from an absurdly overinflated sense of his own abilities, which was occasionally inconvenient. Also, the depth of his greed and feelings of entitlement made him dangerous, but they also made him easy to control, at least for the moment.

Although, she did appreciate his suggestion to have the thing with the machete, her hands-on approach to those who opposed her, become a kind of signature. She hadn't objected. After holding her fury and despair inside for so long, it felt quite wonderful to imagine her son's killers beneath the heavy blade as it severed muscle and chopped through bone.

After she had distributed enough videos, and eliminated enough of her competition, she didn't even have to discount her fees.

And then, finally, after so many years, her search for the Ghost Killers had borne fruit. She had a set of journals with a full account of the massacre in that North Jersey parking lot. She had names. She even had an address.

She dispatched Streyling with a team to capture the killers, but he had failed her completely. Not just once, but twice. Two whole teams out of commission, with nothing to show for it. And Streyling somehow not only alive, but unmarked? Perhaps his usefulness was coming to an end.

It didn't matter. She would get her hands on these Ghost Killers with or without him.

If she had to wade through a river of blood to find her son's assassins, that was exactly what she'd do.

51

PETER

Back at the Intercontinental, after long hot showers and an enormous room service breakfast, they sat in the suite's living room drinking coffee and talking about Streyling's offer.

"I don't think he's lying about the way Kane lives," June said. Her laptop was open on the table. "I spent the last two hours running her background and she's got zero banking, credit, or real estate in her name. What do you have to lose?"

"The chance to put some holes in the guy who tried to kill my family," Lewis said.

"If our guesses are correct, and if Streyling isn't lying about absolutely everything," June said, "he was just a tool. Your main problem is the woman who gave the orders and wrote the checks."

"She's not the one put two rocket-propelled grenades into our home," Lewis growled.

Dinah put her hand on his arm. "Charlie and Miles are safe, that's what matters."

Lewis made a face. "If I let him walk, it's gonna eat me alive."

"Tell you what, I'll smoke him for you, it'd be my pleasure." Nino sat at the small table, holding the last sausage impaled on a fork. "He took those orders from her, he'll just take orders from somebody else when she's gone."

"I can't let you do that," Lewis said. "Not if I agree to his terms."

Nino shrugged. "Maybe that makes it easier, you telling me not to." His plump cheeks were a cheerful pink. "Be real stern about it, give me a good lecture."

Ray shook his head. "I'm with Lewis on this. It's a matter of principle."

Nino looked at him. "Principle goes both ways, Ray. Streyling set a team of killers on Lewis's family. Your sister might be next. You and me both took lives for a lot less."

Lewis turned to Peter. "You're pretty quiet, Jarhead. What's your take?"

Peter got up to refill his mug, but he didn't think more coffee would help. His eyes felt like they were too big for their sockets. The whole group had been up all night. Each one of them needed twelve hours of uninterrupted sleep. But he was pretty sure they weren't going to get it.

"You and Nino are both right," he said. "But really, you're just arguing about how many angels can dance on the head of a pin. We've run out of moves. If Streyling can put us in a room with Kane, we have to take the deal."

Lewis sighed. "That's what I was afraid you'd say."

"Look at it this way," Peter said. "A lot can happen between now and then. With this offer, Streyling is putting his boss in the crosshairs. According to Maurice, the man's got a history of that with the CIA, playing both sides against the middle. Who's to say he won't try for us again, once Kane is out of the picture? If that happens, the deal's off. Shoot him all you want. I'll help."

"Me too," Ray said.

Teddy, lying on his back on the carpet with a syrup-covered plate on his chest and a fresh bandage on his injured hand, began to snore.

Nino tipped his head toward the sleeping giant and dropped his voice. "Gotta say, Lewis, you were right about that guy. He's much easier to take now."

"You kinda want to adopt him," Ray said. "Like a bear cub."

Lewis flashed a tilted smile. "Why don't you take him back to Houston, give him a job at the community center?"

Ray's eyebrows went up. "Are you kidding? Dude belongs up in the woods, with the other wild animals."

Peter leaned over to make sure Teddy was still asleep. "You definitely wouldn't want him to date your sister."

"What, he's a freak?" Nino looked interested.

"For the love of God. Can we change the subject?" June pulled her laptop closer. "I did learn a few things about Kane. Does anyone want to know what I found?"

"Please, yes," Dinah said.

"Well, I started yesterday with her dead husband, Gino Salvati, who you guys hit about ten years ago. According to the coverage after his death, he was thought to be the underboss of one of the New Jersey families. Allegedly, he ran a bunch of rackets in North Jersey, including illegal gambling and loan-sharking. He'd also taken partial ownership of a big recycling center outside of Newark. But his main thing was wholesaling dope up and down the Eastern Seaboard."

Lewis cleared his throat. "He had somebody inside the Port of New Jersey who let him bring in shipping containers from overseas without clearing customs. With him moving that kind of weight, it was a no-brainer for us."

"Salvati stayed home that night," June said. "But his twelve-year-old son, Noah, went along for the ride. He was found dead in the back of one of the cars."

Lewis looked away. "It was a mistake," he said. "Nobody knew he was there, let alone actually targeted the kid. He was just collateral damage."

"When did her husband die?" Peter asked.

"Exactly one year later, in a single-car accident on the Merritt Parkway. According to the article, police believed he lost control of the vehicle and was killed when his Cadillac left the road and rolled a half-dozen times."

"That's not how mobsters kick the bucket," Nino said.

"No," June said. "Although he could have been forced off the road or shot from another car. The cops hold back those details all the time. Maybe he got sloppy, or pissed off somebody important, or somebody else wanted to move up the ladder. He was a mobster, it's an occupational hazard."

"And the wife?" Ray asked.

"Mallory Kane Salvati, although she went back to her maiden name after her husband died. Here she is at the funeral. The Newark paper covered it like celebrity news."

She handed the laptop to Peter. The screen showed a photo of a woman dressed in a tight black dress that accented sleek curves, although it covered her from neck to wrists. Under a neat black hat, her face was perfectly symmetrical. Although she clutched a handkerchief in one pale hand, her expert makeup showed no evidence of tears. The perfect mob widow.

Peter passed the laptop to Nino, who paused for a good look, lips pursed in a silent whistle. "She don't look like our usual targets."

"Her dad was a made guy from one of the New York families," June said, "so she was already in the life. She married young. There was a piece in the Newark paper that suggested the marriage could be part of an agreement between New York and North Jersey."

June took her laptop back. "Anyway, after her husband died, she fell off the radar for a while. Eight months later, she sold the house she had shared with her husband and moved to a rental apartment on the Upper West Side of Manhattan. The money from the house disappeared, as did any money she might have made selling her husband's piece of the recycling plant. That alone would have made her a wealthy woman, but none of it shows up in her financial history. Maybe that's not too surprising, because she'd already gotten a degree in finance from Rutgers while her son was in elementary school, and a law degree after that."

Peter remembered his thought from Maurice's house, that maybe Mallory Kane was more than a mob wife. With June's findings, that seemed a lot more likely.

"She began a small law practice out of her apartment. I found her name on a number of corporate documents out of Delaware and Nevada, entities used to buy hard assets like real estate, then quickly dissolved. I'm not a financial reporter, but it looks to me like a lot of money flowing through, much more than she would have had herself."

June brought up another photo on the laptop. "Using a facial recognition app, I did an image search using her picture from the funeral and came up with this."

She turned the screen so the others could see a street shot of Mallory Kane walking beside a black-haired man who looked like a Palermo bricklayer in a flashy suit. "Here she is in New York with one of the last Mafia bosses still standing, who'd apparently been consolidating whatever power remained from the ashes of all the RICO indictments of the last twenty years."

Peter, sitting beside June with a good look at the photo, noticed that the man's name was in the caption, but not Kane's. The photo editor must have assumed she was just arm candy, because she was dressed to the hilt and looked easily ten years younger than her biological age. Although it was not an arm-candy pose. She was leaning in, her lips pursed in speech, and he was listening attentively.

"However, the Italian Mafia is not a growth industry, even in New York, and she wasn't resting on her laurels." June brought up a second photo, Kane walking out of a restaurant beside a silver-haired gent in a white linen jacket. "This is ten months later in Miami. His name is James Harrison, a Rutgers-educated lawyer with suspected cartel ties, indicted but never convicted, and the featured dirtbag in a high-profile news article about money laundering. So she's jumped from the Italians to the Colombians." Again, Peter noted, her name was not in the caption.

Then June brought up a third image, beside a long black car with a chunky guy in a glossy black raincoat. It was raining, and her face was turning away from the camera as if she were trying to sidestep the photographer but hadn't quite managed it. The facial recognition app had to be pretty good, Peter thought, to recognize her like that.

"Here she is in London the following year, with Maksim Drozdov. He's a minor Russian oligarch, meaning he's only worth about ten billion. So she's climbing the financial food chain very quickly, as well as moving laterally across multiple groups, which is also unusual. All of this advancement, remember, is in just three and a half years."

She pointed at the screen. "The other thing is that she's unnamed in every photo but the first one, at the funeral. This new software is the only reason I managed to find them. But here, with the Russian, that's the last picture I have."

Lewis frowned. "I don't get it. How did we never hear about this woman?"

"She's very good at staying out of sight," June said. "The photo from her son's funeral is the only one where they mentioned her name. The one with the Russian is the last one I could find. Beginning seven years ago, all records of her existence dried up. She sold the apartment in Manhattan and liquidated her bank accounts. No more financial records, no more corporate documents, definitely no more photos online. She found a way to disappear completely."

"What about the feds?" Peter asked. "Will she be on their radar?"

"They like to follow the money," June said. "Treasury will know who she is, and with the cartel connection, maybe drug enforcement, too. But they probably don't know how to *find* her."

Lewis looked at her. "That's it? That's all you have?"

"Well, I only had two hours. But I don't really have other leads to pursue. My journalistic resources are significant, but there's only so much I can do. If you're wealthy and determined, you can stay out of sight. With the company she keeps, she's surely got access to any number of other identities, from any number of other nations. Streyling said she owns a private jet, right? When you're in that elite club, passing through customs is barely a formality. She could be anywhere in the world and we'd never know it."

"What about Streyling?" Lewis said. "Did you find anything on him?"

"He's like Mallory," June said. "Only worse. It's like he doesn't exist."

None of them had brought up the elephant in the room, but it had to be discussed. Peter said, "What about Mallory distributing the notebooks to her criminal network? Would that have the result Streyling suggested?"

"Yes," Lewis said. "From the photos June dug up, we know she's well-connected. We hit a lot of big-time dirtbags back in the day, and most of those outfits take payback very seriously. If only a half dozen came after us, it'd make the last few days feel like a vacation."

That sobered everyone up.

June glanced at her phone and stood. "Listen, I have to go do a thing. I'll be back in an hour." She picked up her jacket and pulled it on. "Lewis, I think you should accept Streyling's proposal, and do it soon. Also, when Teddy wakes up, somebody should take him to buy more darts for that goofy-ass gun of his. They might come in handy." She walked to the door and opened it. "Peter, will you walk me?"

"Sure." He grabbed his coat, clipped the Browning's holster to his belt, and patted his pockets for his wallet and phone. "Where are we headed?"

"I'll tell you on the way."

She walked ahead of him to the elevator and hit the button, then stood staring silently at the floor indicator.

"June," he said. "Where are we going?"

The doors opened with a ding. Peter followed her inside. The doors closed and the car began to drop.

She still wasn't looking at him. "We're meeting Carlo Fratelli in Millennium Park."

"Excuse me?" Peter couldn't believe what he was hearing.

"He's on the DEA task force, remember? Maybe they have a file on Kane. We need all the help we can get on this."

"I don't get it. He's a cop. He wants to roll you up, remember?"

She gave him a sideways glance. "No shit. He's called me six times in the last two days. That's why you're coming, to make sure that doesn't happen."

"And when were you going to tell me?"

"I'm telling you now, okay? Don't be a dick about this, okay?"

"What about Lewis and the others? They are not going to be happy when they find out."

She faced front again. "That's why I didn't tell them."

The elevator came to a stop and she strode into the busy lobby. Despite his longer legs, Peter had to hustle to stay with her.

"This is a very bad idea," he said quietly. "Fratelli wants to put us all in prison. He's not going to start helping us."

"Sure he will. Once he hears the magic words." As they neared the exit to the street, she put on her winter hat.

"June." Peter felt the exhaustion rise up like a wave. "What's your play here?"

She shook her head. "Maybe it's better if you don't know. Go back to the room."

"I'm not going back to the damn room." He took hold of her arm to stop her before she reached the revolving doors.

She slipped his hand, then turned and grabbed the front of his coat with both fists. He always forgot how strong she was.

"We are getting nowhere, Peter. All we have is a name. Every time we try to get a handle on this thing, we get shut down. And you just know Streyling is going to try to fuck us somehow. And, oh, by the way, the clock is ticking on Kane unleashing a whole new wave of kill teams. So I'm going to make a move."

"June—"

"Don't worry," she said. "I'll clear everything with Lewis and the other guys. But sometimes it's better to beg forgiveness than ask permission." She sighed. "Yes, it's a risk. But you and Lewis have stepped into three firefights in the last three days. So now it's my turn. This is my skill set, remember? Talking to people. Getting information and cooperation, finding the win-win. You have to trust me here."

Peter felt the heat of her radiating from a foot away. "I do trust you," he said. "I just—"

He didn't know how to say what he felt. That everything was out of control. That nothing they learned seemed to help. That they were only getting themselves in deeper, with no clear way out.

She released his coat and wrapped her arms around him and pulled him close, her face hot on the side of his neck. "I know," she said. "Me too. We just have to keep at it."

Then she let him go and stepped into the revolving door and pushed hard to get it moving.

52

Millennium Park was a twenty-minute walk from their hotel, the downtown streets hectic with cars and pedestrians and the February wind blowing hard in their faces every step of the way. On their left, past the skyscrapers, buckled white frozen slabs of Lake Michigan reached toward a distant horizon of dark open water.

She'd set the meeting for eight thirty at the playground off Monroe by Lake Shore Drive. But Peter wanted to keep Fratelli on the back foot, so as they entered the park at Randolph Street, June took out her phone and sent him a text. *Change of plans. Meet on the shiny pedestrian bridge over Columbus Drive.*

He replied immediately. *See you in five.*

They passed the chrome pillars and supports for the pavilion, then swung left onto the ramp to the winding, chrome-walled structure that crossed over six busy lanes of traffic. If Fratelli had been waiting at the playground, he'd be coming from the east. On that side, the approach to the bridge curved repeatedly back on itself, serpentine-fashion, limiting any escape. June and Peter were on the more linear western approach, which featured good views of both sides and dozens of spots to hop the sloping rail and disappear into the park. Although they'd still have to contend with the deep and drifted snow.

They waited at the center, perched over the road median below, and watched Fratelli walk toward them, his thigh-length winter coat unzipped despite the temperature. He was short and stocky, in his mid-forties, with the start of a small potbelly. June remembered him telling her that he'd barely made the department's height requirement, back in the day. But he made up for his size with a kind of bantam strut that telegraphed his self-confidence and made him seem larger than he was.

Up close, he looked older than she remembered, with a tired face that sagged as if gravity were heavier for him than other people. But inside their deep sockets, his eyes were quick and curious. In the years June had known him, he'd been a very successful detective, with one of the best clearance rates in the department.

"Well, this is melodramatic," he said, breathing a little hard from the hustle through the park. "Like we're swapping spies at the Brandenburg Gate."

He smiled at June without acknowledging Peter, although she wasn't fooled. Being a detective was all about reading people and figuring the right attitude and approach to get what you needed. Peter was an unexpected addition, tall and bony and rough-looking in his canvas chore coat and jeans. She kept her mouth shut and watched Fratelli decide how to play it.

He said, "Seeing you with this guy answers some questions for me. How a nice girl like you got hooked into that ugly thing with the Albanians. Are you gonna let me help you out of this?"

June didn't smile back. "I'm not a nice girl, Carlo. And I don't need your protection." She tipped her head at Peter. "That's what he's for."

Beside her, Peter was watching Carlo, but also looking past him at the park beyond. His coat was open, too.

"What I need," she said, "is for you to listen for a minute. Without judgment, without coming to any conclusions. Can you do that?"

Fratelli looked skeptical. "Sure."

"Back when I worked at the *Trib*, I gave you some good tips, right? Helped you put some things together, get some good collars?"

June heard herself falling into the language of street police. It was a journalistic tool she'd learned when she was just starting out. Slipping into another person's speech patterns helped her forge a connection with the person she was interviewing.

"Yeah," Carlo admitted, "you did. That last tip on those trunk murders got me a suspect and a conviction."

"And a commendation from the mayor," June said. "So you know my heart's in the right place. Well, I've got something for you now. You'd be in it all the way, because I want somebody I know, someone I can trust. But it's a different kind of thing. Much bigger than a few trunk murders."

Fratelli nodded. "I'm listening."

Peter touched her shoulder, getting her attention, but he spoke to Carlo. "Tell your friends to walk away, Detective. You're not going to want to miss this."

Carlo looked at Peter, eyebrows knitted in mild confusion. "What friends? We're just talking here."

Peter pointed with his chin. "Brown coat, blue hat, by the minigolf. Green coat, blond beard, in the trees to the north. Unmarked sedan stopped by the charging station, down below."

June didn't need to look for them. If Peter had seen them, they were there.

Carlo looked at Peter a moment, then allowed himself a faint smile. "Fair enough. I'm too old to chase you guys through the park anyway."

He dipped his chin to his lapel. "All good here, guys. See you back at the ranch. Beers on me later."

June glanced at Peter, who watched for a moment to make sure the others were leaving, then nodded.

Carlo said, "Please continue."

"Okay, here's the price of admission. You're still on that interagency task force, right? I need you to introduce me to Gottschall, the DEA SAC for Chicago."

Peter didn't turn to look at her, but she knew he wanted to. A meet with the special agent in charge of the DEA's Chicago Division, which covered most of three states, was several orders of magnitude hairier than a conversation with Fratelli. She was out on the edge now.

The detective's eyebrows went up. "That's a big ask. Plus he's a busy guy. Is this about that Albanian thing?"

"No," she said. "It's about Mallory Kane."

Every cop learned, early on, not to let his thoughts show on his face, and Fratelli had a better poker face than most. But it wasn't enough. Reading people was part of June's skill set, too.

He recovered quickly, though. "How about this. Tell me what you've got and I'll run it past Ginty, the unit commander."

At least he didn't pretend he didn't know the name, she thought. "Unit commander, you're so cute. Here's how it's going to go. I'll call you with a time and place. I want you there, and I want Gottschall. Tell him he can bring one other person. And tell him I'm bringing a lawyer, to make sure we're all on the same page."

"Now you've got me worried." Fratelli put on a concerned face, empathy practically seeping from his pores. "What are you mixed up in that you need a lawyer?"

"Again," June said, "so cute. But cut that shit out. I'm bringing you and Gottschall something spectacular. It's a career maker for both of you, and a chance to do some real good. You're both going to want to be part of it. But this is a one-time offer. You fuck around on this, I'm going to the next guy on my list, and you know I have a very long list."

Fratelli sucked on his teeth, thinking. Then he nodded. "Okay, I'll tell Gottschall. But you'll have better luck if we meet after six. He's always got a full schedule."

"That's too late," June said. "Let's make it noon. I'll call you with a location by eleven thirty."

53

They took the long way back, diverting through lobbies and slipping out side exits of multiple buildings as they went. She knew Peter was pissed. He didn't say a word until they were a block from their hotel.

"We should have talked about the DEA piece before," he said. "With Lewis and the others."

"Yeah? And what would have happened?" June asked. "Nothing. They'd have shut me down in a heartbeat."

"Why didn't you just call Oliver?"

Oliver Bent ran something called the Longview Group, a quasi-governmental organization that dealt with problematic emerging technology. Peter and Lewis had done something for him the year before.

"I did call Oliver," she said. "He told me he wasn't running a charity for troubled crooks. I mean, I get it. There's no upside for him, and no political cover if it goes bad. Also, I lied to Fratelli. I don't actually have a bunch of other cops to call. This DEA thing is all we've got."

Peter shook his head. "Lewis is our friend, and I trust him with my life. But don't forget who they are, those guys up in the room. They're the Ghost Killers, June. They're not going to like this."

"I went through Teddy's notebooks, Peter. I read the newspaper accounts. I know exactly who they are, probably better than you do. And I still think this is our best bet. Lewis trusts us, too. Now, are you going to have my back on this, or not?"

When they arrived upstairs, the suite was empty except for Lewis sitting on the couch, looking up from his laptop.

"I talked to Streyling, told him we had a deal. He said Kane'll be somewhere in New York City. He'll know more tomorrow. He said to make sure we take any computers we find. We should get on the road soon."

"Have you talked to Charlie and Miles today?" Peter asked.

"Just now." Lewis gave them a soft smile. "Your mom's got Miles learning to paint. I can only imagine the mess. And your dad's teaching Charlie to use the chain saw, cutting firewood. I'm not sure how safe that is, though."

"My dad teaches a chain saw safety course for the volunteer fire department," Peter said. "Charlie will be fine."

Then Lewis focused on June and frowned. "Something happened. Where'd you guys go?"

Lewis was pretty good at reading people, too.

"I just saw Fratelli," she said. "He's setting up a meet for us."

"Fratelli." Lewis looked at her, his jaw knotted. She saw how tightly wrapped he was, the toll the last few days had taken. "A meet with who?"

"DEA," she said. "The head of the Chicago office."

She watched him process that. The heavy muscles bunched in his shoulders and arms, like a bird of prey preparing to launch itself into the air. Even as he wore a silk T-shirt in a very nice hotel suite, she could see what he had been, before they had met. What he still was, in a way, family or no family.

Finally he said, "We're up to our necks already. We don't need this. We have a path forward."

"Our path forward is more like a Hail Mary, Lewis. Don't get me wrong, my money's on us. But you have to admit this is fucked up. We're going to trust the guy who tried to kill us—twice—to help us put his own boss out of business? The same boss who's apparently in deep with drug cartels and Russian oligarchs? Who's been a half-dozen steps ahead of us at every turn?"

"This crew can handle her," Lewis said. "We've taken on scarier people than this Mallory Kane. Involving the feds just makes things a lot more complicated."

"Things are getting more complicated anyway," June said. "We haven't talked about this because I haven't really seen you guys, but Fratelli keeps calling me. He says the FBI has taken over the investigation in Milwaukee. They've put their financial fraud team onto the corporate ownership of your house. The place is a wreck, and the firefighters flooded it while they were putting out the fire, but now the FBI's got evidence techs inside, going through the remains with magnifying glasses and tweezers. I've seen the news footage. Once they get inside your gun safe, they're only going to get more interested."

The best defense for a criminal was to be invisible, fly under the police radar. From what June had learned, that was the primary organizing principle of Lewis's career, to be the thief nobody knew existed. But once you were under the microscope, with the full force of the law focused on you, all bets were off.

June said, "They're coming for you, Lewis. They're coming for all of us. The path forward stays the same, but we need some cover. Or else we have to give this up and get our butts to Brazil or some other non-extradition country. But here's where Mallory Kane can help us. If she's as big a fish as we think she is, we have some leverage."

"Also," Peter said, "think about your rules. They're designed to keep you from turning into the people you were targeting, right? Well, maybe bringing in the cops helps with that, too. Otherwise, we're no better than Kane and Streyling's hit teams."

Lewis scowled at him. "Were you in on this?"

"She sprung it on me half an hour ago. But you know she's usually right about this kind of thing."

"You don't know the cops like I do. They do whatever they want. There's always a price."

"Not always," Peter said. "You remember those two detectives in Denver? They were stand-up guys. So was that Memphis cop, Gantry. Good police want to do their jobs. We just have to make sure we talk to good police."

Lewis scowled at him. "When you're a white dude, most police are good police. As a Black man from the hood, especially in my particular profession, that ain't my experience at all."

Peter nodded. "I get that. You don't need to go to the meeting. June and I will go. She's got a lawyer coming, too. Nobody needs to know who you are. Or Nino or Ray or Teddy. Right now, it's just a conversation. Nobody's going to agree to anything without your go-ahead."

Lewis turned to June. "How exactly do you see this playing out? What are you hoping to get? Way I see it, they hold all the cards."

Now Peter turned to look at her, too. "Actually, Juniper, I was wondering the same thing. What the hell do we have to trade? They probably know a lot more about Kane than we do."

June gave them her very best smile. "Let me handle that. But as for what I'm hoping to get? Blanket immunity. For all of us. For every-thing. This is how we get out from under the axe hanging over our heads, Lewis. This is how you get free."

He looked away. "After everything I've done? Maybe I don't de-serve immunity."

June grabbed his arm and pulled him around to look at her. "Ev-erybody deserves forgiveness, Lewis. Even you."

Lewis cleared his throat and raised his eyes to the ceiling. "Well, hell, I feel better already."

She got up on her tiptoes and kissed him on the cheek. "Don't be such a pussy, Lewis. I got you, okay? Now, where are the others?"

"Dinah's up at the gym, getting her head straight. The guys are grabbing some sleep." He sighed. "Nino and Ray ain't gonna like this."

"But they'll follow your lead," June said.

"I hope so," he said. "Long as it doesn't connect back to us."

"Did you find any more darts for Teddy's gun?"

"Ray found a supplier in Cleveland. We can pick them up on the way to New York."

"Good," June said. "Our meet's at noon. You guys should probably be gone by then." She flashed the smile again. "You know, just in case."

54

They met in a vacant storefront on Dearborn in the South Loop. June had found the former café online and Lewis had picked the lock on the back door before going to wait in Sandmeyer's Bookstore across the street. He'd sent Dinah ahead to New York with Nino, Ray, and Teddy, but told June he wanted to stay close in case things went sideways.

Somebody had taped brown paper over the café's front windows. The power was on, but the heat was off and the interior had been stripped bare, leaving only a single light bulb, the tile on the floor, and the persistent smell of burned toast. Five men and one woman stood in a rough circle, their breath steaming in the cold.

The lawyer, Schmidt, got things started. "First off, before anything else is said, I want to make it clear that this meeting was requested by my clients, is entirely voluntary, and nothing said today will in any way be construed as a statement of fact or admission of guilt and as such will not be used in a court of law."

He sounded like he knew his stuff, June thought. He'd better, for what they were paying him. He had the paunch and pallor of a man who spent too much time behind his desk, but his blue suit was good and his wavy silver hair was expensively cut. She'd gotten his name from Peter's friend Miranda in Denver, who was also a criminal defense attorney.

"In addition," the lawyer continued, "there will be no audio or video recordings made of what is said today. In return, Ms. Cassidy will consider this entire conversation to be off-limits for publication, even as background information. If we move forward, all parties will sign a nondisclosure. Are we agreed?"

"Sure," said Gottschall, the special agent in charge. "We're just talking. Let's hear what you've got." He was maybe fifty, with horn-rimmed glasses, a shaved head, and the lean slouch of a marathon runner.

June looked at the lawyer, who nodded. She had her phone on speaker and tucked into her jacket's breast pocket, connected to Lewis's burner, so he could listen in. She was also recording. Just in case.

"We have a line on Mallory Kane's location," she said. "Where she'll be in three or four days' time. But we need more background."

"What do we get?" Special Agent Bob Ginty ran the interagency task force Fratelli was on. He was average height and soft-looking, with fleshy features that reminded June of Mr. Potato Head.

"You get Mallory Kane," June said. "Trussed up like a Christmas turkey."

Fratelli's eyebrows climbed toward his hairline. Ginty and Gottschall didn't react at all. Maybe the DEA was used to the idea of extrajudicial action.

"But I'll go first," June said. "Here's what we have on her already." She summarized what Maurice had told them, what she'd learned

THE PRICE YOU PAY

online, then added what she suspected about Kane's relationships with the New York boss, the Miami lawyer, and the oligarch.

Ginty lifted his thick chin and glared at her. "Where'd you get that last part?"

June smiled. "Sources."

"Reporters." Ginty said it like a dirty word. "How do you know where she'll be?"

"We'll get to that," June said. "First, can you confirm what we have?"

Ginty opened his mouth to talk, but Gottschall waved him off. "That matches what we've got," he said. "But her husband's death wasn't an accident. Somebody killed him."

"Why," June asked.

"Good question." Gottschall gave her a wintry smile. "Maybe because we had him cold. He was going to turn state's witness, wear a wire, the whole bit. We were going to indict everybody he'd ever met. Then somebody shot him in the face on the Merritt Parkway."

That overkill certainly sounded personal, June thought. Shooting somebody in the face was the traditional Mafia punishment for a rat.

"According to one of our informants, the wife pulled the trigger," Gottschall said. "We already knew she was in the car. It rolled down the embankment, then caught fire. She got second-degree burns over much of her body before she managed to get out."

Ginty pursed his Mr. Potato Head lips. "Shoot a man driving at highway speed while you're in the driver's seat? Woman's nuts."

"Or determined," June said. "But that's why she disappeared for eight months after he died, right? She was in the hospital."

"A very expensive private hospital," Ginty said. "It never made the papers. She must have paid off every tabloid reporter in the tristate area."

"After that," Gottschall said, "Mallory started washing money.

Like you, we believe she began with the New York families, then moved up the food chain from there. In the process, she removed a half-dozen competitors, at least two of them by her own hand, including that Miami lawyer and a London banker."

"She likes wet work," Ginty added. "Got a screw loose, puts videos on the dark web."

"Regardless of that psychiatric diagnosis," Gottschall said dryly, "she's very smart and very careful. We've been chasing her for eight years. We've had people inside her organization three times. All three vanished without a trace. We know she's washing billions of dirty dollars, but we don't have enough actionable evidence to charge her with so much as a parking ticket. So, without my agreeing to unsanctioned vigilante activity on U.S. soil, if you can help us get a line on Mallory Kane, you have my attention."

June nodded. "Okay. Next, do you know anything about a group of thieves known as the Ghost Killers?"

Ginty rolled his Mr. Potato Head eyes. "They don't exist. That's just a story gangbangers tell to scare each other around the campfire."

"But you know about the bounty on information about the Ghost Killers?"

Ginty turned to Fratelli. "Is this what you brought us here for? This urban legend crap?"

June was looking at Gottschall. "As far as we can tell, the bounty was paid three days ago. The information is real and verifiable. The Ghost Killers exist. And Mallory Kane is trying to wipe them out."

"You're talking about the Albanians," Fratelli said. "They're the Ghost Killers?"

"No," June said. "They were the sellers of the information. The Ghost Killers got to them very quickly, but not quickly enough to prevent Mallory Kane from getting the information she wanted."

"Quite a tale you're spinning," Ginty said. "How does it connect? What the hell are we doing here?"

A slow smile grew on Fratelli's tired face. Obviously, he'd figured it out.

The lawyer said, "The Ghost Killers will collect and detain Mallory Kane for you. They receive complete and blanket immunity for this action, and any and all past actions whether related or unrelated. This includes recent events in Milwaukee and Chicago. In return, the DEA will receive any and all available intelligence harvested, including access to Kane's computers, client information, financials, and all available funds with the exception of a forty percent finder's fee."

"So that's who this shitbag is." Ginty looked Peter up and down. "You kill drug dealers and take their money."

"No," Peter said, "the drug dealers were before my time. But I'm in this now, all the way. You can check my bona fides." He handed Fratelli a piece of paper. "Those are cops who will vouch for me. I was a Marine officer for eight years. The Pentagon has my file, although it's mostly classified. You want something more recent, there's a guy named Oliver Bent who runs a government technology incubator called the Longview Group."

Fratelli looked at Peter as if seeing him in a new way.

"But you got no official standing," Ginty said. "You think you're Batman or something?"

Peter raised a shoulder in a half shrug. "Sometimes people need a little help. I like to be useful. And right now, it looks like you guys could use a little help with Mallory Kane."

Ginty turned to Gottschall. "Boss, we don't even know who these so-called Ghost Killers are."

Gottschall held up a hand. "Mallory Kane's information is very tempting, believe me. But I can't begin to sign off on this, or even pass it up the chain for somebody else to consider. Not only does it break more laws than I can currently count, if news of it got out, the scandal could bring down the whole agency. Not to mention landing my butt in federal prison for a long time."

June had been expecting this. "Let me add a sweetener, in addition to Kane. And maybe some political cover. Call your CIA liaison and give them a name. Kane's fixer. Jay Streyling."

Peter turned to look at her. June gave him a shrug. She didn't need to play by Lewis's rules. She wanted to do the most good for the least amount of damage. What she didn't know was whether this idea would actually work.

"And who, exactly, is Jay Streyling?" Ginty said.

June smiled. "Get on the phone and find out. My guess is, he's on a list. A very short list."

Ginty glanced at Gottschall, who nodded. Ginty took out his phone and walked into the back room.

To June, Gottschall said, "What do you expect will come of that conversation?"

"His boss will call your boss. They won't sign off, but they'll want you to. So you'll be collecting not one significant marker, but two. It's a win-win."

The SAC sighed. "I knew I shouldn't have taken this meeting." He removed his glasses and massaged the red marks left by the nose pads. "Do you have a lot of experience jacking up law enforcement like this?"

Peter covered his snort by clearing his throat a little too elaborately.

June ignored him. "I believe in getting shit done. Sometimes you have to put a little spin on the ball."

Gottschall put his glasses back on. "Tell me something, Ms. Cassidy. I looked you up on my way down here. You're a respected journalist, short-listed for the Pulitzer. How is it that you're involved in something like this?"

"I didn't go looking for it, if that's what you're asking. I met the guy who ran that crew after he retired. He's been there for me when things got hairy. Now I'm there for him. Also, you think of him as a bad guy, but I don't. I've made a list of the people he hit, and I don't see a lot of victims there. Instead, I see a lot of people you didn't get."

Ginty came out of the back holding the phone away from his ear. "He wants to know if they can bring Streyling in alive."

June looked at Peter.

"We'll do our best," he said. "That's all I can promise."

Ginty relayed the message, then put the phone away. "The liaison didn't have to look up the name. He'll call the seventh floor."

"You told him the timeline?" Peter said.

Ginty nodded, maybe done being a dick now that something might actually happen. "They move fast when they might get embarrassed."

"If it happens," Gottschall said, "there will be caveats to your terms. Immunity granted only if the action results in the capture of Kane and the acquisition of reasonably useful intel. In the event of any unwarranted deaths, the deal is null and void. The same goes of any action not taken in good faith. And we're in the loop the entire time."

"Good faith to you might not be good faith to us," June said. "Unwarranted is in the eye of the beholder. Let's stick to clearly defined goals."

"Also, you don't want to be in the loop," Peter said. "When this thing goes down, you're going to want full deniability. Trust me on that."

The lawyer reached into his bag and pulled out a folder. "Here's the agreement on offer, complete with NDAs. I think you'll find it's fair. My clients will remain anonymous, of course, until the terms have been met."

Gottschall took the folder and handed it to Ginty without opening it, then turned to go. "Interesting meeting. I'll call your attorney as soon as I hear."

"One last thing," June said. "I have every reason to believe this will go well, and you'll keep your end of the bargain. But if you fuck my people?" She gave both DEA agents a bright smile. "I'll drag your asses through the newspapers until the bone shows. Are we clear?"

Ginty opened his mouth to respond, but Gottschall silenced him with a raised hand. "We're clear, Ms. Cassidy. As long as you understand that sentiment goes both ways."

Then he and Ginty stepped through the doorway, crossed the street to a waiting car, and drove away. The lawyer shook June's hand, and Peter's, and followed them out.

Fratelli was last. As he turned to go, June handed him a burner phone. "I'll call you on this when it's done."

Fratelli tapped it against his thigh, then slipped it in his pocket. "I hope you know what the hell you're doing."

Me too, June thought as he walked away. Me too.

55

PETER

They took the Chicago Skyway into Indiana, then continued east in the Acura, June driving, the radar detector chirping every few miles. Peter had to keep reminding her that they really didn't want to be pulled over with all those guns in the car.

His phone pinged as they passed Toledo, the tracker app telling him, after a long day's absence, that the package was back on satellite. Crossing the rest of Ohio, he watched the blue dot move from the Indy mailbox shop to the FedEx hub at the airport, then disappear again.

He was pretty sure he knew, now, how Streyling was going to carry his end of the deal. What he didn't know was what that would look like. Where Kane would be, how much security she would have. They still didn't have a location or time.

All they knew was someplace in New York, the day after tomorrow.

As Peter was filling the gas tank outside of Cleveland, the lawyer called June. The DEA was in. Gottschall had signed the agreement. If they were committed before, they were really locked in now. She told the lawyer that Mallory was in New York, so Gottschall should get ready.

Peter took the wheel while the others crashed into much-needed sleep. As darkness fell, the snowy landscape seemed to glow with a surreal light. An hour into Pennsylvania, Lewis took over the driving and Peter crawled into the back to close his eyes. He woke up in New Jersey, where they got off the interstate and drove through industrial streets to the disused freight yard where Mallory Kane's son had died.

It was well after midnight, and despite the busy city and port traffic all around them, the freight yard was a desolate place. The pole lamps were dark, but the ambient light reflected off the ice-glazed gravel, illuminating the dozens of unrepaired bullet holes in the leaning tin sheds along the fence. More than a dozen people had died there. Peter wondered if the blood would still be visible on the ground when winter had ended.

It was after one in the morning before they made it to Hell's Kitchen. The neighborhood was now thoroughly upscale and re-branded as Clinton, or, more recently, Midtown West. Ray had found the fourth-floor two-bedroom online and rented the place for a week. An apartment in an older building with no doorman was much better than a hotel because nobody would notice or care when they came and went, or what they carried in and out.

Dinah had already claimed one queen-size bed for herself and Lewis, and the other for Peter and June. Nino and Ray were snoring fully dressed on the foldout couch. Teddy was curled up like a golden retriever under the dining table, using his green parka for a pillow. Despite their naps in the car, Peter and the others were still exhausted by the last few days, so they went to bed, too.

Peter didn't sleep much.

In the morning, after showers and bagels and coffee, they split into groups and headed out.

The day was cold and bleak, the sky gray and low, cutting off the tops of the new buildings at Hudson Yards. Wind swirled through the concrete canyons, carrying the smell of exhaust and the garbage bags sitting along the curbs, waiting for pickup. They'd outrun the snow expected in Chicago, but it would be here soon enough.

Peter was with June, walking the High Line downtown toward the Meatpacking District, his legs glad of the chance to cover a few miles, when his phone pinged again. The tracker showed the package leaving the FedEx hub at Memphis International. That was south of Indy, the wrong direction.

Peter called Lewis with the news. "Did you hear from Streyling?"

"I just got off the phone with him," Lewis said. "We're still on for tomorrow. He reminded me to grab any computers we find. That's how we'll transfer his cut."

"He give you any more details? Time or place?"

"Says he doesn't know yet," Lewis said.

"You believe him?"

"Doesn't matter," Lewis said. "He's gonna tell us when he tells us. We're just gonna have to be ready."

"Ready for what? A single bodyguard or a six-man team? A high-end hotel or an armored Mercedes?"

"Ain't no different from the sandbox. You prepare best you can, then you improvise. Real question is, who's better at it? And that's us, brother. You can take that to the bank."

Lewis was right, Peter knew. And they were preparing. They already had armored vests and several duffel bags filled with weapons, including their own pistols, a pair of the Albanians' combat shotguns, and the six compact MP5 submachine guns they'd taken from the ambushed team outside of Maurice's place. They also had Teddy's weird-ass dart gun, which had proven to be very useful. When the others had stopped for extra darts and CO_2 cartridges in Cleveland, they'd also found a gun shop and stocked up on extra magazines and ammunition, just in case.

They were making other preparations, too. Lewis and Dinah were headed to a scooter store in the Bowery. The new electric models could hit fifty miles an hour, a good way to cover distance in a hurry in a traffic-clogged city. They'd also hit Duane Reade for first-aid supplies and Ace Hardware for zip ties and gloves and a few hand tools. Nino and Ray and Teddy had taken the car to an army surplus place in Brooklyn, picking up ski masks and oversized coats to hide their armor and weapons on the street. Peter and June were going to an electronics store for better headsets and REI for heavy-duty backpack duffels and other supplies.

On the way back to the apartment, his phone pinged again. The GPS signal had disappeared once more, this time at a mailbox store in Memphis. Peter felt better. The same pattern as before. Still plenty of time for the package to make it to New York overnight.

After lunch takeout from a deli around the corner, June plugged herself into her laptop, Teddy and Ray left to find a boxing gym, and Nino went out for groceries. Lewis and Dinah sat curled on the couch with the phone on speaker between them, the lines in their faces easing as they checked in with the boys. Peter, stretching on the floor, heard enough to learn that apparently Miles had some natural talent as an artist, and that Charlie hadn't accidentally chain sawed himself in the north woods.

But Peter's nerves were ratcheting up, and he knew he needed to get outside. He strapped on the trail shoes he'd bought at REI and headed north on the Greenway along the Hudson, feet pounding the blacktop while the wind off the river cut him to the bone. He kept his eyes on the tangled treeline, where snowdrifts lay deep in shadow, all the way through Riverside Park. By the time he turned around at 125th Street, he realized he'd been worried about an ambush.

His phone pinged again when he was halfway home. The package had reappeared briefly outside the FedEx terminal by the Memphis airport, then disappeared again. In another metal airfreight container, Peter thought. Headed east, he hoped.

For dinner, Nino made linguini with Bolognese sauce and a big green salad and June opened two bottles of wine. By the end of the meal, the pasta was gone, but both bottles were still mostly full.

The vehicles were gassed up and the scooters were charged. The magazines had been loaded. The guns were laid out in rows on the dining room table, looking like a photo shoot for *Soldier of Fortune* magazine.

Nobody felt much like talking.

They went to bed early.

56

The sky was still dark when Peter woke. On the GPS app, the blue dot hadn't reappeared, which he hoped meant the package was still in transit. Beside him, June was snoring.

He got out of bed quietly and went into the living area. Nino and Ray were sacked out on the couch and Teddy was curled into a fetal position under the dining table. Peter made coffee and toasted a bagel and stood looking out the wide apartment windows, watching as the sky slowly brightened and the sun rose, shrouded by clouds, over the vast city.

Lewis came out with his phone open. "Streyling just called. He gave me the address. It's a mailbox store in Greenwich Village."

"What does that mean?" Peter asked. "Will she be there? Or does the store deliver packages?"

Lewis shook his head. "One of her guys will pick it up. His name is Ari Mueller. Streyling is running some kind of game on him, promising him something special in the package. Mueller may or may not have a security team. But he'll know where Kane is."

"What do we know about this dude?"

"Streyling says he's her cyber guy. He told me not to hurt him too badly. Along with the computers, Mueller is probably our key to Kane's operation. Not to mention making sure Kane didn't send out the notebooks to every asshole she knows."

Peter turned back to look at the city, nodding his head. "Okay," he said. "What time does the mailbox store open?"

"Nine o'clock." Lewis looked at the other three men, now awake. "Let's be set up outside by eight."

Peter's phone pinged in his pocket. The blue dot had reappeared outside a FedEx facility by the Newark airport. He held up the phone, showing the others the map.

"The package is in Jersey, right across the river. We're in business."

Greenwich Village was a tangle of angled streets. The mailbox store was on Thompson, halfway between Washington Square Park and Houston, at the fringes of NYU. Thompson was one-way, and narrow with parked cars and a half-dozen outdoor dining sheds set up in the parking lanes on both sides of the street. The sheds had been built as an emergency measure to help restaurants stay open during the pandemic, but had proved so popular that the city had allowed many of them to remain.

By seven fifty, Lewis was drinking drip coffee in a fancy dining shed next door to the mailbox place, staying warm under a propane heater. His electric scooter leaned against the table. Peter was across the street with the other scooter, browsing at the window of a record store with a clear view of the mailbox shop door. June had the Acura idling at a hydrant on Sullivan, a one-way going the other direction, with Teddy riding shotgun, and Dinah was in the four-door pickup at a loading zone on Bleecker. They were roughly equidistant to three subway stations, but they all thought it more likely that Mueller would come in a car.

"We should have bought four scooters," Nino said. He was a half block to the north, sitting in the window of a coffee shop on the corner.

"Screw the scooters," Ray said. "We should have bought one of those heaters." He stood under construction scaffolding at the south end of the street. "I'm not built for this weather."

"You and Nino can rotate every hour," Lewis said.

"I didn't agree to that," Nino said.

Except for Dinah, they all wore body armor and weapons under the oversized coats, which were varied enough in color and style to not resemble a uniform, along with the upgraded headsets on a seven-way call. It was cold enough that Peter was worried about battery life, although they all had backup batteries charged and warm in their pockets.

By the time the mailbox store opened, the tracker app's blue dot had already left the FedEx facility. It disappeared briefly as it passed through the Holland Tunnel under the Hudson, but reappeared at the Hudson rotary and was now making stops along Canal. Lewis had called the store and the clerk had told him that they often got multiple deliveries a day, the first before ten thirty, the last as late as four thirty.

According to Streyling, the cyber guy was short, white, and chubby, and usually dressed like a gangster rapper from the nineties. Recognizing rap fashion was outside Peter's wheelhouse, so his plan was to watch the mailbox shop's door and take a photo of any guy leaving with the white FedEx box wrapped with too much tape.

He wasn't sure how accurate the tracker would be on the street, but he hoped it would help them make sure they had the right guy. Whether Mueller came in a car or on foot, the Heavy Lifters had enough available options to keep him covered.

The sidewalks were busy as the apartments emptied, commuters headed to work. At nine, foot traffic was almost nonexistent. Nobody went inside the mailbox place. It was cold and still. The air smelled damp. Peter knew snow was coming.

The FedEx truck pulled up at nine forty-five and double-parked while the driver walked in with two plastic totes filled with packages. He left three minutes later, the totes filled with what looked like different packages. When the truck drove off, Peter checked the app again and saw the blue dot inside the store.

Peter walked up and down the street to stay warm. Around ten, foot traffic picked up again, Nino and Ray reporting descriptions from their corners. A taxi stopped and waited while somebody dropped off packages. Three pedestrians went inside, but two were women and one was a willowy young Black man. None emerged with a box.

It was after eleven when Nino said, "I got a short white guy in a flat-brim Yankees cap and a huge down parka just came around the corner from Canal. Wearing earbuds. No visible security."

"I got him," Lewis said a minute later. "Fur-lined hood, black track pants, and Timberlands, too. Looking real fly, white dude."

Peter saw him as he cleared Lewis's shed. His boots were unlaced and sloppy on his feet. He was looking at his phone and passed the mailbox shop without a glance. Ten seconds later, he stopped and appeared to check the street address of a redbrick apartment building, then turned around and went back up the street to the shop and went inside.

The glass window was reflective with the light. Peter couldn't see what the guy was doing. He stepped into the record shop and stood at the window and flipped through the racks. They had some pretty good used vinyl. It made Peter want to buy a turntable. He wondered if he'd ever go back to that house on the edge of the ravine.

Five minutes later, the guy came back out with a white FedEx box under his arm. It was the right size, and the edges were shiny with too much clear tape.

It didn't look like the box had been opened. They'd all already agreed that, if the box was open when Mueller left the shop, or it looked like he was going to open the box, they'd pick him up. If Mueller figured out that the package was a fake and called Kane, the plan was dead and they'd have to start over. Otherwise, they'd follow him home, use him to get inside, hope Kane was there.

Mueller, if that's who he was, didn't even look around. He fumbled in his pocket for some kind of vape pen and took a long hit, then headed back the way he'd come.

When he walked past the corner of the teahouse shed and out of Peter's line of sight, Peter took out his phone and checked the app. The blue dot was keeping pace.

"That's our guy," he said. "Nino, pick him up when he passes. He looks totally clueless, but keep an eye out for security. This could still be a double cross by Streyling. Lewis and I will be a half block behind. June, go up to the corner and wait. Dinah, head west to Sixth Ave and hold there. We might have to grab him."

Finding him was the easy part.

Following him home shouldn't be too hard.

What they'd have to do when they got to Kane's place—that would be much more difficult.

57

Ari Mueller wandered up the street with his eyes on his phone, white wireless earbuds visible through his uncombed hair, bobbing his head to music only he could hear. He didn't glance over his shoulder or scan the other side of the street to get a look at anyone who might be pacing him. He didn't pause at a shop window or slip inside a store to force a potential tail to keep walking.

Not a care in the world, Peter thought.

That would change soon enough.

By the time Mueller reached the corner, Nino was fifty feet behind him. Peter was on the scooter a hundred yards back, rolling slow. Lewis had gone the other direction, to loop around and ride parallel, out of view, but ready to pick him up if he stepped into a cab.

As Mueller crossed the street toward Washington Square Park, a long black sedan pulled up to the curb in front of him. The driver-side window slid down, revealing a square-shouldered guy with a salt-and-pepper brush cut and a close-cropped beard.

Security, Peter thought. "Time to step up our game, people. This guy's a pro."

Ari stopped in the road with a hand on his hip, the body language of annoyance. In Peter's ear, Nino said, "Dude asked if our guy wanted a lift." Nino had to take a left at the corner so the driver wouldn't see his face. Peter had already hit the scooter's throttle to take up the slack.

As he closed in, he heard Ari's raised voice saying, "Screw you, Brewster, I can go for a walk without a babysitter."

The security man's face remained expressionless. His lips moved, but Peter didn't catch the words. While he spoke, his eyes looked past Ari, searching the streetscape around him. Definitely a professional.

"She doesn't own me, Brewster. I'm allowed to leave the apartment."

Brewster spoke louder now. "Please get in the car, Ari. This is not a good time. Mallory's concerned about you. It's for your own good."

But Ari just jammed the FedEx box deeper under his arm and walked around the back of the black car and into the park.

Brewster's eyes went to his mirror, tracking Ari's path until he disappeared up the path. Then the window slid up and the long car eased forward until it vanished around the corner.

"June, you take the black car. I'm on Mueller."

Peter went right until he found the next entrance to the park, then turned left through an opening in a low wrought-iron fence. Tall, leafless trees lined the path, their branches crusted white with windblown snow. The benches were empty. Ahead to the left was the Washington Square Arch. He went toward it and saw Mueller sitting on a bench, his vape pen in one hand and the FedEx box on the seat beside him.

At this rate, it was going to be a long, cold trip.

Peter traded duties with Lewis, then began to work his way around the perimeter of the park, looking for the long black car, keeping an eye on Mueller, and thinking about Streyling's trick with the FedEx box. It would be a little complicated to set up and maintain, but nearly foolproof in execution.

You'd rent a half-dozen mailboxes in a half-dozen cities, each with a different credit card. When a package arrived at one location, the store would have instructions to automatically forward it, overnight, to the next box. You'd address the packages to "boxholder" so the different names that had registered the mailboxes wouldn't interfere with the flow.

The beauty of the system was that overnight packages would be nearly impossible to track unless you knew exactly what you were looking for. The police would need to apply for a warrant to learn the forwarding address, and by the time they got one, the package would already have moved on. Every time it was forwarded to a new address, it became harder to follow. Especially if the package's final destination was yet another mailbox store, because there the trail would end.

It was a kind of three-card monte translated for modern e-commerce. You could mail drugs, guns, cash, whatever you wanted.

"He's on the move," Lewis said. "Headed through the arch toward Fifth Ave." Peter trailed behind, watching Lewis keep pace. The wind blew hard down Fifth. Even in his thermals, Peter was cold. Ari would be freezing, even in that ridiculous parka.

"Shit," June said. "I just lost the black car at a light."

"Did he lose you on purpose?"

"I don't know. New York drivers are insane. I should have been closer in this traffic."

"Mueller's hailing a cab," Lewis said. "Going west on Ninth. I'll stay with him."

"Okay," Peter said. "Dinah, where are you?"

"I'm on Sixth," she said. "I should see him any minute."

"Okay, good. Stay with that cab. If we have trouble, I might need you to do something."

The cab went north into Midtown, all the way past Bryant Park. Sixth was one-way, with Fifth and Seventh one-way the other direction, which made it hard to run parallel. But it would have been hard anyway, with all the traffic. Cars bunched up at the red lights, then spread out again, accelerating to the next red. The high-speed scooters let Peter and Lewis weave through traffic, keeping pace, trading positions regularly to conceal themselves from any watchers. There was no sign of the black car.

At 55th, the cab took a left, went three blocks past Broadway to Eighth Avenue, then turned uptown again. More one-ways. At 57th, the cab took a right, headed back toward Seventh. "Either he's trying to lose us or he's getting close to home," Peter said.

June was two blocks back, listening to the play-by-play. "Fifty-Seventh is Billionaire's Row," she said. "Some of those high-rise apartments go for fifty to a hundred million. Many of them unoccupied, investment properties owned by shell companies. There's a lot of foreign ownership, largely untraceable, a good way to wash dirty money."

"Sounds like we're in the right neighborhood," Lewis said.

The cab pulled over in front of a wavy glass-and-steel facade with a huge Nordstrom sign on the front, flanked by tall metal streetlights. Above the building's canopy, the sheer glass face stretched up as if reaching for heaven. Mueller got out of the cab with the FedEx box under his arm and paused for one last hit from his vape. Peter hopped the curb and stopped by the department store's display window as if checking something on his phone.

Ari took another hit, then walked past Nordstrom to a smaller door, the building's residential entrance. The uniformed doorman saw him coming and came out to hold the door for him.

But Peter was there, grabbing Mueller's arm and turning him back to the street. Peter's other hand held his knife, a cheap folder with a pocket clip and a thumb stud that let him open it one-handed. He poked the tip of the blade through the smaller man's coat and into the tender skin wrapping his ribs, just enough for him to feel it.

"Hey, Ari, I'm Peter. We're old friends, and you're walking me inside."

Ari stopped in his tracks, staring at Peter with his eyes wide. "Oh, no," he said. "No, no, no."

He tried to pull away, but Peter was too strong, using the movement to push the knife a little deeper. Not enough to do real damage, but definitely enough to get Ari's attention.

Ari's whole body tensed up. "No," he said. "Wait. She'll kill me."

Peter gave him a wolfish grin. "No more waiting, Ari. You made your choice a long time ago. Walk me in with a smile and you just might live through this."

58

Peter could feel the smaller man shaking. Despite himself, he felt a little sorry for the guy. It was one thing to be a master of the internet, but something else entirely to face the real risks of the physical world.

Lewis appeared on Ari's other side, smiling kindly. "You feeling all right, pal? You don't look so good." He took the FedEx box in one hand and wrapped the other around the little Israeli's other elbow, trapping him between them, then leaned in and dropped his voice to a growl. "Smile for the doorman and play your part, everything gonna be just fine."

The doorman, a solid-looking white guy in his forties, possibly another former cop, wasn't sure about any of it. His eyes flicked from Peter to Lewis to Ari. "Are you all right, sir? Do you know these gentlemen?"

"It's okay, ah, they're friends." Ari was hyperventilating a little, but not enough to notice. "This is Peter."

Peter nodded and eased Ari forward toward the heavy glass door as Lewis raised the hand with the box and gave a broad, friendly grin. "I'm Felix," he said in a plummy English accent. "Ari and I were at Oxford together."

The doorman still wasn't convinced. He focused on Ari. "Remind me, sir. I know you just got here last week. The hundred and ninth floor, right?"

Which told Peter that it was the right building, and now he also knew the floor. It also told him that the doorman didn't know Ari, which would help their little bit of theater. Could it really be this easy?

The Israeli opened his mouth to speak and Peter put the knife in another fraction of an inch. Ari grimaced, but his mouth clapped shut.

"My friend really doesn't feel well," Peter said. "It's something he ate. It's kind of an emergency. Unless you want to get a mop. And some disinfectant."

To his credit, the doorman didn't back away. He was good at his job. And maybe Peter and Lewis had set off his radar. "I'm sorry, I'll need to see some ID from all of you."

Peter didn't want to hurt the guy, but he didn't want him to call the police, either. For this to work out right, the crew needed at least an hour in the apartment, preferably more.

The doorman wouldn't be the only person on duty, either. In a white-glove building like this, at least one porter would be on call for parking cars and carrying packages. There would also be a concierge and probably a facilities manager in an office off the lobby. Any of them could call 911. Even if Peter and Lewis succeeded in taking them all down and locking them in the office, surely somebody would wonder where all the help had gone.

Peter held up a finger, turned away slightly, and lowered his voice. "Dinah, we need you. Make some noise."

Behind them came the rising roar of a big engine. The four-door pickup appeared in the street, moving fast, then hopped the curb and slammed into a tall metal light post at an angle. It made a sound like a hammer pounding a coffee can.

The hollow post, more than a foot in diameter, bent toward the building, but did not fall. Dinah kept the hammer down. The back wheels screeched on the blacktop. The pole was sturdy, but no match for the heavy truck. It bent farther until the metal finally tore and it fell with a shatter of glass and steel against the Nordstrom canopy, where it stuck at an angle, wedged against the building.

Dinah calmly reversed, got clear, then swerved into traffic and drove away.

"Holy crap." The doorman stared up at the spectacle, transfixed, no longer interested in Peter or Lewis.

Peter pulled Ari forward and through the glass doors into the lobby, an opulent space echoing with marble, with Lewis walking backward, keeping an eye on the street. The elevators were toward the back, two banks of five. Ari struggled in his grip, so Peter sunk the knife a little deeper. "Which button, Ari?" Not all the elevators would go up to the hundred and ninth floor.

"This one." Ari pointed and Peter knuckled the down button as a young guy in a uniform, probably the porter, hustled through a side door and out the front. He didn't even look at the three men by the elevators. He'd either heard the crash or had been called by the doorman.

Peter didn't know whether the collision outside would be enough of a distraction to prevent the doorman from chasing them down, although he hoped it would buy them some time. Not that it would make a difference in the long run. He'd seen multiple security cameras on the building's facade and in the lobby, capturing their faces. They were committed now. There was nothing to do but push forward.

DEA Special Agent in Charge Gottschall better honor their deal, Peter thought.

Waiting for the elevator to arrive, Lewis pulled a pistol from his belt and held it down along his leg as he released Ari's arm. "Keys," he said. Ari fumbled in his coat pocket and pulled out a thumb-sized rectangular fob on a ring with a single large door key. In many newer buildings, as a security measure, the elevators required a chip card or electronic fob to select a floor. It would allow the rider access only to his own floor, as well as common areas like the building's gym or spa or private club.

The doors opened and Peter escorted Ari inside. But they weren't going up just yet. Lewis put the fob to the reader and selected the floor marked P4, then hit the door close button. The lowest parking floor would probably have the fewest people.

The elevator dropped. Peter leaned on the knife, just a little, reminding Ari of the situation. "What's the layout upstairs?"

"I, uh, I don't know," Ari said. "It's an apartment?"

"Which unit?" Lewis asked.

"It's the whole floor," Ari said. "One-oh-nine." He was still hyperventilating. His Yankees hat was askew and his coat had fallen partway open, showing a red Chicago Bulls jersey, a half-dozen gold ropes, and a heavy gold medallion with his first name spelled out in diamonds.

"In the apartment," Peter said. "Where does the elevator open?"

"A lobby area, with coat closets and emergency stairs and doors to the inside."

"More than one door to the inside?"

Ari blinked, thinking. "Yeah. Three. To the living room, the kitchen, and, like, the master suite."

"Are the doors kept locked?"

"No. There's always somebody posted there with a radio and a gun."

"How many security people total?"

"Nine," Ari said. "Plus Mallory and me. That's it."

The elevator came to a stop. A cool female voice said, "Sublevel four."

The doors opened to resident parking, fifty feet below the street. Fewer than half the visible spaces had vehicles. Definitely absentee owners.

"Good enough," Lewis said. "We need to move." He handed Peter the elevator fob. "You secure Ari and I'll start searching cars." They'd made a half-dozen rough plans with variations, depending on where they ended up. Lewis dropped his duffel in the elevator doorway and ran.

Peter wiggled the knife. "You're going to behave, right?"

"Yes, yes, of course. Please don't hurt me." Ari was crying now. Peter felt like an asshole.

He put the knife away, then zip-tied Ari's wrists and ankles, then shucked his duffel, found a roll of duct tape, and ran a strip over the little Israeli's mouth. "Can you breathe?"

Ari nodded, eyes wide.

"Good." Peter eased him to the floor. "I'd like to keep you alive. But if you cause me any trouble, that might change. Do you understand?"

Ari nodded again, clearly eager to please.

Peter sighed and adjusted his headset. "Lewis, can you hear me? Lewis?"

There was no answer. Peter pulled out his phone. The seven-way call was gone. They'd lost reception in the parking garage. He fished inside his duffel for the radios and headsets they'd taken from the operators outside Maurice's house. He already had basic first-aid supplies tucked into his coat pockets.

The elevator door dinged and pushed against Lewis's duffel. Peter wondered how Dinah was doing, if June and the others were anywhere close.

He couldn't shake the feeling that this whole thing was not going to end well.

59

Working his way outward from the elevator bay, Lewis tried six cars before he found an unlocked Lexus.

He ducked his head inside and began to search for the garage entry mechanism. In a building like this, it would likely be similar to the elevator fob, but larger and more powerful, so the garage door sensor could read it from inside the glove box or other compartment.

He found it in the center console, a rounded disk the size of a half-dollar. He also found the car keys, a major bonus. Driving was faster and easier than running. He fired up the engine and backed out of the spot, then cranked the Lexus up the ramp toward the exit four floors away, tires squealing on the polished concrete. He had no idea how much time they had.

When he saw the wide steel security door, he hit the brakes and eased forward until the sensor triggered and the door rolled up. June was right outside in the Acura, with Teddy in the passenger seat.

Lewis waved her in. He'd already realized he'd lost the cell connection underground. June held up a finger, telling him to wait.

Behind her, pedestrians strolled by like it was an ordinary day. The entrance was on Broadway, not 57th, so he couldn't see whether Dinah had managed to get away in the blue truck. She was supposed to drive a few blocks, drop the pickup at a hydrant or loading zone, and walk back to the building to watch for the police. She'd really nailed that light pole, though. That woman kept surprising him.

Nino and Ray appeared on the ramp, jogging toward him. They got in the Acura and Lewis backed up slowly, letting June nose forward through the still-open garage door. When she was mostly in, he looked over his shoulder and hit the gas, reversing as fast as the car would allow, all the way down to the lowest level.

He put the Lexus back where he found it, but kept the fob. They'd need it to get out. June put the Acura in the empty slot beside it and they all piled out and ran around the last corner toward the elevator bank. Teddy grinning like an idiot with his tranquilizer gun and his coat pockets bulging with spare darts. Nino and Ray with serious faces, unbuttoning their own coats to reveal the armor and weapons beneath.

Lewis grabbed June's sleeve, slowing her for a moment. "Did you hear anything from Dinah?"

June patted his hand. "She's fine, Lewis. She left the truck and walked away. She's safer than we are." Then she pulled away and turned and began to run after the others.

Lewis felt like he was going to throw up. He swallowed it down and followed June's lead.

Peter stood at the elevator, holding the doors open, handing out radios. Ari lay on his belly on the elevator floor. "This looks like a party," Teddy said, bouncing on his toes. "Like today is my birthday."

Nino stepped over the little Israeli. "How many upstairs?"

"Ari said nine security plus Kane," Lewis said. "One posted in the elevator lobby, right when the doors open." He adjusted his headset. "Teddy leads with the dart gun, it's quiet. If the other side gets loud, we do the same."

The others crowded in, gearing up. Ray said, "Any idea of the layout?"

"All we know is, it's the whole floor," Peter said. "We're doing this old-school, move fast and clear rooms as we go. Keep in mind there's a door from the kitchen and the master to the elevator lobby. Ray and June, you hold in the lobby for runners. Also, watch your fire discipline, everybody. If we start shooting out windows, the cops will be on us in a hurry. Anything else?"

"Don't kill Mallory Kane," Lewis said. "We need her."

They all wore headsets now. Peter did a quick comms check, then stepped inside the elevator. The doors closed immediately. He'd already put the fob to the reader. The button marked 109 was lit in red. The elevator began to rise.

It was weirdly fast, bypassing the first seventy floors in a hurry. Lewis felt his heart pounding in his chest. He worked his jaw and swallowed so his ears would pop. He pulled in deep breaths, to calm himself and oxygenate his blood.

In a few minutes this would all be over.

One way or another.

60

The cool voice said, "One hundred and ninth floor."

Teddy stood front and center, bouncing on his toes with the weird-looking dart gun to his shoulder and that broad smile on his face. Upstate Wilson ready to go.

As the elevator door began to slide open, a bulky man in body armor over a white polo shirt raised a shotgun and fired through the gap, hitting Teddy square in the chest. It was Brewster, the square-shouldered man from the black car.

Time slowed to a crawl. Peter noticed, as if in a dream, that the shotgun had an orange pump handle, a law enforcement convention that told him it was loaded with nonlethal beanbags. Although the term didn't begin to convey the power of the projectile, a small Kevlar package filled with buckshot that could put you on the ground for a solid minute. The man's hip holster held a Taser.

Teddy staggered back but didn't fall, and also somehow managed to fire the dart gun, all barrels. The elevator door continued its slide into its recessed slot, revealing six more security men, similarly armed and armored, fanned out in the small marble-tiled elevator lobby. The dart gun's wide pattern caught the four in the center, with multiple darts each.

Peter had to give it to them, they never looked down at the red-feathered darts in their meaty arms. Although they must have already been feeling the drug, they fired into the elevator. Another beanbag slammed into Teddy's chest plate, but two more flew over his head to hit the back wall of the elevator car with a double thump. As the drug kicked in for real, the shotguns sank and the men's eyes drifted. They were out of the fight. But the elevator door was still opening and the remaining three security men were taking aim.

So much for the surprise attack, Peter thought. The security men had known the Ghost Killers were coming, and planned to take them alive.

Teddy was still standing, his bulk acting as a kind of shield for the people behind him. Peter sidestepped right, sheltering behind the protection of the elevator's control panel, and put three suppressed rounds into the chest plate of the man on the far left, knocking him off balance. It would feel, Peter knew from experience, like getting punched very hard. The man's shotgun went off, *BOOM.* Peter felt the wind on his face as the round flew past his head and thumped into the corner behind him.

On the other side, Lewis had made the same lateral movement and now fired a triple-tap at the man on the right, spinning him sideways as he fired, *BOOM.* The beanbag took out a wall sconce in an explosion of glass.

The last man must have seen the way things were going, because he began to backpedal toward the door. A beanbag round was not going to do it. He fired anyway and hit Teddy in the gut, then released the shotgun and began to scrabble at a big pistol in a drop-leg holster.

Peter felt Teddy buckle beside him. Before he could adjust his aim, Ray leaped past at a run and slammed into the security guy.

Ray drove the man hard back into the marble-tiled wall behind him, knocking the breath out of him, then hooked an ankle and rode him down to the marble floor, using the hard stone as a weapon. Peter and Lewis jumped out and faced the two armor-shot security men still on their feet. Peter's guy had refocused on the fight and was bringing his shotgun to bear, but an elbow to the side of his head bounced him off the wall and made him lose interest. Peter kicked away the shotgun. Lewis had the other man down on the ground, bleeding from the arm or shoulder.

Peter's ears rang from the shotgun blasts. Everyone else in the apartment would definitely know they were coming. He got his man's wrists behind his back with a flex-cuff and looked around the elevator lobby, seeing four exits. A steel door to the stairwell, two normal doors that would probably lead directly to the kitchen and primary bedroom, and a set of closed double doors as the entry to the apartment proper.

He ran to the double doors. Nino was there first, his hand ready on the knob. June was sheltered inside the open elevator with Ari the hacker. Lewis had already cuffed his man. Now he fired a silenced round into a security camera on the ceiling while Ray worked to contain the last security guy and Teddy climbed to his feet with a wince.

With three beanbags to the chest and belly, he had to be hurting. From the wheeze as he breathed, he'd probably broken a rib. But he looked at Peter with his chin raised defiantly. "I'm good."

Peter nodded. "Secure this room. Keep those elevator doors open. Protect June and Ari." It would all be for nothing if they didn't find Mallory Kane and put a stop to this.

Lewis stacked up behind Peter. Ray checked the stairwell, then set up behind Lewis. Ari had said there were nine men on Kane's security team. They'd taken down seven men just now. Which meant two left.

Probably guarding Kane. Peter thought about taking the dart gun, but it still had to be reloaded and wouldn't be much use in a real firefight. He clapped Nino on the shoulder. "Go."

Nino turned the knob and pushed open the door, then stepped aside and peeled around to the back of the stack. Peter went through the hole, weapon up and ready, Lewis right behind him.

To the right was an enormous living area wrapped with huge windows framing the park and city and sky. The only furniture was a long L-shaped sectional couch and a flat-screen TV standing on a pair of milk crates. Beer bottles stood on the floor in the corners. No visible security guys.

There was no sound but the soft hush of the heating system and the wind tearing at the sharp corners of the building.

To the right was a dining room, paneled in polished walnut and large enough to seat twenty people. It was empty but for a plastic folding table and four folding chairs. They looked tiny and cheap in the elegant space. Beyond it, through a doorway, a narrow slice of white cabinets. The kitchen.

To the left was a long hall with a row of doors, probably bedrooms. Peter bladed his hand right, and Nino and Ray angled toward the kitchen. With Lewis on his shoulder, Peter headed down the hall.

They took positions on either side of the first door. While Lewis kept watch on the hall, Peter turned the knob and pushed it open and pivoted inside like he'd done a thousand times before, weapon up in line with his eyes. He saw a short entryway with a closet on one side and a bathroom on the other. Nobody there or in the bedroom beyond. Just a million-dollar view, a pair of thin blankets over a pair of narrow inflatable mattresses, and phone chargers plugged into the wall. Like they were camping out, he thought. "Clear."

They did the next bedroom, and the next, and the next. They were all empty.

"Nobody in the kitchen." Nino's voice in Peter's ear. "Nobody in the maid's quarters past it. Next door is to the elevator lobby."

"Ray, reinforce the lobby," Lewis said. "Nino, come to us in the hall, we're clearing rooms."

Another bedroom and a family room, also empty. Where the hell were they?

Then Nino was there, pretty quiet for a guy his size. The hallway turned left at the end. Around the corner would probably be the primary bedroom and bath.

Peter put his back to the right hallway wall and slipped forward to peek left. Nobody there, just a closed door, painted red. "Ray, status."

"Lobby clear," Ray said in his ear.

"Hall is clear to the corner. It ends at a door. I think the primary bedroom is behind it. Ari said there was an exit to the lobby in there somewhere, so be ready for runners."

"Roger that," Ray said.

Peter and Lewis advanced to the red door, each taking a side. Nino hung back behind the cover of the corner, weapon raised. On the hinge side, Lewis tested the knob. It was unlocked. He looked at Peter, who nodded. Lewis turned the knob and pushed the door open. Peter went through.

More hallway, plush carpet, green wallpaper. Lewis came up beside him and they advanced, Nino taking up the rear. They passed a huge bathroom with a glass-walled marble shower and a tub for two with a wide city view. Empty. They came to a bedroom the size of a two-car garage with a mail-order mattress on the floor and a walk-in closet bigger than Peter and June's kitchen. There were no clothes, no suitcase, no toiletries. And definitely no Mallory Kane.

Peter hadn't thought she was the type to run. He turned to Lewis and Nino. "Where the hell is she? We didn't miss anything, did we?"

Then Lewis's phone buzzed in his pocket.

He pulled the phone and looked at the number. He put it on speaker. "Hey, kiddo. What's up?"

Standing beside Lewis, Peter expected to hear Charlie's voice, or maybe Miles. Instead, he heard someone else.

Streyling.

"I'm afraid there's been a slight change of plans."

61

Lewis's heart fluttered in his chest like a bird in a cage. The flood-waters of panic began to rise.

"Tell me they're okay," he said. "The boys, and the people they were with." Peter's parents.

"They're okay. Maybe a little beat-up," Streyling admitted. "Your kids aren't very good at doing what they're told. Must be a failure of parenting. The older couple was just stubborn."

"You sold us out," Lewis said.

"You mean I didn't honor the double cross? Of course not. I *love* my job."

The call cut in and out. Lewis moved toward the window, hoping that would improve the signal. Outside he saw the white world spread out below him, from the Atlantic to the Hudson and beyond. With binoculars, he could probably find that gravel lot near the Port of New Jersey.

"Put Kane on," he said. "This is between her and me."

THE PRICE YOU PAY

"Lewis, you're not giving orders." Streyling sounded amused. "I am."

"Tell her she doesn't need the boys, or the others," Lewis said. "All she needs is me. I killed her son. I'm the one she wants."

"Well, that's very stand-up," Streyling said. "Although I expected nothing less, having read all about you in those notebooks. But Mallory wants everybody in her apartment, including the woman who crashed the truck into the light pole on Fifty-Seventh Street. Nice touch, by the way. There's a jet waiting at Teterboro, at Signature. Tail number NC1212. Drive right out onto the tarmac. Bring Ari. Leave everything else."

"This was always your plan," Lewis said. "Beanbags and Tasers, put us on a plane."

"Oh, no," Streyling said. "The plan was to take you alive and let Mallory take you apart. Cart the bodies down to the parking garage in duffel bags." A smile filled his voice. "But last night, I got lucky. I found your kids. Through the family cell account on your laptop." He chuckled. "I talked a service rep into turning on their phone locators, used the laptop to find them. Let me tell you, it really made Mallory's day."

Lewis felt the knowledge cut deep. This was all his fault. Going back twenty years, the choices he'd made. He would trade himself for those boys in a heartbeat.

Streyling kept talking. "Anyway, you have an hour to get on that plane. If you're late, Mallory starts taking fingers." He chuckled. "Although she might anyway. She's in quite a state, I'll tell you."

Then the phone went silent. He'd ended the call.

Lewis turned to Peter, who'd heard everything. His face was pale. "Peter, your parents will be fine. We're going to solve this."

"Hell yes, we will." Peter took a deep breath, held it, then let it out slowly. Lewis watched him set aside the fear and the pain. Leaving only anger, which would burn clean and hot, all the way to their families.

Lewis closed his eyes and took a breath, trying to do the same.

But he couldn't stop seeing them in his mind's eye, Charlie and little Miles. Scared and alone and hurting.

Dear God, what had he done?

They split up and made a fast pass through the apartment, looking for anything that might be helpful. The living areas were devoid of anything remotely personal. The security guys' bedrooms had only small suitcases, a few clothes, toiletries, spare pistols and ammunition. Lewis and his crew already had enough guns, but they wouldn't do him any good. There was no laptop or pad, just the security team's phones. The buffer on the Wi-Fi router might hold something useful, but Lewis wasn't the person to harvest that. He'd leave it to the DEA guys. If he decided to call them. If Gottschall honored the deal they'd made. Right now he was thinking they'd just make things worse. At the very least, they'd get in the way of what he had to do next.

"Lewis." Peter held an armful of empty duffel bags. "I found these in the closet of the maid's room."

Lewis took one and shook it out. It was huge. He handed it to Nino. "Stick a couple darts into Ari, then see if he'll fit in there," he said. "We don't want him loose or talking to anyone on the plane. But make sure he can get some air."

He followed the others into the lobby, where June had already taken the security men's phones and dropped them down the trash chute. Now she knelt below the ruined security camera and swiped her fingertips across the tile. She showed Lewis what she'd found. "Marble dust," she said. "They must have just installed that camera. So Kane could watch her guys take us out. Streyling's play must be a plan B."

Teddy and Ray had put a dart into each of the three conscious men, then cuffed the ones who were already out, wrists and ankles. They'd be uncomfortable when they woke up, but they'd be alive, and more important, it would take them a while to get themselves free to get back into the fight. Lewis needed to buy all the time he could.

The whole thing had cost them five minutes and gained them nothing. "Load up, time to go." He stood at the elevator door, holding it with his foot while the crew filed in past him. Then he stepped back and the doors closed behind him. He hit the button for the parking level where they'd left the cars. He still hadn't told Dinah.

The elevator dropped like the bottom falling out of the world.

They took both cars, loading Ari in the trunk of the Lexus along with two duffels loaded with weapons. June had volunteered to pick up Dinah at the Carnegie Diner, where she was waiting for the all clear. To his shame, Lewis agreed. Then they sped up the parkway to the George Washington Bridge and crossed the Hudson into New Jersey. Midday traffic wasn't too bad, and Peter drove the Lexus with a calm focus that Lewis envied.

"Peter," he said. "I'm so sorry."

"Don't start with that. I'm barely keeping my shit together as it is." Peter glanced quickly at the rearview, no doubt making sure June was right behind him. "When it's over, we'll have a good story we won't tell to anyone, all right?"

Lewis cleared his throat. He was definitely not keeping his shit together. "I don't," he said. "I just."

Powering past a cement truck, Peter didn't take his eyes off the road, but his broad, knuckly hand found Lewis's shoulder and grabbed on. "I know you're hurting," he said. "No shame in that. But you know I've got you on this. You and your boys." His grip tightened. "Trying to push down the pain won't help. So take a minute and feel it. Accept it. Because in a few hours, to get them safe, they're going to need you all in. Stone cold and frosty as hell. You read me, brother?"

Lewis swallowed and looked at his lap. He felt the pricking of tears and closed his eyes to hide his shame from his friend. It was all his fault. The car bucked beneath him on the lousy roadway. Peter's strong hand was the only thing holding him in place.

He gulped in a breath, then another. Then Teddy's big mitt came over the seatback and clapped onto his other shoulder. "We've all got you, boss."

And Lewis let himself fall apart, just for a minute, for what he'd done, for what he might lose, while the other men sat silently and the Lexus shifted smoothly from lane to lane as Peter found the fastest route toward home.

62

PETER

The beauty of private air travel, it turned out, was that you didn't have to go through security or wait in lines. You drove right out to where the planes were parked. Nobody checked their IDs or asked any questions. You could bring as many guns as you wanted. Peter figured this was why Lewis had sometimes flown private when it was too far to drive. He'd always had plenty of money up until now.

Peter didn't give a damn about the money, he never had. He was just worried about his parents, and those boys, whom he loved with all his heart. But he knew what his dad would say. *Don't worry about what might be, and stay focused on what is, right now.* The engineer turned building contractor had always been a little philosophical. His mom would just be royally pissed.

The pilot was a windburned guy in a fleece sweater who took one look at Peter's face and headed into the cockpit. The copilot was already there, getting the engines warmed up. Peter was half expecting the other two security guys to take control, but they weren't there. Something told him they'd be on the ground when they landed. With reinforcements.

The wind howled across the open runways, blasting any exposed skin and rocking the plane slightly on its landing gear. Peter and Lewis loaded the gun duffels up the narrow stairs. They had to duck their heads slightly to stand inside. Teddy climbed up with Ari's duffel slung under one arm like a rolled-up rug he was taking to the dump, but he laid it almost gently in the center aisle at the back of the plane. June and the others got the rest of the bags. Dinah's eyes were red and raw. Lewis stood in the aisle and put his arms around her and held her while she cried. Nobody spoke.

Then the engines wound up and the plane began to move. They'd left the keys in the cars. Somebody from the charter service would move them. Or not. It didn't matter. Only one thing mattered.

Once, the twelve-seat Gulfstream had been the state of the art for luxury air travel. But that was many years ago, and its best days were behind it. The cherry veneer was cracked and peeling, and the two rows of tan leather seats sagged from thousands of well-fed backsides. The latch seemed to be broken on the lavatory door, which banged open with the steep takeoff, then banged shut again as the engines backed off and the plane banked hard toward the west.

Ray said, "Okay, what's the plan?"

Peter shook his head. "We don't know enough to make a plan. We'll just have to react. Get ready and stay ready and when our chance comes, we take it."

Nino put his seat back. "I'm going to grab a little shut-eye," he said.

"Good idea," Peter said. He held hands with June across the aisle. Ahead of them, Lewis and Dinah were doing the same. He heard a soft whisper and realized Dinah was praying.

Not for the first time, Peter wished he had some kind of religion, some sense of a just and benevolent God. What little he'd once had, the war had long ago wrung out of him.

All that remained was faith in himself and his friends.

It would have to be enough.

As the plane banked over the tiny airport, the plow-scraped runway looked like thin vanilla frosting over chocolate cake. It was larger than the airfield south of Milwaukee, but not by much.

They landed and approached the terminal, which looked like a modest single-story log house. A dark Dodge cargo van was parked outside. When the pilot opened the door and lowered the steps, two big men in unzipped down coats got out of the van. They were burly and bearded, both wearing wraparound sunglasses in the dim, cloudy afternoon. They had body armor beneath the coats, angular Uzi submachine guns slung around their necks, and pistols visible in holsters on their hips. The sunglasses were another kind of armor, Peter knew, as were the beards, hiding any doubt, fear, or shame.

"Here we go," he said.

Behind him, Lewis's phone rang. He put it on speaker.

It was Streyling. "If you don't do exactly as I say, very bad things will happen to your kids, and to the other two. You don't want that, right?"

"No," Lewis said. "Where are they?"

"You'll see them soon enough. Now walk down to the van, one by one. No weapons. They'll search you and cuff you. Then they'll take you to us."

"Put them on the phone," Lewis said. "I need to know they're still alive."

"Surely you don't think you're in charge here."

"I need to know they're alive," Lewis said again. "If they are, and I have your word that you'll let them go once you have us, I'm all yours."

Streyling sighed audibly. "Wait one."

Charlie came on, sounding just like his dad. "They haven't touched Miles, but he's really scared."

"What about you?"

"Nothing that won't heal," he said. "Peter's mom is fine, his dad got a little beat-up. But don't worry about us. Just come get these motherf—"

From the phone, the dull thud of a fist, a grunt of pain.

"If you hurt a hair on their heads—"

"Oh, please," Streyling said. "You're in no position to make demands. Alive and missing a few fingers is better than dead, right?"

The phone went silent. Lewis stood and began to make his way toward the exit, his eyes like sinkholes without bottoms. One by one, the rest of them followed.

The pilot had retreated to the cockpit doorway, a worried look on his face. He'd seen the men with guns. "What's going on?"

Peter didn't want him to call the cops. But before he could decide how to play it, June said, "It's a corporate bonding retreat. We're being taken hostage and have to escape."

"Oh." The pilot looked relieved. He looked at Teddy dragging the enormous duffel bag down the aisle. Everything else remained piled in the luggage compartment by the exit. "What about the rest of your things?"

June smiled as if she meant it. "Can you take them to the terminal for us? We'll pick them up when it's over. There's a big party at the end."

Going down the steps, Peter realized that Lewis had never asked about the dog, Mingus. Streyling hadn't mentioned him, either.

Whether he'd been captured, escaped, or been killed, Peter didn't know. But he wasn't going to bring it up.

Because if Mingus was still out there, his protective instincts would lock him in on the boys' captors like a cruise missile. His wolfish ancestors had covered a hundred miles a day in search of prey.

Somehow Peter knew Mingus would do no less.

63

The burly men had parked the van so that it blocked the view of the plane from the log cabin terminal.

"No talking," the lead man shouted. His nose and ears had the squashed look of a boxer. One by one, he frisked them efficiently and thoroughly, emptying their pockets, even checking their mouths like a prison guard. If he was uneasy about being outnumbered, he didn't show it. The second man, with nervous lips and cheeks pink from the wind, locked their hands behind their backs in hard metal cuffs and loaded them into the Dodge through the sliding side door.

Peter helped Teddy load Ari into the van, then made sure he was last in line with his coat unzipped, right behind June. That would put him closest to the driver's compartment.

There were no seats in the cargo bay, just a frigid steel floor and walls. No heat, either. The cold was almost certainly part of the strategy to keep them docile, but Peter didn't think it would matter. It took effort, but he forced his breathing to stay slow and steady, which kept the war that lived inside him at a low hum like an idling race car, just waiting for him to step on the gas.

The lead man climbed behind the wheel, and the second man closed the sliding door and got in the passenger seat. Peter looked at Nino and Ray and Teddy, one by one, and saw their own crackling energy held in abeyance. They had all seen too much to harbor any illusions. They knew they would die, and probably soon, if they did not act. Each man nodded at him, ready to do what was needed.

Lewis and Dinah were a different story. They knelt together, shoulders touching. Lewis was hunched over as if about to be sick. Dinah's lips were moving in silent prayer.

Come on, Lewis, Peter thought. Now is the time to switch on. Your family needs you.

But Lewis remained in his half curl. His mind, Peter was sure, was full of snakes.

The lead man half turned in his seat with his pistol in his hand. "Here are the rules," he said. "Stay silent, stay seated. Any violation of that will be rewarded with a bullet. Someplace painful and permanent, like an elbow or a knee."

Then he put the engine in gear and steered them off the tarmac and onto a bumpy country road.

The Dodge had one side window and two rear windows. Outside, the clouds hung low. The sun wouldn't go down for another hour, but it felt like night was approaching fast. The heat in the driver's compartment was turned up full blast, but it didn't do much for the prisoners in the uninsulated cargo bay. The wind rocked the van on its heavy springs.

Peter recognized Ashland from the dozens of times he'd driven through it, visiting his parents. They turned left on Route 2 and drove along the rough and frozen coast of Lake Superior, headed west.

"Where are we going?" Peter asked.

The passenger said, "You'll find out. And shut up."

"How can you work for these people?"

The driver turned and stared at Peter. "Her money spends like any other. I know you guys were in the service. You think working for Uncle Sam was any damn different? We were enforcers, killers, for the oil interests, for the defense contractors."

Peter wasn't going to argue that point. "Kane's not just moving money," he said. "She's taken two innocent boys prisoner. Haven't you seen the videos? You know what she's capable of."

"She lost a son," the driver said. "An eye for an eye, that's what the Bible says. Now shut the hell up before I tell my partner to put a bullet in you."

Peter shut up. The van drove on. They crossed the slough at Fish Creek, with scrub brush and frozen water on both sides of the road, then turned onto Highway 13 and headed north on the two-lane toward Washburn and Bayfield, where Peter had grown up. Where his parents still lived. He hoped.

Outside, it just got darker.

June cleared her throat. He looked at her, and her eyes flicked to his groin. He knew she wasn't having romantic thoughts. She was reminding him of the handcuff key.

Peter hadn't forgotten. Ever since he'd gotten cuffed in the back of a police car in Iceland, he'd taken to sewing a hard plastic key into the bottom of his shirts. He also had a small knife blade built into his belt buckle that had gotten him out of trouble before. The problem would be getting to either one with the guards watching and his hands behind his back.

June glared at him as if he could read her mind, then turned away from him, motioning him closer with the fingers of one bound hand. He shifted to snug himself against her. All they needed for this to go wrong was for the passenger to look over his shoulder. He felt her hands fumble against his untucked flannel shirt, feeling for the buttons. The key was in the placket, below the last buttonhole.

The van hit a pothole and bounced. Peter and June crashed together and fell apart. The passenger glanced into the cargo bay, then returned his eyes to the windshield, staring at snow-covered farm fields and bare trees. Peter crept closer to June again.

The van was swaying. The highway was bumpy enough in the summer season, generally more patch than road, but it was much worse in winter with a recent snow and budget cutbacks. He looked down and saw her hands reach out to him and find the placket. Despite the cuffs, despite working blind and behind her back. Like Ginger Rogers, who did everything Fred Astaire could do, but backward and in reverse.

One hand grabbed the fabric while the other pulled it through the fingers, feeling for the lump at the bottom. Then the van lurched again, like it had hit a drift, and Peter tipped forward. June lost her hold and knocked her head against the van's sidewall. "Shit," she muttered.

"I said no talking," the driver shouted.

June snapped, "I hit my head, asshole." A trickle of red ran down her scalp. "Don't you know how to fucking drive?"

Peter suppressed a smile. June was pissed off and spoiling for a fight. She'd spent a lot of time at the dojo the last few years, and Peter had watched her take down skilled men twice her size.

But the driver didn't rise to the bait. He just turned in his seat and pointed a pistol at her. "I don't actually need you, lady. You want to know how much worse things can get? Just keep talking."

Then he pressed down harder on the gas, and the ride got even bumpier.

Peter looked at June and shook his head.

They were going to have to wait until they stopped.

64

They passed through the town of Washburn and continued north, snow-beaten cedars and pines gathering at the roadsides like pedestrians at a car wreck. Unpainted cabins hunched deep in the evergreens, as far apart from each other as possible. A grimy roadside bar flew past, just a handful of rust-eaten cars in the lot. Up here, prime tourist season was maybe eight weeks long, and the money didn't trickle down evenly to the locals.

Before the curve into Bayfield, the driver turned off the highway onto Hatchery Road. If anything, the ride got worse. Because this was the shortcut to his parents' place, Peter knew all the humps and potholes, and the driver managed to hit every one. He was doing it on purpose, Peter was pretty sure. The van itself became an instrument of discipline, picking them up and slamming them down on the hard metal floor, banging them into the walls and wheel wells, like a human pachinko game. The driver kept glancing into his rearview, enjoying the effects.

When the van finally began to slow, Peter looked out the window and saw the house he'd grown up in, set in a grove of tall maple trees.

Today wasn't a teaching day for his mom, which meant, normally, she'd be painting in the attached studio his dad had built, with the wide array of full-spectrum work lights blasting through the windows like the arrival of an alien spacecraft or the Second Coming of Christ.

But there were no lights from the studio. Or the house. Or his dad's workshop in the renovated barn. Each building was just a looming shadow surrounded by drifted snow.

Streyling would have waited until everyone was home before he and Kane and the two burly assholes knocked on the door.

Maybe Peter's dad had managed to grab the 20-gauge he kept by the door. He was strong and fit from decades of building houses, and he'd always been able to handle himself. But now he was over sixty, with a wonky shoulder and a trick knee. He'd have been no match for the security team. And he would have known that he could do more to help his wife, and the two boys entrusted to his care, as a live prisoner than a dead hero.

If Mingus was inside, they'd have had to shoot him. Otherwise he'd have torn into anyone laying a hand on those boys, or Peter's parents. But Mingus had always kept his own schedule, often jumping Lewis's fence to vanish for days at a time, in any weather, and he was no different up north. Peter just had to keep the faith that they were all still okay.

The van came to the long driveway and made the turn. The drive was neatly plowed. The house grew in the windshield. Peter thought they were going to stop. He thought he'd get to see his parents.

But the van didn't stop. It crossed the plowed gravel yard beside the barn and continued on toward the narrow tractor path that led into the meadow behind.

The dark house disappeared behind them.

The driver never said a word.

The daylight was almost gone.

Ahead through the windshield, Peter saw the torn rutted dirt of the path.

Someone had run a four-wheel drive with a snowplow down it recently, clearing the way. Probably his dad's beefy old F-100, the truck Peter had learned on. It hadn't been parked in its usual spot beside the shop. He could see the mark of the vehicle's wide knobby tires behind the rough snowy scrape.

At the far end of the meadow, the tractor path ended and the forest began. The land under the snow got lumpy and irregular. The driver, probably not Peter's dad, had probed with the plow for a way forward, but hadn't found a road. So he simply lifted its plow and hit the gas and pushed into the deeper snow. There was just a single set of tracks, which meant that, whoever it was, he was still in there.

But the cargo van wasn't four-wheel-drive. It couldn't handle the conditions in the woods. The driver clearly knew it, because he pulled to the left at a wide flat spot and threw the transmission into park.

Peter knew his parents' land intimately. They owned eighty acres, which didn't sound like much. In reality, beyond their own acreage lay vast, wild, and pathless woods, dotted with tangled swamps. Owned by a timber company that seemed unaware of its existence, it had been untouched by human hands since the first clear-cutting of the land more than a hundred years ago. There were no houses to the east until the next road, almost five miles away, and the same to the north and south. The whole wilderness was maybe twenty square miles.

Peter had camped in there as a kid, and hunted deer with a bow. It was an easy place to get lost in. Maybe that was the idea.

The driver took out his phone and made a call, listened for a minute, and put the phone away without saying a word. Then he looked at the passenger. "Keep your gun on them. If they so much as look at you funny, shoot somebody. I'll just be a minute."

He got out and walked around, and opened the side slider. The wind immediately whistled through the van, sucking out any residual heat that might have somehow collected inside the metal shell. The driver peered inside, but didn't see what he wanted, so he walked around to the back and opened both rear doors. With his pistol in his hand and his Uzi hanging inside his open parka, he looked at Lewis and Dinah, kneeling side by side, heads bowed.

"You two," he said. "Out."

65

LEWIS

Lewis wanted to kill the driver, but he knew he shouldn't.

If he could get his cuffed hands around to the front, he could probably manage the killing itself, but that wouldn't help his boys. And it definitely wouldn't help Dinah and June and Peter and Nino and Ray and Teddy, defenseless under the wary gun of the second man in the passenger seat.

He was banking on Kane and Streyling being unwilling to murder two innocent boys.

It wasn't much, but it was all he had.

He unbent himself from his crouch and knee-walked past Ari's duffel bag to the open doorway. "You don't need her," he said. "You only need me. I'm the one who killed Kane's son."

The driver grabbed Lewis's arm roughly and pulled him out of the van. With his hands behind his back and his legs trailing, he couldn't catch himself, but he managed to twist in the air and land on one shoulder, rather than his face. He'd fallen between the tire tracks that disappeared into the trees.

The driver looked down at him, shaking his head. "I thought you all were supposed to be badasses. Where I'm standing, you just look like sheep."

He grabbed Lewis's arm again and dragged him away from the doors, then turned back to the van. "Now you, sweetheart. Come on, I won't bite. You want to see your boys, right?"

From her knees, Dinah looked at the driver. Her tear-streaked face was composed, and despite the handcuffs, she held herself with that regal dignity that she'd had since she was a girl. She sat and put her legs over the threshold and stepped out into the howling wind as if every action was of her own choosing.

Six feet away, the driver pointed the gun at her. "You. Kneel in that tire track, your back to me." He watched Dinah comply, then turned to Lewis. "You, kneel in the other tire track. One move I don't like, I shoot her."

Lewis did as he was told.

With the pistol still aimed at Dinah, the driver bent and shoved Lewis forward into the packed snow, then knelt on the small of his back and, working one-handed, uncuffed one of Lewis's wrists. Then he stepped back to what he probably thought was a safe distance.

But the gun was still pointed at Dinah. And her boys were still out there somewhere. So Lewis did nothing.

"Take off your coat," the driver said.

Lewis pushed himself back to his knees and gave the man a look. He was already half-frozen from the trip in the unheated van. The driver tipped his head at the tire tracks curving into the woods. "My boss says that everything you want is at the end of those tracks. But you'll never get there if you don't do what I say."

Lewis couldn't dispute that. With the metal cuff dangling from one wrist, he shrugged out of his coat and set it aside. A gust picked it up and rolled it halfway across the meadow.

"Now the rest of it. Everything. Or I put one in her shoulder."

Lewis couldn't look at Dinah. He climbed to his feet, slowly and carefully, and peeled off his fleece sweater and the thermal top beneath it. The wind blew right through him. He turned and sat in the snow, his fingers already gone clumsy from the cold as he fumbled with his boots. He shucked them off, followed by his socks, his pants, and his thermal bottoms. Already his abdominals were starting to tremble.

But still he straightened up and stood naked and barefoot in the snow.

The driver just grinned. "Now, down on your front again."

Lewis forced himself to lie in the snow. His skin felt like it was being sandblasted. It was a good control mechanism, he thought, as the driver knelt on his back and pulled his arms into position. The cold would slow his reflexes and reaction time, sap his strength and coordination, and make him dumber with each passing minute as his body diverted the blood from his brain and limbs to protect the organs at his core.

Then the weight was gone and the driver had moved over to Dinah, unlocking one cuff. "Now you, same thing. But you can leave your underwear on. Just so you don't think I'm some kind of pervert."

"I know exactly what you are," Dinah said calmly, her voice cutting through the rising noise of a gust through the trees. "I'd pray for your soul if you had one."

"This ain't her fault," Lewis said, struggling to his knees. "I'm telling you, I'm the one killed Kane's son. I should be the one who pays the price."

The driver kicked Lewis in the hip, a hard professional blow, the toe of his boot like a billy club to the bone. "I got orders. You think this is a game? The longer this takes, the colder you get."

"It's okay, Lewis." Dinah unzipped her coat and gave it to the wind.

When she was down to long underwear, tight enough to reveal any weapon, the driver cuffed her hands again, then waved the pistol forward at the narrow twin paths made by the tire tracks.

"Head thataway," he said. "Walk to the light, maybe a quarter mile. There's a fire will keep you warm."

"Lewis." Peter's strong voice cut through the night.

He looked for his friend in the depths of the van.

Peter raised his chin. "Semper fi," he called.

The Marine Corps motto, meaning always faithful. But not just a motto. A promise.

Lewis nodded, then turned back at Dinah. "Time to go."

She was staring at him. He'd never gotten used to the weight of her eyes. Then she pivoted to face the dark woods ahead of them, and began to walk.

As they left the meadow and stepped into the woods, she said, "Please tell me you know how we get our children out of this mess."

The tire tracks curved ahead of them. His feet burned in the snow. "Peter has a plan." His stomach muscles were trembling uncontrollably now, making it harder to speak.

"What is it?"

"I don't know. We just have to keep the boys alive until he comes through. In the meantime, we do what we can to improve the odds."

He checked over his shoulder. The van had already disappeared behind the evergreen branches. He dropped on his butt with his legs out front. Strangely, he didn't feel any colder.

Dinah took a few steps before she realized he'd stopped. "What on earth are you doing?"

Lowering his shoulders, he bent his spine and forced his naked hips backward through the circle of his cuffed arms. With his wrists now under his knees, he leaned forward and scraped the cuffs around his bare heels to bring the cuffs to the front of his body. Stretching had always been a big part of his workout, but he could never have managed this trick without being stripped naked.

Dinah was already sitting, doing the same thing. She made it look easy. She could have been a dancer.

He pulled her up and swatted the snow off her butt and thighs. His own backside felt like a steak forgotten in the freezer. "Can you run? Not fast, but big. We need to make our own heat."

They began to jog, high-stepping like Clydesdales, swinging their arms from side to side. Now he couldn't feel anything below his ankles. His feet were like clubs striking the ground. He and Peter ran outside all winter long. He'd thought he was used to the cold. But not like this.

The tire tracks straightened. Ahead of them, an orange glow filtered low through the evergreens. A fire, the driver had said. They kept moving and the glow got brighter, then the trees ended and they stood at the edge of a clearing. The tracks turned to the left, leading to the big knobby tires of an ancient pickup with a plow on the front and a salt spreader bolted into the bed. Peter's dad's truck. In the middle of the clearing was a bright leaping bonfire. On the far side stood four figures, dark behind the light.

Lewis took Dinah's hand. His own were shaking. "My love, I'm so sorry."

"Do *not* apologize to me right now." Her face was fierce, a warrior queen, but the tears had begun to fall again, turning to ice on her frozen cheeks. "Right now, you get down to *business*."

He nodded and tugged her hand and began to walk toward the bonfire.

It was waist-high, the flames licking upward and flickering orange against the surrounding circle of snow-frosted cedars. The figures behind it threw monstrous shadows like a nightmare made real. They made Lewis think of the ritual sacrifices of some ancient Nordic tribe, blood prayers to ensure the return of spring.

Then he was close enough to see them.

On the left, opposite Dinah, stood Mallory Kane in a down jacket, a large automatic pistol in one hand, her other arm tight around Miles. Charlie was next, hands fisted at his sides, shoulders back, looking more like his father than Lewis had ever seen. Then came Streyling, holding the neck of Charlie's sweater with one hand and a black Glock to Charlie's head with the other.

Mallory pointed the gun at Lewis. "Come closer."

He took another step, then another, feeling the heat of the fire. His front tingled with pins and needles as his skin began to thaw. But it wasn't enough. The shaking in his hands had spread to his limbs. "It's going to be okay, boys."

"No," Mallory said. "It won't." The orange firelight turned her face from shadow to light and back again. Her fine blond hair shone like spun gold. "Here's how it's going to go."

She smiled then, and Lewis felt a different kind of cold fill him. Colder than the coldest winter night could ever be.

"You took my son from me," Mallory said. "But I'm going to do you a favor. I'm going to let you choose which of your children gets to live."

66

STREYLING

His fingers hooked into the neck of Charlie's sweater, Streyling hoped she'd start with the bigger one. Without the need to control the boy, Streyling would be free to act. He wouldn't mind shooting Charlie. The kid had been a discipline problem from the beginning, and Streyling had no patience for people who wouldn't do what they were told.

He knew he was walking a tightrope. Mallory on one side, Lewis the Ghost Killer on the other. Still, he was confident in the controls he'd put in place, the men in the van, the crippling power of the cold, the parental burden of seeing your children held hostage. Even Mallory's agitated state worked in his favor. Her emotions would hamper her decision-making.

To get what he wanted, all Streyling had to do was be the last man standing. Mallory and Lewis would be focused on each other. With any luck, they'd take each other out without any help. Once things were rolling, he'd be the one to finish it. He was a very good shot with a pistol. He'd never known Mallory to fire a gun, although she could be brutal with her machete. But a machete had no finesse.

Streyling, on the other hand, was a former Agency man. Finesse was his skill set.

This was a risky set of moves, he knew. But he liked risk. Nothing ventured, nothing gained. And Streyling always won in the end. Because he was better than everyone else.

He'd found the boys, after all. And it was his idea to take them, to use them as a method of control. Just like it was his idea to sideline most of Mallory's security team in New York with that attempt to capture the Ghost Killers. After the debacle at Maurice's house, Streyling had known how it would end. It didn't matter how good her team was. The Ghost Killers had proven themselves to be better.

Streyling was the mastermind, not Mallory Kane.

She just didn't know it yet.

But she would soon find out.

Her laptop was hidden in her bag in the back of the old truck. Ari had told him that she never went anywhere without it. Streyling was almost certain of the password. It would be her son's name, or his date of birth, or the date of his death, or some combination of the three. Her obsession had made her predictable.

If he was wrong about the password, it wouldn't matter, because Ari was stashed in the back of the van with the other Ghost Killers. Streyling had planned that, too.

The older couple had been an interesting wrinkle. The man had been a fighter, Streyling had to give him credit. Not that it made a difference when you received a shotgun butt to the face. He went down hard, and the woman went down beside him, using her own body to shield him from the next blow. Admirable, Streyling thought, but stupid. What was it about Midwesterners? The long winters did something to their minds, made them crazy.

He wasn't happy that Mallory hadn't let him kill the older couple, though. No witnesses, that was Streyling's rule. But he could go back and finish them off when it was over. He had plenty of ammunition.

Now all he had to do was start pulling the trigger.

What he couldn't decide was, who should he start with?

67

The Ghost Killer stared at her across the fire. Even naked in the cold, with his children facing a bullet from her gun, he conveyed strength. Dignity. The woman, too.

Not like Jay Streyling at all. Streyling had no center. He tried to fill it with toys and clothes, women and gambling. But none of those lasted.

Once, she had thought family would last, or at least her relationship with her son.

She had been wrong.

She glanced at Streyling now. In the firelight, his face was as transparent as glass. She knew exactly what he wanted, and how he planned to get it. She had planted the seeds for it herself, with a very different outcome in mind.

She had needed him for many years. She needed him today, too, for a little while longer. But there was a reason she'd kept him at arm's length. He was like a rattlesnake, striking out of instinct rather than reason. She'd always enjoyed watching his face as her team frisked him. It was like reading his mind, seeing the resentment, the sense of grievance as they dug their hands into his pockets and patted his groin.

Now he was standing ten feet away, a gun in his hand. Her computer was in her bag in the truck. That laptop was Streyling's holy grail, the key to everything Mallory had built. Although she had backups, she ran her entire business from that machine. And Streyling wanted to take it for himself. Just like every other man she'd met. Too dumb to build a business of his own, so he would steal hers instead.

He would try to kill her soon, she knew. But he was scared of the Ghost Killers, so he wouldn't take action before she eliminated the men who had taken her Noah.

Once that was done, she wasn't sure she cared what happened next.

She was shaking, but not from the cold. She had the younger boy clutched against her like a talisman. She didn't want to know his name, but she couldn't help learning it. He reminded her of Noah. They had the same dark eyes, the same skinny unformed body. It was just good luck that Noah was the same age when he died—when he was killed, she reminded herself—because it made the equivalency clear.

A child for a child. A life for a life.

Her revenge was so close she could taste it.

But it didn't taste the way she'd thought it would.

There was none of the sweetness she had savored when she'd swung the machete at those men who'd tried to take what was hers. Instead, she was filled with a profound sadness.

Was this who she had become? A woman who would kill a child?

Or maybe this ruthless woman was who she had always been. And she had been lying to herself for all these years, about the ends justifying the means.

The boy's body was pressed against hers. She felt his trembling like a mouse in a cupped hand. So fragile, so easy to extinguish.

It wouldn't be easy. But it was necessary, wasn't it? She'd taken a vow. Only to herself, but weren't those the vows that mattered most? To revenge her son. To wipe Noah's killers and their families from the face of the earth. It was the only way she would be free.

So she would force the Ghost Killer to choose a son. She would absorb the Ghost Killer's pain, feed on it, so that it might somehow salve her own irredeemable anguish. Revenge was the only way to save herself. She hoped it would save her, anyway. The alternative was unthinkable. She had been imagining and working toward this moment for so long that she could not conceive of another outcome.

But she would not stop with Miles's death.

When the Ghost Killer had been broken by his grief, as she had been broken, he would think of his older son, Charlie. He would then, perhaps, allow himself to hope for the boy's survival.

That was the moment when she would take Charlie's life, too.

It would be easier than killing Miles, she hoped. Charlie was so much larger than her Noah had been, so much closer to manhood.

Then, when the Ghost Killer was broken for a second time, she would take the woman's life. And break him again.

With each death, the Ghost Killer would be diminished, reduced to shattered remnants, as she herself had been reduced.

When the time came for her to end his life, it would almost be a mercy.

Then she would kill Streyling, return to the van, and kill the rest of them, too.

And at last she would be free.

68

PETER

The van's engine was still running and the heat in the driver's compartment was on high, but it never reached the prisoners because the sliding door was still open. The wind sucked out any possible warmth, leaving Peter shivering despite his coat and long underwear. If he was going to generate his own heat, he needed movement.

The passenger had set his gun in his lap and was warming his gloved hands by the vent. The driver scratched his nose with the barrel of his pistol and stared at Peter as if he were a cow in a slaughterhouse. Which Peter might as well be, if he didn't take action. But he couldn't do anything until the driver lost interest in his cargo.

He wondered if his parents were out in the woods, too. His mom hated to be cold. His dad's problem-solving mind would be ticking along like a Swiss watch, trying to find a way out. They would be worried about him, he knew. And where were the boys? He pictured

Charlie, looking so much like his jarhead dad. And Miles, who looked more like his mother, with her same kind nature.

Finally the driver turned to face the controls, set the pistol on the console, and began to fuss with the heat, trying to maximize the flow to his position. Peter felt a touch on his hip. June. A gust rocked the van, and he turned toward her, using the wind to keep his own shifting body weight from alerting the guards.

Her back was now to Peter's front again. Her capable hands reached for his shirt and found the button placket, then began working her way down toward the bottom, where the folded hem made an ideal place to hide a small plastic key. If her hands were as cold as his, this would be a challenge.

But at least the van wasn't moving, so they weren't fighting the bumps in the road. Her fingers found the slightly thicker section where the key was tucked between layers of fabric. He felt the tug as she got to work on the threads. June wasn't the kind of woman who had her nails done regularly, but she liked them long enough to peel an orange or, in a moment of passion, grab hold of his backside. She'd never minded leaving a mark.

"Hey," the driver said. "What the hell are you doing?"

Peter turned his head and saw the man eyeballing him, the pistol in his hand. "We're freezing our butts off back here. I'm just trying to share a little body heat."

June pulled sharply at his shirt. Peter kept himself in place. "No talking," the driver said. "Move away from her. Last warning or I start shooting."

June released his shirt, then poked him in the belly with a blunt knuckle. Peter knee-walked himself around to face the driver, allowing his bound hands to brush against hers. He felt her cool fingers against his wrists, exploring the cuffs. He looked down at the floor.

"I'm sorry," he said. "Please don't shoot anyone. We just want to get home."

The passenger stared balefully out the window toward the trees. "Not much chance of that."

The driver frowned and turned back to the front, glaring at the other guard. "Hey, moron, let me do the talking, okay?"

As if Peter didn't already know the plan was to kill them all.

He sighed and dipped his head, pretending a hopelessness he didn't feel. Behind him, working backward, June pulled at one of the bracelets.

Don't let them clink, he thought. Even though the van's engine was on, and the heater's fan was loud, and the wind rushed through the treetops outside, the sound of metal on metal would be unmistakable.

Then he felt the tightness ease from his left wrist. He kept his arms in place so she could remove the key without dropping it. He waited for her to press it into his left palm. Then he raised his hands behind his back so the cuff wouldn't hit the floor, and gathered the loose bracelet in his right hand. He kept one eye on the driver. The van rocked again, giving him the chance to shift just enough that he could see the cuffs on June's wrists.

It was a lot easier to put the key in the keyhole when you could see it.

When her right wrist was free, he gathered the loose cuff and put it in her left hand, then put the key in her right. She would free the others. But first, Peter had to act.

His own arms still behind his back, he straightened up and took a deep breath, pulling in oxygen. He didn't like being on his knees, but it would take him too long to get to his feet, and the ceiling was too low for him to stand anyway. He braced his toes against the floor, hoping the soles of his boots would grip. If they didn't, this whole thing was going to be over very quickly.

In his mind, he pictured the driver's compartment, the placement of the guns, then mentally rehearsed the movement to free the knife in his belt buckle. Which hand he would use, what he would do next. The consequences if he failed. He reached for the war inside himself and felt that inner engine roar to life, revving high the way it always did. He tasted copper in his mouth. That gasoline rush of adrenaline. Alive, I am alive.

Then, in a single, smooth motion, he brought his hands around to his front, pulled the T-handled knife free from the buckle with his left, and leaped forward to the driver's compartment, where his right hand grabbed the neck of the passenger's coat and his left hand jammed the two-inch blade against the side of the man's neck, right at the carotid artery. A dozen years ago, the Marine Corps had taught Peter this method for a very quick and almost painless death.

"Both of you, hands up or I kill him."

"No, wait," the passenger said, hands twitching in midair.

The driver reached for his gun on the console.

Peter slashed the double-edged knife sideways at arm's length into the driver's neck, biting deep beneath the skin, aiming for the artery. The hot gush of blood told him he'd hit his target. Then he whipped the knife back to the passenger, who was fumbling for his gun. "Stop."

The war in his voice froze the man in place like a rabbit trying not to be seen by a wolf.

"Do you want to die?" Peter asked.

Very carefully, the man shook his head. The well-honed blade made a thin red line on his skin.

"There's only one way to stay alive. Hold up your hands, wrists together."

He did as he was told. The van rocked as June went out the open slider, popped the passenger door, knocked his pistol to the floor, then slapped a pair of cuffs on him. They must have been hers, because she no longer wore any.

Peter checked the driver. He wasn't moving. The van rocked again, and Teddy reached past June and took a handful of coat and pulled the guard face-first into the snow. "You dickhead," he growled, and wound up to kick him in the head.

"Teddy, stop." Peter's voice was sharp, but quiet. "Search him for weapons, empty his pockets. Find something to cuff him to, then grab that Uzi. We need to get moving."

"What about Ari?" Nino asked. "He's still passed out."

"Close the van doors and leave the motor running, he'll be fine until we get back."

Ray opened the driver's door and pulled the crumpled body down to the ground, then began to unsling the Uzi from around the shoulders. Peter reached forward and plucked the pistol from the console.

The crack of a gunshot echoed through the trees. Then another, and another.

Without a word, Peter was off and running, following Lewis's and Dinah's footprints through the snow into the darkness of the forest.

69

LEWIS

I'm going to let you choose," Mallory Kane said, "which of your children gets to live."

Naked and shaking, Lewis stepped closer to the bonfire and stared at Kane across the blazing barrier. Her pistol was half-raised in one hand, and she held Miles tight to her body with the other.

"Those boys didn't do anything to you," Lewis said. His frostbitten skin flared as the fire began to warm his front. Any closer and he would burn. He didn't trust his muscles to do what he needed them to do. "I'm the one who killed your son. It wasn't on purpose, but I did it. Let them go. We can end the whole thing right here."

"No." Her voice was loud over the crackle of burning wood. "You *choose*."

Miles's eyes were wide with fear, tears streaking his face. Beside him, Charlie looked like a clenched fist. The firelight showed dark bruising and split skin on his cheek where someone had hit him.

Streyling's left hand was clawed into the neck of Charlie's sweater and his right hand held a pistol jammed into the boy's temple.

Lewis ached for them. He turned to Dinah. She was focused on her boys, maintaining her calm for their sake, but Lewis could see the tightness in her face that meant she was terrified.

Mallory put the barrel of the pistol to Miles's narrow chest. "You fucking *choose*." Her voice rose, high and ragged. "Which one dies? Tell me *right now* or I'll kill them both."

Lewis couldn't speak. He needed time, but he didn't have any. A sly smile played on Streyling's lips. Unarmed against two killers with guns, Lewis willed his frozen muscles to thaw.

"*You choose*," she screamed, sounding barely human.

Maybe, Lewis thought, it was a mistake to allow himself to love Dinah and the boys. To allow himself to be loved in return.

After all the shit he'd done in the bad old days, Lewis had never felt truly worthy of it. Of the peace he'd found sitting at the supper table, the four of them holding hands as Dinah said grace by candlelight. Or the joy that rose, unbidden, when Miles leaned against him on the couch, or Charlie asked him to shoot hoops in the driveway, or Dinah put her lips to his cheek when she got home from work.

But maybe now, with all this pain and sorrow his old life had brought down on their heads, he might finally be found worthy. The way others had been found worthy over the centuries. Through sacrifice.

He could do that.

He would do anything, give everything, to see his family walk out of these woods.

Maybe that's how this was always going to go.

Maybe, for the man he had been all those years, this was the only way.

He dug his toes into the snow, trying to find solid ground beneath. First Streyling, he thought. Then Kane.

Until Dinah cleared her throat and said, "Mallory? I don't understand. Why are you doing this?"

Mallory looked at Dinah as if she'd sprouted horns. "Because I want *that man* to feel what I feel." She jabbed the gun toward Lewis. "I want him to hurt like I hurt when I think of my Noah."

Dinah nodded. "My first husband, the boys' father. He died a few years ago." Her voice was calm and clear and carried across the crackle of the fire and the silence of the snow. "He was killed. I don't have to tell you how much that hurt. I loved that man dearly, and those boys loved him, too."

She stood tall and proud in her black thermals, focused entirely on Mallory, taking a step toward her.

"I still think about him every day. I live with that pain, with his loss, every day. That pain is part of me, it's woven into me. It's all I have left of him."

"A husband is *not* a son," Mallory said.

"No," Dinah said. "You're absolutely right about that. But maybe I know, at least a little, how you might feel. Your Noah was taken from you, through no fault of your own. That *hurts*. But harming one of these boys? It won't free you from that pain. It will only pollute his memory. Right now, you still have something of Noah, something pure and clean. If you kill one of these boys, you lose that."

Mallory stared at Dinah, unmoving. The flickering firelight changed her face from shadow to light and back again. But her pistol was a little lower now, as if the weight of it had begun to tire her.

As Dinah took another step forward, her voice softened, but still somehow rang out in the cold night. "You don't have to do this, Mallory. *You* get to choose, too."

Maybe it was a trick of the flames, but Lewis thought Mallory's shoulders might have slumped slightly. Her hand clenched in Miles's coat, holding him tightly against her body, began to open, just a little. The gun continued to lower, as if it were getting too heavy to carry.

Lewis didn't dare to speak. Please, he thought. Please, God, don't harm those boys.

Then he glanced at Streyling, who was watching Mallory. The sly smile was gone. His lips were twisted up like he'd tasted something foul.

No, Lewis thought. No, no, no.

His bare feet were still blocks of ice, but they'd found rough grass beneath the slick snow. His thighs were warmer now, and his stomach, and his chest, and his arms. He could leap and grab if he had to.

On the far side of the bonfire, Streyling's fist was tight on the neck of Charlie's sweater. The muzzle of the pistol still ground into the side of the boy's head. Tensed against the push-pull of Streyling's grip, Charlie was taut as a bowstring, his eyes angled sideways, locked onto his captor's face.

Lewis saw it in Charlie's posture first, his balance shifting unconsciously toward Streyling, and Lewis knew Streyling had released the pressure on the pistol. Then he removed the gun from Charlie's head and extended his gun arm past Charlie's upper back. Aiming at Miles, or Mallory, or Dinah.

Charlie got it. His arms were free. He was strong, quick, a talented athlete. Before Lewis could react, Charlie windmilled his left arm behind his back, trying to knock Streyling's gun arm up and maybe grab hold of it.

Lewis leaped across the fire, empty-handed.

Because Streyling's other hand still held tight onto the boy's sweater, he would have felt Charlie's move almost before it started. Charlie had size and power, but Streyling was very fast, and his Agency-trained skills were honed by decades of field experience. Instead of keeping Charlie close, he pushed him away, which gave Streyling room to free his gun arm.

Lewis watched all this happen, each detail startlingly clear. He didn't feel his feet scatter the burning coals. He was locked onto Streyling.

But Streyling saw him coming. He got the gun around and fired twice.

BANG BANG. Lewis felt two hard punches in his torso, but no pain. He felt strong and clean. He got a hand on the gun and pushed it down.

BANG. Lewis felt a third punch in the thigh. Then he had the gun in both hands, but so did Streyling, with his finger inside the trigger guard.

BANG. BANG BANG. Was he hit? He didn't know.

"Run," he shouted. "Charlie, Miles, run."

The gun was everything. Streyling held on, fighting for his life, but Lewis had more lives to fight for. He hooked a foot behind Streyling's ankle and rode him down with a knee to the balls, pushing the gun to one side. Then he began to force the barrel toward Streyling's head, whose hands held the gun in front of him as if his hands were clasped in prayer.

Then the gun was under Streyling's chin. Lewis fumbled for the trigger, got his finger over Streyling's. Streyling tried to roll him, Lewis kept his position. Streyling tried to twist his head to the side, but Lewis had the barrel screwed deep into the other man's soft tissue. There was no escape.

Shooting this motherfucker *definitely* qualified under Lewis's rules. But he couldn't pull the trigger.

Because of the boys, he thought.

He didn't want them to see it. To have to live with the memory. They already had to live with so much.

Oh, God, he thought, the boys.

He looked to his left and saw Mallory standing with her pistol in her hand, now pointed at Dinah's chest. Dinah was just a few feet from her, saying something that Lewis couldn't hear over the roaring in his ears. Mallory still had hold of Miles's coat. He was trying to twist away, but she wouldn't let him.

He looked to his right and saw Charlie in a crouch, frozen, eyes white with panic.

"Charlie," he said. "Go help your mother."

"You're shot."

Oh, Lewis thought. That's why he felt so tired.

Streyling bucked beneath him, trying to push the pistol back from his chin and succeeding, inch by inch. Lewis was getting weaker. He was losing blood fast. The pain was starting to arrive.

"Charlie, your brother needs you. Go help your mother. Go on, *move*." Lewis needed to focus on Streyling. To decide what to do before it was too late.

Charlie's face was anguished. "Dad," he said.

Streyling was making progress. He got another inch, then another, until the barrel was pointed into the air between them. Then Lewis abruptly twisted the gun sideways, changing the trajectory, and pulled the trigger. *BANG BANG BANG BANG.* Until the receiver locked back, the chamber empty.

Streyling screamed and arched his back, four new holes in his upper arm and shoulder. It was better than killing him, Lewis thought. And it'd make it harder for him to hurt anyone else.

There was a blur of motion and Peter was there, kicking Streyling in the head, bending to tear the pistol from their tangled hands. Lewis fell to one side. He was all wet. The snow was red. "Dinah and Miles, help Dinah and Miles."

Peter knelt at his side, breathing hard, his eyes grave. "They're okay, Lewis. They're safe."

Lewis rolled to look and saw June pointing a pistol at Mallory, who closed her eyes and opened her hands. Her weapon fell to the ground and Miles tore away from her grasp.

"Charlie, help me." Lewis got his elbows under him and began to pull himself toward Dinah and Miles. He didn't mind the cold anymore.

Then Dinah was beside him. "Don't move, baby. I've got you."

Now the pain showed up for real. It rose through him and tried to carry him away, but he didn't let it. He wanted to stay right there and look at Dinah forever, her face bright. Charlie looking wide-eyed over her shoulder, holding Miles close and tight.

His loves.

His life.

Then he knew. It was all worth it.

There was something else he needed to say, but he had trouble forming the words. The DEA deal. Gottschall needed Mallory's laptop. Without the information on it, and the money it controlled, the immunity deal was off. Everyone else would be screwed.

He looked at Peter. "Find the laptop. Call Fratelli."

"For real, Lewis?" Dinah looked at Peter, voice like a scalpel. "Give me your coat. Then find the keys to that truck. I know there's a trauma center in Ashland." She turned back to Lewis. "You are not allowed to die, do you hear me? I will not allow it." She put her hand on his cheek, hot as the sun. He leaned his face into it.

Streyling started screaming again. Teddy appeared with a pistol hanging from one hand. He stared down at Streyling for a moment, then extended his arm. The gun barked and Streyling went silent.

Lewis heard an engine start. Dinah packed snow into his wounds. He grabbed his boys' hands. Then Nino leaned over him, and Ray. Why did they all look so sad?

But it was Teddy who knelt coatless in the snow to put one arm under his knees and the other around his shoulders.

He felt himself rise into the air. Like he was floating, or flying.

Like he was finally free.

70

PETER

Peter pulled the Chevy into the driveway behind June's new Subaru and killed the engine in the dark. He'd just finished hanging the kitchen cabinets at his big renovation project on the other side of the river and would start running baseboard tomorrow. It felt good to be putting an old house back together, making something better than it had been. More than that, when he was done, it would be beautiful.

He got out and stood on the walkway in his shirtsleeves, enjoying the unseasonably warm weather in the fading daylight. It was the end of March, and the snow was gone except for the last patches deep in the shadows of the ravine. He knew there would probably be at least one heavy April snowstorm before spring arrived for real, but after the long, cold winter, tonight's warm breeze felt like spring enough.

He saw the lights coming through the big windows that wrapped the back of the house. He'd taken on Lewis's job of dropping the boys at school in the morning, and June picked them up at the end of the day. It was also her turn to make dinner, which generally meant take-out of some kind.

His stomach growled and he glanced at the time on his phone. Dinah's shift ended at six, but because the intensive care unit was understaffed, she often stayed late to lend a hand. She always texted June with an update so the boys wouldn't worry.

It was an adjustment, having them move into the house Peter and June shared, but a welcome one, he thought. Dinah and June had gotten even closer, and Peter loved all the extra time with the boys.

Charlie and Miles were quieter than they used to be. June said they both seemed more like themselves now, compared to just a month ago, although Peter didn't think they'd ever be back to who they'd been before. How could they, after what they'd been through? How could any of them?

But the boys were young, which helped enormously in recovery from that kind of emotional trauma, at least according to the therapist Dinah had found them. Their brains were still growing and developing as they continued to mature into the young men they were meant to be. The experience would always be a part of them, but it didn't have to define them.

Peter had talked with his own shrink in Oregon a few times, which helped. But sometimes, in quiet moments at work, or making a meal for the family, he had to stop what he was doing, bow his head for a moment, and allow the sadness to take over. The tears would well up as he thought about how he'd almost lost the people he loved. After a few minutes, he'd wipe his eyes and remind himself how lucky he was, how lucky they all were.

They'd left Streyling dead in the clearing with Teddy's bullet in his brain. For all Peter knew, he was still there. Unless the bears had gotten to him.

After Peter had driven Lewis and Dinah down to the ER in

Ashland, he'd searched his dad's pickup and found a high-end laptop deep inside some very expensive luggage tucked behind the salt spreader. June had taken the van and arrived at the hospital thirty minutes later, along with Peter's mom and dad, who'd been handcuffed to a gas pipe in their farmhouse basement, and Charlie, who had a facial fracture where Streyling had hit him with a gun. Miles rode along, too, because there was no way June was going to leave him at the farmhouse with Mallory Kane.

It turned out that Charlie had dragged Mingus into the bathroom to keep him from getting shot while attempting to rip the throats out of the two security guys. When June unlocked the door to let the dog out, she discovered that he'd nearly chewed the knob out of the wood, trying to get free to chase down those guys.

At the hospital, Peter asked June to take the laptop back to the farmhouse. He figured she was the best person to persuade Ari to transfer Lewis's percentage before calling Fratelli, who pulled the trigger with the DEA. Gottschall had showed up in an Agency plane after midnight with a half-dozen goons and legal papers confirming the Heavy Lifters' promised immunity. The DEA team left with Ari and Mallory Kane in custody. Gottschall had actually given June his card, asking her to please reach out the next time she found a jackpot like this.

Since narrowly avoiding killing a child, Mallory had shrunk into herself and stopped responding to questions of any kind. Ari, on the other hand, promised to cooperate fully in exchange for a suspended sentence and a job with the feds, teaching them Mallory's financial tricks. He also confirmed that the scanned notebook pages had not been dispersed into the criminal underworld. The DEA had probably kept a copy, but that was unavoidable.

Peter's folks returned to their regular life as if nothing had happened, although Peter had given them access to an account that would ensure them an extremely comfortable retirement, if they ever actually chose to stop working, which seemed unlikely.

Nino was back running his restaurant with more than enough money to pay off his creditors.

Ray had bought his sister a house, and set up a foundation to fully fund the center in Houston.

Teddy was on his way to Alaska in a used camper van that already smelled indelibly of the four mixed-breed dogs he'd adopted from a shelter.

Before he left, they'd burned his notebook pages in a bonfire in the backyard.

After walking through the side door into the house, Peter dropped his backpack by the table with June's shoulder bag and set his lunch box and thermos on the counter. June leaned close and he felt the smile on her lips when she kissed him. "Thai food tonight," she said. "I ordered it myself."

He gave her a squeeze and smiled at the boys, who sat on the floor by the new couch that crowded the corner, doing their homework. "How was school?"

Miles looked up. "Pretty good, Pete." Miles had started calling him Pete, which was annoying and also amusing. Charlie didn't even look up, probably due to the headphones turned up full blast. After dinner, he and Peter often played one-on-one in the driveway. Charlie spotted him six points and still beat him easily.

Which was all fine with Peter. He pulled two Sprecher Ambers from the fridge, walked them over to the couch, and held one out. "You earn this today, old man?"

In the last light coming through the floor-to-ceiling windows, Lewis sat with his back to one arm of the couch with his legs stretched out across the cushions. One was in a long cast that held his shattered tibia in place while it healed.

"Damn right I did. That mean rehab lady 'bout killed me today." He took the beer from Peter. They clinked bottles and drank.

As for the rest of Lewis's wounds, all the stitches were out, although he had at least one more surgery scheduled. He'd lost his gallbladder, a chunk of his liver, and fourteen inches of his small intestine. His right lung had collapsed in the truck on the way to the hospital.

The medevac chopper had flown him and Dinah down to Froedtert Memorial outside Milwaukee, the best trauma center in the state. Lewis died twice on the flight, and twice more on the operating table. Afterward, the surgeon told Dinah he'd never seen a human being fight so hard to stay alive.

Peter settled himself on the far end of the couch, making sure not to disturb Lewis's injured leg. "What else did you do today?"

Lewis patted the large black book on his lap. "Just this."

Working with the notes he'd made in the Chicago hotel, along with occasional phone calls with Teddy, Nino, and Ray, he'd started writing down everything he could remember about his former life, although without using any real names or places, of course. He'd already filled two notebooks and was working on a third. "Funny how it helps. Putting it on paper gets it out of your head, you know?" He shook his head. "I shouldn't have been so hard on Teddy."

"Are you going to call Fratelli back?" The Chicago detective had left several messages, hoping Lewis could help him clear cold cases in the cities where he'd worked.

Lewis frowned. "I don't know, Jarhead. Talking to the cops kinda goes against the grain."

Miles looked up at him. "I think you should do it, Dad. The therapist told me everybody gets to choose their own story, choose who they want to be. So, like, who do you want to be?"

Lewis put a hand lightly on the boy's shoulder, a tilted smile playing softly on his lips. "That's a real good question, Miles. I'll have to think on that."

Then the side door opened and Dinah bustled in with her enormous purse over one shoulder and two giant bags of takeout in her hands. "I ambushed a delivery guy outside. Smells like Thai food. Who's hungry?"

Outside, the darkness had become complete. But inside the house, with the smell of takeout and the sound of voices raised in laughter, it didn't matter.

They were together.

They were home.

ACKNOWLEDGMENTS

First, an apology. If you're one of my readers who has been waiting an extra year for a new Peter Ash adventure, I'm sorry it took so long.

Some books almost write themselves.

This book, despite my best efforts, was not one of them.

With that in mind, I'd like to thank the good folks at Putnam and Head of Zeus for their kindness and patience, including my previous editor, Danielle Dieterich, and my new editors, Mark Tavani and Aranya Jain. Thanks especially for leaning into the final round of edits with extraordinary care and skill. I'm very much looking forward to another bout of surgery with you on the next book.

Thanks, yet again, to Putnam's superlative sales, marketing, and publicity crew, including (but not limited to) Katie Grinch, Shina Patel, Alexis Welby, Ashley McClay, Sally Kim, Benjamin Lee, and Ivan Held. You put my work in front of readers, and for that I am supremely grateful. Thanks to Claire Sullivan, Erin Byrne, Tiffany Estreicher,

ACKNOWLEDGMENTS

Emily Mileham, Maija Baldauf, and Steven Meditz for making this book both gorgeous and readable.

Thanks to Dana Kaye and her crack team at Kaye Publicity, including Katelynn Dreyer, Hailey Dezort, and Eleanor Imbody, for extending the outreach for this book into many new corners of the world, both real and virtual. You are rock stars, every one of you.

Thanks, as always, to my fearless and ferocious agent, Barbara Poelle of WordOne, for being the underside of the duck.

Extended and enthusiastic thanks to the many independent booksellers who put my work into the hands of readers. Local bookstores are the lifeblood of the book world, and their knowledge and passion have been instrumental in my success and the success of almost every other writer you love to read. Plus, buying local keeps those dollars—and jobs—in your community, so please please patronize your local independent bookstore!

Extra special thanks, of course, are due to Daniel Goldin at Boswell Books in Milwaukee and Barbara Peters at The Poisoned Pen in Scottsdale, who have been champions from the very beginning. I am in forever your debt.

Thanks to Bill Schweigart and Don Bentley for being good dudes. Read their stuff or miss out.

Thanks to Gregg Hurwitz for being a font of wisdom and patiently answering my many questions about publishing and Hollyweird. You are also a good dude.

Thanks to William Kent Krueger, Michel Koryta, Robert Crais, and many, many other writers for telling me their stories of books that died on the vine. Thanks to C. J. Box, who is that rare writer who has never missed a deadline, for making fun of me for missing mine—and reminding me that none of this stuff is all that important in the overall scheme of things. Thanks to every writer who talks openly about the many challenges of doing this difficult job, because it helps the rest of us understand that we're not crazy.

Thanks to the Milwaukee writer crew, especially Erica Ruth Neubauer, Tim Hennessy, Chris Lee, and Liam Callanan, for food and drinks and book talk.

For all those people who are sadly addicted to facts, I have taken many liberties with the truth in the service of the story. Sorry about that. Also, I know it takes longer to transfer the contents of an investment account than I've shown here, but it's not very dramatic to wait three days for confirmation.

Many thanks to Rachel at Midwest Skydive in Sturtevant, Wisconsin, for walking me through their hangar and introducing me to the Twin Otter. If I ever jump out of an airplane again, Midwest Skydive is the place I'll do it.

Massive and enormous thanks to Erin Olson for our extraordinarily helpful conversations. You have changed my life and I cannot possibly express my gratitude enough.

Thanks to my brother, Bob; my sister, Maryl; and the rest of my non-writer friends for their roles as unpaid sales associates and pep talkers.

I never know where to include Margret, my Sweet Patootie. Really, babe, you should be the first person acknowledged here, because without you, life would be sad and lonely and most of all, *boring*. Or the last person acknowledged, because, as I am finally learning, you are (almost) always right. So thanks for being you, and for spending a quarter-century married to me.

Thanks to my son, Duncan, for our outdoor adventures, and for our many conversations about art and creativity. I learn something new from you every time we talk.

Thanks to my mom, Lucia Petrie, for being an ongoing inspiration. You're who I want to be when I grow up. Thanks to my dad, Pete